THE MISSION

THE DEFENDER SERIES

BIRTH OF THE DEFENDER
Prequel

THE MISSION
Book 1

DEFENDED
Book 2

TREASONOUS ACTS
Book 3

IN EVIL'S GRASP
Book 4

MISSION ABANDONED
Book 5

BIRTH OF A REVOLUTION
Book 6

THE MISSION

THE DEFENDER SERIES

Book 1

Reggi Broach

second edition

Defender Christian Publications
Harrison, Tennessee, USA

Published by Defender Christian Publications, Harrison, TN, USA

First edition printed 2017.

ISBN: 978-1-950038-00-8 (paperback)
ISBN: 978-1-950038-02-2 (eBook)
ISBN: 978-1-950038-01-5 (hardback)
LCCN: 2017901519

PUBLISHERS NOTE:
This is a work of fiction. Names, characters, places, and incidents either are a product of the author's imagination or are used fictitiously, and any resemblance to actual persons, living or dead, business establishments, events, or locales is entirely coincidental. The publisher does not have any control over and does not assume any responsibility for author or third-party web sites or their content.

R. B. Enterprises books are available at special discounts for bulk purchases, for sales promotions, or corporate use. Special editions, including personalized covers, excerpts of existing books, or books with corporate logos, can be created for some titles. For more information, contact R. B. Enterprises at:
SpecialSales@RBEnterprises.info

TABLE OF CONTENTS

"Before I formed you in the womb, I knew you; before you were born, I set you apart; I appointed you as a prophet to the nations."

- Jeremiah 1:5

ACKNOWLEDGMENTS

I want to express my profound gratitude to several people for their help in contributing to the development and publishing of this book, and hopefully its sequels. I am not solely responsible for this book and I make no such claim. I compiled this book with a large amount of fear and trembling.

I would like to thank Chaplain Jerry Minchew, author of *Knighthawke* and *Knighthawke Vanishing Shadows,* and his wife Vickie Minchew for their advice, constructive criticism, encouragement, and inspiration. Without your help, I'm not sure I would have had the courage to go through with this endeavor. Thank you for letting God use you to help me.

A special thank you to those who had a hand in editing and proofing for me. Thanks to Janelle Musick, Becky Chaffin, and Pastor Darren Schalk, author of *Dear God, We Need to Talk* for their help toward making sure the book is readable.

Thanks to my brother Nathan, an aerospace engineer, for his technical expertise in my gravitational calculations. He took my calls and texts at various times of the day or night. Thanks also to his wife Shannon for listening to him mumble to himself as he tried to work out the technical aspects of whatever I asked.

For all those times I sat there staring into space thinking, I would like to express my appreciation to anyone who was near me and answered the query, "I need a word that means ____ " The ones who suffered the most were my daughters, Rachel and Kayleigh, and my niece, Alea, although there were others. Thank you, Alea and Matthew, for allowing me to borrow your Legos to design the layout for my ship.

Thank you to all my friends from church, and my nursing and respiratory therapist friends from work, for listening to me ramble on about the progress of my book. I appreciate your interest and encouragement. It has meant a lot to me.

A very special note of appreciation goes to my son, David Alexander Broach. He allowed me to use his name for one of my main characters. When we chose names for our children, we chose them carefully and prayerfully. Each of their names has powerful meanings in the hope they would live up to those names. David means "beloved," and Alexander means "Helper and Defender of Mankind." Although the character isn't about my son, he does serve as a Defender of Mankind in the US Navy and is very loved and admired by his family.

My wonderful husband Ron deserves so much credit for this book. He encouraged me to start writing and listened to me talk incessantly about the lives of imaginary people. He proofed portions for content and effectiveness numerous times. He laughed at the funny parts and cried at the sad parts. His wonderful, caring spirit, his patience, commanding presence, and sense of fairness are part of the inspiration for my characters.

There are many others who have offered encouragement to me, and you may not realize it, but it meant more than you will ever know.

I want and need to acknowledge Jesus Christ, the Holy Spirit, and God Almighty as the inspiration and sole reason for writing this book. It is my desire to share His message to an audience who may not otherwise know who or what He is and why the Lord matters. I cannot rewrite the Bible and have no intention of doing so. It is my goal to point the reader to the true writer of this message and keep in line with the true gospel message.

Commonwealth Interstellar Force Ship

Tech Specs: *SS Evangeline*

Explorer Class Ship with long range space, planetary atmospheric, and aquatic maneuvering capabilities.

Drive Capabilities:
- Tachyon
- Matter/Antimatter

Ship Weapons Capabilities:
- Minimal laser
- EMP and tachyon defensive weaponry
- Electromagnetic shields and deflectors

Personal Weapons Capabilities
- **Tri-Emp:** A personal weapon, projectile based with three levels of electro-magnetic pulse charge.
- **Laser Rifle:** a longer range weapon with a laser and Tri-Emp capabilities.
- **Personal Shield Generator:** a glove-like device generating a shield for personal use, capable of being adjusted to different sizes and sensitivity.

Ship Accessory Equipment
- **Shuttle:** can be flown in space, atmospheric, and aquatic environments. Used for ship to planet movements and short flights on planets. Mainly used as personnel transport, with limited cargo capacity. The co-pilot controls the computer, shield, and laser weapons.
- **Surf-ve:** an amphibious surface vehicle for transportation of personnel or cargo. It has a retractable canopy over the passenger compartment. The co-pilot's chair has computer, shield, and laser weapons control.
- **Whipper:** single person transport that uses anti-gravity hover technology. It can move and hover over land or water.

Personnel Accommodations:
- 14

Mission

To establish a Commonwealth presence on all technologically undeveloped worlds, or worlds that have not chosen to ally with the Commonwealth despite non-spatial developments. To report any world where the invasive forces of the Liontari have a foothold.

Crew Manifest

The crew is to consist of two teams. The primary team is the ship's crew, and the secondary team is the diplomatic mission team. Each team is to act as support personnel for the opposing team as needed.

Commonwealth Interstellar Force Headquarters				
Office of Personnel Raesii CIF Training Base CIF *SS Evangeline* Crew Manifest				
Name		Rank	Ship's Crew	Diplomatic Crew
Last	First			
Alexander	David	Captain	Captain	
Alexander	Brynna	Commander		Diplomatic Team Leader
Dominick	Lazaro	Lt. Commander	Chief Engineer	
Flint	Braxton	Lt. Commander		Architectural Engineer
Adams	Jason	Lt. Commander		Physician
Flint	Alexia (Lexi)	Lt.		Psychologist
Ryder	Thane	Lt.	Pilot	
Adams	Laura	Lt. JG		Nurse, Botanist
Holden	Marissa	Lt. JG	Navigation	
Dominick	Cheyenne	ENS		Linguistics
Ryder	Aulani	ENS	Comm & Computer Tech	
Holden	Jake	Chief Petty Officer	Security	

PART ONE: THE LAUNCH

THE MISSION

"You're too soft!" Admiral Deacons stared at the young captain.

"Sir?" Alexander asked.

"You passed all your tests, your psyche evaluation, and no one found anything to stop you from taking a command position."

"Isn't that a good thing, sir?"

"I didn't derail your plans because I thought that somebody—somewhere—would take care of it for me."

"Are you pulling me off the command track, sir?"

Admiral Deacons spoke, slowly and deliberately. "No, I'm not. I can't, even if I wanted to. I just wanted you to know, I could have, and I should have. I want you to know why. You're very intelligent. You think fast on your feet. You know the regulations and follow them. You have a good command presence."

The Admiral paused again, a concerned look still engraved on his face.

Captain Alexander wasn't sure if he should wait or ask the question burning in his mind. The Admiral got out of his chair, moved to the window, and began to stare out it intently. Captain Alexander stood a little over six feet and had thick, dark brown hair. He was broad shouldered and definitely not a light-weight, but the Admiral had a way of making him feel small.

Captain Alexander took a deep breath then asked, "So what is it about my performance that concerns you, and what can I do to alleviate your concerns, sir?"

Admiral Deacons turned to look at him and said, "Okay, enough with the 'sir.' Take a seat. Off the record, I've known you since you were born. You're a fine young man, and I'm proud to be your uncle. I was also extremely proud when you entered the Commonwealth Interstellar Force instead of following in your father's footsteps and joining the infantry. The infantry just doesn't stretch a man the way the Brigade does. Do you realize this upcoming mission will put the lives of eleven crew members in your hands? Whether they live or die will depend on the decisions you make."

"Yes sir, I understand completely. I guess I don't understand what it is you think I'm not understanding."

"I watched some of your training exercises. Whenever your team couldn't accomplish their goals, you would move in, do their jobs for them, or assign someone else to help. You can't do that in the field. The people under your command must be able to do their jobs so you can do yours. You can't coddle them. There is no place for that in the field. You always achieved your mission, but your team wasn't properly trained or functioning as a team!"

The Admiral's voice was starting to sound angry. David took his uncle at his word and began to speak frankly.

"Uncle Rob, I think I see the problem. You weren't directly involved in the training, so you didn't see everything. You watched the testing scenarios where we were being graded on the overall outcome, not on individual accomplishments. After those scenarios were over, I kept my people late to go over the things that went wrong. We repeated them until they went the way they were supposed to go. My team put in many extra hours getting it right even though we weren't being retested. They griped and complained, but in the end, I think they felt a greater sense of satisfaction."

"There aren't any second chances in real life. If you don't get it right the first time, there are no practice runs, no timeouts, no way to fix it, and make things better."

"Which is why I put in the extra time to get it right here and now." David paused. He wasn't sure if his next statement would help alleviate his uncle's fears or add to them. He decided his uncle was already so worried, that it couldn't possibly be any worse. "Uncle Rob, I realize these people's lives are hinging on my every move… and personally, it scares the life out of me. I keep trying to second-guess myself. What if I choose wrong?

What if somebody dies? What if I could have saved them, and I didn't?"

The Admiral looked at him and asked, "Could you send one of your people to do something you know would get them killed? Could you send one of your team to die? Could you let your wife die if it meant saving the rest of your crew?"

David took a deep slow breath before answering. "It isn't something I would want to do. I like to think I have the strength to do what I had to," He finished softly, "even if it costs me my wife."

"Could you live with it?"

"I don't know about that, sir. I'll have to see if that day ever comes."

"I hope it never comes to that, son. I really do. I've just been afraid you were too soft to let someone die if necessary. This mission is a simple, straightforward mission. It's not like going into an undercover situation or a war zone, but there are genuine uncertainties. It's also deep space. Anything can go wrong. First contact situations are risky."

"I know what's being asked of me, Uncle Rob. I'm not saying I'll do everything right, or that I'll even survive the first week, but I know how important this mission is. I'll do everything in my power to see that it succeeds. I'm going to do the job I was trained to do."

"The Supreme Executor and the entire Commonwealth have put a lot into this project, so I would expect nothing less from you. I hope you last longer than a week. It would be a terrible waste of money and resources if you only lasted a week." A small halfhearted smile formed on the Admiral's face. The smile was nearly eclipsed by the deep concern still permeating his eyes and demeanor.

Captain Alexander, sensing his uncle had made his point and was attempting to end on a positive note, stood up and said, "Well sir, I hope I last longer than a week too. I would hate to waste a perfectly good marriage agreement." David flashed a large sheepish smile at the Admiral.

The Admiral's face relaxed a little more. He extended his hand to the young captain and said, "Yes, that would be a waste. I wish you the best... Captain... Alexander."

David took the Admiral's hand firmly. "Thank you, sir. I'll make you proud of me. I promise."

"You already have. Just come back alive and in one piece."

"Yes sir!" Captain Alexander snapped to attention, saluted, and executed a flawless egress from the Admiral's office.

Captain Alexander walked back to his own office contemplating the Admiral's words. He didn't have any regrets about his decisions, but he didn't want to dismiss the Admiral's concerns lightly. The Admiral, after all, did have quite a bit more experience than he did. He decided to get back to finishing his final preparations for departure. David tucked the thoughts away in his mind for future reference. He looked over the finalized crew roster. Most of his crew had remained the same over the past few months, but his final requests weren't completely honored. The captain was still attempting to familiarize himself with his newest crew's names and specialties. As he looked it over, his computer posted a hail from his new wife. He touched the screen to answer her. Brynna's face appeared on the screen, and she greeted him, "Hey David, got a second?"

"Sure Brynna, what's up?"

"I was just wondering approximately what time you might be home this evening and if you were going to want something to eat when you get here."

David looked at her pleasant face and grinned, "I can bring my files home to finish up if you want."

"I thought I would cook tonight since it might be a while before I get to do any more real cooking."

"I see. Well, maybe I should stay here, and I'll probably be REALLY, REALLY late so you probably shouldn't save me any leftovers." His grin got even bigger.

"David! Have you got something against my cooking?"

David laughed. With a twinkle in his eyes he answered, "No, I'm just teasing. I really don't know much about your cooking. We've only known each other for what... three, four months?"

"That sounds about right."

"Well, let me gather up my files, and I should be home in thirty to forty minutes."

After finishing his conversation, he sat there for a moment reflecting on the recent events. He met Brynna just four months ago, and they had taken an instant liking to each other. She had beautiful, thick, wavy brown hair, green eyes, a kind soft face, and a warm, friendly personality, although she was quite capable of being firm and serious when she needed to be. After two months, they both agreed to a short-term marriage contract, which they initiated just two weeks earlier. David liked Brynna so much he hoped it would last longer than the initial contract length. Their mission required each person be married to someone on their trip. The mission planners believed it made the crews more relaxed and settled if they didn't have to deal with on-board romances, jealousy, etc. A new marriage and a new mission would keep the crew busy and have a longer "honeymoon" period for the new marriages. David knew there were some societies with lifelong marriage contracts. He wasn't quite sure what to think about such a strange concept. He admired anyone who would honor any contract for his or her entire life, but to remain married to only one person? Forever? He liked Brynna... a lot, but stay with her forever? The thought wasn't unpleasant, just odd. David took a deep breath, collected his files, shut off his computer and lights, then headed out of his office.

The next morning was the beginning of a flurry of activity. All of the mission crews were packing a very Spartan array of personal belongings to take with them aboard ship. Their other personal belongings were packed away in a long-term storage facility. In the weeks or months prior, as each couple signed their marriage contracts, they were assigned to furnished apartments on the Commonwealth Interstellar Force Training Base. This arrangement encouraged the newlywed couples to put as much in storage early on and kept their personal belongings from causing marital disagreements.

The ships were not particularly spacious. There would be six couples aboard each ship. Each ship had six crew quarters and one guest cabin available. The crew quarters were not much larger than a hotel suite. The guest quarters could double as an office or meeting room as long as it wasn't occupied. The ship also held a gymnasium, a cargo bay, shuttle bay, a dining hall, and a large multipurpose room. This room could serve as a ball court for various sports, meeting room for the entire crew, or even a dance floor. There were strict orders issued this room was NOT to be used for any long-term storage. It could only be used for storage in an emergency. The crew was going to be in tight quarters for a minimum of two years. The walls of the room could be programmed like a computer screen with beach scenes or mountains; whatever pictures were stored in the computer's memory banks to give the impression of being in a large open space. The air recycling system could also be reprogrammed to produce warm ocean breezes or cold mountain temperatures. It was not the same as those luxury holographic auditoriums, but it was a pleasant experience, which could relieve some claustrophobia or cabin fever. There was also a medical bay, which could hold up to six patients at one time as well as the appropriate workspace for medical research, lab work, and facilities for synthesizing medications.

They basically had three days of leave before departure to put all of their affairs in order and say farewell to their family and friends. The evening of the third day they were to report back to base for a farewell banquet. David and Brynna liked to get things done early. They had their personal clothes and uniforms packed and sent aboard ship. Their files were already loaded onto the ship's computers. They packed a small bag with their dress uniforms for the banquet and civilian attire for visiting with friends and family. The first day of leave, they cleaned the apartment and made sure everything was out, then stopped by the Office of Advanced Planning to be sure their affairs were in order both legally and financially. They were getting paid while they were gone, but where they were going, they would have no place to spend it. They should have a nice nest egg by the time they got back.

After they finished taking care of business, they caught a shuttle to David's family's home where they spent the night. The next morning, after some tearful goodbyes, they headed to Brynna's family's home. The visits left everyone full of tension. David had only briefly met Brynna's family when they got married. Brynna knew the Admiral and had run into him on numerous occasions, but she also had just recently gotten to know David's family. They had visited each other's families a couple of times for dinner since then. It still felt like meeting with strangers. The fact that they were about to be gone for two years certainly didn't relieve any tensions.

David and Brynna tried to respect each other's family time by staying out of the way, helping with meal preparations, and cleaning up while the other spent time visiting. Brynna's father pulled David aside to give him a stern admonishment to take care of his little girl. As they prepared to leave the next morning, David assured both of Brynna's parents he would indeed bring her back safely.

As they headed back to base, their conversations alternated with long periods of silence. Their emotions bounced back and forth between feelings of loss, fear, and excitement over their upcoming adventure. Once they arrived on base, they each went to their respective offices to prepare for the banquet and close out their already sparsely adorned offices. David went over the crew manifest again to be sure each crewman had checked back into the base. Once satisfied all was in order, he breathed a little easier. He decided to look over Brynna's mission staff to be sure there were no problems on her side. This mission was going to be different from any other missions he had been on. He had carried out search and rescue missions, carried diplomatic envoys, and conducted missions of mercy, police actions, and missions to observe spatial anomalies. This mission and crew were split in half. His job was to provide transportation, security, and mission support for Brynna and her team. Her team would provide support to the ship's crew while they were being transported to each mission location. Sometimes he felt like a glorified chauffeur, but deep down he knew there would be more to his mission than just transportation. When the ship was on the ground, except for matters of safety and security, Brynna would be in charge. When the ship was moving, he would be.

David wasn't sure about the wisdom of a "shared" command. Ultimately, he would have the final say in any decision, but out of respect for her position, it wasn't an action he would take lightly. All ship's captains had been counseled regarding this particular dynamic of their command. Since the Mission Team Leaders also served as the ship's first officer, they hoped this would help to unify the two groups and add to the understanding of each leader's priorities and position. He had received additional counsel on the matter since the Team Leader, in this case, was his wife. David and Brynna had discussed the matter a couple of times, and they seemed to have an understanding of it. Time would tell if that were not the case.

The evening began with a social hour. It wasn't a sight that was seen very often. This particular group had uniforms explicitly designed for their mission. The mission uniform colors were teal and black. Their daily uniforms were half teal and black, but the dress uniforms were predominantly black with teal trim around the collar and a stripe down the outside of the pant leg. The uniforms were also adorned with gold rank insignia, award insignia, and ribbons. The ranks were displayed on the top of the sleeve just below the shoulder. The standard Commonwealth Interstellar Force uniform colors were bright blue and black. The Admirals wore black with white trim. Many of the course instructors were present in traditional blue and black dress uniforms. The sea of dark uniforms was a sharp contrast to the brightly lit banquet room.

After everyone had a chance to visit, they were directed to take their seats at the tables scattered across the room. As David and Brynna were seated, David glanced around noticing an unusually large number of security officers posted around the room. Surely there weren't any security threats here. It struck him as odd, but with the banquet starting, he had to let go of the thought. The Admirals Board and their guests were taking their seats at the head tables adjacent to the podium.

As they finished eating, Admiral Deacons rose and walked to the podium. He greeted the room full of nervous and excited crew members as warmly as one could while wearing a dress uniform and maintaining his Admiral's dignity. The Admiral admired each one of the individuals picked for this mission. There were twelve teams of twelve going out, and he knew every one of them personally.

These men and women were like his own children, although he did take an extra special interest in David and Brynna. He planned to give a more personal send off to each crew as they departed, so he kept his comments broad and brief. He thanked them for all the hard work they had done and wished them the best on their long journeys. He finished his speech by saying, "I know every single one of you will make me and the Commonwealth proud." His speech was punctuated with a vigorous round of applause. Each crew member sensed the Admirals genuine spirit and the feelings were mutual.

As the applause settled the emcee stepped up to introduce the next speaker. "Tonight, we have a very, VERY special guest speaker. We were not sure if his schedule would allow him to be here tonight, so we kept the information to as few as possible. I am sure you all know him, so please stand to honor and welcome our Supreme Executor of the Commonwealth, Luciano Hale."

There was a half second pause of shock followed by a long, loud, thunderous applause as the side doors opened and the Supreme Executor, surrounded by a security detail, entered the room. An additional security detail positioned themselves in strategic places around the periphery as the Executor approached the podium. The audience was still somewhat in shock. The Supreme Executor rarely made personal appearances. Why did this mission manage to land on his radar? Everyone was dying to discuss it, but they didn't dare. They were also anxious to hear what he had to say. It certainly gave them something to talk about later tonight. As the applause again died down Executor Hale began to speak.

"Please, be seated. Thank you for the warm welcome. It is an honor to be here this evening. I would not have missed this night for anything short of intergalactic war. This is not going to be a formal address, I promise. Everyone just sit back, relax, and I hope this is a speech you will enjoy. I, at least, would like you to get your money's worth. Oh, wait, forgive me you didn't pay to be here tonight. I'm paying you. That's right, well then, at least allow me to get my money's worth."

Slow, cautious smiles began to spread across the room. The Supreme Executor flashed a disarming grin. The Executor had a pleasant looking face. His dark, wavy hair was starting to give way to a newer salt and pepper color along his temples. His smile had a way of drawing one in and making them comfortable. His eyes, on the other hand, were dark and mysterious, even cold. It could be the nature of the job he held, all those secrets and the unpleasantness of hard decisions made, or was it something else? The Executor had been equipped with a portable voice projector prior to entering the room. It allowed him to move about freely and still be heard. His security officers weren't keen on the arrangement, but the Executor didn't want to set himself above his audience. He wanted his actions to bear the same weight as his voice.

"I have had my eye on this project from the beginning. I watched your training, the construction of your ships and all the preparations going into this project. Admiral Deacons, you and your people are to be commended for all the amazing work you've done. Let's give the Admirals Board a round of applause for all their hard work." The Supreme Executor turned to face the Admirals Board and started the applause himself. As the applauding started to fade again, he quickly added, "Give each other some applause. Each and every one of you has worked hard and deserve to be commended." As it grew quiet again, the Executor continued, "This project has been a very personal one for me from the beginning. I suppose you are wondering why this is so personal."

Executor Hale spoke very slowly and paused to make eye contact with as many people as he could. The smile dissolved. His face took on a somber and sullen appearance. He began to speak again in a serious tone. "What I am about to tell you, is a part of the mission you haven't heard before and does not leave this room. You are under oath to keep this confidential. There is an enemy, in our galaxy, and in our space. These forces are unknown to us. We don't know how they are getting through or where they are coming from. What we do know is, they are coming through like spies, slowly, cautiously. They've gained the support of some of the smaller, uncivilized planets. I suppose you're wondering why a few uncivilized populations are anything to worry about. The Commonwealth has had the policy of noninterference with the development of the younger planets. We've bargained with them, visited them on occasion, but we have not shared our advanced technology. We haven't told them of the other worlds or taught them our ways. Once a society develops enough to start reaching for the stars, we step in to introduce them to the Commonwealth. At that time, they learn the laws of the Commonwealth. Their leaders are re-educated in the ways of structuring their governments. We help them achieve the higher standards expected by the Commonwealth. We teach them about sharing in common all our resources, and we help them identify resources they have to share. These societies often don't have the ability to maintain peace on their own worlds. We assume the burden of maintaining peace by helping them establish one worldwide government loyal to the Commonwealth. We provide troops to help them stop civil wars. We provide intermediaries to help them solve disputes. We guide them in establishing a planetary discipline force to confiscate the weapons of revolutionaries and maintain a crime-free population. We even remove the hardened criminal elements from their society, re-educate and relocate them. All of that is now in danger because of our new enemy. These new forces are taking control of the smaller insignificant populations and gaining their allegiance. We have worked hard in the Commonwealth to see everyone is cared for equally. Since the establishment of the Commonwealth nearly three hundred years ago, we have virtually eliminated poverty, war, and crime. I get reports from our explorer vessels visiting our neighboring galaxies of wars and divisions among their people. This galaxy is ruled by the unity of its people. I have worked hard to see you free from worry associated with war, violence, division, and disorder. I want you to be free to choose your own path. I will not tolerate those who stray from the path of order and discipline created by the Commonwealth. Each of you has chosen a military life, and you understand the need for order and discipline. These invaders threaten that order and discipline. We captured some of their spies, and they proved too dangerous for us. After interrogating them, they had to be neutralized in the only way possible. We had no choice, but to execute them."

A stunned silence fell across the already subdued crowd. Even the occasional clinking of china or sloshing of a water glass faded away. No one moved. The Executor paused, allowing his words to sink in. Executions were almost unheard of. Their society had become so advanced and sophisticated; executions were deemed unnecessary.

"I know you must think I am a cruel monster to go to such extremes, but we tried rehabilitation and re-education, prolonged solitary confinement, and medications. None of it stopped them. They managed to turn their guards into their allies; they tried to turn everyone they came in contact with. We tried to study them to find out how their methods worked, but the more our people learned, the more they were pulled in to the other side. Regrettably, some of our very own people had to be... executed."

Executor Hale, his voice cracking, looked down at the floor and paused. He appeared to be blinking back tears. Soft mumbling rippled across the audience. After he composed himself, he began again in a strong voice. "This has to end, now! Our people don't deserve to be executed! I didn't want to issue the order. I had no other choice. Our people are not expendable. I care deeply about the well-being of our citizens. The Commonwealth's goals are for the betterment of its people, all its people. This includes the uncivilized and undeveloped worlds in this galaxy. We have been caring for them before they even knew it. When we received word of disasters, famine, disease among the lesser worlds, we discreetly sent in food, medicines, and other aid to help them. All we ever asked of them in return for our help is to remember the Commonwealth. This new enemy has begun working against us, trying to corrupt our future citizens. They are creating a division of alliances. These small populations are rejecting the Commonwealth, who came to their aid, in time of need. This isn't their fault. These civilizations are young and easily influenced. They still garner primitive beliefs in gods. They worship the suns, moons, stars, animals, or statues. This is the fault of those who have infected them. This unknown enemy has caused this. We must rescue these infant societies before it's too late. It's up to us to save them from their own shortcomings and innocence. They don't understand what is at stake. They don't see the big picture like we do. We have to stop this invasion before it spreads. This is an infection and must be cut out! We have to save them!" He shouted and pounded his fist on the table closest to him. His voice had been growing in intensity throughout his speech until it reached a thunderous crescendo punctuated by the pounding of his fist and the dishes rattling on the table.

The audience stood to their feet one by one and began applauding. As the applause began to wane the Supreme Executor raised his hands to motion for silence. Everyone settled back into his or her seats as he began to speak again. His tone was calm and matter of fact.

"You were told, we are initiating a first contact type mission and offering goodwill gestures to lesser civilizations. We are going to give them small advances in technology, simply to better their lives through improvements in health, farming, building, irrigation, and so on. We are going to introduce ourselves to them, help them, and earn their trust. We don't want to push ourselves on them, but in return for our help, we are going to ask them to warn us when our new enemy shows up. We will develop societies who will choose to be loyal to us. Your mission is not primarily a military mission. You are the advance scouts. When you joined the Interstellar Force, you gave an oath to be defenders of the Commonwealth. These twelve teams are the first line of defense of the Commonwealth. If you run into the enemy, you are to leave and report it at once. We will quarantine the planet, allow no one to enter or leave, and hopefully contain it. We will stop this evil darkness, overshadowing our galaxy, and putting a blight on our society. In the defense of the Commonwealth, do I have your full support?" His voice was again rising in a crescendo.

The crowd gave a resounding, "Yes sir!"

Admiral Garcia picked up his glass, raised it, and loudly proclaimed, "For the good of the Commonwealth!"

The audience got to their feet and joined him in toasting, "For the good of the Commonwealth."

Supreme Executor Hale did not belabor his point. He finished his speech very quickly by proclaiming he knew they would make him proud. The Executor had other important engagements to attend to so he left as suddenly as he had arrived.

The rest of the banquet was shrouded with a feeling of restlessness. The crowd wanted to discuss what the Executor had presented, but they were too uneasy. It was hard to wrap their brains around the information. The most difficult thing to swallow was the executions. Executions were unheard of. Criminals were punished through incarceration for a time, then rehabilitation, relocation, and possibly re-education. Many times, it was determined mental illness was the cause for crime, and those were treated medically if possible. Everyone wants to see justice served. Criminals were detained and punished based on the severity and nature of the crime. A lesser crime meant extensive counseling, testing, and appropriate education. If the staff were convinced rehabilitation had occurred, the individual could be relocated to another planet, set up in a job, and given a place to live to make a fresh start. There were some who felt this was not harsh enough because from time to time someone would commit a crime just to get a "fresh start." Relocation decisions were based on the type of crime and whether it was believed the individual was unduly influenced by his environment. If the crime was severe enough, or the criminal repeated his or her behavior, total re-education was the only alternative. Total re-education involved deep hypnosis to revamp the entire personality and psychological profile. An individual of this caliber would be relocated, and if it were believed the traits were genetic, they would also be sterilized. There were a couple of penal colonies if all methods failed, even that was rare.

The rest of the night was less eventful. Everyone enjoyed the time to relax and visit with the friends they had each made during all the training. As the night came to a close, everyone retired to his or her new shipboard accommodations. Because of the previous night's events, the crews were allowed to sleep in a bit. The day would consist of putting away those few items they carried with them the last few days and a final once-over of the entire ship. There were also a few last-minute meetings. The Admirals Board called a meeting with all the ship's captains. Captain Alexander was reasonably certain the topic of discussion would pertain to the Supreme Executor's speech. He wasn't wrong.

●●●

David walked into the Admirals Board meeting and hesitated before taking a seat. He glanced around the room to find the most strategic place to sit. The front of the room contained a head table for the Admirals board. The body of the room had a U-shaped table facing the head table. He chose a seat on the far side of the table facing the door. He tried to select a seat that didn't appear too eager or too reluctant. Captain Alexander was one of the youngest and newest captains in the Interstellar Forces entire fleet. He noticed a majority of the captains in the mission fleet were younger new captains. He suspected they had been pushed through their training faster just to populate the mission crews. What he didn't know or suspect was the true intent of the admirals' plans. They chose young, inexperienced commanders who would be quick to obey their orders and were too inexperienced to ask questions.

There were five admirals assigned to the Admirals Board including David's uncle. Admiral Garcia was the lead admiral on the board. The room was called to attention as the admirals entered and moved to their seats up front. Admiral Garcia was seated in the center of the front table. As the admirals were seated, Admiral Garcia called the meeting to order.

"Be seated."

Admiral Garcia opened his notes, took a sip of the glass of water positioned in front of him then began.

"I'm sure all of you have questions regarding the Supreme Executor's speech last night. I will be giving you your specific orders. The threat to our people, our civilization and our way of life is genuine. Although they have not come at us with weapons, they are moving in slowly, quietly, in a truly insidious manner. They are led by one known as the 'Timeless One' and as such, is said to have great power and knowledge. As with any great leader, he promises his followers peace, freedom, healing, a good life, etc. You all know the usual platitudes for the weak-minded. The 'Timeless One' also claims to be on the side of Light and Truth and the other usual nonsense. They insist all the galaxies belong to the Timeless One and those who do not ally themselves with him will be destroyed. This galaxy belongs to the Commonwealth, to the people of the Commonwealth. They are threatening our destruction. We have worked hard to maintain peace and prosperity. If they intend to threaten that peace, we will put a stop to it quickly and permanently. We found these insurgents on worlds all across the galaxy, so it's already spread too far. They appear to only be on the lesser worlds, but we have to find out the extent of their reach. We believe this new enemy is somehow forcing these civilizations to follow them. The ones we have encountered seem to be incapable of choosing anything, but to serve our enemy."

Admiral Garcia paused and took another sip of water. "Your assignment is this: #1 – Do what you can to meet and earn the trust of the less advanced planets and colonies. #2 – Warn them about our enemy and get their cooperation to report the enemy's movements to us. If we can destroy them at that level, then let them help us. #3 – Be on the lookout for populations already infiltrated by the enemy. If you find one that has been infiltrated, get out and report back to us immediately. The interface you leave behind will include the basic educational information you were instructed about in your training. It will serve as a communications device, and it will also be programmed to monitor daily activity and conversations. If certain keywords or phrases are identified, it will automatically notify us. We will dispatch a crew to confirm it, and deal with it appropriately."

Captain Logan, who was sitting beside Captain Alexander raised his hand and asked, "Sir, how can we be sure if what we are dealing with is the enemy? There are so many primitive beliefs, cultures, and religions, how can we be sure we've found the actual enemy?"

Admiral Johnson spoke up, "Admiral Garcia, may I address this one?"

"Of course, go ahead."

"Thank you, sir. I have studied the enemy very carefully. They ally themselves with a being we have been unable to locate. Our scanners cannot pick up anything, yet they seem to be in constant contact with this being. At first, we thought it was just some sort of mental illness. We tried to treat it as such, but there were unexplained occurrences. We put them into a mental health facility and placed them in solitary confinement until we could get them under control. Then somehow, they would be found sitting in the common areas talking to the other patients. We returned them to their rooms, placed guards outside the doors, and made sure the video surveillance was activated. The next morning, we saw a video record of these individuals walking right out of their rooms and into the common areas again. The guards were awake and alert, but have no memory of seeing anyone leave the room. There was no evidence the guards were bribed, blackmailed, coerced, drugged, or hypnotized. We had to confine all the patients to their rooms and close down the common areas. After we took those precautions, we discovered they were moving freely from one room to another. Once we discovered how dangerous they were, we moved them to our most secure facility while sedated. Unfortunately, they converted some of the patients, and we were not able to help them. They had to be put down. It is a little hard to tell you exactly what you are looking for because we have had a difficult time isolating them ourselves. We discovered them when we reached out to a world that was beginning space travel. As we attempted to integrate them into the Commonwealth, we encountered resistance like none we've seen before. Their world had several territorial leaders as we have seen so many times and some of those leaders refused to commit to the Commonwealth. They claimed to be allied with a being that would not permit them to ally with us. The resulting conflicts on that world caused the entire planet to go to war. There is always a period of unrest and adjustment when we are guiding a new world into becoming an advanced civilization. These world leaders believe they are big fish in a big pond and, when we come along, they must learn to accept being a small fish in a very big pond. There's always some resistance, although with time and guidance they get through it. We did everything we could to integrate their own world leaders into the new leadership positions, but they would not sign the loyalty oaths. Ultimately, they had to be removed as leaders. These are the individuals we studied. They gave us a description of their ally in very vague terms. He is an advanced being of over-whelming power and knowledge, yet they cannot give a physical description of him because they've never seen him. His name is Pateras El Liontari. He communicates with his followers telepathically. They have reported visits from an emissary of Liontari known as Sotaeras. For these individuals to be able to move from room to room without being observed would indicate some sort of manipulation of matter, energy, and mind control. The primary things to look for are these same supernatural abilities, refusal to swear allegiance to the Commonwealth and the names of Pateras El Liontari and Sotaeras. Does that answer your question, Captain Logan?"

"Yes sir."

Admiral Garcia resumed his portion of the briefing, "We've faced enemies before. We have gone to great lengths to establish this Commonwealth to see there is peace in this galaxy. All the enemies of the Commonwealth have declared themselves openly. We have never seen an enemy come at us in such an indirect manner. It's hard to stop them when we don't have a target to shoot at. I cannot stress this to you enough. Do NOT try to get intelligence from the enemy. Do not linger once you've found them. Get your people out before they are turned against you. They will appear weak and inoffensive, but they are masters of deception. When you find them, get out quickly and notify us immediately. If any of your own people are taken over, you can leave them behind or if you're already in space, quarantine them and report back immediately. No one is to have any contact with one who has been corrupted. Do you understand?"

The captains responded with a firm, "Yes sir!"

Admiral Garcia began to close the briefing with his final instructions. "You are to inform your crews of everything you have heard in this briefing. I hope none of you are ever taken over, but should it happen; your crews need to know how to handle you. Is that understood?"

"Yes sir!"

"There is one more thing. If you determine your crew is at risk and you feel there is no other recourse, you are hereby authorized to perform executions as humanely as possible of your crew. This is to be used as a last resort. Be aware; there may be a board of inquiry convened to determine if you were justified in taking such an action. Make sure, and document everything."

David, unnerved by these last instructions asked, "Admiral, do we know how this corruption happens? Is it some kind of brainwashing, an alien parasite, or mind control?"

"No, we do not know how it happens. We have performed extensive scans and did not find any sign of parasites or alien presence. No drugs have been in any of their systems. Some of the corrupted never came into direct contact with any of the prisoners. They merely viewed the surveillance videos and became corrupted."

"Sir, how do we fight an enemy we can't see? How do we quarantine someone who can get out of locked doors?" David continued. He was becoming quite troubled, as were several of the other captains.

"You don't fight this enemy," replied the Admiral. "That's our job. You just find them and leave the rest to us. We have plans in place to deal with the situation. If you cannot keep them confined, sedate them. If sedation doesn't work, put them in stasis, maroon them or space them. Do the best you can. If you do not follow these orders, you will be relieved of command. Do I make myself clear?"

"Yes sir," the captains responded.

The Admiral opened the floor for any remaining questions. The tasking seemed relatively simple and straightforward. Given the Admiral's harsh tone no one else felt inclined to ask anything. Hearing none, he moved on. He gave each captain the coordinates for the sector to which he or she would be assigned as well as supplemental information from the archives about their assigned sectors. The sector information included star charts, historical data, and demographics on the planets, and their populations.

When the meeting concluded, no one hung around to talk or say any lengthy goodbyes. There was plenty of work left to do, and the work now included a staff meeting with the crew. David headed back to his ship to get started.

His ship was named the *Evangeline*. All the ships were explorer class ships and bore similar positive names. He assumed the intent was to cast a positive psychological image for what would be a long, tedious mission. Every little bit would help.

Surface shuttles constantly ran from the offices carrying supplies and personnel out to the twelve ships sitting on the tarmac. David hitched a ride on one back out to the *Evangeline*.

Each of the ships was identical except for identification markers. David still thought the *Evangeline* was the best-looking ship in the fleet. She was designed for maximum efficiency to maneuver in atmospheres, water, or in space. Her design reminded him of a mixture of certain sea creatures. She was dark gray in color with teal trim. She was wider than she was tall. The shuttle bay on top gave her a bulge, which reminded him of a dorsal fin. The ship did vertical takeoffs and landings, so her landing gear consisted of three pedestal style props. Although she didn't have a tail like most sea creatures, with the cargo bay ramp extended, it slightly resembled a tail. From the top, she looked more like a half moon.

A retractable stairwell extended from the primary airlock to the ground. David climbed the steps as he had numerous times before, but today he savored every step. This time it was for real.

The ship was now his to command. The primary hatch was an airlock, which had both an inner and an outer door. David crossed the threshold of the second door and paused to take in the sight, smells, and sounds of the ship. The lowest level of the ship held the cargo bay, crew quarters, infirmary, guest quarters, dining hall, and engineering. David stepped aboard a lift and rode it up to the third level of the ship. Level two contained the gymnasium and the multipurpose room. The gymnasium was tall enough to extend up to the third level. The bridge and the Captain's office were both on the third level. The fourth level contained the shuttle bay and a couple service conduits.

David stepped onto the bridge drinking in the atmosphere. The station closest to the door was an auxiliary station, which could take the place of any bridge function, or all of them if necessary. In front of that were three stations. The Captain's chair was in the center. To the left of the Captain's chair was the Commander's station and, on the right, was the Communication's station. Across the front of the bridge were the weapons, helm, and navigation.

The Communications officer, Ensign Aulani Ryder was the first person to see the Captain step onto the bridge because her station was angled toward the center of the bridge rather than the front of the ship. She promptly called out, "Captain on the bridge!" The bridge crew stopped their activities and snapped to attention.

David paused for a moment before responding. "As you were." Once they were in deep space, he planned to dispense with that formality, but until the crew reached a point of knowing all the limits and boundaries, he would leave it in place.

As Captain Alexander took his place on the bridge, he distributed the travel coordinates to the pilot, Lt. Thane Ryder and the navigator, Lt. Junior Grade (LJG) Marissa Holden. Thane had come highly recommended as a pilot, scoring top marks in all the training exercises. The only drawback was that although Lt. Ryder was good at his job, he tended to get cocky at times. He took more chances than most pilots, but he did respect the chain of command. Thane was just under six feet tall and rather lean. His dark brown hair looked almost black. His smile could quietly pull you in and make you comfortable in his company whether you wanted to be or not. Marissa, on the other hand, was not nearly so self-assured.

She liked Thane well enough, although she didn't like the way he stretched and misinterpreted the regulations. Marissa was very much a "by the book" type person. She also had very dark brown hair, which she kept pulled neatly back out of her face. Marissa knew she and Thane were going to be working together a lot, so she made sure to focus on her job when she was around him and not on his "childish" behavior.

David pulled the navigation charts up on the three-dimensional displays on the bridge. He wanted to discuss initial routing with the primary navigator and pilot; Lt. Holden and Lt. Ryder, as well as their backups. Since the ship had two crews serving as each other's backups, Captain Alexander wanted both present for the initial trip planning.

The secondary navigator was actually the mission crew's botanist, Lieutenant Junior Grade, Laurel Adams, but she preferred to be called Laura. The secondary pilot was her husband, Lt. Commander Jason Adams, who also served as the ship's doctor. It seemed like an odd backup, but the doctor took his job as a physician so seriously, his position as a pilot was more like a hobby. He still took it seriously, but to him, it was "fun." Dr. Adams and his wife had been married for two years already. He and Laura took trips together in a small ship of their own. He was their pilot, and she was their navigator. Her career of choice was a botanist. They chose to join this project together because they both love a good adventure. They were the type of people who were extremely intelligent and interested in a wide variety of things. They both seemed to enjoy a challenge, and this mission would certainly be that.

Thane's wife, Ensign Aulani Ryder, was the ship's Communications and Computer Technician. She would be serving as a Linguistics and Computer Technician support for the mission staff. Aulani was working away at the communications console passing messages back and forth between the crew and the mission base staff. Her hair was pulled back in a short ponytail which bounced happily with her every move. Thane and Aulani had only been married as long as David and Brynna. Aulani was easy going, but stable. She seemed to keep Thane from getting out of hand.

David had a communications console at his station, and instinctively he reached for it to call Jason and Laura to the bridge. He checked himself when he realized it was time for him to let his people do their jobs. He looked up at Aulani, "Ensign Ryder, have Lt. Commander Adams and Lt. Adams report to the bridge."

The ensign looked back at him and responded with a cheerful, "Yes sir." Captain Alexander wanted to be very careful here at the beginning of the mission to set the appropriate tone. He called each crew member by their rank and last name. Since the crew had dual roles, he also addressed them with the position they were serving in at the moment. The doctor could have been called either Dr. Adams or Lt. Commander, and if they had been in the heat of battle, David wouldn't have cared less about names or titles so long as the right person responded at the right time and got the job done. He fully expected to lighten the tone as everyone settled into his or her roles.

Jason and Laura entered the bridge together and joined the others at the display console. Captain Alexander showed them the sector they were to be assigned to travel. The galaxy had been laid out in twelve different sectors. There were three layers of four quadrants each, roughly like a sandwich cut into quarters. The top bun divided into four parts, the meaty section of the sandwich divided into four parts, and the bottom bun also divided. The systems in the top and bottom of the galaxy were fewer and farther apart, so the territory had a greater depth to be covered. The center of the galaxy had more systems closer together, so they had less depth; but they did extend furthest from the center of the galaxy. The intended route was to start at the closest systems and work their way outward bypassing worlds already space-faring and active members of the Commonwealth. They discussed the first six possibilities. Once David decided the appropriate priorities, he left the actual route planning up to the navigation staff and excused himself.

"Ensign Ryder."

"Yes, Captain?" She responded.

"Based on our loading schedule, what would be the best time to schedule a full staff meeting?" David needed to bring his people up to speed on the new information he had from the meeting with the Admirals board. Aulani checked the manifest and routing information then told the Captain, "Sir, we should have everything on board in an hour and a half."

"All right, schedule it for two hours from now. That will give everyone a chance to have everything stowed away before the meeting. Make the notifications; we'll meet in the dining hall."

"Yes sir." She replied and started to work.

David returned to his console and reviewed the results of weapons tests and the engine diagnostics. Everything seemed to be running very smoothly. Despite the good reports, David wanted to check in with the Engineer and Security Chief anyway.

David punched the communications console and spoke, "Chief Holden, this is the Captain."

A second later, Chief Petty Officer Jacob Holden, aka Jake responded, "This is Chief Holden."

"Chief, I was just reviewing our weapons complement, the test fire stats, and the design specifications. Everything seems to be in line. Have you seen anything giving you cause for concern?"

"No, sir. Everything seems to be working perfectly. Lt. Commander Dominick and I did, however, set up an additional back-up power circuit to the ship's laser cannons. I'm not expecting us to need those cannons very often, but I don't want them to fail if we do. Perhaps I should have checked with you before we did it, but it doesn't compromise any other ship systems."

"That's fine," David replied. "So long as I know about it and it doesn't cause any other problems. Did you test the new circuits?"

"Yes sir. They are operating at the same peak efficiency as the primary and the standard back up."

"All right, good job Chief. Send me a copy of those relays and put a copy in the data banks. Let me know if you have any problems or concerns."

"Yes, Captain."

"Captain, out."

David looked at the data for engineering, atmospheric recycling, water reclamation, and artificial gravity. Everything again appeared to be in order. Not wanting to discount anyone's "gut feelings," David hailed the Chief Engineer. "Lt. Commander Dominick, this is the Captain." David waited patiently for a reply, but after a full minute without a response, he hailed again. "I repeat,

Lt. Commander Dominick, this is the Captain. Please respond."

"This is Lt. Commander Dominick, Captain, go ahead."

"Is everything okay down there, Commander?"

"Yes sir, I'm sorry, sir. I didn't hear your first hail. I had my head down in a bulkhead accessing a loose circuit board."

"Lt. Commander, I was just looking over the specifications and performance analysis for all the engineering systems. Everything seems to be working at maximum efficiency. Does anything stand out in your mind?"

"No, sir. Everything is looking good. I just had the one loose circuit board, and now that's fixed. I was just about to go through the systems on the shuttle. Would you like to go with me to take her out?"

"No, thanks, Lt. Commander. I appreciate the offer, but I have some other things to attend to before the staff meeting." David would really have loved to take the shuttle out for a test run, more than he cared to admit. He had started out in the Brigade as a pilot and enjoyed it, but since he chose the command path, he wasn't able to fly as much as he would like. He didn't regret his choice, but it did have a few drawbacks.

Since supply requisitions and delivery scheduling had to go through the communications officer, it was more expedient for the comm officer to serve in both capacities. Ensign Ryder served as the primary supply officer, and Ensign Dominick was her assistant. The next thing on David's checklist was supplies. If the ship wasn't adequately supplied, it was going to be a very short trip, or the mission was going to be a very big failure. All twelve ships were being outfitted exactly the same, so there wasn't really a reason to expect failure in that respect. Of course, there was always the chance the wrong supplies could be loaded onto the ship. It really wouldn't work out well to have twice the weapons and no food.

David moved from his station carrying his datapad with the supply list displayed and approached Ensign Ryder's station.

"Ensign Ryder?"

"Yes, Captain?" She replied.

"How are we coming on the supplies? Any problems?"

"Fine, sir. Ensign Dominick is verifying receipt of the supplies in the cargo bay. Everything should be loaded in about an hour. I sent updated copies of the supply list to each department noting what has already been loaded and I plan to send a final copy as soon as we're done loading. I would like everyone to review it to be sure nothing's been overlooked."

David made a note on his datapad to be sure it was mentioned in the staff meeting. "Okay, I'm putting you down to make that announcement at the staff meeting. Anything else?"

"No, sir, everything seems to be running exceptionally well." Ensign Ryder paused and another look formed on her face that was a cross between puzzlement and concern.

"What is it?" David queried.

"Well, sir, I'm typically an optimist, but when things go too smoothly, it just makes me a little... concerned. I keep thinking; something always goes wrong, at least a little something. There's been nothing go wrong at all. Everything has come in correctly and on time or even early, nothing has been misplaced or damaged. It's actually kind of... creepy."

The thought was a little unsettling to David, but since he had to maintain the confidence of his crew, he did what any good captain would. He tucked his true feelings away and said, "There's been a lot of work and planning go into this project, and the best people we have are working on it. I think we just have a good handle on things. It doesn't hurt to keep your eyes open though."

"Captain?"

"Yes, Lt. Holden?"

"Sir, we have our first three target sites lined up. We thought we would go to Galat III first then Medoris IV, second and Drea III, third."

Any planet not already a member of the Commonwealth was given the name of its sun and a number based on which planet it was from the sun.

Lt. Holden continued, "We thought we should start with the closest planet then work our way outwards in somewhat of a spiral pattern." Lt. Holden reached for a control on the display and manipulated it to demonstrate the intended flight plan.

"What are your reasons for starting there?" David didn't disapprove of their choices, but he wanted to know the flight crew's train of thought, and he also knew he wasn't above making mistakes in his own thinking. It never hurt to have another set of eyes review a situation.

Lt. Holden having just come through her crew training, along with the rest of the crew, was accustomed to explaining her actions. "Since we aren't sure about the extent of the incursion or the possible reaction the enemy may have to being discovered, we should proceed cautiously. This course keeps us closer to our reinforcements if we need them. It also increases our chances of developing allies more quickly who haven't been touched by our enemy."

David's eyes locked on hers for a moment. He searched her face for doubt then shifted his search to each one of the navigation crew. Each one gave the impression of being confident in their decision. "Sounds good, let's do it. Get that information ready to disseminate to all departments at the staff meeting. Also, get the coordinates put into the navigation computer and get our course plotted. Let me know what time we could be ready for departure. Good work."

David wanted to do a thorough walk-through of the ship. He decided to start outside. He went out to walk around and under the ship, examining every seam or ripple in the hull. After examining everything he could from the ground, David procured a portable lift and examined the top and upper sides of the ship. Once he was satisfied everything was in order, he re-entered the ship and examined every inch of the inside, except for the crew quarters. He wasn't comfortable invading his crew's privacy, and he seriously doubted anything was obviously wrong in those areas.

The two hours he had until the staff meeting went by rather quickly. It would not be good for the Captain to be late to his own meeting. David walked into the meeting thirty seconds before it was scheduled to start. Lt. Ryder was the first to see him enter and called out, "Captain on deck!" The room snapped to attention.

"As you were. Everyone take your seats." This room served as both a dining hall and a meeting room. It contained four small rectangular tables. Ultimately, they could comfortably seat sixteen people in this room. They could cram a few more in if necessary, although more chairs would have to be pulled in from storage or crew quarters. Since the crew was divided between the four tables, David chose a central location to address the room. He set his datapad down but remained standing. He moved through his agenda quickly and efficiently allowing no time for idle chatter.

Although they had only known each other a short time, Brynna was still capable of picking up on the subtle nuances of David's demeanor. She knew from the minute he walked in the door; something was bothering him. She tried to convince herself it was just nerves, stress, or David's way of "taking command." She wasn't doing a very good job of convincing herself.

David saved the information from his meeting with the Admirals board for last. It was probably the hardest thing he was going to have to discuss with the crew. He had been rehearsing this part of his speech for several hours, and he wasn't sure he had it down the way he wanted it yet. David hesitated long enough to get a deep breath then began. "I know you all have a lot of questions about the Supreme Executor's speech last night. I received a briefing this morning that gave more detailed information, which I will pass on to you along with your orders. Our primary mission is to gain allies and determine the extent of our new enemy's progression. If we locate the enemy, we are to evacuate our crew immediately and report their location back to headquarters. If any of the crew is taken over by the enemy, they will be left behind with the local population. If we are in space, they will be quarantined with no contact from the rest of the crew. Commander Alexander..."

David's eyes locked on Brynna's as she responded, "Yes, Captain?"

"You have the responsibility to relieve me of my command if I should become affected. I also have the authority to execute, as humanely as possible, any crew member I deem too great a threat to the rest of the crew. Commander, if I become that threat, this responsibility falls to you."

Brynna did her best to maintain her composure; however, she did grow slightly pale. To send a crewman into a life or death situation was one thing, but to simply execute them was another. She responded with a reluctant, but firm, "Yes sir."

David wanted to lighten the mood a little, so he added, "Just don't execute me just to get your next promotion." He gave her a wry smile.

Taking his lead, she grinned back at him and said, "Just don't make me mad."

The crew laughed softly and began to relax again. David continued his instructions by giving them the identifying characteristics of their enemy he had received that morning. He completed his briefing by saying, "This is going to be a long tour in close quarters. We need to get along, respect each other's space, and I want us to have some fun. Our mission is a serious one, but we should have plenty of good experiences. Are there any other questions?" David's eyes contacted every other crew member's eyes one at a time. Seeing no one with a questioning look in their eyes, he said, "All right then, as soon as all the supply lists are reviewed and turned in to Ensign Ryder, I will report us as ready to depart. Everyone to your primary stations."

Ten minutes later, Ensign Ryder reported she had received all the lists, and everything was in perfect order. Captain Alexander had her send the "Ready to depart" message. The return message was to "Stand by to receive Admiral Deacons."

"Set scanners for incoming vehicles or personnel 360 degrees, air and land." David had things to do but didn't want the Admiral coming on board without a proper greeting. After another 10 minutes, Chief Holden piped up and reported, "Ground shuttle approaching, sir."

"Thanks, Chief." David jumped up and headed to meet the Admiral. "Ensign Ryder, tell the crew to prepare to receive the Admiral and have Commander Alexander meet me at the main airlock."

"Yes, Captain." Aulani touched a control on her panel and spoke, "All hands, prepare for Admiral Deacons. Commander Alexander, report to the main airlock."

David stood by the airlock, which was standing wide open and breathed the fresh air one last time. Going off-world, one never knew what the air would be like on another planet. The air on a ship always seemed a little stale. Brynna joined him a few seconds later. She too took a deep breath and sighed. "I'm gonna miss that fresh air."

"Me too. Are you nervous?"

"A little, but I'll get over it."

The Admiral approached the airlock and stood just outside. "Permission to come aboard?"

"Permission granted. Welcome aboard, Admiral."

The Admiral stepped inside. David saluted, and the Admiral returned his salute.

"Well, David, I'm impressed. Your ship was the first to report being departure ready."

"Thank you, sir."

"Brynna, did David fill you in on what could be expected of you?"

"Yes sir."

"Would you be able to execute your own husband if it became necessary?" The Admiral studied her face carefully.

Brynna hesitated, and then looked David squarely in the eye. "If he becomes a clear danger to the crew then, Yes sir, I would. I don't know how much use I would be afterward though." She looked back at the Admiral to gauge his reaction. She had just told the Admiral she was able and willing to kill his nephew.

Admiral Deacons paused momentarily to gauge the accuracy of her response. It was a hard question to ask and answer. He would have been more concerned if she had responded too quickly or too confidently. He appreciated her candor and would not have expected anything less from her. "I sincerely hope it never comes to that. Before we get too 'official,' I do want to tell you both how proud I am of you. No matter how this mission turns out, David, you've been like a son to me, and Brynna, I think of you as a daughter."

David wasn't quite sure if he was responding to the "Admiral" or to his "Uncle." He chose the safer path, stuck out his hand to shake the Admirals hand and said, "Thank you, sir. I feel closer to you than I do to my own father."

The Admiral grinned at David's guarded behavior in silent approval. He took David's hand, firmly grasped it, then pulled him in for a brief embrace, halfway between a hug and a pat on the back. When the Admiral released David, he turned to Brynna who followed the Admirals lead giving him a tighter hug than David's and a quick kiss on the cheek. She quietly whispered, "Thank you, sir." She stepped back and regained her military bearing.

David and Brynna escorted the Admiral throughout the ship. The Admiral personally greeted every member of the crew, thanking them for their hard work and wishing them the best. He didn't want to slow their departure, so he kept his comments brief yet sincere. He also had other ships to visit, and it had the potential of being a very long day. Reaching the end of his tour, the Admiral wished David and Brynna the best and bid them farewell.

The couple returned to the bridge to prepare for departure. The ship's crew members were at their primary duty stations, and the mission crew members were working with them any place it was feasible to have the added support. Chief Holden, Lt. Holden, Ensign Ryder, Lt. Ryder, and Captain Alexander made up the primary bridge crew. There was only room for one pilot at a time. Currently having no patients, Dr. Adams manned one of the vacant bridge stations. Two multipurpose stations located on the bridge could be used as a redundant control station of the other bridge functions. Commander Brynna Alexander took her station to monitor their departure. Lt. Commander Dominick and Lt. Commander Flint remained in Engineering. Ensign Cheyenne Dominick, Lt. Laura Adams, and Lt. Lexi Flint went to the dining hall to watch their departure from the Computer screen together. It wasn't that the ship had never been off the ground before, but there was still a high level of "first time" excitement in the air. Once Captain Alexander determined everyone was in place and ready for departure, he settled into his chair. "Ensign Ryder, contact the Launch Commander and request permission to launch."

"Yes sir." She pressed a button and began to transmit. "Launch Command, this is the *Evangeline*, requesting permission to launch." Considering the magnitude of the occasion, she put the audio on all ship's comm units so no matter where on the ship anyone was located they would hear the response. David hadn't ordered it, but given the circumstances, he had no complaints about her choice. The excitement was so thick in the brief seconds before Launch Command responded, David was afraid they would have a hull breach if it lasted any longer. Then came the anxiously awaited response, "*Evangeline*, this is Launch Command... stand by."

Lt. Ryder glanced over at Marissa and softly said, "Stand by? Are you kidding?" Marissa gave him a stern glance but didn't respond.

"Take it easy, Lieutenant," David spoke calmly. His gut reaction was very similar to Thane's, but he kept it from showing.

Another second later Launch Command came back on the comm line, "*Evangeline*, this is Launch Command, you are cleared to launch on launch pattern Alpha. Please confirm."

Ensign Ryder responded, "Launch Command, we confirm, cleared to launch on pattern Alpha."

"Lt. Ryder, engage the thrusters. Lt. Holden, set course for launch pattern Alpha and lay in a standard orbit."

Thane and Marissa started to work. The ship began powering up, and a distinct hum and vibration made its way throughout the ship.

"Take us out, Lieutenant."

As the engines reached a rhythmic sound, Thane pulled back on the throttle. The ship groaned, shuttered briefly then settled into a noticeable hum. The movement of the ship through the atmosphere created resistance against the ship's hull. It could be a little intimidating if you weren't used to leaving the atmosphere. As they began to clear the atmosphere, the hum began to fade until it was hardly noticeable. As they reached their intended orbit, everyone's nerves began to settle. There were plenty of reasons to be nervous. The ship had been test piloted a couple times, but it was still brand new. Some of the crew members were newer than others, and they all were somewhat new to each other. They had spent time working together for the last couple of months, but it takes time to build trust. The crew had not reached a point of total trust.

David touched his comm panel and said, "All hands do a broad-spectrum system check and report in."

The three crew members in the dining hall were assigned to physically check every room not already occupied. They wanted to be sure if the computer monitoring systems weren't working they had as much advanced warning as possible before they left orbit. The crew was checking for hull breaches, failures in the artificial gravity, even broken lights. They split up and went to their assigned routes and walked into every room including crew quarters. The three women, upon completing their respective routes, reported back to the Bridge.

After receiving the reports from Engineering and the women doing the spot checks, Aulani reported back to the Captain. "Sir, Engineering and the auxiliary crew have reported all systems checks are complete and reporting no problems."

"Excellent. Lt. Holden, set course for Galat III. Ensign Ryder, let launch command know we are leaving orbit and setting course for Galat III. Lt. Ryder, take us out of orbit. As soon as we have cleared the solar system, engage the tachyon drive. Engineering, prepare for initialization of the tachyon drive."

Lt. Commander Lazaro Dominick's voice came through the speaker, "Engineering here. Acknowledged."

The bridge's retractable shield opened for a direct view of the stars while they were making their way out of the system. The external cameras were also on and available for the rest of the crew to see the view of the system as they left. Some of the crew had never been out of their solar system. David's history logged numerous trips outside the solar system, although he never tired of the view. It was quite a sight to see the planets roll by. Some of the larger planets were relatively close to them. One was a gas giant whose size nearly filled the observation window. The planet's swirling clouds gave a colorful show as they passed by. The last two planets were on the far side of their rotation, so they cleared the system a little early.

Thane moved a slide on the control panel to increase the buildup of tachyon particles. Tachyons naturally travel faster than the speed of light, but to use tachyons as a source of propulsion was another trick entirely. The tachyon field was generated by a matter/anti-matter engine. The tachyons were then channeled across the external frame of the hull starting at the nose of the ship and flowing toward the rear. Once the channels reached full capacity, there would be one focused burst of energy to propel the ship toward the edge of the galaxy. As they passed the last planet, the tachyon field began to build. When the energy levels reached the appropriate level, Thane moved the slides on his console. The ship vanished in a bright flash of light resembling an exploding star, but on an infinitely smaller scale.

It took a large tachyon burst to get the ship started on its journey, but fewer tachyons to maintain and even gain speed. The initial energy build-up would be used to start the ship's movement, but a lesser, steady flow would keep the ship moving and increase its speed. It was a really fast way to travel, but it did have some drawbacks. The field balances had to be strictly maintained, first in the matter/anti-matter engines, and second in the tachyon channels across the ship's hull. Naturally, there were redundant systems, but if a main feed were interrupted the entire ship could end up shredded with slices of it spread halfway across the galaxy. Due to the sensitive nature of this particular drive mechanism, the ship would always have someone at the helm and in engineering while the drive was active.

THE MISSION

THE CREW

Once the initial excitement of their departure was over, the crew could settle into a rather dull and monotonous trip. It was going to take them nearly three weeks to reach Galat III. David used the time to cross-train the crew as much as possible. It also served to ward off boredom. There had to be at least three people on duty at all times: a pilot, an engineer, and a Command Officer. The Command Officer didn't have to remain on the bridge, but he or she did have to be awake, alert, and aware of their status. Once the ship's course was set, it pretty much ran on autopilot, but someone needed to be in close proximity in case something went wrong. Captain Alexander gave each crewman a primary assignment as well as one shift per week as a trainee.

Lt. Lexi Flint was assigned as the ship's morale officer. During this part of the voyage, she had to see no one went stir crazy. Lexi planned an informal get together for the second day in the dining hall. She scheduled it to start at the end of one shift and end after the beginning of the next shift, so everyone had a chance to join in. Everyone got together to play card games and despite the lack of space to store "extras," they did have some light refreshments. Two days later she started scheduling various sporting events in the gymnasium. Sometimes it was a team sport, and other times it was individual competitions. Everyone seemed to enjoy the time to socialize, although some took the competitions more seriously than others.

Security Chief Jake Holden was one of those. He had a difficult time seeing the games as "just for fun." Thane and David were on the same level athletically as Jake. Thane was faster and cocky. David was slower and more calculating, but his strategies usually bought him definite advantages. Jake tended to lose patience when David didn't take obvious openings. One of the games they played frequently was called "Zone." The floor would be color-coded by lighted panels that would change randomly. There were four receptacles a ball had to drop into in the four corners of the court. The trick was to bounce or ricochet it into the receptacles while standing in the correct zone. In order to score points, you had to be standing in the same color zone as the receptacles when you threw the ball. If the zones changed in the middle of your shot, you either didn't score, lost points, or you could even score points for your opponent. You were guaranteed at least sixty seconds after a zone change before the colors would change again, which made for more frantic plays.

From one game to another based on duty schedules, the team members would change up with every game. Lexi didn't want to get any long-term rivalries developing on such a long journey in tight quarters. The main idea was to have fun, get some exercise and constructively use pent up energy. Although her goals were well-meaning, Jake and Thane managed to end up at odds whether they were playing against each other or on the same team. David ended up stepping between the two of them on numerous occasions being careful not to use his authority as captain in the games. It was inevitable his position of authority still had some bearing on the other players though. David never actually threw a game, but he played for fun not just to win. He wasn't as afraid to lose as Jake apparently was. Once David saw how seriously Jake was taking the games, he tried to encourage him to relax. Somehow Jake wasn't taking his advice to heart. Several of the women enjoyed playing "Zone" as well. Marissa preferred to take a treadmill into the multipurpose room and programmed various scenic views into the projection system, so she could run along beaches or forest trails. The projection system made it seem like she was actually going somewhere, and the air recycling system added to the realism. The only things missing were the smells and the feel of the ground under her feet.

Over the course of a week, Thane realized and silently appreciated the fact that the schedules had changed, and he was no longer playing zone with Jake. When Jake was involved, it had become more work than fun. Jake began to realize the change in scheduling as well. Thane had beaten Jake in their last game, and Jake wanted a rematch. Neither David nor Lexi had told the two about the schedule changes. They both thought it would be best to make the changes quietly, and not draw attention to it. Unbeknownst to either of them, Jake approached Laura to see if she would mind letting him take her spot.

"Hey, Laura, can I ask a favor?" Jake put on his best boyish smile, which was disarming.

"Sure, Jake, what is it?"

"I was wondering if I could take your spot playing Zone today." Laura hesitated, "I was really looking forward to this game. Jason and I have a lot of fun playing against Thane and Aulani."

"Oh, okay. I don't want to interfere. I just thought since we were only two days away from our destination you might be preparing for the mission and... well... Thane, uh... beat me the last time we played. I've been itching for a rematch, and our schedules just haven't worked out." Jake flashed another grin at her.

Laura knew the two had not played well together and wondered whether the scheduling issues were coincidental or by design. Jake didn't seem like he was spoiling for a fight, so Laura slowly relented.

"Well, maybe you're right. I do need to review some files for our land mission. We're going to be on this mission for at least two years. It's not like we won't have plenty of opportunities to play again. Sure, go ahead and take my spot. Just play nice, okay?"

"I will. I promise." Jake smiled again. As Laura turned and walked away, Jake's smile faded, and the grudge he had been holding became visible on his face.

Jake changed his clothes and went onto the Zone Court to get warmed up. A few minutes later Jason walked onto the court and was surprised to find Jake there.

"Hey Jake, how are you?"

"I'm good. How about you?" Jake continued moving about the court throwing the ball into various goals.

The safety equipment for the games included a helmet and face mask, kneepads, and elbow pads. The equipment was color-coded by team. Jason and Laura had been assigned as the yellow team on this particular day. Jason was somewhat confused to find Jake practicing in the Zone Court wearing yellow.

"Jake?"

"Yeah?" Jake stopped throwing the ball and turned to face him because he knew what Jason was about to ask.

"I thought Laura and I were playing today."

"Oh sorry, Doc. I guess she didn't get a chance to tell you. I'm playing in her spot. She said she wanted to review some files before our landing and I really wanted to play anyway. I hope that's okay." Jake wasn't quite lying, but he certainly wasn't putting the facts in quite the right perspective. He paused hoping it wasn't a problem. "Oh, okay. I understand. I was just looking forward to spending some time with Laura. I was pretty sure she and I could give these guys a run for their money."

"Well I may not have the same appeal as Laura, but I think you and I could still have fun teaching these guys how to play." Jake smiled again.

The last game Jake and Thane played had left a very bitter taste in his mouth. The game had happened almost two weeks earlier. Thane had beaten him in the last few seconds of the game. Thane knocked Jake down as he scored then laughed when Jake was sent sprawling across the floor. Thane didn't mean to embarrass Jake and was generally good-natured about such things. He offered Jake his hand to help him up off the floor, but Jake slapped it away. Marissa had been watching the game. His new wife had witnessed his humiliation, which only added fuel to the fire. No man likes to be embarrassed in front of his woman. In an attempt to preserve his ego Jake rolled to his feet to confront Thane.

"That shot is invalid! You committed a foul!" Jake shouted.

"What? I did not. You're just clumsy. You tripped over your own two feet. Don't blame me for your screw-ups." Thane didn't like to lose, but if he lost fair and square, he was typically a good sport about it. He didn't however, take it well when his abilities were called into question. When Thane would lose a game, he would first express his anger or disappointment by kicking or hitting a wall or some other inanimate object. After the brief initial outburst, he would congratulate the winners and tell them it had been a good game. He might even compliment them on a particular strategy or shot. He would then spend the next two hours kicking himself for things he should have done better. He could question himself, but he wasn't about to allow someone else to do that, especially after a win.

Lexi had been teamed up with Jake for this game and Aulani was Thane's partner. Since Thane and Aulani had been married for only a couple months like most of the other couples on the ship, there was still an unspoken desire to "prove" one's self to their mate. Thane wasn't ready to start disappointing his wife either. Lexi tried to reduce the tension between the two men by saying, "It's okay, Jake, we'll beat them next time. We know his strategy now. He can't pull that move on us again."

Thane and Jake had been in each other's faces, but when Lexi spoke, Thane started to back away and turned to leave the court.

"No! He needs to apologize, and we get a penalty shot!"

As soon as those words came out of his mouth, Thane whipped back around angrily. Aulani could see whatever was going to happen next wasn't going to be pleasant. She grabbed Thane's arm and softly pleaded with him to let it go and walk away. At her pleading, Thane's demeanor softened slightly. He approached Jake more slowly and spoke with a much lower tone of voice than originally planned and calmly told Jake, "Look... I'm sorry I knocked you down, and I'm sorry if I embarrassed you." Thane glanced over to the observation area at Marissa who was sitting there looking stunned. He lowered his voice so only Jake could hear him. "Just take your loss like a man."

David was serving as the scorekeeper and referee. He was seated in the upper observation area, watching the exchange intently. He was ready to interfere if necessary.

As soon as Thane whispered his comment, Jake reared back and swung his fist at his opponent. Thane was ready for him. He dodged the fist and countered with a swing of his own. He gleaned a glancing blow off Jake's chin. David was ready for their actions. He sounded the time out alarm, three times louder and longer than normal. The buzzing sound was so loud each one had to stop what they were doing and cover their ears. As soon as the two men stopped fighting, David got on the speaker. This time, he used his authority as Captain. "Gentlemen, that's enough! I want both of you to hit the showers and get cleaned up. After you've cooled off, report to my office in one hour."

Both men stood there eyeing each other cautiously. David spoke into the intercom again. "Move now, gentlemen."

Aulani reached out and tugged at Thane's arm. Thane backed away cautiously. Once he had backed away, Jake angrily picked up his things and headed back to his quarters. Luckily their quarters were in opposite directions. Marissa wanted to go with Jake but decided he needed a few minutes to himself first. She waited for about fifteen minutes then went to check on him.

When David sounded the buzzer so loudly, he didn't realize it had been heard in other parts of the ship. Brynna was the commander on duty. She was on the bridge when it went off. The distance between the bridge and the gym was enough to distort the sound to the point of being unrecognizable. It sounded like a low hum, accompanied by a vibration. Jason was the pilot at the helm. As soon as they heard it, he and Brynna did a scan and systems check to try and locate the source of the disturbance. While Jason was doing his systems checks, Brynna hailed engineering to see if Commander Flint could isolate the disturbance. Commander Flint hadn't heard or felt anything. He surmised the usual hum and vibration of the engines might have masked the sound Brynna was inquiring about. Nevertheless, he assured her he would check all systems and review the data recorders for the exact time of the disturbance. When she could not isolate the source, Brynna felt she should notify the Captain.

"Commander Alexander to Captain Alexander."

"This is Captain Alexander. Go ahead, Commander."

"Captain, we recorded a low hum and a vibration of unknown origin approximately seven minutes ago. We're doing a systems-check of all systems, but so far, we've seen no anomalies. The sound was not observed in engineering, but Lt. Commander Flint is running diagnostics and reviewing data recorders."

"Belay the data record review. I know what the sound was." David felt a little sheepish when he realized he had gotten the attention of half the ship. He intended to get the attention of the two men who were trying to hurt each other. David didn't want the data reviewed of what happened on the game floor. He considered it a private matter, and it was going to be hard to keep things quiet with such a small crew anyway. David explained what happened and ordered Brynna to continue the diagnostics. He thought it would make for a good drill.

An hour later, Captain Alexander was sitting in his office preparing himself to address the altercation. Thane reached the Captain's door and took a deep breath. He reached up and pressed the button outside the door, letting the Captain know he was there. The Captain pushed the corresponding button to open the door. Thane knew he was no longer addressing a game referee, but his Captain.

"Lt. Ryder, reporting as ordered, sir."

David glanced up from his computer screen and said, "At ease, Lieutenant." He went back to looking at his computer. Lt. Ryder stood there for what felt like an eternity. In actuality, he was standing less than a minute. Presently the door chimed again, and David admitted his next expected visitor. Jake stepped into the room somewhat casually. Upon seeing Thane's stance, Jake snapped to attention and reported to the Captain with the appropriate military bearing. David had Jake stand "at ease." He waited another full ten seconds before he began to speak.

"Gentlemen, in case you hadn't noticed or have somehow forgotten; we are on a small ship with a skeleton crew. We are going to be in tight quarters for more than two years. We have only been on this ship for one week. Are you planning on being at each other's throats in one month?"

Both men responded, "No, sir!"

"Apparently, I haven't made my expectations very clear. Since we are running a skeleton crew, no one is expendable. This is such a small ship and the quarters are so tight, we have to get along. Chief Holden, your job is to see to the safety of the entire crew. Safety doesn't mean you simply keep them alive. It also means in good shape, mentally and physically. It means keeping them safe from yourself. Security is your chosen career path. I need to know, right now. Can you do this job?"

The Security Chief hesitated slightly. He expected a lecture about being a good sport, not a question about his career choices. Finally, he responded, "Uh… Yes sir."

"You hesitated, Chief. Are you certain? Can you protect Lt. Ryder with your life if necessary?"

This time the Chief didn't hesitate. "Yes sir, I can, sir." His enthusiasm was less than David wanted, but it was better than his previous answer.

"Lt. Ryder, at some point in time your life may be in Chief Holden's hands. Can you trust him with your life?"

Thane preferred to trust himself, but he knew someday he might very well owe his life to the Chief. He responded with a sullen, but timely, "Yes sir."

The Captain continued, "Lieutenant, you are an officer in the Commonwealth Interstellar Force. I expect more from you than such childish behavior."

"Yes sir. I'm sorry to disappoint you, sir."

"I accept your apology, but I think you owe apologies to the Chief and every other crewman who witnessed that display. Chief, so do you."

A very brief flash of distaste crossed Thane's face. He wasn't quite ready of his own accord to let it go yet, but he realized the Captain was right. Thane turned to face the chief.

"Chief, I'm sorry. I didn't intend to knock you down or embarrass you in any way. When I saw you were upset, I could have handled it better. I should have handled it better. It won't happen again."

The Chief wanted more from Thane, but he knew he wasn't getting any more. Still looking annoyed, he replied, "Apology accepted. Sorry I got in your face like that. I was ticked off."

It was weak as far as apologies go, but Thane was determined to be the bigger man. He was, as the Captain pointed out, an officer. Thane offered his hand to Jake. Jake shook it.

The Captain was watching them intently. He gave them one last admonition. "Think carefully about what I've said. If this happens again, you will find yourselves confined to quarters on your off-duty hours. You think this ship is small now? It will get a LOT smaller."

Jake and Thane promptly responded, "Yes sir."

"Lieutenant, you're dismissed."

"Yes sir." Thane snapped to attention, did an about face and exited hastily. He walked a few brisk steps down the hall then stopped to take a deep breath. As far as dressing downs were concerned, it was probably one of the best ones he'd ever had. It still wasn't any fun, and Thane had to admit it was deserved. After gaining his composure, he moved on to make his other apologies.

The Chief thought his haranguing was at an end until Lt. Ryder alone had been dismissed. David's tone softened slightly.

"Chief, we talked about this. These games are meant to relieve boredom, get some exercise and have fun."

"Yes sir. I understand, sir."

"Do you? You aren't acting like you understand. You're acting like our lives depend on whether or not you win. Space travel is dangerous enough without you adding more stress to our lives. You keep this behavior up, and no one is going to want to play with you or against you."

"Yes sir. I got it." Jake started looking and sounding more annoyed.

"I hope you do. If you can't play for fun and be civil, then you had better find another way to relax." David paused to let his words sink in. "I expect you to take yourself off the game rotation if you can't handle it. If I have to do it, you won't like it."

"Yes sir." Jake sounded more contrite this time. He paused then ventured where he shouldn't have. "Sir, did you review the data record? He fouled me..."

"Chief! This isn't about one foul, one win or loss, or one game. I don't care who won or lost. I care about you being part of this twelve-man team. You need to care more about the stress relief, the exercise and having fun! Or, didn't you hear me the first two times I said it?"

"Yes, Captain!"

"Take yourself off the game roster for the next 48 hours." David was border lining on actually being angry now. He paused long enough to compose himself and then offered one last comment.

"I did review the data record. You both headed for the same position simultaneously. Thane got there first, and you got the wrong end of things. He didn't foul you. You actually fouled him. It's just part of playing the game. Learn to relax, Chief. If you can't do it on your own, then start making appointments with Lt. Flint for professional counseling. You are a great security chief and a valued member of this crew. You're better than this."

David let his words sink in for a moment, then wrapped it up.

"Any questions?"

"No, sir."

"Then you are dismissed."

Jake snapped to attention, saluted, and left. His head was buzzing with everything the Captain had just said. Part of him wanted to agree with the Captain and let go of his anger and hurt feelings. Another part of him felt like justice had not been served. He wasn't going to rest until he got it.

Once the Captain was alone in his office, he sat there scowling at the closed door. He could tell by the look on Jake's face this wasn't over. He hoped time might soften Jake's mood. He was afraid 48 hours wasn't going to be long enough.

"Computer, locate Lt. Lexi Flint."

A diagram of the ship appeared on the computer screen with a blinking dot in the dining room. This wasn't a high enough priority for David to disturb Lexi if she had just gone to bed. Since she was in the dining room, he didn't mind briefly disturbing a meal.

"Captain to Lt. Lexi Flint."

Each crewman had a wrist bracelet containing a comm unit among other functions. Lt. Flint was eating her dinner when her comm unit beeped at her. She wasn't used to hearing it, so it took her a second to decide what the sound was and where it was coming from. As soon as she recognized the source, she answered it promptly. The display indicated the communication was coming from the Captain.

"This is Lt. Flint, Captain, go ahead."

"Lt. Flint, after you have finished your meal, I need to see you in my office please."

"Yes, Captain. I'll be there in 10 minutes."

"Take your time, Lieutenant, this isn't urgent."

"Yes sir."

"Captain out."

Brynna entered the Captain's office just after the two men had been dismissed. "How did it go with Lt. Ryder and the Chief?"

"The Lieutenant is fine; he handled himself appropriately. The Chief, on the other hand, is having trouble seeing the big picture."

When he mentioned the Chief, a flash of emotion crossed his face briefly. Brynna saw it and understood. No words were necessary. She also understood the difficulty of maintaining privacy on such a small ship, so she didn't want to ask too many questions. "Is there anything I need to know?"

David briefly filled her in on his expectations for each man and the intended repercussions if they failed to meet his expectations. He also let her know of his intention to speak to Lt. Flint regarding the Chief's anger management.

When Lexi entered the Captain's office a short time later, she knew what the subject matter would be. The Captain gave her the same explanation and expectations he had given Brynna with one addendum. "Lt. Flint, I need you to do one more thing for me. I want you to rearrange the game schedule so Chief Holden and Lt. Ryder are not playing at the same time. I will do my best to see they are not off duty together, but I can't cover all the hours unless I assign them extra duty shifts. I would rather keep this incident as low key as possible. I expect the Chief to contact you to take himself off the game schedule. I don't expect him to make an appointment with you for counseling. I don't want to make it an order... yet. I would like you to make an extra effort to... I don't quite know how to say this."

David paused for a moment to find the right words then continued. "The Chief likes to feel in control. I know he gets angry when things get out of his control. If I ordered him to 'get counseling,' he would resent it and fight it every step of the way. I left it up to him to make that choice, for now. I want you to try to keep an eye on him and let me know if he becomes a danger to this mission, himself, or the crew. Be his friend and adviser, even if you can't be his counselor in an official capacity. Do you understand what I am asking you to do here?"

Lt. Flint nodded as she replied, "Yes sir, I believe so, sir. The Chief is a proud man and doesn't like to admit weakness, so you need me to be his friend and offer suggestions giving him opportunities to improve by his own choices. My husband and I can get to know Jake and Marissa as a couple to avoid looking suspicious. If I approach Jake individually, his defenses would instantly go up. Believe me, sir, I am familiar with his type."

David looked slightly startled at her candor. "How are you so familiar with his profile, Lieutenant?"

Lt. Flint replied matter-of-factly, "I studied his profile before the mission began." She paused allowing the next question to form in the Captain's head and then answered it before he had time to ask it. "I am familiar with the psychological profile of the entire crew, even yours, sir. It's my job to know the crew as well as alien sociology."

David's training and preparation for the mission had been spent predominantly with ship's crews, not with mission's crews. The times he trained with the mission crews were when they were training in their back-up positions as ship's crewmen. He fully expected they knew how to do their mission jobs, but this was a little closer to home than he expected. David's eyes locked on hers for a long moment, then he replied. "It seems you are very good at your job. With that in mind, I expect you to keep me informed if anyone starts to show signs of endangering this mission or crew. If I show those same signs, you are to inform me respectfully, and you are to inform the Commander immediately, even if, at that time, I order you to say nothing. With this mysterious mind-controlling alien out there, I don't want to take any chances. Do you understand?"

Lexi knew the Captain believed in being straight forward and thorough, but he didn't want to waste time rehashing things. She answered simply, "Yes sir. Is there anything else sir?"

"No, Lieutenant, I think that covers everything plus a little extra. I am confident you will do a great job. You're dismissed."

"Yes sir." She left his office with a slight grin. She liked the fact that she could rattle the Captain just a little. She would have been worried if she had rattled him a lot. The fact that he was slightly surprised, but not offended was good. She knew they now had a professional understanding of each other. She also knew she had his trust. It had not been a particularly long conversation, but it did accomplish quite a bit. Over the next couple of weeks, she spent as much time with Jake and Marissa as she could without looking suspicious. She needed to gain Jake's trust and confidence without looking like it was anything romantic. They had been advised to marry prior to this voyage just to prevent "on board romances" from interfering with ship's operations. Most of the relationships were new and not secure, and she didn't want to be the cause of a marriage dissolution less than a month into the mission. Braxton and Lexi spent time with Jake and Marissa whenever the four were off together. Lexi also spent time with Marissa, which gave her some insight into Jake's mindset. She took the opportunity to give Marissa advice she could discreetly pass on to Jake. Hopefully, she was making a difference.

It had been over a week since the incident with Thane. Taking Laura's spot was the chance Jake had been waiting for. Jake was excited as he warmed up with Jason. Now he would show Thane who was truly the better player. Lexi was scheduled as the scorekeeper and referee the day Jake wormed his way into the Zone Game against Thane. Thane and Aulani walked out onto the game floor and stopped when they saw Jason and Jake warming up.

Aulani spoke first, "I thought you two weren't supposed to be on the schedule together."

Thane looked at her, "I don't know that for a fact. The Captain didn't tell us not to play each other. It just seemed like somehow we never did play together anymore after that. It could have been just a coincidence, or maybe Lexi did it just to keep the peace."

"Please don't let him antagonize you, Thane," Aulani pleaded with him. "It's not worth the trouble."

"I won't start anything, and I promise to be nice. Okay?"

Aulani tried to read his face. She wasn't sure how firm his resolve was to stay out of trouble. Finally she said, "Let's just relax and have fun. Ignore him and his attitude. I don't want to win badly enough to upset either of you."

Thane looked slightly annoyed. "I am not going to throw a game just to avoid upsetting his fragile ego."

Now it was Aulani's turn to look annoyed. "You may not throw the game, but if it starts getting ugly out there, I may."

"I won't let him get to me, but I won't throw the game either. I will let any insults he throws at me go right past me. Okay? Are we good?"

Aulani's face relaxed a little. "Okay." She knew her husband well enough to know he meant what he said. She also knew he had his limits as to what he might overlook.

Lexi came into the upper observation deck and settled into the "game officials" booth. It really wasn't much more than a chair and a computer terminal. The computer did most of the work, but the close calls needed an extra human element. She was running later than she intended and got engrossed in getting the game parameters set up. She didn't immediately notice Jake was taking Laura's place. The players took their positions on the court and Lexi sounded the buzzer to start the game. About thirty seconds into the game, she realized the change in players. She wasn't quite sure what to do about it. No one was violating any orders, so she wasn't sure it was reportable, although she was concerned. She did query the computer for the duty roster to see who the commander on duty was. Brynna was the current duty commander. David's schedule showed he was currently sleeping. Lexi decided the best course of action was not to draw a lot of attention to the situation and deal with the unauthorized schedule change personally after the game was over.

She also sent an informative message to Brynna, just so she would know if something were to go wrong.

Jake was playing hard and did his best to try and cover Thane when he was playing in a defensive position, but Aulani kept running interference. Jake was so determined to cover Thane, Aulani scored several times because Jake left her unguarded. They got down to the last part of the game and Jason was getting frustrated with Jake. During a timeout, Jason and Jake appeared to be arguing over the game. They were several points behind and had very little time to catch up. As the game resumed, Jake took over guarding Aulani, but his attention was still focused on Thane. Aulani took advantage of his distracted mentality and scored again. Jason threw a frustrated look at Jake. Jake refocused himself and scored two more times, and Jason scored once. The score was now tied, and they were faced with a two-minute overtime. Jake scored the final winning point, but in the process tripped Aulani and she hit the floor, hard. She shook her head to clear it before attempting to get up. Since she had heard the final buzzer, she wasn't in a hurry to move. Thane rushed to her side. Jake was busy celebrating his victory. Jason, the ship's doctor, joined Thane at Aulani's side. Aulani insisted she was fine and just needed to catch her breath. Jason and Thane helped her to her feet. Jake, realizing he was the only one celebrating, turned to see the two helping Aulani up and his visage changed. He looked at her and quickly began to apologize.

"Aulani, I'm so sorry. I didn't mean to run over you. Are you okay?"

"I'm fine, Jake. I just tripped. It's nothing a hot bath can't fix." She tried to be pleasant, but she could feel the tension in Thane's arm, which was wrapped around her, holding her up. Thane had been unusually quiet during the game because of his promise to Aulani. He continued to hold his tongue, and Aulani was proud of the restraint he was showing. The Ensign was a little wobbly, but Thane was able to keep her steady. Jason gave her a final admonition to call him if there were any changes in her condition or a failure to improve, then he let go of her. Jason stood squarely between Jake and the departing couple. The look on his face was difficult to read, but Jake knew he was about to get blasted – again.

"What was that about? I have the feeling I was being used somehow. You certainly weren't focused on the game. You were more focused on getting in Thane's way."

"Sorry." Jake attempted to walk around Jason and move on. Jason wasn't done yet though.

"I think you owe me an explanation and a better apology than 'Sorry.' What was going on out there?"

"Look, Thane owed me a rematch, and this was his last game before we arrive at Galat. I'm sorry if I caused you any problems."

"From now on, keep me out of your grudge matches," Jason snapped. He grabbed his gear and walked out leaving Jake standing there. Jake slowly picked up his gear and started to move toward the door. He didn't move fast enough because Lexi stood there blocking the doorway, glaring at him. Jake cautiously addressed her, "Hey, Lexi, how are you?"

"It's Lt. Flint, in this case, Chief."

Jake's posture quickly adjusted to compensate for her tone and statement. "Yes, Lieutenant?"

"Chief, I was ordered to arrange the schedule so you and Thane wouldn't play together. You had no business trading places with other players without my authorization."

"Take it easy. You followed your orders. You arranged the schedule like you were told. The Captain won't hold you responsible for my actions." Jake was quickly getting annoyed. This game had certainly not gone as he intended.

"This isn't about me disobeying the Captain's orders. This is about you disrespecting me and my job on this ship. I am the ship's morale officer as well as the ship's psychologist. It's my job to keep people working together in a cohesive manner. I can't do that if you're going to work against me and abuse the trust of those around you. It's your job to keep this crew safe physically. It's my job to keep them mentally safe."

"All right, I got it. No changing the schedule around. It won't happen again." Jake tried to push past her to get out the door, but Lexi wasn't quite done yet.

"Chief, if anything like this happens again, I will order you to start counseling. Work out this ridiculous ego problem. No one is out to get you. Do you understand?"

"Yes, ma'am." Jake snapped to attention and saluted her. Now he started to feel like no one was going to respect him as the security officer. He was certain they wouldn't if they found out he was seeing a psychologist.

Lexi, knowing the Captain wanted her to maintain a friendship with Jake, tried to smooth things over. "Jake, there's a line between friendship and duty. I feel like you are taking advantage of our friendship to get what you want."

Jake started to interrupt her, but she didn't let him. "Just a minute, Jake. I have a duty to this crew, and our friendship can't interfere with that duty. I truly hope this will not be the end of our friendship."

Lexi watched his eyes for a moment then stepped aside so he could pass through the door unhindered. Jake stepped into the doorway and stopped. He glanced back over his shoulder and mustered his most heartfelt apology. "I really am sorry, Lexi. I shouldn't have taken advantage of your good nature. I didn't think it would be that big of a deal. It won't happen again." Jake paused then added one more thing, "I hope we can still be friends." Jake wasn't as competitive with women as he was with men. He considered himself to be a protector of the weak. Women were generally not as strong physically as men. His competitive nature seemed to attach itself to strong, able-bodied men. Thane took the brunt of Jake's nature because he was the most athletic, next to David. Jake viewed Jason as a science geek, even though he was quite physically fit. Lazaro and Braxton gave Jake similar impressions because of their intellect and their rank. All of the crew had to be physically fit, but somehow, they didn't affect Jake the same way. David would have, but since he was the Captain, Jake felt a sense of restraint around him.

As the Chief walked away, Lexi decided she should follow up with another message to the Commander. She went back to her office and carefully constructed a message to let Brynna know there were no altercations in or after the game. She did indicate Aulani stated she had tripped and the doctor felt only minor injuries resulted. She also noted she had verbally reprimanded the Chief for not clearing the schedule change through her.

Brynna saw the initial memo and debated about whether to go down there or not. She decided not to intervene unless an actual problem arose. When she received the second memo, she was glad she had chosen not to go. The crew, specifically Lexi, was doing their job. She was also relieved to know there had been no problems. She did flag the memos for David to read when he came on duty. She knew he wouldn't be pleased.

As expected, the Captain wasn't pleased, but he let the matter stand as it was and didn't ask any other questions. Jake halfway expected to get called into the Captain's office and was surprised when he didn't. The next time they ran into each other though, David gave Jake a hard look that spoke volumes.

THE CREW

PART TWO: THE FIRST PLANET

THE PLAN

The last three days before reaching Galat III, David adjusted the shift schedules so the crew's sleep schedules would be more uniform. He wanted the schedules in line with the sleep and wake cycles of the area where they planned to land. It would not be good for negotiations if the envoy was falling asleep.

When they reached the planet, David put the ship into a standard orbit. They knew from the information they received prior to departure the area on Galat III they were going to was a more heavily populated area. It was a stationary hub of high commerce on a planet populated by farmers and nomadic tribes. A ship's crew of twelve could not explore the entire planet, so they had to choose areas giving them the broadest possible sampling. The people on Galat III were a simple people, but they weren't ignorant or superstitious. Traders had visited them from space periodically, to trade for crops, so the Galatans weren't afraid of the ships or strangers. There was also a good chance they would not need a translator. The ship spent one day in orbit compiling information before they attempted to make contact. The ship's crew reviewed the local topography to find a place to land. They needed a landing site that would keep them close to the settlement, but stable enough to support the weight of the ship.

Brynna's mission team was relieved of their ship's crew positions and began to work on their own primary tasks. David's crew provided Brynna with sensor scans of the planet's weather, geology, demographics, and any other information which might prove useful. In order for their mission to work, they would need to gain the trust of the inhabitants by providing whatever services they could. Brynna briefly reviewed the data herself then distributed each report to the appropriate personnel. Since this planet was accustomed to visitors from space, they did have some reports in the computer's database. Brynna brought her crew together in the dining hall after they had reviewed their respective reports. David was slightly conflicted at this point. He had been in charge for the last three weeks and now he was taking a back seat to Brynna. David really felt like he should be involved in her staff meeting but didn't want to undermine her authority. He shouldn't have worried. Brynna saw the wisdom of including the secondary mission crew.

Brynna began her staff meeting with a brief rundown of her goals and the changes in the chain of command. "Let's get started. I want to remind everyone where the ship's functions and crew safety are concerned, the Captain is still in command. As far as the mission on the ground is concerned, I am in command. When we are working with the natives on this planet, use your own discretion as to whether you call each other by name versus title. The population will not be militarily oriented and may be more comfortable with names. If you have doubts about the situation, defer to title.

You have probably already noticed the presence of the ship's crew members in this meeting. I invited them to join us because, for this portion of our journey, they are our support team. They will be involved in all of our meetings, if possible. Ensign Ryder will be working closely with Ensign Dominick. The Captain and the Chief are responsible for our safety, so it's in everyone's best interests if they know where we are at all times. Lt. Commander Dominick will also be working closely with Lt. Commander Flint. The first item needing to be addressed is communication. Ensign Dominick, what's our status?"

"Well, Commander, since we have documentation of others visiting this world, we have their language files, and some demographics already available to us. This will save us time in translation. The files are already programmed into everyone's comm units. The data communications module, or as some have called it the 'drop buoy,' is partially programmed. Until we know what their needs are, we can't finish programming. It will probably only take a couple hours to finish it up. I've already established a generic data-base of things like basic first aid, water purification and safe food preservation supplied by Dr. Adams, some files on irrigation, cross-pollination of plants, crop rotation – you know, just your basic agricultural information. We can customize those files when we get planet specific information from Lt. Adams. I also have the files of designs for boats, bridges, buildings, simple mechanics, refinement of metals, etc. Lt. Flint helped me classify the files for the appropriate developmental levels. I also tied in the translation files so it can be used to translate for the indigenous population."

Chief Holden looked confused and said, "I thought we didn't need the translation files."

Ensign Dominic replied, "We are giving them the ability to have a translator for their own use between their own people or other visitors from space. These people are known traders. This could keep a human translator from cheating them or taking advantage of them. I just think of it as another service we offer."

Brynna looked at Ensign Dominick and said, "That is an excellent idea. I'm glad you did that. Let's make that standard for all buoys. Anything else?"

Ensign Dominick finished up her part of the briefing, "That's pretty much it. I will have to get planetary specifics to complete the buoy."

Brynna resumed her briefing by laying out her intended course of action.

"My plan, when we get planet-side, is to find the local leaders and request a meeting. I will present our proposal to them."

"You don't want us to start surveying the area as soon as we land?" Lt. Adams queried.

"No, I want to earn their complete trust. I want the leaders and the local population to know we respect them despite our advanced capacities," the Commander explained.

The Lieutenant nodded. "Exactly what are you proposing? I mean, how are we searching for this new enemy?"

"Our proposal is a simple trade. We are explorers. We need some fresh supplies for our ship, just food and water. I am sure everyone would enjoy some fresh fruits and vegetables and maybe even some steak?"

Several of the crew smiled, nodded, and even licked their lips. The food they brought with them was prepackaged food merely requiring opening and heating. They were nutritious, simple, and even tasty, but after three weeks they were ready for some raw fruits and vegetables.

Brynna continued, "We offer knowledge and perhaps some labor in exchange for our supplies. We will accept pretty much whatever they offer to pay us. We will request they allow us a chance for some R&R. That will give us a chance to get to know them and their way of life. All we have to do at this point is to keep our eyes and ears open and ask questions. After we complete our surveys, if we haven't learned anything about the Timeless One, we will make a formal inquiry about him. If they don't have any knowledge, we'll leave the data communication module with them as a gift. We'll instruct them how to use it and program it to notify us if certain keywords are heard in any language. We can then move on to our next target."

Brynna moved on by asking, "Lt. Flint, what information do we have on their level of technology?"

Lexi glanced at her files and then replied, "They are extremely low on the technology scale. I have ranked them at high Level II. They are capable of smelting, weaving, sewing. Buildings are made of various materials: brick and mortar, wood, some of the outer populations are living in tents or grass huts. They have a written language, but schooling ceases around puberty. One thing I noticed, and we can confirm the accuracy after we land, is I don't think they have learned how to make glass. If they don't know how to make glass that would definitely be something we could offer them."

Ensign Dominick looked puzzled and asked, "Why is glass such a big deal? How could they not be able to make something so simple?"

Lexi explained, "First of all, most discoveries are made by accidents. I suppose no one had the right accident to discover glass. Second, we use so many synthetics now, it's hard to realize the breakthrough glass would bring to such a society. They have windows that open and close to let light in, but they also let in insects, small animals, and the weather. They don't have the ability to make the materials we use for windows, so we can't give them that. They can also use it to form vases, drinking glasses, jewelry and so on. Does that answer your question?

Cheyenne nodded.

Brynna picked up the briefing again, "Do we have anything at all on their farming methods, irrigation, sanitation, vehicles, or architecture?"

"I am afraid only very basic information. They are using plows pulled by various livestock. I don't have any information on irrigation or sanitation. Vehicles are also various constructs pulled by livestock. As far as the architecture is concerned, all I have are the basic building materials."

"What about cultural taboos, deities, or important customs?"

Lexi looked at her notes then bit down on her lower lip for a second. She wasn't quite sure how to address this next issue, but it was definitely going to be an issue. She decided to deal with the minor issues first and get them out of the way.

"As far as deities are concerned, there are a variety of deities worshiped. Some worship the moons, stars, sun, the planet, invisible imaginary gods, statues, just about anything you could name. My recommendation is, ask before you touch anything that looks like it might be special or important. Do not harm any animals or even kick them out of your way. I don't have a comprehensive list of deities, but some worship animals."

"Important customs... when greeting someone formally, you approach them with your arms held outward and the palms facing upward. This indicates you are being open, honest, and straightforward with them. An informal greeting is similar to a handshake only higher up on the forearm and again with the right hand."

Jake piped in again, "Why the right hand? I've noticed several civilizations go predominantly with the right hand."

Lexi responded, "That's a good question. Genetically speaking, most humanoids are predominantly right-handed, so they carry weapons with the right hand. Since these people are traders, an open right hand is a sign you are not here to take what doesn't belong to you, but you are interested in making an honest trade."

"The last thing you need to know may present a problem." Lexi looked directly at Brynna.

Brynna took notice of the concern on Lexi's face then said, "Whatever it is, I'm sure we can deal with it. What is it?"

"This culture does not accept women as leaders or spokesmen. Women are subservient to their husbands. They don't hold offices, vote, etc. Women aren't much more than slaves. Commander, they have been exposed to other cultures from the traders who have visited, but whether they will trade with you, I just don't know. They do operate on a caste system so perhaps they would recognize your rank as having value."

Brynna gave her words careful consideration before responding, but it didn't take her long to come to a decision. There were only three other people capable of leading this part of the mission: Lt. Commander Dominick, Lt. Flint, and Captain Alexander. Lexi couldn't lead this one for the same reason Brynna couldn't. Brynna and David had already discussed keeping Lt. Commander Dominick on board the ship. That left David to lead the team.

"Well, I guess it is a good thing I invited the Captain to join our meeting. Captain, can you handle being my front man?"

"Yes, ma'am. If you would prefer, I can stay behind and let Lt. Commander Dominick go with you instead of me."

"No, I think that might only confuse matters. I want you to take the position of lead negotiator."

Brynna turned to Lexi and asked, "Are they going to be okay with women in the landing party?"

Lexi glanced through her notes again, "Yes, they will. It's considered a status symbol to travel with one's spouse and even better if you have children with you. Only the rich can afford to take their families with them. Women are respected in the role of a healer. I don't know how they feel about men as healers."

"It looks as though we have everything backward. We should have had a female doctor and a male commander." Brynna looked over at David and grinned, "Do you want to trade jobs?"

David shifted uncomfortably in his seat, "No-oo, thank you for offering though. I like handling my eleven crewmen and my one ship. You are quite welcome to handle the next twenty planets with billions of civilians speaking however many different languages with all the different customs. No, no, thank you."

"Well, when you put it like that, it does sound like you got the easy job." Brynna grinned again and waited for his retort.

David started to object but realized if he did, she could rib him for cowering away from taking the harder job. Instead, David decided to steal her thunder by admitting to cowardice. "Oh, you betcha. I'm no fool."

There were several laughs around the room as Brynna gave David a dirty look, "No, you definitely are not a fool."

Brynna finished up her briefing and let the crew go to work on their individual projects. Dr. Adams put a medical bag together consisting of a medical scanner, first aid supplies, antibiotics, antivirals, pain relievers, and other various medications and equipment. His wife, Laura, had a scanner programmed for plants, herbs, insects, and various microorganisms. Her scanner could diagnose plant diseases, soil problems, and infestations. All the scanners were basically computers with scanning capabilities, but they only had a limited amount of memory, so they could only be programmed for one focus or another.

Jake carried a scanner, but it was programmed to pick up heat or energy sources, weapons, and movement. It detected the kinds of things that would make a security officer nervous. Jake issued weapons to each member of the crew. They carried two weapons, the first was called a Tri-EMP, which can fire programmable projectiles. The Tri-EMP fires three different levels of electromagnetic pulses (EMP). Setting one programs the projectiles with a low-level electrical charge, which would stun a normal human. Setting two is an electrical charge that would take down something the size of an elephant. Setting two wouldn't usually kill a normal human, but it would take several days for them to get back to normal. Setting three produces an electromagnetic charge that would kill a human or an elephant or take out a piece of electrical equipment. Hopefully, they would never need to use the top setting. Basically, the Tri-EMP is adjusted to the desired setting and programs every projectile as it fires them to the programmed setting.

The second weapon was a laser, which was also programmable, to a degree. The laser was small and sleek and could be set for a small fine beam resulting in an increase of intensity or a wider spread less focused beam. Its strength could also be increased or decreased. The laser was used more as a tool than a weapon because it could be used for anything from lighting a campfire to being attached to the Tri-EMP and used as a sight guide. Jake, as the chief security officer, carried another weapon of sorts. The weapon was the same size and shape as a boxing glove. Jake carried it attached to the left side of his belt. To operate it, he would slide his hand into the recessed area and grab onto the control rod. The device would clamp down around his wrist and hand for stability. When activated, it emits a small deflector shield capable of protecting four to six people depending on the settings. Jake also carried a couple small knives and a basic tool kit. He took his job very seriously.

Aulani retrieved the native language files from Cheyenne and programmed everyone's comm units with the local language. Although it was highly probable a native who spoke their language could translate for them, there was always the chance they might be momentarily without a translator. The comm unit translators would basically record whatever was said, then it would repeat it in the appropriate language using the original speaker's voice. It also had the option of placing an earpiece into the ear so you could hear the translation, but the speaker would not hear the relay.

Lt. Commander Flint prepared his scanner with files pertaining to the engineering tools of his trade. His scanner would read the makeup of soil, building materials, and tools. It would also gauge sizes and weights. He packed some tools considered to be antiques by Commonwealth standards, but they would serve as teaching tools for their project.

Since David was going to have to take the lead this time, he and Brynna sat down to go over detailed strategies. The natives were accustomed to strangers and strange customs. They both hoped Brynna taking a quiet lead, and the other women performing their duties would be viewed as another "strange alien custom" and not the beginnings of a feud.

THE PLAN

GALAT III

Early the next morning, David put the ship down in a clearing just outside of their target city. It appeared other ships had landed there before. The area was layered with flat rocks and stones to form a landing pad of sorts. The stones kept the ship from sinking into the soil. The cargo bay opened to reveal an amphibious multi-terrain vehicle they referred to as the surface vehicle, or "Surf-Ve" for short. They had already loaded what little equipment they needed the night before. Thane, Aulani, Marissa, and Lazaro were staying with the ship. The rest of the crew climbed aboard the Surf-Ve and headed toward town. Brynna drove, and David took the seat beside her. It was always exciting to land on a planet you've never seen before. Today, the excitement was a little higher than usual. A first contact situation doesn't come along very frequently. The Commonwealth presence permeated the entire galaxy. New contacts normally only showed up when a planet achieved space travel.

As they neared the edge of town, Brynna chose to park outside the city and away from the buildings. The buildings were close together, and the people used various beasts of burden for transportation in the city streets. She preferred not to spook them with the Surf-Ve. The crew got out of the vehicle and walked toward town. As they started down the street, several people watched them curiously from a distance, but no one wanted to approach them. They made their way to what appeared to be a town square. After they reached the square, they looked around for a few minutes to locate a town hall or a place of leadership. They also looked for someone willing to direct them, but no one seemed interested in helping.

Brynna looked at Lexi and asked, "Suggestions?"

Lexi looked around, "We may have caught them a little early. The shops are not quite open yet. I would say, give it a few minutes. It may take a little time for word to get around."

Just as Lexi had spoken those very words, a boy approximately ten years of age came around a corner and stopped. After staring at them for a couple of seconds, he took off running like he had a purpose. In a moment, they heard a boy's voice shouting something.

Brynna smiled and said, "I think the word is getting around. Make sure your translators are activated."

"Do you want them audible or inaudible?" David inquired.

Brynna thought for a second then answered, "David, make yours audible, everyone else inaudible unless we split up then you should go audible. This way they know we can hear and understand them."

A few minutes later, the crew noticed several people coming their way. They were being led by the same boy seen moments ago. The man, who appeared to be in charge stopped, said something to the boy and sent him scurrying off. They were too far away for the translators to pick up the voices at random. If they were standing in a crowd, having the translators pick up and translate numerous conversations simultaneously would be chaotic at best and gibberish at worst. The range was routinely very short to prevent such problems, although it could be reprogrammed to increase the range or focus on a particular voice.

The Commonwealth had established one language known as Intergalactic Standard (I.S.). Anyone who traveled beyond his or her planet was required to be fluent in it. It didn't matter to the Commonwealth how many local languages you spoke. You also needed to know I.S. Working in an area dealing with off-worlders, one had to be fluent. Schools were required to teach it as equally as they taught spelling and grammar in the native tongue.

The man who appeared to be in charge moved into the town square and spread his arms out with his palms up. He greeted the crew in Intergalactic Standard, despite not being raised on a Commonwealth planet.

"Welcome to our city. My name is Donnel. I am the Magistrate of this town. How can our city serve you?"

The man was older. He appeared to be around sixty years of age. His curly, salt and pepper colored hair was just long enough to barely touch his shoulders. He wore a well-kept beard, which matched his hair color. He and his companions wore simplistic linen tunics with intricate embroidery on the hems, sleeves, and lapels. He had a friendly countenance and a warm smile but seemed a little concerned by their presence. David could see the concern on his face and wanted to put the man at ease. He turned to face Donnel and turned his arms out palms upward as he approached. The peculiar posture felt odd to David, but he smiled anyway and greeted the man.

"Greetings to you, Magistrate. My name is David Alexander. I command a ship known as the *Evangeline*. We landed just outside of town. We have been traveling for several weeks and are in need of some rest and relaxation as well as some food and supplies. My companions and I wondered if we could work out an arrangement with your people. We have no goods to trade, but we could offer services instead. Could we discuss our needs and our offer with you?"

Brynna and Lexi both caught themselves holding their breaths, waiting for the Magistrates response. The Magistrate looked at the crew and then back at David. He had every reason to be cautious. Those who landed in the ships from the skies often had weapons capable of causing a great amount of damage. Most of the visitors who came were regulars, but sometimes they would get troublemakers. It pleased the Magistrate they used native customs and courtesies. It also pleased him to see the strangers waiting to be recognized and asking permission before making themselves comfortable. He was more at ease because David's party traveled with women. Raiding parties didn't usually travel with women.

The Magistrate finally responded.

"What is your title?"

"My title is Captain."

"We welcome you and your people, Captain. Let us go to the meeting hall to discuss your proposal. We will bring you refreshments and get to know each other better."

"Thank you. We appreciate your hospitality. I do have one question though. We have devices to help us understand your native language. Is it all right if we use them as necessary? Will it frighten any of your people?"

The Magistrate smiled, "I appreciate that you asked permission. Most of our people have seen such devices before so they will not fear them. You may get some curious children following you around though."

David smiled in return, "Thank you. I think we can handle curious children. I just didn't want to cause any widespread panic."

The magistrate accompanied the crew to the meeting hall. As they entered the structure, the brightness of the outdoors made seeing nearly impossible for a few seconds. The hall was very dark and rustic in appearance. The room was lit by numerous candles and by windows, which were more like holes cut into the walls. The windows were covered by small wooden doors that could be opened or closed as needed. As their eyes adjusted to the darkness, they began to see the details of the room. The room was square. At the center of the far wall was a raised platform. The platform was two steps higher than the rest of the floor. A table with several chairs was neatly arranged on the platform. Each of the other three walls had rows of benches facing the center of the room. In each corner was a door to the outside and what appeared to be a wood-burning stove.

The magistrate took his place at the head table along with a few of the other men. Some of the men with the magistrate appeared to be guards. They carried small weapons on their belts and remained by each of the doors. David and Jake were both a little concerned by the weapons and two other things. The doors were set up to be barred shut from the outside, not the inside. The other thing they were concerned about was the windows. The windows were too small for a human being to crawl through. Jake was always calculating escape routes, attack routes, and other security vulnerabilities. Both David and Jake knew there was a line between taking safety precautions to protect oneself and ensnaring an enemy. They both silently hoped the magistrate was only cautious. They were armed well enough to easily put down an attack against the primitively armed people, but it wasn't without the risk of losing a life. It also meant negotiations wouldn't go well. There had been no reports of aggressive behavior from these people. It still made them a little apprehensive.

The magistrate motioned them to the benches directly across from the table. "Please, have a seat."

David sat on the front right corner, and Jake moved to the second row on the far left of the bench. Brynna started to sit next to David and Lexi to her left. The faces of the other men at the table began to show shock and disapproval. The man closest to the magistrate leaned over and whispered. David looked over at Lexi and whispered, "What did we do wrong?"

"I'm not sure. I would guess maybe the seating arrangement. Apologize and ask for instructions."

David stood back up and addressed the Magistrate. "Magistrate, we are unfamiliar with your customs. We do not wish to offend anyone, and it appears we have done something that does not meet with your approval. Please forgive any offense we have caused. Can you instruct us on what the appropriate actions are here?"

The men's faces began to relax as David spoke. The Magistrate smiled. "You are a wise and insightful man. I appreciate the lengths you are going, to please us. It is not appropriate for women to be seated in front of or beside men. The men are responsible for conducting business and should be seated up front."

David looked at the crew and nodded for them to rearrange themselves. Jake grudgingly moved to the first row but sat on the edge of his seat so he could move quickly if he needed to. Brynna and Lexi moved to the second row and sat as close to David as possible. Braxton had initially taken a seat next to Lexi on the front row, so he simply moved closer to Jake so that Jason could join them.

Once everyone was seated again, the Magistrate began to speak. "We welcome you to our home. Let us first begin with introductions. As I mentioned before, I am Donnel, the magistrate of this province. My role is to keep everything in balance. I am a spokesperson and judge over the council. I cast deciding votes when the council is deadlocked. I also decide disputes that cannot be handled at a lower level.

"To my left is Nasha. He is the Minister of Justice. He settles disputes, punishes crimes, and defends our people from their enemies.

"To his left is Duard, the Minister of Trade and Finance. His job is to keep trade going in this province. He takes care of the docks, storage houses and such. He collects the rental fees, which pays for the upkeep of those areas.

"Joren is the Minister of the Farmlands. He manages what crops are grown on our farms and aids in transporting them to market. He helps the farmers with problems with their crops. He also manages the territories assigned to herders. I think his job is the hardest and we have to keep him the happiest, or he tells the farmers to plant all the same food, and we eat only one food for a solid year."

Everyone smiled and laughed softly as the Magistrate continued his introductions.

"Eston is the Minister of the Township. Eston manages the towns and roads. He also sees that we have tradesman in all the right places and apprentices are properly trained. Both Eston and Joren are responsible for the education of those they serve.

"Since you are unfamiliar with our customs, as Magistrate, I will take on the responsibility of your education and training in customs and courtesies." The Magistrate left the platform and joined David. David stood up to confer with him.

The Magistrate spoke quietly to David and the crew explaining the proper way to address each member of the council both individually or as a unit. Donnel taught them the correct way to make introductions that included women.

"It is an honor to meet all of you. I am David, Captain of the ship *Evangeline*. This is my wife, Brynna. She is my second in Command. I know our ways may seem strange to you, but our people grant authority based on training and abilities rather than gender. My wife answers to me, but she is very knowledgeable and well-trained. I trust her with my life and my crew's lives. We respect the fact that this is not your way and ask you to respect our way as well."

The Council members looked back and forth at each other with uncertainty. They whispered quietly among themselves for a moment then Nasha spoke for the council. Nasha spoke

Intergalactic Standard as fluently as the Magistrate. "Do all of your women have such qualifications?"

"Each member of my crew is trained in different areas and have received the best training in their areas. I can tell you about their training as I introduce each of them."

"You may proceed with the introductions." Nasha seemed somewhat reluctant to concede that the women had such important standing.

David continued with his introductions, and each crewman nodded as they were recognized.

"This is our crew's doctor, Jason Adams."

David's translator was set to alert him if he used words not easily translated or to concepts that were cultural taboos. He caught it flashing out of the corner of his eye about the same time he noticed puzzled looks from the council. The word "doctor" was flashing, and the alternate word of "healer" was offered. David quickly corrected his mistake.

"He is our healer, and his title is doctor. Behind him is his wife Laura, she is trained in the study of plants, how to grow them and how they can be used. Her title is lieutenant. This is Braxton Flint. He designs buildings and other structures. His title is Lieutenant Commander. This is his wife, Lexi. She..."

David hesitated. He knew full well if the term doctor wasn't an option, the term psychologist wouldn't work either. Lexi recognized his struggle and quietly whispered to David, "adviser or counselor."

"She studies people, advises and counsels them. Her title is also Lieutenant. This is Jake Holden, my security officer. His title is Chief. His wife remains aboard our ship. This is Cheyenne Dominick. She studies languages so we can communicate wherever we go. Her title is Ensign. Her husband, along with two others, remains on board our ship. I can introduce you to the others later."

The council members whispered back and forth again. David looked over at the Magistrate and quietly asked, "Did I do something wrong again?"

The Magistrate studied the council's faces for a moment then looked at David.

"They are concerned because you travel with a man and a woman who are not married to each other. I think it is a good thing you let them know they each have a spouse close by."

After a moment, Nasha spoke, "We are honored to meet you, and we accept that your ways are different. We will respect your ways. We cannot guarantee our people will understand or accept it, but we will send an emissary of the council with you to bridge the gap between your people and ours.

"I understand you wish to have a business arrangement with us."

"Yes, Councilman Nasha, we do. What we propose..."

Councilman Nasha held up his hand to stop David from speaking. The Magistrate reached out and touched David's arm. David stopped and looked puzzled.

Councilman Nasha spoke up and said, "We are in agreement. Negotiations shall begin now."

He stood raising both of his hands as if to silence the entire room. As soon as he made the gesture, the men guarding each door turned, walked outside, and shut the four doors behind them. The crew was more at ease with the guards leaving until they heard the doors being bolted from the outside. Jake jumped up, and his hand touched his weapon, but he didn't draw it. The Magistrate, with his hand still on David's arm, felt David tense up. He realized his new charges were alarmed and moved to intervene, diffusing the situation.

"My friends, please, no harm is intended. This is how we conduct business. This method has proven very helpful to us. No one leaves until an agreement is reached. It ensures a person's motives are pure. There are exceptions of course. We will have no food or water until an agreement is reached, even if the agreement is we will go our separate ways and no longer do business together. It keeps people from hanging onto things out of sheer greed or stubbornness. When faced with long hot meetings without food and drink, a person must decide just how badly they want to hold out. Is this acceptable?"

David looked at the earnestness in the Magistrates face then the council's looks of confusion. He glanced at Jake who gave him a slight shrug of uncertainty then he looked back at Brynna and Lexi. The women were tense, but each gave him a slight nod of approval. David looked back at Jake and nodded for him to sit back down. Jake took his hand off his weapon and sat back down, but he did not relax. Finally, David responded to the Magistrates question. "I'm sorry for the confusion, Magistrate. Yes, this is acceptable."

"I am sorry if we gave you cause for concern. It has always been our way, and perhaps we take it for granted. Also, please, as I am now your liaison to the council, call me Donnel."

"Thank you, Donnel, for your patience with us. Councilman Nasha, may we begin again?"

Councilman Nasha, still uncertain as to what the crisis was all about, took his seat and began again. "Captain David, you wished to present a trade proposal? Please begin your proposal."

"Council members, our crew is on a twofold mission of exploration and diplomacy. We have been sent by our government, known as the Commonwealth, to meet the people on all the worlds in this galaxy of stars."

David's translator was alerting him to the word galaxy. David had already picked up on it from the faces of the councilmen.

"As your world contains many provinces and each province has many cities, so it is outside your world. Each sun is a star and has many worlds surrounding them, the stars make up galaxies, and there are numerous galaxies in the universe. The Commonwealth is a government made up of representatives of all the worlds who travel the stars in this galaxy. We seek now to get to know those who do not yet travel those stars."

Councilman Nasha interrupted David, "For what purpose?"

"In previous years, when a world began space travel, we would then introduce ourselves to them. Most worlds have previously believed they were alone in the galaxy and it has caused fear and incidents causing a loss of life. First contact situations are dangerous. We have never come as conquerors, but those who are new to space travel are often warlike and unstable. We seek to introduce ourselves to the less advanced worlds now so when the time comes you will know we are out there waiting for you. Does that answer your question?"

Councilman Nasha nodded. "So, what is it you seek from us?"

"You have already been visited by traders before, so you already know about those who live on other worlds. You do not need us to teach you about that. We wish to introduce you to the Commonwealth and consider you friends of the Commonwealth. As friends of the Commonwealth, you would be entitled to our help with less benevolent traders. We could also send you help to deal with serious illnesses, famines, crop failures, floods, or other great disasters. We can leave a machine with you that will do two things. First, it can contact us across great distances if you need us to return. Second, it is like a record of knowledge, if you tell it your crops contain an infestation of some sort, it could tell you how to treat it. It does not know all the answers, but it may know many of them.

"What we specifically would like from you is to accept our friendship and our gift, and we have been traveling for three weeks. We would like to have a time of rest and relaxation and to refresh some of our supplies. We can offer our services to you in trade. If you will allow our people to see your crops and methods of farming as well as your methods for building, refining metals and other craftsmanship, we may be able to help you improve your methods. Perhaps we can make things go more smoothly or efficiently. I believe there is one thing we can already introduce to you. If our information is correct, we have a substance that is easily made, but you have not as yet discovered how to construct it. Commander Braxton Flint can show it to you if you like."

Councilman Nasha nodded to David, who in turn nodded to Braxton. Braxton felt like this was more of a mechanical engineer's job or at least a public relations job. He was used to glass coming to his projects already prepared for installation. He could extol the virtues and shortcomings of glass, but how it is made was not within his comfort zone. Nevertheless, he was a trained officer in the Commonwealth Interstellar Force and fully intended to do whatever duty he was assigned, to the best of his ability. He carefully lifted his bag from the floor, pulled an insulated container out. The container held several glass items. The first item he pulled out was a drinking glass. The second item was simply a square glass pane. The third was a mirror similar to the glass pane. The fourth item was a small glass flower. The fifth item was a small telescopic device.

"Gentlemen, may I approach your table to show you the items I brought?"

Nasha again nodded his approval. Braxton picked up his five items, carried them over, and set them down carefully on the table. He picked up the drinking glass to begin his demonstration.

"This cup is made of a substance we call glass. It is not the sturdiest substance and can be broken if dropped, but it does have advantages. You can see more clearly what is in the cup. Sometimes a drink will taste differently because of the material a cup is made from. This does not happen with glass. You can also see when washing the cup that it's clean. Another advantage to a cup made of glass is it's not porous like other materials, so it's not as likely to harbor disease-causing microorganisms."

Braxton's translator had fixated on the word "microorganisms," and he was temporarily at a loss for how to define it to a people who couldn't make microscopes to see what a microorganism was. He hesitated and looked back at David for assistance. Dr. Adams quickly understood his dilemma and responded. "Excuse me, gentlemen; I think I can help explain if you will allow me."

Councilman Nasha smiled and responded, "Please do. Most of your words I understand, but some of them make no sense." The Councilman seemed to enjoy watching Braxton fumble. Nasha had a taste for ironic humor and did enjoy watching these people from an advanced society be intimidated by such a simplistic lifestyle.

Jason stood in front of his seat to explain microorganisms. "All life forms are called organisms because they have different systems or organs which work together to maintain life functions. Man has a heart to pump blood, lungs to breathe air, and a stomach for food. These and other organs work together to keep a man alive and well. Microorganisms are life forms so small you cannot see them with just your eyes. Some insects are incredibly small and difficult to see, but if you see a dog scratching or biting himself, you know he has fleas. Just as an insect bite or sting can make one sick, sometimes microorganisms can make one sick, and they are small enough, thousands of them can live in the tiniest pores, cracks or crevices."

The council looked confused and talked in their own language to each other. Minister Eston finally spoke.

"Who told you this? Was this part of the ancient texts?"

Now it was Jason's turn to look puzzled. He took a moment to gather his thoughts then responded. "I learned about it from my instructors as a boy. Our people have studied these things for hundreds of years, but I do not know of any ancient texts."

Minister Joren joined in at this point. "How can you study what you cannot see without the texts given by the Originator?"

Jason began to understand their confusion. "Oh, I understand your question now. We cannot see them without help. Commander, show them the telescope and explain about the shape of the glass."

Braxton picked up the telescopic device and described its construction and function. Once they saw the demonstration and understood the magnifying power of curved glass, they became very excited. It was like watching young children making new discoveries. Once they became comfortable with their new knowledge, Commander Flint moved on to the next item.

"Glass can be made into sheets and placed into walls like the openings you have in this building to make windows. These windows can allow light to come in but keep weather or insects out."

Braxton went on to explain they could be placed on hinges or overlapping tracks to open or close them if needed. He then introduced the mirror to them. They were all quite sure the women would love the windows and mirrors. The Council was less excited about the drinking cups. The men were more excited about the telescope. The last item was the glass flower. Braxton picked it up and held it where it would reflect as much light as possible in the dimly lit room.

"This has no real function at all except to make a woman smile.

It is merely decorative, and you know how women love flowers. This flower doesn't have to be watered. It doesn't die, but it is fragile. I suppose if you ever have competitions where a man can show off his skills, this would be an excellent place to test them. It could also give your economy a boost."

"How hard is this glass to make?" asked Eston.

"It isn't as hard as refining metals and the materials are plentiful. We can teach you the specifics, but basically, you heat sand into a liquid state then mold it."

Minister Eston looked at Minister Nasha in disbelief. Sand was nearly as plenteous as water. Surely they could not have missed making something so simple. There had to be more to this.

Minister Nasha looked at the crew and the items sitting on the table. This new substance could be quite useful. He looked back at David considering his next words very carefully.

"You are willing to teach us how to make this... glass? What is it you want in return?"

Braxton left the items on the table and moved back to his seat as David stood up to respond.

"Our people want to establish a good relationship with yours. We would like to establish an alliance with your people. That is the main goal of our visit. We would like to spend a little time getting some rest and relaxation. Our physical needs include approximately ten to twelve barrels of water and to leave our ship parked for a few days. We would love to have some fresh fruits and vegetables. As far as those are concerned, we will accept whatever you are willing to give us. We have food aboard our ship, but it would be nice to have fresh food. We are willing to offer other advances where we can."

Nasha studied him carefully. It was hard to trust someone who seemed willing to give them so much and ask for so little in return. There had to be a catch or drawback somewhere. "What would be involved in this alliance?"

David sensed their hesitation. He hadn't wanted to reveal the full nature of their visit until later, but he was afraid they already knew there was a condition hanging out there. David didn't like Brynna being seated behind him. In an effort to be able to see her face, he paced back and forth as he spoke. He finally caught her eye. She knew what was weighing on his mind and she nodded her approval to him.

"Gentlemen, the Commonwealth seeks to bring peace and prosperity to all its members. We also seek to know our allies, the people, the history, and the things that make people unique. We have heard rumors of one called Pateras El Liontari and that he is very powerful. We seek to know who this is and to gain him as an ally. Can you help us with this?"

"What will you do if we decline your offer?" inquired Councilman Nasha.

"We will move to another city and make the same offer. If no one agrees on your world, we will leave and go to another world. No harm will come to you from us. We intend only to earn our keep and make alliances." David responded simply.

Councilman Nasha looked at the other council members then responded, "Please allow us to consider your proposal. We will give you an answer shortly. Magistrate, could you rejoin us for our deliberations?" The Magistrate politely excused himself from the crew and returned to the table. As the Council talked quietly, David sat down then turned to face the crew. The crew moved in closer so they could also talk quietly.

"Thoughts?"

Brynna replied first, "I think it's going well, but they do seem rather cautious."

Jake looked very skeptical and added, "I think they're hiding something."

David studied Jake's face briefly then asked, "What gives you that idea?"

"That last part about Pateras El Liontari, you asked them if they could help us and they didn't give you an answer."

Lexi jumped in, "That's probably what they're discussing now. If they know nothing about Liontari, they may not want to admit it. They may be afraid our aid goes away if they can't help us."

Jake countered again, "If that's what I was afraid of, I would just ask outright."

Brynna didn't want everyone looking nervous and uptight in front of the council, so she decided to put the matter to rest firmly but in a lighthearted manner. "David, I think it was better to ask about Liontari up front, so they aren't afraid we're hiding something. It also takes the burden of waiting until the last moment off our shoulders. They could feel betrayed or used if we waited until later to make the inquiry. I also think they are disturbed by the fact an advanced society would want or need anything from them. Let's just wait and see how things go. I think we had better appear nonchalant about the whole situation. We need to be willing to leave if that's what they want and willing to help in whatever ways we can if they allow it. Does everyone understand?"

Everyone nodded in agreement. David, being a bit of a cut-up and seeing the need to get everyone relaxed again, added one more thought. "I hope we come to an agreement soon before we have to give them air conditioning." All of the crew either laughed or smiled except Braxton who was intently looking at the ceiling. Brynna finally asked him, "What are you doing?"

"Huh?"

"Lt. Commander, why are you staring at the ceiling?"

"Oh, uh, I was thinking about how to give them air conditioning."

David jumped, looked at Braxton and said, "I was just kidding about the air conditioning."

"Well, I was just thinking how easy it would be to rig a ceiling fan. We could mount a windmill on the roof and run a pulley or gear system through the roof to turn it. I know they have candles hanging on the chandelier for lighting and a ceiling fan would interfere with that, but if we improved the lighting set up. It could work. I was also thinking about ways to improve the lighting using mirrors and glass. I thought if we could…"

"Okay, all right, we got it. Good job, you are definitely on the right track. I really was kidding about the air conditioning."

Brynna followed David's flustered comment, "Braxton, if they agree to our proposal, you can leave them with plans and drawings for your ideas. We don't have to physically accomplish every idea before we leave. You and Lazaro can get together with the council and decide what projects need the most immediate attention."

Brynna glanced up at the council table. The council seemed to be having a lively discussion. They were speaking in their native tongue so she couldn't understand what they were saying. She had, out of courtesy, turned her translator off. Some of the council were waving their arms around rather emphatically while others were sitting quietly and just listening. When out of the corner of her eye she noticed Jake was staring at his wrist. She got up and moved to sit behind him and whispered. "Jake, what are you doing?"

Jake looked up slightly startled, "What? Uh, I'm just monitoring."

"Monitoring what?" At this point, Brynna had stopped speaking in Intergalactic Standard. She began speaking her own native language of Raesin. She had grown up on the planet Raesii, which also housed the Commonwealth Inter-Galactic Force Training Base. Jake came to Raesii to attend the Academy in high school and learned Raesin, so they both spoke the same native language. Several of the crew, including David, could call Raesii home.

Jake had a look on his face that said, "I know you aren't going to like this, but I'm doing it anyway." Jake also replied in Raesin, "I'm monitoring the council's deliberations. You can see how animated their conversation is. If they mean to harm us in any way, I want to know as far in advance as I can."

Brynna did not want Jake eavesdropping on their conversation, but she understood his job as a security officer. After thinking for a moment, Brynna said, "Jake, I appreciate your diligence, but just program your translator to key in and alert you on specific terms. I don't want them to have any reason not to trust us."

Jake hesitated for a short second then punched a couple buttons on his translator. He looked back at Brynna and said, "Yes, Commander."

Brynna admired his dedication and tenacity, but sometimes it was a fault. She did want him to know she appreciated his attempts to protect her and the others. "Thanks, Jake. I appreciate what you were thinking, but they did allow themselves to be locked in a room alone with us. They have less protection than we do. Our weapons could wipe them out in a matter of seconds."

"I suppose you have a point. I just didn't want to be caught off-guard." All the translators were programmed with keyword recognition programs. They had to be activated by the user though.

David had been talking quietly to Jason and Braxton when Brynna had abruptly gotten up and moved. He heard them speaking in Raesin but was too far away to make out what they were saying. David's family had moved to Raesii when he was a teen, so it was not his native language.

In a moment, when Brynna returned to her seat, David turned his back to the others and turned toward Brynna to ask, "What was that all about?"

Brynna wanted to keep it low key so she simply replied, "It's not important, I'll explain it to you later."

David had a touch of curiosity, but he contained himself and let the matter stand as it was. He nodded and acknowledged her decision. This part of the mission was her baby, not his. He turned back around and rejoined his previous conversation. Jake watched the exchange to see what happened, thinking he might be in hot water again. When David didn't even glance his direction, he decided he wasn't in trouble. Jake let his attention wander a bit since, as Brynna had pointed out, the council was really at their mercy, instead of the other way around. He started to get bored and stood up to stretch his legs a bit. He was suddenly startled to discover David was at his side. He was suddenly unsure of his previous conclusion about not being in "hot water." He looked at David and hesitantly said, "Yes, Captain?"

David wondered why Jake was so jumpy. He surmised it could have something to do with his previous conversation with Brynna, but he didn't want to bring anything up about it.

"Jake, I was just thinking. As cautious as our hosts have been, I would say they have been burned by visitors before. Perhaps there might be some security help you can offer to them. We obviously can't offer them weapons, but we can offer defensive strategies and teach them how to protect themselves."

"Sir? I thought my priority was the protection of the crew. You want me to hand them strategies they could feasibly turn against us?"

David was speaking in Intergalactic Standard (I.S.), but Jake had answered in Raesin. David wanted to keep things open and above suspicion in case they were overheard.

"Keep it in I.S., Chief. I understand your concerns. The safety of the crew is your primary concern, still, keep your eyes and ears open. Nothing in their history indicates they are violent or warlike. I don't think they would harm us without a good reason. I want them to know they have nothing to fear from us and if we are teaching them to defend themselves, they'll know that. Let's keep things open and straightforward."

Jake responded again in I.S., "Yes, Captain. I can already think of several things they could improve on to protect themselves. I can discuss it with Councilman Nasha if we come to an agreement."

David smiled. "Great Jake, I knew you would already be thinking that direction."

It had not been very long at all when the council finished its deliberations. The Magistrate was apparently comfortable with the crew's understanding of the proceedings, for now. He kept his place with the council. The Magistrate stood to address the crew.

"The Council has a couple of questions."

David stood to answer the Council's questions. "Of course, what would you like to know?"

"You are offering us the knowledge of how to make this glass and other knowledge. Could you tell us what other knowledge?"

"Our security officer is prepared to teach you some things to protect your city and your people better. Our healer is available to treat illnesses and instruct in ways to prevent some illnesses. Our engineers can help improve your processes for construction, forging, harvesting, and transportation. The rest of my crew can help assist these men, or if you have a special project, they can help you with it. We are leaving this to your discretion."

"And all you want in return is some food and water and perhaps some entertainment?"

"We would like some fresh air and sunshine. We do need some fresh water. Any food or entertainment you offer would be appreciated very much."

"You also want us to be allies, and you want knowledge."

"Yes, we value friendship and knowledge," David replied.

"We value those things as well, but we recognize knowledge brings power, and you are already advanced far beyond us. If we give you what little knowledge we have, that gives you even more power over us."

David pondered his words for a moment. "I understand your concerns. At some point, we will have to trust each other in order to have an alliance. We have no intention of using what we learn against you."

Even as David spoke those words, he was concerned he might be wrong. If they found their enemy here, what would the Commonwealth do about it? The Executor had taken a rather harsh stance. David hoped they were just searching for a home base they could quarantine or find the leaders and take care of them to stop the spread. He took a small amount of comfort in the fact he and the crew genuinely meant no harm to these simple people. Something about it still gnawed at him.

The Magistrate looked at the council and then said something in their native language. The men each nodded. The Magistrate turned back to the crew and smiled. "Then we have an agreement." He moved off the platform, then reached for a rope hanging from the wall. He pulled it three times. A bell somewhere above them and outside rang. The crew heard the four doors being unbarred and opened to allow some fresh air and sunlight in. By this time the crew was uncomfortably warm and sweating. The Magistrate returned to the platform. He held out his right hand and motioned for David to join him with his left. David joined him on the platform and reached out his right hand. They grasped each other's right forearm completing the Galatan equivalent of a handshake.

"We will celebrate our agreement with some refreshments and tonight we will have a banquet to introduce you to our citizens. Will all of your crew be able to attend?"

David had his back to Jake, but he was sure he could feel Jake bristle. Jake was thrilled when David left some of the crew in the ship. He felt more of the crew should have been left there in case the mission proved to be too dangerous. If Jake had his way, the landing party would have consisted of himself, Braxton and Brynna. David smiled and assured the Magistrate the entire crew would be there. Moments later he contacted the crew remaining behind and sent Jake out to pick them up with the Surf-Ve. He watched Jake's demeanor change as he gave the order. Yes, there it was, Jake was bristling.

The council members left their table and began to greet each crew member similarly, even the women. David gave the Magistrate a puzzled look. The Magistrate explained to David since the women held titles and jobs, they would be granted the same respect as the male members of the crew. He also cautioned David they would still need to travel with a male member of his crew and either a council member or one appointed by the council. The Magistrate was concerned that not every citizen would have the same respect for a female leader. He also tactfully suggested to the young Captain that he advise the women to use the utmost care in their manners. They would get much more cooperation from asking rather than telling.

Presently several women and children entered the room carrying pitchers of water and trays of fruit, cheese, and bread. There were also pitchers of milk and something smelling like buttermilk only the color was not right. David steered clear of that one, but Jason had to try it.

The crew spent the next hour socializing with the council. David asked the Magistrate for a moment to confer with his crew before they split up to get to work. The rest of the crew had already arrived. Brynna divided them up and assigned them to the individual ministers. She briefed everyone on their projects and instructed the women on how they would be expected to act. That part was difficult for her. She wasn't used to being a second-class citizen and didn't like telling the women to behave like second-class citizens.

Brynna assigned Thane and Marissa to Duard, the Minister of Trade and Finance. Over the next few days, the two looked at the usual routing of goods to market. They reviewed maps of the area with Duard to determine better routes. Thane was accustomed to overseeing the loading of cargo into cargo bays, so he also looked at Duard's warehousing. They even took Duard up in a shuttle from the ship to get an overhead view of the area. Duard was a little reluctant to go at first, but he wasn't about to look weak in front of Marissa. Thane saw how nervous he was and wanted to have a little "fun" with him by making it a "wild" ride. Marissa agreed to go along with it under one condition. The condition was that Thane would clean up any mess Duard made as a result of his "wild" ride. Thane didn't care for the idea, so he kept their flight as calm as possible. He didn't want to get blamed if Duard got airsick.

As the shuttle lifted off, Duard looked as though he might get sick anyway, but as they moved about and nothing catastrophic happened, he started to relax. Marissa tactfully kept asking him questions to get his mind focused on the job instead of the flight. By the time they were done, he actually seemed to be enjoying himself. Several children playing in a field nearby came running when they saw the shuttle land. Minister Duard described his trip to the awestruck children who then proceeded to beg him to take them on a ride. The Minister, having seven children of his own, had a weakness for the pleas of children. He asked Thane if he would mind taking them up in his flying craft for just a short trip. Thane was glad to. However, Marissa wasn't sure this fell into the category of improving the lives of the inhabitants. Thane insisted it was a goodwill gesture, which would improve relations with the natives. Reluctantly, she agreed.

The shuttle was small, and there were more children than seats, so some had to share. One child crawled up into Marissa's lap, and Duard scooped up two more small children. Marissa looked at the child she held. The child appeared to be a little girl about three to four years of age. She had long, curly, brown hair, big brown eyes, and the cutest dimples when she smiled. Marissa turned her translator on, so she could understand what the little girl said. Marissa looked at Thane and reminded him, "These children aren't very secure in their seats so don't do any wild acrobatics."

The translator indiscriminately picked up Marissa's comment and translated it. The little girl in Marissa's lap got excited, grabbed Marissa's arm, and started chattering in Galatan. In a second, the translator reproduced the little girl's voice, "Your bracelet is talking to me!!!" As soon as the translator started relaying the message the girl started chattering again then clasped her hands over her mouth. "That's me! That's me talking. What am I saying? I not say that. Is it stealing my voice?"

Marissa reassuringly hugged the girl and then pointed at the bracelet and explained what its function was to her. The translator then repeated the message appropriately. The little girl giggled then grabbed Marissa's arm again looking at it closely. Finally, she asked Marissa, "Is there a bird in there? Sometimes birds copy what you say." Marissa laughed and assured her it wasn't a bird.

Thane wanted to make this a short, but memorable trip for the kids so he headed for the river. He made a quick circle around the town then headed slowly up the river close to the water's surface. There was a mountain range just up-river, so Thane took them up into the mountain pass briefly. He came out of the mountains at a high altitude. A boy about ten years of age was sitting directly behind Thane watching closely as he manipulated the controls of the shuttle. After a while, the boy could contain himself no longer and asked, "Can I try to do that?"

Thane wanted to let him give it a try but knew he was already pushing the boundaries of his mandate. "Sorry, son, I can't do that. After we land though, I can teach you how to make a sky craft of your own."

The boy got very excited. "Really?"

Marissa's reaction was similar; only her reaction contained a mixture of skepticism and disdain. She leaned over and whispered to Thane out of the translator's range. "You can't be serious, Thane. Do you want him to get himself killed?"

"I was just going to teach him how to make a toy glider or kite or something. By the time he's old enough to adjust it to his size, he'll be wise enough to test it on something other than himself. You worry too much."

"You don't worry enough." She whispered.

By the time they finished with this second shuttle flight and got the shuttle back in the shuttle bay, Duard had decided to walk back into town and call it a day. He wanted to tell his friends about his sky ride. Most of the kids took off to their homes to brag about their excursion to their friends and family. The one little boy, who was the brother of the girl who had been sitting on Marissa's lap, stayed behind with his sister to wait for Thane to keep his promise. Thane had the boy and his sister gather some sticks while he collected some thread and fabric from the ship. He showed them how to make a rudimentary glider and gave them a few basic lessons on aerodynamics and steering. Next, he showed them how to make a kite and fly it.

After the children left, Thane and Marissa went back to cleaning and settling the shuttle into its berth in the cargo bay. Marissa was amazed at how much time Thane put into playing with the two children. She considered Thane to be an overgrown child himself then decided it wasn't that big of a stretch after all. Marissa was curious though about one thing. As she watched the kids running off toward home, she decided to ask him about it. "Thane."

"Yes?"

"You took quite a bit of time playing with those kids. Why did you spend so much time with them?"

"Well, we're supposed to give these people small advancements in their technology. They may not take to the skies in this generation, but I may have planted the seeds for the next generation. It was also fun. They're cute kids."

"I figured out the fun part. You're right. They are cute kids. Did you ever think about having kids?"

"Aulani and I have talked about it. It's a big commitment, especially with both of us having a career in the military. We want to, but maybe a little later. We both love kids. I've seen Aulani with my nieces and nephews. I think she will be a natural at being a mother."

Thane had a distant look on his face, and he began to smile as the image in his mind's eye progressed. Marissa smiled when she saw Thane's face. It was nice to see this side of him.

Almost as an afterthought, Thane looked back at Marissa and asked, "What about you and Jake? You ever think about having kids?"

"I can't – uh – that is, we haven't really talked much about it."

Thane cocked his head and looked at her. There was something in her tone of voice suggesting she was holding back. "Are you okay with that?"

Marissa stopped and just looked at him trying to decide how to answer him.

Thane realized he might be getting a little too personal. "I'm sorry, Marissa, that's really none of my business. Forget I asked."

Marissa felt like she should still offer some sort of reply because she knew what he had seen on her face. "I guess Jake and I are in a similar position as you and Aulani, only more complicated. I can't have children so we would have to adopt. Jake hasn't wanted to talk about it. I just wish he would at least discuss it."

Thane wasn't quite sure how to respond. "I'm sorry, Marissa. I didn't know. I shouldn't have gotten so personal. I didn't mean to..."

"It's okay, Thane. Jake won't talk about it, and sometimes I need to. I think he sees it as a situational impossibility so why discuss it. He seems to think he's protecting me by not talking about it."

Thane decided to give her a graceful way out of the conversation. "I guess Jake is a tiny bit pragmatic." He looked at her and grinned.

Marissa, realizing what he was trying to do, looked back at him and smiled. "Jake? Pragmatic? Whatever gave you that idea?"

The two continued working silently for a couple minutes then Marissa softly said, "Thanks, Thane." She smiled at him, grateful he had cared enough to give her a gracious exit from the conversation.

Thane smiled. "You're welcome." They finished up and headed off to their respective cabins to clean themselves up.

Jason and Cheyenne had been introduced to Slaina, the chief healer. She was the only woman to hold a position of esteem in this society. Slaina was an older woman about 50 years of age, who served as a midwife and healer of the city and the farms surrounding the city. She was training another woman named Essa, who was about 30 years old, to be her replacement. Essa was already a trained midwife and appeared to be quite pregnant. She told them this would be her seventh child. Cheyenne paired with Jason to deal with the translation of medical terminology. Jason and Cheyenne went with Slaina as she made rounds through the town and the surrounding countryside. He taught her how to make some basic medications for pain relief and to fight infection. He also gave her stern warnings about letting people use them unnecessarily.

Slaina initially felt threatened by Jason. She had been "instructed" by the town council to grant him every courtesy and to learn whatever he had to teach. She wondered what a man could possibly know about midwifery. Essa respectfully followed the lead of her mentor. Jason tried to be very careful not to embarrass the women. He made sure he afforded them the respect they deserved by their esteemed positions. Their medical abilities were so basic and rooted in mysticism; it was hard not to feel superior to them. As he followed her on her rounds, he deferred to her "expertise" in front of her patients and tried to offer her assistance on her own terms. After she went back to her home, he asked her questions about her treatments, their origin, and effectiveness. Once they established some common ground, Slaina opened up to him, and he could begin teaching them. He taught Slaina and Essa about the causes of disease and some of the basics of disease prevention. He also advised her to spend time teaching the community in basic first aid, resuscitation techniques, and cleanliness. They eventually covered a lot of area including proper food storage and preservation, boiling water, and frequent hand washing.

After the crew had been in place for a little over a week, a boy about fourteen years of age came to the ship in the middle of the night looking for Jason. The boy was Essa's son, Korion. Essa was in labor, and things weren't going well. Korion told them Slaina sent him to bring Jason back with him. Brynna sent both Jason and Cheyenne. She also sent Thane to drive the Surf-Ve since he was familiar with the terrain and their best pilot. They put Korion in the front seat to direct them. They had not been to Essa's home because she always came to Slaina's home to start making rounds. Jason had not done an exam of Essa with his equipment only a brief physical examination. She had been reluctant to allow him to even touch her. She insisted her baby wasn't due for almost a month, but his exam roughly indicated she was already due, or her baby was going to be very large. Without his equipment, he couldn't be sure. Without diagnostics, no one could be sure what was going on. This time, he brought his equipment and fully intended on using it.

As the Surf-Ve pulled up outside their home, which was on the edge of the city, Dr. Adams could hear Essa crying out. He also heard an older child crying and calling for her mother. Jason quickly told Cheyenne to have Thane take Korion and the other children to a neighbor's home. As he came inside, Slaina reported to him what was happening. Jason kept his translator on and had it transmit into his ear-piece. Slaina had a look on her face that said she had seen this before and knew it usually ended badly. Slaina tried at first to speak in Intergalactic Standard. She wasn't very fluent in it and had trouble saying what she needed to. Jason touched her arm gently and told her to speak in her own language, and he would understand.

Slaina took a deep breath. This wasn't easy for her to admit defeat and defer to this man who was an off-worlder. She began again to explain to him.

"Essa has been laboring for many hours. Her last baby came so quickly. I thought I wouldn't make it here on time. This baby doesn't have its head down as it should. I have tried everything I know to do."

The doctor looked Slaina in the eyes, gave her arm a gentle squeeze. Which relayed a message to the worried healer that said, "Thank you for trusting me. I will do my best for your patient." He felt Slaina relax slightly and saw the relief in her eyes. Jason then asked Slaina to speak to Essa on his behalf. He could only help her if she were willing to trust him. Essa was reaching a point of exhaustion and was lying there barely conscious between contractions. Slaina roused Essa and told her there was nothing more she could do. Slaina told Essa to trust Jason to help her. Essa shook her head at first. Slaina knew she would have to be straightforward and blunt with Essa. Her long hard labor was making her judgment cloudy. Slaina sat down on the bed beside Essa and grasped her hand. She firmly patted her cheek to bring her around.

"Essa… Essa… You must let Doctor Jason help you, or both you and the baby will die. I cannot help you. Essa… do you understand?"

Essa nodded weakly.

"Will you let him help you?"

Essa had sweat pouring down her face and could barely see, but she looked at Jason. She could clearly tell he was concerned about her. Essa looked back at Slaina and saw one small tear slowly rolling down her cheek. The fog in her mind cleared enough to make sense of it, and she nodded at Slaina again. Slaina turned to Jason and nodded. Jason quickly went to work. He pulled out a small round trans-dermal patch and placed it on the skin inside her wrist. He told her it would help ease her pain and slow the labor. He needed her labor to slow down so he could try to turn the baby. He pulled a second patch out and put it inside the other wrist. This one would relieve the exhaustion, increase her oxygen levels, and settle her stomach. It only took a few seconds before she began to relax and some of the color returned to her face. Jason continued to use Slaina's help. He had Slaina help Essa to drink some water. He instructed Slaina to get Essa to drink as much as she could.

By this time, Cheyenne had gotten all the children into the Surf-Ve with Thane and on their way to Essa's sister's home. Essa's husband, Taldor, had been the one holding the crying toddler they heard when they arrived. Taldor was torn between the crying child and his wife's needs. When he carried the child outside to the Surf-Ve, she became distracted by the strange vehicle and the excitement of the other children. She allowed Korion to hold her in the front seat of the vehicle. Taldor was very relieved. He wanted to be at his wife's side during this difficult time. Cheyenne and Taldor entered the bedroom as Jason began to scan his wife with the medical scanner. Taldor was not happy about this man being in his bedroom, touching his wife, and seeing her like this. It wasn't proper, and he spoke his feelings quite adamantly in his native tongue. Jason looked at Slaina. Slaina had regained her professional composure by this time and stood up to deal with Taldor.

Slaina pulled Taldor just outside the door to the bedroom and began to speak to him. Taldor kept his eyes on the doctor the entire time they spoke. Cheyenne asked Jason what she could do to help. Jason asked her to set up the portable lanterns from the ship for him. Taldor's voice came through the doorway and sounded quite agitated. Cheyenne looked at Jason and asked, "Should we be worried about that?"

Their translator was too far away to pick up the conversation, but Jason glanced at Taldor and Slaina then assured Cheyenne, Slaina had things well in hand. Slaina was explaining the situation in very explicit terms to the upset husband. When he finally came to realize he would lose both his wife and unborn child without the doctor's help, he settled down. He still wasn't happy, but Slaina assured him the doctor was only trying to protect his wife and child. Slaina sent Taldor to the head of the bed to help support Essa when it was time to deliver the baby. Taldor meekly took his place as he had done for each of his previous children, helping to hold her up when it was time to deliver the baby. He was too tired and beaten at this point to argue with her. It was emotionally and mentally taxing for him to hear his wife's cries of anguish during childbirth and it hadn't taken this long since the time Korion was born. He just wanted this to be over for her sake.

Jason looked at his scanner, which was positioned low on Essa's abdomen. He reached up to push on her belly to test how well the baby might move. He pulled back quickly and grabbed the scanner again. He moved it around above her abdomen. Cheyenne saw his eyebrows raise and he smiled slightly.

"Jason, what is it?" Cheyenne asked softly so as not to cause alarm.

Jason looked up at her and then at Slaina and Taldor. "There are two babies."

Jason's translator was only translating one direction, and Taldor did not speak Intergalactic Standard. He knew Jason said something important. Not knowing what it was he looked to Slaina for help. Slaina smiled weakly and translated for him. Taldor was torn between being happily surprised and worried because his wife had still not safely given birth. Slaina was caught in the same emotional dilemma.

Jason completed his evaluation of the situation and prepared to help his patient deliver her babies. He gave Essa a stronger medication for pain and proceeded to instruct Slaina about his intended course of action. Jason sent Cheyenne to help hold Essa in Slaina's place. He asked Slaina to help him with the babies. Once everyone had their place and knew what they were to do, Jason manipulated the babies and got the first one into the desired position. He gave Essa a few minutes to rest and drink some more water, then he removed the trans-dermal patch slowing her labor, but he left the ones for pain and nausea in place. Moments later, Essa gave birth to a beautiful baby boy. Jason handed the baby off to Slaina who cleaned him up, stimulated him to breathe and cry a very healthy cry. Jason scanned Essa again to be certain about the second baby's position. This baby wasn't as cooperative. Jason tried to manipulate the second baby into position, but it refused to be turned. According to his scans, both babies were good sized and quite healthy.

Jason looked at Slaina. He told her what was wrong. Surgery was the only way to deliver the second baby safely. Jason replaced the patch to slow Essa's contractions while he explained the procedure to Slaina with the help of Cheyenne and the translator. Slaina had heard of this being done, but she had never seen it. He assured Slaina he had done this procedure before. He asked her to explain to Essa and Taldor what he was about to do. Taldor objected and looked like he was ready to throw the doctor out of the room. Slaina stepped directly in front of him. The tall, muscular Taldor was a stark contrast to the petite Slaina. She still had such a commanding presence the large man was compelled to back down. Slaina put his son into his arms and told him this was the only way to give him the second child safely. Taldor looked at Essa, who was again showing fear mixed with exhaustion. Essa just wanted this to be done. She begged Taldor to let the Doctor do what he thought was best. Taldor reluctantly nodded his approval. He sat down on the bed next to Essa. He put their son in her arms then he wrapped his arms around the both of them.

Jason treated Essa with a neural inhibitor, stopping her pain without affecting the baby. He instructed Slaina on each step he was taking as he did it. He also glanced periodically at Taldor and Cheyenne to make sure they weren't going to pass out from watching the surgery. Both seemed fine. Presently, Essa gave birth to her second baby, a little girl. Jason handed the baby off to Slaina. This time Slaina handed the baby to Cheyenne to clean up. Cheyenne looked startled at the squirming baby in her hands. Jason saw her dilemma and briefly told her what to do. Slaina was more interested in Jason's work. Cheyenne quickly cleaned the baby up and handed her to her anxious waiting mother. Jason finished up Essa's surgery as quickly as he could while still trying to explain what he was doing and why to Slaina.

After he completed Essa's surgery, he, Cheyenne, and Slaina left the room to go clean themselves up and take a break. Jason continued to teach Slaina. He had used his own equipment, which included a laser scalpel and cauterizer. Jason explained she would have to use a knife instead as well as needle and thread. He warned her that without his pain medications, this procedure would be extremely painful, and her patients might fight her. Cheyenne helped him explain all the complex medical concepts. It was so late by this time, Jason was afraid information was going to get lost. He was trying to cover the information while it was still fresh on their minds. He finally decided they all needed to get some sleep. Slaina said she would stay the rest of the night with Essa. Jason told her he would stop by later in the day to check on them.

Thane was back with the Surf-Ve. He had apparently been back for a little while because he was sound asleep inside it. He woke with a start when they climbed in. As soon as he was coherent, Thane asked if everything was okay. Cheyenne was still working off an Adrenalin rush and seemed eager to talk. The doctor was tired and ready for a nap, so he was happy to let her answer. When they arrived back at the ship, Jason gave a brief report to David and Brynna, then wandered off to get a quick shower and some sleep. Thane had no trouble making his way back to his bed. Cheyenne had to sit down with a book for a little while before she could settle down and sleep.

The next morning Jason and Cheyenne got up late and had lunch. They headed out to see Essa. When they arrived, Essa was sitting in the kitchen eating, and the babies were snugly tucked into a cradle beside her. Taldor was carrying in a load of firewood for the stove. Slaina was cleaning up the dishes. Five of their six older children were playing outside. Taldor picked the children up after breakfast that morning. The toddler was wandering around the kitchen and staying very close to her mother. Every now and then she would walk over to the cradle, point to the babies, and say something. The translator couldn't make out what the child was saying, so Cheyenne finally asked. Slaina told her, she was saying "babies." It appeared she was amazed at their sudden appearance in their home. Taldor seemed glad to see them this time. Jason did a quick scan of Essa and the babies who were all doing great. The babies started to stir, so Essa picked them up. Cheyenne moved closer to admire the two. She told Essa, via the translator, how beautiful they were. Cheyenne asked her what she named the babies. Essa looked at Cheyenne and Jason, smiled and said, "Jason and Cheyenne." Taldor moved over behind Essa and smiled in agreement with her. Jason offered Taldor his hand and told Taldor they were honored by this.

As a result of their efforts, Jason made more progress than he expected with Slaina and Essa. He and Cheyenne brought the computer module with them one day and demonstrated how to use it. Before Essa's babies were born, Jason felt like he was forcing information onto Slaina. She asked very few questions and showed little to no initiative toward anything he suggested. Now they were both full of questions and ideas. Jason made a mental note to suggest Slaina's new knowledge of Basic First Aid and Resuscitation be incorporated into their school programs. He planned to speak to Eston and Joren about this as soon as possible.

When Jason did get the opportunity to speak to them, Slaina was with him. He told them his proposal to have Slaina come into the schools to teach health subjects as well as the First Aid and Resuscitation. At first, they were confused by the request; then they found it amusing. Now, it was Jason's turn to be confused. Jason asked the Ministers to explain to him why this was so amusing. Minister Eston explained, "You want us to teach healing to boys? Healing is a woman's job."

Jason looked quizzically at the Ministers, "Who teaches the girls?"

"What they learn, they learn from their mothers."

"Who teaches the women how to read and write?" Jason continued.

"Women do not need to read and write. They need only to learn to cook, sew, and heal. Why would they need to learn to read and write? Her husband will take care of her." asked Minister Eston.

Jason knew he had entered dangerous territory, so he tried to stay practical with his point and stay away from the political reformation. "What happens if a man is sick or dies and leaves a wife and daughters? What if his wife needs to collect from those who owed him money to pay their debts? If she cannot read his ledgers to know who owes him money, how can she collect? I suppose she could ask another man to read them for her, but how will she know if he is cheating her? What if a woman never marries and has to sew or do other chores to earn money to live?

How will she know if someone is cheating her, or how can she know if she has enough money to live?"

Ministers Eston and Joren knew these were problems. Women who believed they were being cheated were sent to Nasha to settle such disputes, and there were too many such occasions to be counted. Perhaps the doctor had a good idea here. Minister Joren spoke first but carefully watched Minister Eston for a reaction, "Your words do have some merit. We will consider teaching the girls in a separate school, basic reading, and writing. Slaina could teach them some of these health topics you spoke of, but I see no reason to teach the health topics to boys."

The doctor was afraid to press his luck, so he decided teaching, at least the entire female portion of the population, was a good enough win for now. Cheyenne didn't see it that way though.

"Minister Joren, may I ask you some questions?"

"Yes, Ensign Cheyenne, you may."

"How many healers are in this area?"

"Just Slaina and Essa." He replied.

"Do the boys or men ever get together and go swimming without the women?"

"Of course they do, boys love to run off and play when they should be doing their chores." He seemed puzzled by her questioning the obvious.

"How many of your women participate in wars or battles?"

"None, of course, wars are no place for women!" He was losing patience with this line of questions.

"My point is this. If you have only one or two healers, how many lives are lost waiting for her to arrive? If the boy who falls into the water and drowns is reached soon enough, his life might be saved. If the warrior wounded in battle received the right care immediately after an injury, perhaps he would live to fight again. There is no replacement for a trained healer, but what the doctor suggests is training for all people that could preserve life until a healer arrives."

Joren smiled slowly. "I thought you were simply an ignorant woman. You are much wiser than I gave you credit for. Minister Eston, I will allow Slaina and Essa to teach in my schools. What about you?"

Minister Eston was not so easily convinced. "I will consider it."

Slaina was elated at the developments of this conversation. Once she, Cheyenne, and Jason were alone again, she told him she could find other avenues to convey this knowledge. She assured them she would be aggressive in her endeavors. Jason was concerned he may have started a women's revolution. The doctor decided he should report this development as soon as possible so Brynna and the Captain would be prepared if they were blamed for such a sociological upset. He excused himself from the two women and contacted Brynna via his bracelet's comm unit.

Brynna and David were with the Magistrate overseeing the installation of the first new windows in the council chambers. Braxton was also installing a ceiling fan powered by a windmill on the roof of the building. David was holding onto a support rope while the fan was being secured. Brynna stepped away when Jason asked if she was alone. David heard the communication come in but could not hear what was being said when she stepped away. The next thing he heard was Brynna saying, "You did WHAT?"

David forced his attention back to holding his support rope steady and waited for whatever was coming next. A couple minutes later the fan was secured, and the support ropes were released. Brynna walked back over to David looking vexed. David was almost afraid to ask. He didn't want to interfere with her job but decided to at least ask. She didn't have to tell him if she didn't want to. "What was that all about? It wasn't something Jake did, was it?"

Brynna looked at him somewhat wide-eyed and just blinked. Finally, she was able to put her racing thoughts into words. "No, it had nothing to do with Jake. It was Jason."

"Jason? He didn't get any more babies named after him, did he?"

"No, and after this Taldor may change their son's name to something else."

"Jason is a very easy-going, level-headed officer. What could he have possibly done?"

Brynna, still looking vexed, looked David squarely in the eye and said, "I think he started a women's emancipation movement."

David's jaw dropped. "He did what?" David's voice carried further than he meant for it to and he started getting stares from the others in the room. He lowered his voice, pulled Brynna further into the corner and repeated his question.

Brynna recounted what Jason had told her. David just shook his head. "I know we're supposed to start moving them toward Commonwealth standards, but I don't think they meant for us to go that far with it."

Brynna agreed. She really hoped this would not be a problem. "We better have a response ready if it does become a problem. Do you think we should be proactive and address it first?"

David pondered it for a second then offered his thoughts on the matter. "I suggest you have a response, but don't address it first. If they don't see it as a problem, let's not suggest it."

Brynna agreed then added, "I'm going to head back to the ship to get the details of what happened from Jason and Cheyenne. I'll give you an update as soon as I have more information."

That evening, the council met to discuss all of the recent events. Although they had some concerns about the new changes, they were quite happy with their new arrangement. The council believed their world must have some importance to have the Commonwealth take such an interest in them. They were more than happy to emulate the Commonwealth in whatever ways they could. They liked the new technologies they were receiving and wanted to show themselves worthy of more. They were willing to even educate the girls in reading and writing, teach men how to save lives and prepare for a healer to come. It was growing in them almost like an addiction, and it had only been a couple weeks. The Council also decided their guests had spent so much time working they weren't getting enough relaxation. This had been part of their arrangement with the crewmen. The council decided to plan a celebration. The community had a routine of working for six days, a rest and relaxation day on the seventh and then the eighth was considered a Holy Day. They decided to invite the crew for the next rest and relaxation day to the celebration.

The next morning, the Magistrate came to the ship to meet with David and Brynna. David invited him in to tour the ship. He finished the tour in the dining room where they could sit down and talk while they ate breakfast. Donnel told them about the Council's meeting. When he mentioned the impending changes to their educational system, Brynna bit her lip. David, seeing her reaction, reached under the table and gave Brynna's hand a gentle squeeze. David cautiously inquired, "Is the council comfortable with all of these things? I know change is often difficult and resisted. We did not come here to make things difficult. Our intention is only to make things easier."

The Magistrate did confess there were concerns, but an agreement had been reached, or the council would have still been sequestered in the council chamber. He almost seemed ashamed to admit there had been some reluctance. After his report on the council meeting, Donnel extended the invitation to the Seventh Day Celebration. He expressed his concerns about their agreement. "We agreed your crew would get a chance to rest and relax in exchange for the help you have given us. They have not rested. We cannot fail to keep our part of the agreement. We would be dishonored."

David responded as any gracious man would have. "We are the ones at fault here. We learned your seventh day is for relaxation, but we got caught up in our desire to do our best for you. We have neglected our own needs. We would be honored to attend the celebration. We are the ones who have put you at risk of being dishonored. Please forgive us."

David thanked him for the invitation and accepted on behalf of the entire crew. He also made sure to inquire about any cultural necessities, like bringing gifts or food, or correct attire. Donnel told David to wear whatever was comfortable. Since their clothing was so different, it didn't matter anyway. He also told them they should not bring anything.

Donnel was happy to hear David's reply. They finished their discussion, so the Magistrate got up to return to his duties in town. David and Brynna escorted him off the ship. The Magistrate started to walk toward town, and almost as an afterthought he turned back to David. "There was one more thing about our agreement I do not understand."

"What is it?" David asked.

"You have sought knowledge about our people and our history, yet you have never come to our Holy Day celebrations. I don't understand. Our Holy Day is a celebration of all we are. You seek to know our allies, but you do not come to meet them."

Now it was David's turn to be puzzled. He looked at Brynna who gave him the slightest shrug then a quick and subtle nod. David responded slowly in order to give himself time to think. "I hope we did not cause any offense. We are unfamiliar with Holy Days. The Commonwealth has no Holy Days, but we know they are highly valued by others. We did not want to interfere in something that might cause offense. If you think we would benefit from it, then we will come."

"I will be glad to introduce you to how we celebrate our Holy Days. This will be a good Holy Day for you to come to. Arni is coming. I am told he will arrive tomorrow." With that, the Magistrate happily turned and walked away.

David and Brynna wanted to pursue him to ask who "Arni" was but decided they would find out soon enough.

The crew was nearing the end of their mission, so they were staying closer to the ship at this point. It was time to let the people of this community start working on their own with their new "toys." Brynna called a staff meeting of everyone available. Jason and Cheyenne were still trying to make up for Slaina's initial reluctance to listen to Jason. At the staff meeting, everyone gave positive reports. Lazaro and Braxton reported numerous improvements in machinery, processes, and basic structural comforts. Along with the introduction of ceiling fans and windmills, they introduced simple machines such as pulleys and screws. These were such simple things, but these people hadn't been out of caves that long.

Laura reported she had introduced the concepts of crop rotation, plant grafting, and cross-pollination. She also discovered a plant having medicinal properties and passed the information on to Jason who presented it to Slaina. Jake reported several security measures and strategies he had introduced to Minister Nasha. Nasha's troops operated with spears, knives, swords, bows, and arrows. Jake introduced them to recurve bows, crossbows, and catapults. Lazaro improved on their smelting which made their swords and spears stronger.

David and Brynna had met with Minister Duard regarding ways to improve trade negotiations, banking, and finance. There didn't seem to be much to "enlighten" him on because his practices were already quite sound, although perhaps too trusting. When they suggested maintaining stricter policies in those areas, Minister Duard politely, but firmly declined. Thane also reported he had introduced the beginning concepts of aviation to several children, and he felt it would plant the seeds of imagination and exploration for the next generations.

Brynna concluded the meeting by letting the crew know they had been invited to a celebration on the next rest and relaxation day. She also told them they had been invited to the next Holy Day celebration. The crew was happy to hear about the celebration, but they were also concerned about it. Aulani and Lexi were curious and eager to attend. Jake and Lazaro were not interested in participating at all. Brynna informed the crew she had accepted both invitations and they would happily attend.

Later, outside the ship, Jake and Lazaro quietly suggested to the Captain they could stay behind on the Holy Day and prepare the ship for launch. David stopped, looked at both men sternly to respond to their request. "Gentlemen, your Commander has told you what is expected of you. I cannot prepare the ship for departure until she says it is time to go unless we are in mortal danger. Are we in some kind of danger I should be made aware of?"

Lazaro looked away sheepishly and mumbled a low, "No, sir."

Jake looked a little confused. He wasn't sure if the Captain was implying he think of something to justify their request or if he was merely annoyed with them. From the piercing look on the Captain's face, he decided it was the latter and managed to utter a disgruntled, "No, sir."

David finished the discussion by saying, "In that case, gentlemen, I trust you know where you need to be." The two men started to walk away.

David decided to make sure he was very clear on the matter, "And gentlemen, don't ever try to pit one of us against the other like that again."

The two men replied with a resolute, "Yes sir!" They left quickly.

The town council had recently delivered the requested food and water to the ship. After the men walked out of sight, David continued his inventory of the food and water. Brynna stepped out from behind the stacked supplies. David looked up from his datapad and smiled at her. She was always a pleasant sight to his eyes. "Hello, Beautiful."

Brynna smiled back at him and then blushed slightly at the sound of his greeting. They had been so busy working they had not had much time for personal interaction. Brynna casually asked about the supplies. David told her they had all they needed and more. As Brynna started to walk away, she stopped to ask one last question. "Were you planning to tell me what those two just tried to do?"

David looked up from his datapad long enough to meet her gaze, "No." Then he promptly went back to his datapad.

Brynna knew by his reaction he felt it had been handled appropriately and nothing more was needed. She decided one more thing needed to be said. "Thanks for backing me up, Captain Alexander."

David stopped. The significance of her reply was that of a Commander to her Captain, not a wife to her husband. David was fairly sure they both had a good understanding of their roles on board the ship, but it was also nice to know Brynna was secure in it as well. "You're welcome, Commander." Once again, they exchanged brief smiles then went back to business.

Two days later, the entire crew attended the rest and relaxation celebration. It started with a lunch set up near the landing pad. The council wanted to make sure the crew rested, so they planned the celebration near the ship and started it with a late lunch so they could sleep in. The afternoon was filled with games, talking, and some of the women brought sewing projects. The female crew members knew very little about sewing. They knew how to make minor clothing repairs, but nothing about making clothing from cloth or decorative sewing.

Thane had developed a reputation among the children for creating kites and toy airplanes. Several of the children commandeered him to help them create new aviation projects. Aulani began to miss her husband and found him sitting on the ground under a tree surrounded by children. What had started out as five or six had now grown to twenty or thirty children. Thane looked up at Aulani and smiled, "Did you come to help?"

Aulani smiled back, sat down on the ground, and said, "Sure, I'd love to help." As the children began to run out of supplies to build their projects, the women began noticing their cloth scraps were disappearing. Marissa saw children coming and going. Once the women started looking for their scrap material, Marissa realized the children were not staying, but would dart in and out of the women's sewing circle. She had seen some of the smaller ones even crawling around under the makeshift tables. Lazaro had introduced scissors to the blacksmiths, and three of the women now owned scissors, but one pair was somehow unaccounted for. The woman, who could not locate her wonderful new sewing tool, was torn between telling the other women how handy they were and trying to find her missing tool. . Marissa decided to follow one of the children. She followed him to the same tree where Thane and Aulani were sitting, working on their kites and airplanes. Marissa couldn't help but laugh and join in with them. She did give the child who was holding the scissors a firm recommendation to return the scissors quickly to their owner.

David, Jake, Braxton, Lazaro, and Jason joined in a game with the other men. The game involved a ball being thrown up into the air, and then it had to bounce once before it could be touched. Once it bounced, you could hit it, kick it, or pick it up and throw it into an area at the end of the field. All the men seemed to enjoy it. Laura was dying to join the game, but it was not permitted for women to play. Jake even seemed to relax and enjoy himself. He never lost his temper or gave any signs of unsportsmanlike conduct. David complimented him on playing a good game when Jake's team won.

That evening everyone gathered in the town square for a party, which included dancing and refreshments. Each couple was thrilled at the chance to spend time with their spouse, even the couples who didn't enjoy dancing, danced. The crew relaxed and had the most enjoyable evening since before their launch date. As the evening came to a close, the Magistrate approached David. "I trust you and your crew have enjoyed yourselves today."

David assured him they definitely had. They continued to discuss the day's events and laughed periodically at the more humorous aspects of the day. Donnel's demeanor then sobered as he made a final serious inquiry. "Do you feel we have honored our part of the agreement?"

David was caught a little off guard by his question. David had been leaning back in his chair. He sat up straight and looked Donnel in the eye. "Absolutely. Why do you ask? Is there something you're concerned about?"

Donnel was concerned. He leaned in and spoke in a low voice so he wouldn't be overheard. "Your people have given us far more than we expected, and it far outweighs what you have asked for in return. Is there anything more you require? We feel we owe you more than what we have given."

"The only things we still seek are your continued alliance with the Commonwealth and knowledge of Pateras El Liontari."

Donnel leaned back in his chair resolutely. "Then tomorrow, we will fulfill the final requirements of our agreement. At the Holy Day Celebration, we will pledge our alliance to the Commonwealth and introduce you to Arni. He can teach you all you need to know about Pateras El Liontari."

David tried to conceal his excitement at making such progress so quickly in their mission. He smiled and told Donnel, "I look forward to meeting this Arni then."

The Magistrate stood up to leave and said, "We should get some sleep. Holy Day will begin quite early tomorrow. The celebration changes regularly. Tomorrow, we celebrate at Sunrise at the western cliffs. We will watch the sunrise over the western mountains and rejoice in all the Originator has given us. We will celebrate the alliance he has given us with the Commonwealth."

The Magistrate reached his hand toward David. David grasped his arm in their traditional gesture and responded to him, "We are definitely looking forward to your celebration tomorrow."

As the Magistrate, walked away, David started searching the crowd for Brynna. As soon as he spotted her, he worked his way through the people to pull her aside. Brynna was obviously enjoying herself. Her face glowed with a look of peace and contentment. When she caught sight of the intense look on David's face, her face changed to a look of curiosity. He pulled her away from the crowd just as the Magistrate stepped onto the platform with the musicians. As the Magistrate encouraged everyone to say their goodnights and head home, David excitedly whispered to Brynna that they were about to get the information they needed. Brynna became excited. She wondered if any of the other mission teams had found out anything yet. Both she and David had a sense of satisfaction as they headed back to the ship. Once aboard the ship, Brynna updated the crew on the situation and strongly recommended they all get some sleep.

GALAT III

ARNI

The next morning, everyone boarded the Surf-Ve. Jake had been up late preparing and managed to be in possession of more weapons than he had hands to carry them in. During the entire mission, each crew member carried a weapon for personal protection, but they never had cause to draw their weapons. David saw Jake's vigilance and strongly cautioned him about overreacting. If Jake overreacted, they might never get the information they needed.

At breakfast, the crew all seemed rather sluggish, so Lexi thoughtfully made some extra coffee and put a container in the vehicle for their ongoing consumption. They weren't used to getting up before sunrise and with the previous night's festivities running a little late, they were having trouble waking up. Lexi thought it might be a good idea to get some conversation going. She attempted to get their brains in gear by asking thought-provoking questions. Her attempts were rewarded by receiving short answers in response. Aulani didn't know why Lexi was asking so many questions, but she did notice her queries were not getting the desired response. Aulani joined Lexi on her quest. Slowly the crew started responding and even began quiet conversations between each other.

The sky began to take on the gray cast that always preceded sunrise making things easier to see. The closer to sunrise it got, the heavier the crowds became. There were horse-drawn wagons, parents pulling small wagons or carts with sleeping children, older children running back and forth chasing each other and small domesticated pets. The number of people present was more than they had ever seen in the area. They also noticed many tents and campsites alongside the road. Aulani looked the crowd over and voiced the same thing everyone else was thinking. "There aren't this many people in this area. A lot of these people must be travelers."

There were so many people and domestic animals; Thane was afraid of an accident. He finally had to pull the Surf-Ve over and park it. The crew grabbed lanterns and joined the mass of people gathering at the cliffs. As they walked up the side of the plateau to their destination, the sky lightened up enough for the crew to get a look around. As the crew slowly made their way up the mountainside, Brynna caught Lexi and whispered, "Thanks, we needed that."

Lexi smiled and said, "Next time, I may prescribe a regimen of calisthenics."

Brynna blinked. "Umm, I think coffee and conversation worked well. I'm good with this option, really." Lexi laughed at her reaction.

The area by the cliffs was almost a field. It was a plateau with patches of grass scattered across it. The land was mostly rock, so it couldn't be used for farming. It did have a fantastic view overlooking a large valley with a river running through it. On the other side of the valley was the beginning of a majestic range of mountains.

As they reached the edge of the clearing, the crew moved along the outer edge of the crowd to make room for the people coming behind them. They wanted to stay near the edge. They considered themselves to be visitors and observers, not participants. Lexi surveyed the demographics of the populous to make sure they wouldn't offend anyone based on seating arrangements or some other cultural belief. The crowd appeared to be there on a first come, first served basis, and grouped by families. The crowd consisted of a mixture of mindsets. Some were focused on an unseen facet of the gathering. Some seemed to be excited, while others simply were not awake yet.

Donnel saw the crew keeping their distance and waved at them to join him near the edge of the cliff. The crew began to move toward him when Donnel saw Jake rush to the Captain's side and say something. The Captain stopped and spoke to him for a moment, then put his arm on Jake's shoulder in a reassuring manner and they continued moving toward Donnel. Donnel smiled. Jake was very much like Nasha, always cautious, or perhaps suspicious was a better word. Although, Donnel wondered why Jake was still suspicious of them after all this time. The crew greeted Donnel as they approached. Donnel returned their greeting and invited them to sit with him. He explained the celebration would be conducted in the language of the people, and it might be difficult for their translators to help them from such a distance. Brynna quietly instructed everyone to set his or her translators to interpret in silent mode. Donnel gave them a few basic instructions about what would and would not be expected of them.

"You may participate if you wish, but do not feel as though you must do anything that makes you uncomfortable. All we ask is that you do not disturb the others around you. If you have questions, there will be time to answer them later. I will help you as the day allows; however, I am officiating this celebration so I will be busy for a good part of the day. Do you have any questions before I begin?"

The crew shook their heads. David responded on their behalf, "I don't believe we have any questions right now, but I am sure we will have some later. Please don't let us keep you away from your duties."

The Magistrate nodded to them and stepped away. He was normally quite confident and relaxed, but today he seemed nervous. The crew sat down and made themselves as comfortable as they could on the hard ground. The sky was showing a beautiful array of colors now, as the sun was about to crest the top of the mountains across the valley in front of them. The Magistrate stood with his back to the sunrise and raised his hands in the air. Across the field, everyone sat down except for what appeared to be designated men standing at prescribed distances from the Magistrate and each other. Moments later they discovered the men were there to relay the Magistrate's words to the crowd further out. Braxton made a mental note to introduce some concepts of sound projection to the Magistrate later.

Once the crowd took their places and got quiet, the Magistrate began to address them. David noticed that even the children stopped playing and sat down to watch and listen, without being told.

"Greetings my friends. Welcome to those of you who have traveled great distances to join us today. Today is an extra special Holy Day Celebration. We have guests from the stars who have joined us to watch and learn about us and about He who brings us the Word of Light and Life. It is also the expected time for Arni to come to us. Let us watch the sun bring light to the sky and give thanks and praise to He who brings us the Words of Light and Life."

All around the crew people began to react differently. Some began to speak audibly, some began to sing quietly, and some just sat there serenely watching the sunrise. Some even cried. Brynna enjoyed a beautiful sunrise as much as anybody, but she never saw a reason to cry about it, unless, perhaps, you were in fear of losing your life and never seeing another one. Lexi was fascinated by the diverse reactions of the people to a sunrise. Jake looked like he had ingested too many cups of coffee. Brynna had an audiovisual recorder and was discreetly recording as much as she felt she could get away with. Cheyenne was using her translator to try to pick up and record the words and songs of those closest to her. She signaled Aulani to do the same thing. Some people bowed down with their faces to the ground. It appeared they were worshiping the sun. Brynna could see Lexi was obviously puzzled by this behavior. She wanted to ask about it, but she didn't want to disturb anyone, especially since that was the one thing they were warned not to do. Brynna made a mental note to ask about it later.

Once the sun had risen fully into the morning sky, the crowd got quiet again, and the Magistrate began to address them again. "For the benefit of our visitors from the stars and the young children, today we will review our history and the prophecies. Let the children come to the front."

As the children came running forward, the adults moved back to give them room. Jake seemed extremely jumpy. Having children so close to this cliff wasn't doing anything to help him calm down. Marissa touched his hand to try to get him to relax a little. It didn't help. He jumped like he'd received a stout electrical charge. David was starting to get annoyed with Jake. He knew his security chief was just trying to keep everyone safe, but he was becoming a liability. David managed to catch Jake's eye. The message came through loud and clear without a word being spoken.

Donnel looked at the children and asked, "The sun and stars are givers of light and life, but who gave us those stars?"

Several children responded eagerly with their answers, "Pater. Pateras."

Donnel called one of the older children by name and asked, "What is Pater's full name? Tell us all so we can all hear who we thank for our lives."

The boy stood proudly and said, "Pateras El Liontari. He is the Speaker of the Words of Life and Light."

At the mention of the name "Pateras El Liontari," the crew's attention became riveted on the Magistrate and the children. They completely ignored the people around them. As the Magistrate continued to talk and quiz the children in front of him, Jake slowly scooted up beside the Captain, trying to be careful not to attract attention. He very quietly whispered in Raesin, "Captain, our orders were clear. We have to leave."

David wanted to gather more information. He didn't feel threatened in any way, but Jake was right, their orders were clear on the matter. He also didn't want Jake to think he was improperly influenced. David quietly replied, "There are too many people, we can't make it back safely yet. Wait until the celebration is over. We will tell them, we've been ordered to return to the stars. Just stay alert."

The Magistrate noticed the disturbance but continued to quiz the children. Things suddenly took a bizarre twist when the Magistrate talked about Pateras being the one who holds all knowledge and how he sent the crew from the stars to give to the people out of his abundant knowledge. The crew sat there in shock. They suddenly realized these primitive people believed Pateras El Liontari sent the crew to this planet. David wondered how they could believe that when the crew had very pointedly started out by asking questions about Liontari. Now they were baffled. Did these people really know anything about Liontari? Were they just hearing stories about him and filling in the blanks in their own unenlightened way? Maybe they weren't in any danger. The Magistrate then spoke the words everyone had been waiting to hear. "Today is a great day, the son of Pateras himself is here to speak to you. WELCOME back to us Arni Liontari." Arni moved to the front of the crowd and took over speaking.

Now, this was a new piece of information. Pateras El Liontari had a son? Arni appeared to be in his late twenties or early thirties. He dressed in a simple tunic like the other men on Galat. His dark hair barely reached his shoulders, and he wore a close-cut beard. He was about David's height and build, but unremarkable in appearance.

He reviewed their entire belief system. Pateras was attributed as being the Giver of life and death, the Giver of blessings and curses, light, truth, sorrow, and joy anything the people had whether good or bad was given by Pateras. He also told them about the prophecies that a great evil and darkness was coming, but Pateras sent him to deliver them from it. He also spoke of a horrible fate awaiting those who rejected the deliverance Pateras offered. He admonished the people to choose who they would serve and encouraged them to serve Pateras only. He warned them their loyalties could not be divided. Was it just a coincidence that his eyes landed on the crew when he spoke those words? Arni gave them one last prophecy. Pateras, the creator of all, was now tired of the evil spreading throughout the stars. "I have told you my Father sent me to reclaim his people. The war has already begun. Soon your lives will be required of you because of me. I was sent to finish this once and for all. The war will last a long time, but the day I die will be the day the war will be won."

The crowd got deathly quiet while Arni continued. "Death cannot stop me. I have already begun calling the twelve twelves to leave the Evil One and follow me. I will defend he who defends you. His sentence of death will be mine." Arni's eyes landed on David briefly before he continued speaking. "As surely as I die, I will live again." Upon hearing of Arni's resurrection, the crowd cheered then settled back down to listen again.

After Arni finished speaking, he turned the gathering back over to the Magistrate. The Magistrate concluded by dividing the crowd into what appeared to be prearranged groups. Each person could join whichever group they wanted based on their greatest need. There were groups for older men, older women, younger men, younger women, married couples, children's groups. It appeared the groups operated as a support group or a focus group dealing with problems faced by their particular demographic. They seemed to address problems with raising children, marital discord, or anything the individuals felt they needed advice or support with. There also seemed to be some sort of component of deity worship, even in this activity. The groups would talk for a period of time, and then they would stop and encircle a couple or an individual and place their hands on the person or persons at the center. Those that could not reach the individuals in the center would place their hand on the back or shoulder of the person directly in front of them. It looked as though they were trying to pass some sort of energy and transfer it from person to person. Once they established these links, they would all begin to speak simultaneously. It wasn't some sort of chant because they were saying different things. There were too many voices and too much interference from ambient noise for the translators to pick up what was being said.

Lexi and Cheyenne moved to the outside of one of the groups to try to pick up what was going on. The two women moved close to a women's group. Slaina and Essa were together in this group, so Cheyenne felt comfortable getting close to them. She tuned her translator into Slaina's voice and recorded as much as she could to analyze later. Lexi followed Cheyenne's lead and programmed hers to Essa's voice. Slaina had her eyes shut while she was speaking. Sensing the presence of the two women, she opened her eyes. Slaina's hand had been on Essa and another woman, but as she stopped speaking, she pulled her hands off the other women. Slaina turned to Cheyenne and smiled. When Essa felt Slaina's hand pull away, it got her attention as well. Somehow their presence appeared to disrupt the entire proceeding. The women all finished speaking and turned their attention to the two women. Cheyenne looked at Slaina and the other women. Using her translator, she apologized for interrupting them. The insightful woman smiled again and said, "It is all right. We are all here to seek answers to the difficulties we face, and to help each other. It is apparent you are seeking answers as well. Please, ask whatever you wish. If we don't know the answer, we will find someone who does."

Cheyenne and Lexi looked at each other. Lexi nodded for Cheyenne to start asking questions. Cheyenne wasn't sure which questions were the most pertinent, so she just started by following her own curious nature. "We don't understand what you are doing. What does this accomplish? Why do you all speak at once? Who are you talking to? What is the significance of this formation?"

As the translator relayed her questions in Galatan, several of the women began to smile, and a couple of the younger women even laughed openly. Cheyenne looked puzzled and then voiced her sentiment, "Why are they laughing?"

Slaina glanced over to the ones who laughed and in a stern voice stated, "They laugh because they aren't mature enough women to know when to control themselves." Hearing the sternness in Slaina's voice the two women's faces fell. They blushed slightly from embarrassment and looked at the ground until they no longer had the unwanted attention. Slaina turned her back to the two women so only Cheyenne and Lexi could see her face and smiled again. Once Slaina had made her point, she continued to answer Cheyenne's questions.

"We bring our struggles and problems to share with the others.

If someone has dealt with the problem before then, they share whatever insights they have."

Cheyenne interrupted Slaina, "That much we understand. We have similar things, but what were you doing when we walked up? What about your formation?"

It was Slaina's turn to look puzzled. Nevertheless, she attempted to explain as much as she could.

"After we have discussed whatever we can, we take our problems to he who has the Words of Light and Life. We give our problems and needs over to Pateras. We are speaking to Pateras."

"But you are all speaking at once, and you aren't saying the same things. No one can understand that many people speaking at once. What device do you use to communicate with him? Does he record your messages and listen to them later? That would require some very advanced technology. We haven't seen any evidence of advanced technology here. Has he left some communication device with you?" Cheyenne countered.

"You're right. No human could, but Pateras El Liontari isn't a mere man. He hears all our words, even the ones we don't speak. He knows all our thoughts. This is for our benefit, not his.

He knows our words even before we speak them. We need no devices to speak with him."

Lexi and Cheyenne weren't sure what to think. The Commonwealth had traveled throughout the entire galaxy, and the only sentient beings ever found were humans of varying shapes, sizes, and races. The concept was almost laughable. However, with the recent discovery of this new enemy, "Pateras," could he be a non-human, or was this just their primitive way of thinking? These people had never seemed superstitious. They seemed like highly intelligent people just underdeveloped from a technological standpoint. Lexi didn't want to offend them, so she cautiously ventured further, "No one can do that. Have you seen him do this in person?"

Slaina's face took on a very odd expression as she tried to form her next explanation. Suddenly a man called out to Slaina. "Mother!" Slaina turned around quickly to see a man bounding toward her. Her face brightened visibly as she turned and headed to meet him. While the two exchanged warm hugs and greetings, Essa moved closer to Lexi and Cheyenne to continue the explanations.

"Arni is Slaina's only son. He travels a lot, and she does not get to see him very often. I can try to answer your questions until she returns."

"We were trying to understand why you stand together with your hands on each other's backs and shoulders speaking altogether." Lexi also wanted to ask about Arni because his name was mentioned in relation to Pateras El Liontari. There were so many questions her mind was racing. She was afraid she would forget to ask something important.

"Arni taught us to speak to Pateras in this way. He taught us to care for others."

Lexi saw this as an opening to move the conversation toward who Arni really was and asked, "It sounds like Arni has great authority here. What is his title?" This culture respected titles so, this seemed to be the most appropriate question to ask.

"Arni has many titles. I do not know which title is the most important." Essa paused a moment to weigh her answer. "He is our Teacher, Healer, our Guide, and Messenger. I suppose Messenger would be the most important title although Healer is perhaps what we are more dependent on."

Lexi continued to probe Essa, "Did he get his skills as Healer from his mother? I thought men were not healers."

"No…" Essa paused and appeared to be searching for the right words. Their conversation was going through the translators, so it was not a language problem. Finally, she found what she thought were the right words. "Arni heals, but not like his mother. His mother treats illness and injuries and cares for the ailing, but she does not actually heal people. Arni does not have his mother's skills. He heals by speaking healing or touching the sick. His healing happens immediately."

Lexi felt her heart speed up even more. She really wanted to see this for herself, but at the same time, she knew the warnings the Commonwealth had issued about the Liontari.

As the two women continued talking, Cheyenne stepped away to bring David and Brynna into the conversation. She looked up and saw the Magistrate was already bringing them to meet Arni. Brynna signaled the others to rejoin them. Thane and Aulani were observing a children's group. They were trying not to be a distraction, but many of the children had become so attached to Thane and Aulani, they were excited to see them. Marissa slowly followed them. She wasn't sure if she should try to observe a different group, but she really felt more comfortable around the children. The little girl who sat in her lap during the shuttle ride saw her approach and insisted she sit with her. Marissa smiled at the girl and complied with her request. The rest of the crew spread out to observe other groups.

As the crew came back together, the Magistrate attempted to introduce them to Arni who was standing with one arm still around his mother. Unfortunately, when Thane, Aulani, and Marissa moved away from the children's group, several tried to follow them. Thane attempted to discourage them, but as soon as the children saw Arni, they became even more excited. Several came running toward him shouting his name, which distracted numerous people. Arni excused himself for a moment, hugged several of the children and spoke softly to them. After Arni spoke to them, he sent the children, still bouncing with excitement, back to their group. Marissa noticed, although the youngsters were back in their group, their attention was still focused on Arni. She glanced at the woman who was leading the children's group and noticed Arni's presence also distracted her.

Before he could attempt to make introductions again, the Magistrate suggested they move away from the crowd to the edge of the clearing. He told Arni the crew had many questions for him. Once the introductions were made, Brynna instructed the crew, except Cheyenne, to return to the groups they were observing. Cheyenne, Brynna, David, and Jake remained with Donnel and Arni to talk. As they headed toward a grouping of rocks under a large old tree, Jake pulled David aside to hastily voice his reservations.

"Captain, we need to get off this planet. We don't need to follow this man around and listen to anything he says. We'll become infected, or compromised, or whatever it is he does to people."

"Jake, I understand your concern, but I don't think the Commonwealth knew we might get the opportunity to speak to someone so close to Pateras El Liontari. We might be able to get a lead on their base of operations and stop them in a matter of weeks instead of two or more years. I would say that's worth risk. Wouldn't you?"

Jake pondered his question for a brief second before answering. "So long as we aren't turned against our own people first."

"If you think it's that big of a risk, go back to the ship and prepare a message to send back to base containing all reports to date and one more indicating what we have learned here today. If we don't come back or act out of character when we do, then send the message."

Jake objected. "I'm not comfortable leaving the crew here unprotected."

"Jake, after today, we're done here. You can stay with us and gather more intel, or you can go back to the ship as a last resort. The choice is yours, but I think we will be okay for just a little longer."

Jake was not happy and wanted to take things one step further to make his point. "Fine! I'll wait a little longer, but if I think for one second you or any other crew member has turned, I won't hesitate to shoot you."

David knew he meant every word. He also knew if he balked in any way, Jake could interpret his actions as being compromised. "I get it, Jake. Just make sure you have all the appropriate documentation, so you don't end up facing charges later on. My last log entries all indicate I am still in full control of my faculties and quite loyal to the Commonwealth. Understand?"

"Yes, Captain."

The Magistrate, noticing the two men had stopped to talk in what appeared to be less than cordial dialogue, approached the two men cautiously. "Is everything all right, Captain David?"

"Yes, Magistrate, everything is fine, just a slight difference of opinion."

As they reached the edge of the clearing, they each found places to sit on rocks under the shade of a tree. Arni looked at each crew member. Despite his approximate age of thirty years, the same age as most of the crew, his visage appeared far more mature. He had a kind face, but one seeming to bear the wisdom of age. There was something about his eyes though. It seemed as though he could see right into ones very heart and soul. David also thought he could see a look of sadness in his eyes. David knew Pateras had great power. Could Arni also have great power? Did he know, why they were here? Would he try and stop them?

The Magistrate introduced the crew to Arni. "These are the people I mentioned to you. They have been very kind and helpful to us. Please thank your Father for sending them here for us."

Arni smiled. "I will thank him for you, but please thank him yourself when you talk to him."

The crew looked at each other quizzically. David looked at Arni and thought, "He's an opportunistic shyster. He's taking credit for our presence." David wanted to challenge the Magistrate's misconception but decided there were larger issues to deal with.

"I understand you have questions for me." Arni began.

David was surprised to hear Arni speaking his own native language, perfectly. He reached down to adjust his translator. He set it to simply record and not translate. He wanted to keep a record of the conversation to review later. Arni's language skills distracted David, forcing him to refocus his thoughts. He began his questions with an apology. For the benefit of the Magistrate, David spoke in Intergalactic Standard. "I'm sorry. I was surprised by your language skills. Do you travel off-world?"

"I have been to many worlds."

"Is this your homeworld? We've seen no evidence of advanced technology here. How can you get to other worlds?"

"I am at home on every world, but I doubt that is what you were asking. My mother gave birth to me on this world. How do I travel to other worlds? I sometimes catch a ride with traders or my Father takes me to other worlds."

"So Slaina is your mother. Who is your Father?" David expected to find out Arni's father was a visiting trader who met a local girl and fell in love.

Arni looked at David, then Brynna, Cheyenne, and Jake. "You already know the answer to that question. My Father is Pateras El Liontari." David's eyes and Arni's eyes were locked on each other. Jake felt the blood drain out of his own face. David never flinched and boldly asked, "And who is Pateras El Liontari? Where can we find him?"

"The only way to get to my Father is through me. I alone can present you to Him."

Arni looked at Cheyenne who was just as pale as Jake felt. "You have a question?"

Cheyenne was almost too scared to speak. "Slaina said Pateras isn't human."

Before anyone could react to Cheyenne's information, several people were heard screaming and yelling near the edge of the cliffs. David and Jake took off immediately in the direction of the screams. Cheyenne still had her eyes glued on Arni. Arni looked at her, smiled slightly and said, "I'm not here to harm anyone. You have nothing to fear from me." With that, Arni walked toward the commotion.

Braxton, Jason, and Lazaro were at the front of the crowd. Everyone was talking excitedly. Another woman was standing at the edge of the cliff crying hysterically. A man was standing with his arms wrapped around her. He was holding her tightly to keep her away from the edge of the cliff, tears quietly rolling down his face. When David and Jake reached the front of the crowd, Jason and Lazaro told them what had happened. Several children had been playing near the edge of the cliffs, and in all the excitement, one of them had gotten closer than he was allowed to the edge. He tripped and fell over the edge. The child's body lay mangled on a ledge about fifty feet down. Jason pulled his scanner out trying to get a reading on the child. It was either too far for the scanner to get an accurate read, or the child was already gone. Braxton and Lazaro were working on a way to get down to the child. Several families had brought blankets to sit on which were quickly cut into strips and tied together to serve as a rope. Jake and Jason went down the rope to the boy. Jason's scanner had not been too far away. The child was indeed gone. The scanner revealed extensive internal injuries, broken bones, skull fractures, and death was caused by a brain injury. Jason looked up at David and shook his head. There were several men besides the crew helping with the rescue attempt. The men located two sturdy tree branches to be used to form a makeshift stretcher. They knew the child was already gone, but this was the only way to recover his body in a dignified manner. After pulling the stretcher up from the ledge, they set it down gently on the ground. His mother and father knelt over him crying uncontrollably. They grabbed his lifeless body and cradled him in their arms. The boy appeared to be ten to twelve years old. Slaina joined the distraught parents, wrapping her arms around them both and crying with them. Slaina was the midwife who had delivered the boy. He was the only child the couple had. As David and the other men pulled Jason and Jake up from the ledge, more people gathered around the grieving couple, resting their hands on the couple and each other as the group became too large for each one to reach the couple. They began to all speak at once as the crew had seen them do in the groups earlier. As the group stopped speaking and began to move away from the hurting family, David noticed the couple seemed very calm and almost at peace. Jason approached the couple to express his condolences.

"I am so sorry for the loss of your son. I wish I could have saved him, but some things are beyond even the knowledge of the Commonwealth."

The man thanked Jason for trying to save his son, and for bringing the boy's body back to them. His mother looked up at Jason, and despite the tears remaining in her eyes, she smiled at him and said, "My son is beyond the stars with Pateras. He will be happy there."

Jason, not sure what to say, just agreed with her. "Yes, I am sure he will be happy there."

Arni moved with ease through the crowd toward the couple and their son. Lexi heard whispers among the crowd as Arni passed by her. Her translator was having trouble isolating one voice among so many again, but she had picked up enough of the language to recognize they were talking about Arni. She knew Arni was an important person, but in light of the tragedy, she wondered why he was still the topic of conversation. Arni reached out his arms to the couple as he drew near them. The couple collapsed into his arms and cried again. Lexi moved closer to them to allow her translator to pick up their conversation. She wasn't sure it was the appropriate thing to do in the face of such a tragedy, but she couldn't help herself. She knew she would hate herself for it later. What Lexi heard next was unnerving. The boy's mother looked at Arni and pleaded with him. "Arni, I know my son is safe with your Father, but please, he is my only child. Bring him back to me."

Jason was still close enough to overhear the conversation. He turned to the boy's father and said, "I have some medications that can help your wife get some rest and cope with her grief."

The man looked at Jason, his wife, then at Arni before he responded. "I will wait for Arni's decision."

Jason was taken aback by his response, but he had to comply with their wishes. Jason stepped aside and whispered to Brynna, "They are in shock. They both need a sedative. They think Arni can give them their son back."

Cheyenne was standing close enough to hear the doctor's worried comments. She couldn't help, but think, "What if he can give them their son back?" She wasn't about to voice her thoughts though. Jake was too anxious to shoot somebody, anybody. The thought also crossed her mind that maybe she was being compromised. As soon as the thought crossed her mind, she saw Arni look directly at her.

Arni had been listening to the distraught mother's pleas. He took her hands and spoke softly to her. Cheyenne wasn't close enough to make out what he was saying. She did see Lexi standing close enough, and her translator was recording. At the precise moment his eyes locked on Cheyenne's, she heard him raise his voice and say, "I will bring your son back to you."

The one thing that didn't occur to Cheyenne until later was she heard Arni make his announcement in her home language of Madrathean. Once she realized what she heard she began to doubt herself. If he had truly spoken in Madrathean, the local population wouldn't have understood him. Why would he talk to the locals in a foreign language? Did she imagine it? Was he playing tricks on her mind?

Arni knelt down next to the boy, picked up the boy's lifeless hands and said, "Father, send back this child according to your great plan." The boy suddenly gasped and stretched as though he were waking up from a good sleep. He opened his eyes to see Arni and his parents kneeling beside him. The boy sat up, excited to see Arni he hugged him immediately. His mother and father wrapped their arms around the two of them and cried again. Only this time, they were tears of joy.

Cheers of joy and excitement swept through the crowd like wildfire. Across the crowd, you could hear people shouting, "He's alive! The boy is alive! Arni healed the boy!"

Jason, hearing the commotion, whipped around and grabbed his scanner. He scanned the boy from head to toe. He stared at the scanner results for a moment then looked up at David and Brynna in disbelief. The entire crew was stunned at this turn of events.

From the look on Jason's face, David knew he had no explanation for what had just transpired. He knew Jake would be on him in a second to insist they leave, and he would not take "wait a minute" for an acceptable answer. The young Captain made his move first. He touched the comm unit on his wrist and ordered everyone back to the Surf-Ve except for Jason. He ordered Jake to get the crew back to the ship. He informed the security chief he and Jason would start walking that direction shortly. Jake reliably objected, but David quickly and quietly put a stop to Jake's predictable rant. "Chief, we're dealing with a power we don't understand. From what I have just seen, it's possible this power could swat us like an insect. I don't want to arouse any suspicions. I need you to get the crew back quickly and quietly to the ship and prepare for an immediate launch as soon as the doctor and I return. Once the crew is back and working on launch preparations, come back to get us. The doctor and I will make the appropriate farewell excuses, and we will start walking your direction."

Jake looked hesitant to leave his Captain behind, so David followed it up with one last plea. "Jake, I need you to get my wife and the rest of the crew to safety." As soon as Jake heard the Captain use his name instead of his title, he knew the Captain was taking the situation very seriously.

David was taking the situation seriously, but not as seriously as Jake. The Captain was more worried about Jake than Arni. He was amazed by Arni's power and recognized its potential, but for some reason, he didn't fear it. The man brought a dead child back to life. He hadn't harmed anyone. This brought to mind the question, "What was he capable of? Was he trying to harm anyone? If he had brought a boy back from the dead with a touch, could he also take life with a simple touch?"

Jason continued to scan the boy, and since Arni was in close proximity, he took as many scans of Arni as he felt he could get away with. Jake escorted the crew to the Surf-Ve as fast as he could. Some of the children tried to follow Thane, Aulani, and Marissa. Thane had to firmly send them back to their families. Thane took the controls of the vehicle and headed for the ship. He, Aulani, Laura, and Marissa had been too far away to know exactly what had happened. They only knew there had been a large commotion and now they were leaving. Brynna sat in the front right passenger seat. Jake and the other men took strategic positions throughout the vehicle. Thane and the three women recognized the tension emanating from the rest of the crew. Once they were underway, Thane asked Brynna, "Commander, what happened? Why are we leaving? Where are the Doc and the Captain?"

Brynna responded in a somewhat sullen tone, "Jake's going to go back to pick them up shortly. We have a confirmed contact with Pateras El Liontari. We have to prepare for immediate launch."

Thane was suddenly concerned about the Captain and the Doctor's welfare. "Why did the Captain and the Doctor stay behind?"

Brynna wanted to say David had stayed behind to investigate further, but she knew that wouldn't go over well with Jake. Instead, she gave him the answer David himself had given, "To give us a chance to get away without arousing suspicions."

"Why did he keep Jason with him? Why didn't he keep Jake?" Laura interjected.

Her face was getting paler by the moment. Of all the couples on board the ship, Jason and Laura had been married the longest. They had reached a point in their relationship where they had formed a strong attachment to each other and relied on each other.

Brynna saw the look on Laura's face and decided she needed to put her mind at ease as well as take command of the situation before anyone panicked. "The Captain would not have kept him if he had felt they were in immediate danger. He and the doctor intend to get as much information as possible until the last second. He does, however, want the ship ready to launch when they rejoin us, so we have work to do when we get back, and we need to do it quickly."

Some of the crew were shocked at what they had just witnessed, and some were just uncertain. No one was responding quickly as they tried to process the new information. As Commander, Brynna didn't need them to understand what had just happened. She needed them to understand what was about to happen and what was expected of them. She needed to have them focused.

"All right, everyone listen up. When we arrive, Lt. Ryder, Lt. Holden, and Ensign Ryder report to the bridge, Lt. Commander Dominick report to Engineering and get the engines ready to go. Chief take the Surf-Ve back to get the Captain and the Doctor. Lt. Commander Flint, use whoever you need to make sure the supplies are secured and have the cargo bay ready to receive the Surf-Ve when it returns. Any questions?"

There was little movement among the crew, and no one said anything. A couple of them nodded their heads, indicating they understood their assignments and had no questions. Brynna wasn't satisfied with their response, so she reiterated in a slightly stronger tone. "Do you understand your orders?"

The crew finally realized they were dealing with the Commander now, not the team leader. They responded with a firm, "Yes, Ma'am." The two and a half weeks on the planet had taken its toll on the crew's military mindset. It only took a moment to get it back though.

While Jason was still trying to take as many scans as he could, David approached the Magistrate to bid him farewell. Arni turned to face Jason and smiled. "Did you get all the information you seek?"

Jason was slightly unnerved at getting caught scanning more than the boy, but he faced his confrontation bravely. "I doubt it, but I think you know that already."

"I am a man. I eat, I sleep, and when the time comes I will die, but it will not be the end. My time is growing close, but their time is even closer." Arni said as he sadly looked at the crowd around them. "I brought this boy back, so his family could live their last days in joy and peace."

Jason's next words nearly got stuck in his throat, "Are you going to destroy these people?"

Arni shook his head. "No. You will." With that brief response, Arni walked away from the doctor and went to join the anxious group of children.

David rejoined the Doctor, who was now visibly shaken. "Doc, are you okay?"

The doctor muttered a soft, "Yeah."

The Captain was not convinced. David grabbed the doctor by his upper arms and shook him. "Doc, are you sure you are okay? I need to know."

The doctor's eyes focused on David, "Yes, I'm fine. Can we leave now? I'm ready to get off this planet."

David breathed a sigh of relief. He seriously doubted the doctor would want to leave if he had been compromised. The two men began walking to the edge of the crowd. As they moved away from the large group, they turned around to see everyone gathered around Arni, giving him their full attention.

As they started down the road, Jason wanted to get his mind off his conversation with Arni, so he started a conversation with David. "What did you say to the Magistrate?"

David was glad for the distraction. "I apologized for our sudden departure and told him the Commonwealth needed us to head to another destination as soon as possible."

"Did he seem all right with it? Was he suspicious?"

"He seemed perfectly fine. He thanked us profusely for everything we had done for them and invited us back."

David was bothered by something about the whole situation but couldn't really put his finger on what it was. He decided he needed to see a complete picture from the entire crew before too much emotion clouded the situation. He needed to get back to the ship and fast. "You feel like jogging?" Jason welcomed the chance to get back to the safety of the ship sooner.

The two started jogging until they met up with Jake returning in the Surf-Ve. Jake was concerned to find them running. He was already pushing the Surf-Ve as fast as he dared and could not get to them any faster. As soon as he reached them, he punched the braking mechanism, which caused the wheels to lock up on the vehicle. As the vehicle came to a stop a massive cloud of dust was thrown into the air, covering the Captain and the Doctor. They climbed into the Surf-Ve coughing and wiping their eyes. As soon as they were in the vehicle, Jake took off again. The two passengers grabbed the nearest canteens to clear the dust from their faces, throats, and eyes. As soon as the coughing settled down, David looked at Jake and asked, "What was that all about Jake? Are you trying to kill us?"

Those were not the words Jake expected to hear. He thought he had saved their lives by helping them escape from whoever was behind them. Jake, still looking bewildered, responded, "I was trying to protect you from whoever was chasing you."

Since the Captain had called Jake by name instead of rank, Jason felt comfortable interjecting his own sentiments, "We were just anxious to get back home to the ship. We weren't running from anyone. Nobody was trying to kill us, except maybe you."

David decided to lighten the mood a little, "Yeah, Jake, some security chief you turned out to be. That would be an embarrassing death too, death by dust. That's just humiliating." David wiped his face again and tried to hide his grin. Jason laughed at the thought too.

Jake felt himself relax a little and added, "How would that look for me? A security chief who can't protect his Captain from dust." He tagged his comment with a sheepish apology. "Sorry, Captain. Sorry, Doc."

As the Surf-Ve pulled up to the ship, David metaphorically put on his Captain's hat. "Chief get the Surf-Ve secured then check in with the Commander to see what else needs to be done. Doctor, get your gear stowed away and report in. As soon as we are on course for our next destination, you can get a shower."

David headed to the bridge. As soon as he stepped onto the bridge, he asked Brynna, "Commander, what's our status?"

Brynna wanted to ask him about his appearance but refrained. "We will be ready for liftoff as soon as the Chief and the doctor report in. Our cargo is locked down, the shuttle is secured, Lt. Commander Flint did the external inspection. We have a course laid in for Medoris IV. Orders sir?"

"Take us up, Commander. Make for Medoris IV, but don't engage the tachyon drive until you have orders from me. As soon as we have achieved orbit, I am going to get a quick shower; then I want all available personnel in the dining hall."

Brynna wanted to clarify her orders. She had expected David to command the launch. "You want me to take the ship up?"

David moved to the auxiliary station. His mind was already three steps beyond that point mentally. He whipped around and caught himself before he made an unwarranted smart remark. He managed a short quick, "Yes. Commander." Brynna caught a brief glimpse of David's mindset and took charge of the situation.

An hour later, the available crew was assembled in the dining hall, and the ones who could not leave their posts were connected via video conference. The Captain and Doctor were both showered and in their uniforms. During their stay on Galat, the crew had sometimes worn civilian attire. Some of them were still in civilian clothes. The Captain wasn't worried about their uniforms at this point. His primary goal was to address the reports and duty roster. David assigned the first full duty day without assigning anyone for cross training. When he addressed the crew, he offered both an explanation and exultation.

"First, I want to commend each one of you for the excellent work you did on Galat III. You did your jobs and did them well. Second, I need each of you to put your reports together as soon as possible. Do not discuss any of the events that occurred on the planet with each other until all reports have been turned in. After all the reports have been turned in, we can all sit down and discuss it together if you wish. Remember to be as factual as possible, no opinions except in the final section where it asks for a personal opinion. The last thing I wanted to do is to bring you up to speed on our status. Our current destination is Medoris IV. I do not want to get out of this system until our reports are filed and we have heard back from CIF headquarters. Once we have the go-ahead, we will proceed to Medoris IV. I expect this portion of our trip to take three to five days, six days at most. As soon as your reports are turned in, start doing the prep work for Medoris. Any questions?"

The Captain seemed disturbed by the day's events, so no one bothered questioning his orders. They all needed time to process the things they witnessed. It seemed each one needed to put their thoughts down in the reports just to help them make sense of things, if sense could be made. Once the reports were collected, David and Brynna went over them together. David began noticing certain small discrepancies in their reports. The one catching his attention first was the language Arni had been speaking to them in.

At first, David thought it was merely an error until he challenged it. "Brynna, you put this down in your report wrong."

"Put what down wrong?" Brynna moved to look over David's shoulder to see the computer screen.

"Right here. You put down Arni was speaking Raesin when we first met him. He was speaking Jurantian." Juranta was where David had been born. He had grown up there until his teen years when his family moved to Raesii. Juranta was a small mining planet, which wasn't very well known. It was the reason David was caught off guard when Arni first spoke to them.

"Did you have a short circuit in your brain or something? He was speaking fluent Raesin, not Jurantian. Have you been working too hard or something?" Brynna gave him a patronizing pat on the head and started to walk away.

David turned around and caught her arm, "Brynna, I distinctly heard Jurantian." His eyes were deadly serious.

"You're joking." Brynna looked at him and the grin on her face faded. "You're not joking. I heard Raesin, honestly. What does Cheyenne's report say? She was with us."

David looked at Cheyenne's report. David was willing to consider that either one of them could have been working so hard and had just misinterpreted what they heard. When he read Cheyenne's report, he knew it wasn't the case. Cheyenne's report indicated Arni was speaking neither Raesin nor Jurantian, but perfect Madrathean. David had not allowed himself to be affected emotionally until now. Now he experienced a mixture of shock, awe, amazement, and even a little fear. David decided he needed to be done with those feelings even before they were really started. It was obvious they were dealing with the superior power of their new enemy, and he had to be proactive, not reactive. David called Cheyenne into the office to verify her recount of the event.

Cheyenne entered the Captain's office and reported to him officially. The Captain invited her to have a seat around his worktable. Once she was seated, the Captain began his questions, "Ensign, I need you to clarify a couple things on your report." Cheyenne sat very still. She swallowed hard and said, "Yes sir. I'll try, sir."

"The Commander and I were noticing you indicated Arni was speaking fluent Madrathean. Are you certain about that?"

"Yes sir."

"Were you using your translator?"

"It was in record mode only sir." Cheyenne was looking paler by the moment. Brynna was becoming concerned by the gaunt look on her face.

"Do you still have the recording?" David seemed nonplussed by her appearance. His decision to tuck his feelings away was now firmly set.

"Yes sir. I downloaded the files from the translator to the ship's computer." As soon as they had the file pulled up and replaying, Cheyenne lost another shade of color from her face. The recording was speaking in Intergalactic Standard. David and Brynna looked at each other without speaking. Cheyenne was at a loss for words.

David looked at her and asked one last question. "Is there anything else we should know?"

Cheyenne thought back to the moment when she wondered if she had been compromised and Arni had looked at her. It could have been a coincidence, really it had to have been, but now with her mishearing Arni speak... Cheyenne stood up slowly, her hands shaking, and tried to speak.

Brynna interrupted her attempt, "Are you all right? Cheyenne? Cheyenne?" That was the last thing Cheyenne remembered.

As Cheyenne's eyes began to open she heard voices around her. As soon as she could see clearly, she saw her husband, Lazaro, standing over her holding her hand looking worried. On the other side of her was Dr. Adams asking her how she felt. Cheyenne wanted to sit up, so the doctor raised the head of her bed about 30 degrees. Cheyenne told the doctor she was feeling weak, shaky, and slightly nauseated. The doctor stepped away to get her something to make her feel better. When he stepped away, Cheyenne saw the Captain and Brynna standing in the doorway looking very serious.

She wondered why Jake wasn't present. Tears started to roll down her face slowly, and she gripped Lazaro's hand tightly. Lazaro sat down on the edge of her bed and hugged her tightly. "Cheyenne... What is it? What's wrong?" Cheyenne was crying so hard by this time she couldn't speak, she just kept looking at the Captain. Lazaro followed her gaze. "Captain, whatever is bothering her concerns you. What happened in your office?"

David looked at Brynna then back at Cheyenne and Lazaro. He shook his head and answered, "I don't know. Brynna and I found some discrepancies between several reports and wanted to get some clarification before we turned them in. She just stood up and passed out. Maybe she thought she was in trouble."

David walked over to Cheyenne's bed and picked up her hand. "Cheyenne, you didn't do anything wrong. Please tell us what's going on."

Cheyenne managed to finally get two sentences out between sobs. "Please don't let them execute me. I wasn't taken over." She buried her face in Lazaro's shoulder again.

Lazaro stroked the back of her head gently and looked helplessly at the Captain who glanced at Brynna. Jason returned just in time to hear her plea. David was torn between handling this as Captain or friend. He decided she needed the authority figure more than the friendship. It was his authority she feared, so that's what needed to free her from her fears. The Captain released her hand and assumed a more authoritative stance. "Ensign Dominick."

Hearing his command voice, she reacted like any good soldier, although still distraught, "Yes... sir?"

"Are you telling me, you think you are capable of manipulating energy and matter? Are you capable of controlling minds telepathically and no longer loyal to the Commonwealth?"

David's blunt tirade seemed to offend both the Doctor and the Lt. Commander. Behind him the Doctor began to defend his patient, "Captain, she's in no shape for this right now."

Lazaro stood up to face the Captain in Cheyenne's defense, "Captain, what are you saying? My wife isn't the enemy."

David responded quickly and firmly, "Stand down, gentlemen." He reiterated his request to Cheyenne more gently than the first time, "Ensign, answer my questions."

Cheyenne looked at the Captain, tears still flowing silently down her face and answered, "No, sir, I don't think I can do any of those things, and I'm still loyal to the Commonwealth."

"Are you trying to manipulate me?" David's tone grew softer.

"No, sir" Cheyenne answered softly.

"Are you telling me you are no longer capable of defending the Commonwealth?" David continued to drill the young Ensign.

"No, sir."

133

"What makes you think you've been compromised?" David didn't want to put her through the discomfort of answering questions, but he needed to know.

"Because I saw all the things he did and heard the things he said. I believe he is capable of whatever he says. I started wondering if I was being compromised and right at that moment he looked at me like he knew what I was thinking. Slaina said Arni's father wasn't human. If he isn't human, what can he do to us? Is he doing something to us already? Did he do something to me?"

David postulated for a moment, relaxed his stance, and then grasped her hand again. "Cheyenne, we were told Pateras has telepathic abilities. I think he wanted you to doubt yourself. I think perhaps he did know your thoughts, but if he knows who we are and what we represent, why didn't he stop us? Why didn't he take control of all of us? As long as you are loyal to the Commonwealth, you haven't been compromised. I am not going to execute anyone based on a maybe. I think Arni caused those discrepancies in the reports. I want to be able to let headquarters know about it upfront, so they don't have reason to believe we've all been compromised. Cheyenne, you are safe. You haven't been compromised."

At that, everyone in the room relaxed. David felt it was best to leave the room and give her a little time to process. Brynna followed him out.

●●

David and Brynna went back to David's office to talk. David sat down in his chair feeling somewhat defeated. Brynna sat down quietly, waiting for his reaction. Finally, he spoke, "This crew is running scared. They aren't going to function well if they're scared, not to mention the toll that stress takes on a body. I don't know if they're more scared of the unknown or me. What do you think is the best approach?"

Brynna thought for a moment. "Let's pull Lexi in on this."

David reached for the log to see if Lexi was available. She had just come off her duty shift, so the Captain asked her to join them. Once Lexi arrived, David brought her up to speed on the most recent events. Lexi sighed when she realized the scope of the problem. "What are your recommendations, Lieutenant?" David asked.

"I recommend you set the record straight with the crew the same way you did with Cheyenne. I also recommend everyone sit down and discuss what they saw openly. I personally saw an incredible demonstration of power, although nothing actually frightened me."

David nodded in agreement. "I will put out a memo for everyone to assemble in the dining hall at the end of the next shift except for those who are on duty and they can link in via computer again."

At the end of the next shift, everyone was assembled as ordered and discussed Arni. The most prominent thing they discussed was his ability to bring a dead child back to life. Jason assured the crew the child had numerous fatal injuries. The child's injuries could not have been faked. David and Brynna shared what they learned about hearing Arni speak in different languages. Cheyenne and Lexi shared what Slaina and Essa had told them.

Cheyenne was hesitant to share her fears that Arni knew her thoughts with the others, especially with Jake in the room. David gently pushed her to share her experience. Jake had just come off his shift and was anxious to get some sleep. He was sitting with his chair leaned back against the wall and balanced on the chair's back legs. He was keeping the chair balanced to help him stay awake. Jake had seen what Arni had done with the boy, so this was nothing new to him. When Cheyenne finished sharing her story, Jake abruptly set his chair down on all four legs. He was suddenly more alert than he had been moments ago. As his chair hit the floor, Cheyenne jumped visibly and looked at David. David got up and moved around behind her. Putting his hand gently on her shoulder, he began to encourage the others to share and gave Cheyenne a sense of reassurance that she was safe.

"I know this was hard for Cheyenne to share, but we need to know everything Arni and Pateras may be capable of. It's a frightening thing to think someone may know your every thought. This may have been merely a coincidence, but if we don't share our experiences with each other, we can't track behavior patterns."

Jake settled back into his chair, but he kept one eye on Cheyenne. Cheyenne tried hard not to look at Jake. Jason decided it was time to share what Arni had said to him. Jason told the crew he had scanned Arni with his medical scanner, which indicated Arni was completely human. He also told them about getting caught scanning the man. The hardest part was to tell the crew that Arni indicated the people were about to die, and Jason would be the cause.

Jake, now more willing to participate in the discussion, leaned forward, "How is the Doc supposed to be responsible for getting those people killed? He protects life. He doesn't take life."

David looked at the doctor, "Doc, tell us exactly what he said."

The doctor got a pained look on his face, took a deep breath, and went through the conversation step by step. Jason finished his recount of the conversation by saying, "I asked him if he was going to destroy the people and he said, 'No, you will.'"

Jake shook his head and said, "No, that just sounds ambiguous.

It could mean you personally, or the crew, or the Commonwealth."

Marissa, who was sitting near Jake, said, "You mean, we'll be responsible if something happens to them?"

David saw the discussion was going to take a drastically negative turn. "Ladies and Gentlemen, I don't see how that's possible. I have no intention of causing these people any harm. We aren't going back to that planet unless ordered by the Commonwealth. We are not responsible for any harm that may befall this population. Are we clear on that point?"

David looked at each individual in the room and the two on video screens until he received an affirmation of agreement. As soon as he had everyone in agreement, he began to close out the discussion. "So, what can we conclude about Arni based on what we have seen so far?"

Everyone looked at each other saying nothing for several moments. David didn't want to supply answers. He wanted the crew to say what they thought. Jake was the first one to speak up, "Arni does have some kind of incredible power, but whether it's the ability to fool our senses and scanners or to actually bring a kid back to life... I can't say for sure."

Lexi picked up from there, "Jake's right. He may not have healed a dead child, but he may have just convinced everyone he did. His powers may be all telepathic. The doctor may have seen the scanner read what Arni wanted him to see. Captain, you and Brynna may have just thought you heard different languages. It may be that the recorder picked up Intergalactic Standard because that was what he was actually speaking."

Aulani was monitoring from the bridge with Thane and asked, "So if he is that powerful, why weren't any of us turned?"

Lazaro, following the meeting from engineering, jumped in. "That's a good question. One I'd really love to know the answer to."

"Perhaps it takes time for him to gain control over people. He was born here, so he's had a lifetime to gain control over this population." Lexi proposed.

"That doesn't explain how his allies can take over the minds of others." David countered.

"What do you mean by that?" Jake inquired.

"The allies taken into custody by the Commonwealth and later executed, had the power to pull others over to their side" explained David.

"Maybe we aren't important enough," Aulani suggested.

"And patients in a mental hospital are?" David countered again. In a moment, David decided to completely close the discussion because they didn't have enough information to draw any firm conclusions.

"Bottom line is this: We don't know where Pateras is from, but we do know he's not from this planet. He is extremely powerful and threatens the security of the Commonwealth. We seem to be safe from his influence at this time. The last thing you need to know is this; as long as you are loyal to the Commonwealth, you are safe. The subjects the Commonwealth previously encountered would not sign loyalty oaths to the Commonwealth. I am also making an executive decision. Unless one of you is an imminent threat to the ship or crew, you will not be executed. If two ranking officers are in agreement someone has been compromised, they will be left behind on a planet already noted as compromised. I will not execute anyone unless the ship or crew is undeniably in danger. You will be sedated and quarantined until you can be dropped off. I will not have this crew afraid of each other. We will not be torn apart because of fear. I also need whatever information any of you have. I can't give a complete report to the Command Staff back home if you are afraid to tell me what I need to know." David gave his words a minute to sink in.

Jake jumped to his feet to object. "Sir, those were not our orders. You can't mean that."

David worded his answer very carefully. "Chief, I understand your concerns, but the Admirals back home could not have anticipated this. I can't operate with a crew who doesn't trust each other and are afraid to say something that could save all our lives. Do you want to go running blindly into a situation because somebody is afraid to speak up?"

Jake wasn't quite sure how to answer the Captain, so he countered with another question. "Why would someone be afraid to speak up?"

David again chose his response carefully. "It's possible someone might feel whatever they said could be viewed as being compromised, even if they haven't been. This decision is going in the ship's log, and if there are to be any actions taken against another crew member, there will be two notations of agreement noted in the ship's log by the two people in agreement. Any questions?" Hearing none, David dismissed the crew.

Jake walked directly up to the Captain to again voice his dissent. David waited for the room to clear before addressing Jake's concerns. "Jake, you have the crew scared to death you're going to shoot them over an off the cuff comment or lighthearted joke. You're too paranoid and high strung. You need to give the impression to the others you're going to think before you act. They feel like you are going to shoot first and ask questions later."

Jake's mouth dropped open in shock and disbelief. "That's ridiculous! No one could possibly think that."

Jason had left the room with the rest of the crew but returned when Jake and the Captain failed to exit. "You're wrong Jake. I've seen evidence of it myself. The crew shouldn't be afraid of its only security officer, but they are. They don't feel secure around you."

Jake was taken aback. He turned his back, walked a couple steps away, and stood there a moment wondering what he should say or do. He finally turned back around and asked, "What do you want me to do?"

David shook his head slightly. "I'm not sure how, but you need to gain the trust of the crew. Do something to let them know you aren't going to throw their lives away like yesterday's garbage."

"Do you mind if I ask, who is it that's afraid of me? I just want to start trying to fix this with the ones who are the most afraid."

David hesitated. He really didn't want to put Cheyenne into a more frightening situation than she'd already been in.

Before David could formulate his response, Jason jumped in. "I am, for one. I'm sure there are others."

David decided Jake didn't need to know about the incident with Cheyenne. He looked from Jason back to Jake and answered honestly. "So am I. There are others. Knowing specific names isn't relative."

Jake scoffed. "You aren't serious. Why would you be afraid of me, Captain? Or you either, Doc?"

"Jake, I wasn't physically afraid for my life, but I was concerned about your actions to the point it affected my command decisions. I really don't want placating you to be a part of my thought processes. I don't want to be afraid of you, or you to be afraid to trust me either. I need to know you're going to trust my decisions until they are undoubtedly wrong. The crew needs to know you trust them the same way. I set up the two people in agreement protocol, for this very reason. I suppose it's good for everyone to know where you stand, but please find a way to show the crew you are fighting for them… not against them."

"Yes sir, I understand, sir," Jake replied meekly.

"You might also see if Lexi can give you any suggestions."

"Yes sir. Thanks for being straight with me, sir."

"Thank you, Jake. I know you have the best of intentions."

After Jake left the room, Jason asked David, "Do you think that will sink in?"

David shrugged his shoulders. "I don't know. I hope so. He seemed receptive to what I said, but you never know."

●●

Later that evening, David compiled all the reports. He planned on sending them out the next morning when he went on duty. He put the reports away and got ready for bed. Brynna was already in bed sleeping. He tried to slip into bed without disturbing her. He slipped carefully under the covers and lay down. Brynna rolled over and snuggled up next to him. Without opening her eyes, she softly mumbled, "I wondered if you were ever coming to bed."

David wrapped his arms around her and whispered, "I'm sorry I woke you."

"It's okay," Brynna responded softly. "I wasn't quite asleep yet." Brynna could feel the tension in David's arms and asked, "Is everything okay?"

"I just wanted to get those reports ready to go. I'll be glad to get them off my mind."

Brynna responded with a drowsy, "Uh-huh."

David realized Brynna was far too sleepy to continue the conversation. He apologized again for disturbing her and whispered a soft, "I love you." He kissed her forehead and told her goodnight. Brynna managed to open her eyes long enough to give him a sleepy smile and a goodnight kiss. Moments later they were both sound asleep.

David found himself dreaming of the good times they had just experienced on Galat. He and the crew were eating and dancing at their celebration. They really did enjoy themselves on the planet. The people there were wise and intelligent, a little backward, but they did know how to have fun. As David relived the fond memory in his dream, suddenly, from everywhere a pack of wild dogs attacked the townspeople. David couldn't tell which direction the dogs had come from or where they were going. He wanted to stop the attack but was unable to move. The dogs were not attacking any of his crew, only the townspeople. Seconds later, David looked around. The area that had just been full of life was now blanketed in death. Everyone except his crew was lying on the ground, dead. Blood was everywhere.

One of the wild dogs was bigger than all the others and appeared to be the alpha male. The alpha male howled and barked sending all the others away from the town. The dog turned to look directly at David. He snarled and began moving toward him. David backed away from the dog and looked for ways to protect himself and his crew. The crew, including Jake, seemed to be frozen in place from shock and terror. They were each looking at him for help. The dogs were all gone except for the one about to charge David. Suddenly, David could move again. He reached for his weapon, which was no longer on his belt. He had nothing to protect himself, no knife, no laser, no shield, nothing. David looked down at his hands. They felt wet. His hands were covered in blood. He hadn't touched any of the victims around him so why were his hands bloody? The dog leaped at him, knocking him to the ground. Just as he hit the ground, David woke up and instantly sat upright in the bed. He was drenched in sweat and shaking. He looked over to see if he had disturbed Brynna again. Brynna was facing away from him and still sleeping soundly.

David got up quietly and went to the bathroom. He shut the door before turning on the light to keep from disturbing his sleeping wife. He leaned over the sink and turned the water on and looked down at his hands. They were still just as clean as when he had gone to bed. The dream seemed so real he half expected to see blood on his hands. He breathed a sigh of relief. He picked up a cloth, wet it with cold water and began to wash the sweat off his face. The cloth covered his entire face briefly. As he pulled it down from his eyes, he looked at his reflection in the mirror. David's face paled as the face of Arni appeared over his shoulder in the mirror. David froze in place as he weighed his options. Arni looked at him with sad eyes and spoke simply and quietly, "If you send that report, there will be blood on your hands. Please choose wisely." With that, he was gone. David turned around. He was alone. The door had never opened or closed. The Captain hastily got dressed and headed to the bridge.

Thane and Aulani were on duty together. They were surprised to see the Captain walk onto the bridge. Thane was the officer in charge for this shift as well as the pilot. David handed Aulani a data rod containing the reports he had just compiled. "Get this ready to send. I'm going to attach a message to it in a moment."

Aulani responded with a puzzled, "Yes sir."

Thane turned away from his console and inquired, "Sir, what's going on?"

David brusquely replied, "I need you to run a ship-wide scan to look for intruders, unexplained energy signatures, or anything out of the ordinary. Aulani, review the last twenty minutes of communications data and see if there were any hidden communication signals."

Aulani turned back to her console and started her newly assigned tasks. Thane got the computer started working on the scans. David looked at the duty roster then headed down to engineering.

After David left the bridge, Aulani looked back at Thane and asked, "What was that all about?"

Thane just shook his head. "I don't know, but it looks important; stay on top of it."

Lexi was the engineer on duty. Her primary job was so mentally involved she chose engineering as her secondary job. It gave her a chance to work with her hands and exercise the other half of her brain. When David walked into engineering, he found Lexi lying on the floor working under her console. She was just putting the cover back into place as he knelt down beside her. The Captain immediately inquired if everything was all right. Lexi assured him it was merely a loose connection and she had fixed it. The next question was why the Captain was in engineering after putting in such a long day himself.

David sat down in a chair across from Lexi's console to talk to her. Lexi thought he looked tired and even beaten. She became concerned before he ever opened his mouth. Before Lexi settled into her chair, David jumped up and started pacing. Lexi gave him a moment to collect himself then asked, "Captain, what's bothering you?"

David paced another lap then came to a stop, "I hope I'm not losing my mind." The Captain proceeded to tell her what happened to him. Lexi wasn't foolish enough to dismiss the incident in the bathroom as part of David's dream. She knew he was awake and coherent.

After David finished speaking to her, he sat back down in the chair and asked, "Am I losing it, Counselor?"

Lexi smiled slightly and told him, "Captain, if one can ask that question, the answer is 'no.' You are not losing your mind. I tend to think it is the stress of the situation, but knowing what we've learned about Arni, he may be messing with your mind. I don't think he can commandeer anyone's mind. Maybe he's trying to do the only thing he can, like cause confusion and plant fear in your mind."

"So, the sooner I am no longer a threat to him, he'll leave me alone?"

Lexi leaned back in her chair. "You're asking me if I know what Arni's plan is. Well, I don't. I don't know what he's trying to do. Captain, whether it's your mind playing tricks on you, or Arni messing with you, I think in either case the sooner we put this behind us and focus on our next mission the better. If Arni is trying to stop you from filing your report, then get it filed. Once it's done, there's no reason to bother you anymore. If you're just unsettled, file your report so it can be out of your mind."

David nodded in agreement. "You may be right. I'm going to finish this right now." David got up to leave but stopped in the doorway. He turned slightly to look back at Lexi. "I just have one more question. What if Arni is right? What if there will be blood on my hands?"

"Captain, we were ordered to stay away from the Pateras influence, not hunt it down and destroy it. I can't see you killing innocent people even under orders from the Commonwealth. I know the Commonwealth had to execute a few individuals, but they wouldn't destroy an entire civilization. Perhaps Arni meant Pateras himself would destroy them to protect his own secrets. You can't be held responsible for that."

"Thanks, Lieutenant." David moved on through the doorway. He went back to his office and recorded two messages, one for the Commonwealth and one for the Magistrate on Galat III. In the message to the Commonwealth, he emphasized it could be dangerous to even approach the system and strongly recommended the system be put under strict quarantine. He also informed the Commonwealth he intended to send a warning message to the people of Galat III to disassociate themselves from Pateras. The message for the Magistrate was a warning that the association with Pateras El Liontari could bring his people into danger, and he vaguely referenced the warning from Arni. The message to the Magistrate would be relayed to the data module left behind for the population's use. He did not tell the Commonwealth about the warning from Arni.

David took a second data rod up to the bridge with the two messages. He gave them to Aulani to transmit to the appropriate places along with the reports to the Commonwealth. Thane and Aulani completed their scans and reported finding nothing unusual. Captain Alexander was not surprised by their report. He thanked them for their diligence and started to leave the bridge. Thane stopped him. "Captain, what are we looking for?" It seemed to be a less intrusive way of asking the Captain to explain himself.

The Captain didn't want to go into too much detail, so he briefly explained, "I received a warning message from Arni, not to send in our reports. I wanted to know how he projected the message to me directly."

Thane and Aulani looked at each other then back at the Captain. Thane assured the Captain they would look again and expand their search. David thanked them again and headed back to his cabin.

David got ready for bed a second time. He wasn't sure he was going to be able to sleep this time, so he turned on some soft relaxing music and snuggled up to Brynna. He finally drifted off to a fitful sleep. He dreamed one brief dream then nothing more until morning. In his dream, he was standing alone in a small room. As his eyes focused, he realized he was standing in a prison cell. He heard Arni's voice say, "When your day of reckoning comes, I will be there for you. Rest for now." David slept hard and long.

Over the next couple of days, everyone seemed unusually subdued. Captain Alexander was exceptionally quiet. Brynna wasn't used to seeing him brood. She waited anxiously for him to snap out of it. As soon as the crew received their new orders, David got back to business as usual. His orders were simple. He was to proceed to their next destination, Medoris IV.

PART THREE: THE SECOND PLANET

MEDORIS IV

Lt Commander Jason Adams was the pilot on duty when their new orders came through. Captain Alexander had Jason immediately set course for Medoris IV at top speed. Their new destination was only a couple of days away, so the crew got started on their first contact protocols and preparations. David was anxious to forget the last mission and start on the next one.

On the surface, he was business as usual, but the crew still felt tension exuding from him. Brynna pulled him aside to talk to him. David assured her he was fine. He had not told her about the dreams or message from Arni. He attempted to get back to work, but she wasn't about to let him off too quickly. "David, I feel like you're keeping things bottled up and they're going to eat away at you. Is there something you need to tell me?"

David knew if Brynna checked the ship's logs, she would find out about the warning Arni had given him. No one, but Lexi, knew about the first dream. He hadn't told Lexi about the second dream. David decided Brynna would only let it go if he gave her at least a little something. He finally relented. "Brynna, after I came to bed the other night, Arni sent me a message. He warned me not to send those reports in."

"How did he do that? Did he use the data module?"

"No, he appeared physically in our quarters then disappeared."

"Are you sure it wasn't a dream?"

"I'm quite sure. I was already up washing my face. I was very awake."

Brynna's brow furrowed. "Did he say anything else?"

David had the urge to start pacing again. He managed to stop himself after taking only two steps away from Brynna. He turned back toward her.

"Arni said if I sent the reports in, there would be blood on my hands. The blood of the people on Galat III." David turned his back toward her again.

Brynna walked over and placed her hand on his arm. She turned him around to face her. She placed her other hand along the side of his face and gently caressed his cheek. "David, you can't hold yourself responsible for something that hasn't happened. We were ordered away from the planet, and we recommended a system-wide blockade. If Pateras is as powerful as we think, he should be able to protect this planet from anything that could befall them. We aren't going to cause them any harm. You aren't going to hurt these people. You are worrying for nothing. Forget about it."

David looked into her eyes. Brynna was a beautiful woman, but he found himself too distracted to see her beauty. David forced himself at this moment to focus on nothing, but her face. He finally managed to see nothing, but her smiling face. He smiled back at her. "You always seem to know how to cheer me up." He took her hand from his cheek, squeezed it, and then gently kissed it. "I'd love to spend more time letting you cheer me up, but we have a staff meeting to get to."

Brynna wasn't sure he was totally relieved of his burden, but he was right about the staff meeting.

●●

Everyone available gathered again in the dining room to discuss Medoris IV. Brynna, being the team leader to this part of the mission, chaired the meeting. They began with Lexi's information about the culture.

Lexi described the culture as similar in technology to Galat, but with colder weather and not as civilized. The glaciers at the northern and southern poles covered nearly a third of the planet. The inhabitants were concentrated around the equator. Some were cave dwellers. Some had developed housing resembling hives because the structures wound around in a circular pattern going higher and narrower as it reached the top. The third group moved with the warm weather. As nomads, they were primarily hunters following migratory animal herds. Since survival was a daily struggle, they did whatever they thought they needed to live, even if it meant stealing or killing. Lexi also noted that struggles between each of the populations were prevalent. There were not a large number of inhabitants on this planet because most of the landmasses were iced over. There was a sizable land mass separated from the rest of the continents that was totally uninhabited by humans.

Laura looked into the geological aspects of Medoris. The growing season was short, and starvation would become an issue toward the end of the long winters. Laura recommended they survey the area to determine if there was any vegetation that could be used for food not previously identified. She also recommended they explore food preservation techniques and implementing the use of greenhouses. The hive dwellers had mastered the use of glass making. However, they apparently did not know they could use it to prolong their growing season at least on a small scale. It would be a major endeavor to build a greenhouse big enough to house entire grain fields.

Braxton mentioned a number of the cave-dwelling populations were in areas containing hot springs. He asked if he might get a chance to visit them to see if there was a way to maximize the usage of the springs. He commented on the development of the hive dwellings as an excellent way to stay warm and for protection against raiders. The Lt. Commander noticed the migratory patterns of the herds frequently crossed paths with the grain fields of the hive dwellers. He recommended walls could prevent this annual occurrence.

Thane recommended making contact at a location currently in its peak growing season and near the mountain cave dwellers. Jake was concerned it would be a hotbed for raiders and violence. They nearly got into a heated debate over the matter until Brynna put a stop to it.

"Jake, I understand your concerns, believe me, I do. Thane, what are your reasons for going into the middle of all that?"

"We don't have the resources to cover all the populations on any planet, but if we can get the nomads to learn the art of being traders instead of simply taking what they want, they could spread the knowledge we leave with them to the other populations as they travel. My thought was we present ourselves as mediators to stop the wars and raids, and one of our conditions is they spread the knowledge we leave with them. If we can stop the fighting in this one place where all the populations can see it, then it can spread planet-wide."

Brynna paced back and forth for a moment pondering his proposition. "I like the idea, but Lexi, what about the mentality of the populations. Do you think they might be open to it?"

Lexi thought for a moment. "This population is very self-absorbed. If we can play into that ideology, I think it might work."

"What sort of hierarchy and cultural arrangement are we dealing with?" Brynna asked.

"They are very protective of their own. They have something akin to a tribal lord or chieftain. There are no limitations on who can rule. The strongest rules, so Brynna, you must be strong and decisive. We each need to wear recognizable weapons visibly. We can't be afraid to pull them and use them."

Jake jumped in, "Commander, I recommend we keep our normal weapons with us, but not visible. Don't use them unless there's no choice. I suggest we keep large knives on us and visible."

Brynna went a step further. "Of course, chief. Could you also hold a couple refresher courses on handling knives? I am also assigning the Captain, Lt. Ryder, and Lt. Holden as part of your security detail. Security is going to be their primary responsibility on this mission. I am going to take Lt. Ryder's suggestion. It may be a hotbed, but I think it will be the best place to start."

The chief seemed ecstatic his security suggestions were taken, and his concerns were being addressed. He always felt like the crew viewed him as a necessary evil instead of a valued crew member.

"Commander, I have a couple questions. What exactly are we offering in trade? My other question is; what kind of exposure has this population had with off-worlders?" Cheyenne inquired via the ship's communications network. She and the Captain were currently on duty on the bridge.

Brynna responded first. "Lexi, what can you tell us about their off-world exposure?"

"The cave dwellers have had regular visits from traders looking for the mineral tetrabradium. The others have had no documented exposure to off-world visitors."

Brynna continued to answer Cheyenne's questions. "We are going to offer them the same things as before; only our emphasis is going to be on uniting a divided planet."

Lt. Commander Dominick interrupted via comms from Engineering, "Commander, did Lt. Flint say tetrabradium?"

Brynna stopped and glanced at Lexi who nodded before she answered the engineer's question. "Yes, Mr. Dominick, she did. What is the significance?"

"Well, we can convert it to use in the tachyon emitters. We aren't low, but our initial trip to this side of the galaxy caused a measurable drop in the reserve tanks. If we could get our hands on about thirty pounds of the stuff, it would bring our reserves back up to one hundred percent. It's not the stuff we normally use, but I can make it work."

Brynna looked slightly startled at this new information. "How much do we have in our reserves?"

"We still have seventy-two percent of our reserves, which is above our primary supply so if we can't get it, we'll still be fine. I just thought since the opportunity presented itself we should try to use it. If we get into an emergency situation, we might need it, but for regular use, we would be fine without it."

This information got David's attention. He knew the trip to this part of the galaxy would drain part of their reserves, so this was not unexpected. He still preferred they restock and keep the ship at maximum efficiency. He waited patiently for Brynna's response. He wanted to take advantage of this opportunity too, but this was one of those areas where his and Brynna's responsibilities overlapped. Brynna, being trained in command as well as David, chose the wisest course of action.

"We definitely will see what we can do to get some. In the event they are unable or unwilling to trade, Captain, could you get some scans of the uninhabited areas of the planet, so we might collect it ourselves?"

David was glad to hear her decision. He didn't have any doubts about her command abilities, but there was always the thought in the back of his mind that she would have to disagree with him sooner or later. David responded to her well-phrased request, "Yes, Commander, I'll get on it as soon as we are in scanner range."

Brynna looked back to Cheyenne, "Do we have language files available?"

Cheyenne shook her head. "No, I am afraid we don't."

"What are our options to collect the language data?"

"We can go down and try to communicate as best we can until the translators pick up enough to establish the files, but that could be seriously problematic. We could also discreetly plant some communications buoys to basically do the same thing with fewer problems."

Brynna noticed a puzzled look cross Braxton's face. "Do you have a question, Lt. Commander Flint?"

"I don't understand why it would be more problematic to go in person with the translators. Wouldn't it be a faster way to establish our presence?"

Cheyenne jumped in to answer him before anyone else got the chance. "Primitive worlds may have superstitions or cultural taboos we could stumble into. The use of our translators themselves could create fear, especially if we show up not knowing their language then in the course of a couple days we are suddenly able to use them. It might be viewed as some sort of magic or sorcery. It could be dangerous."

Braxton's face contorted again. He was having a little trouble adjusting to the idea technology could be viewed as foreign or evil. He seemed to handle the idea of teaching new technologies to an underdeveloped population, but to have someone fear it? That was an odd concept for him. He knew of worlds where technology was openly rejected because the people wanted to live simple lives. The people on those colonies had voluntarily walked away from technologically advanced planets. It wasn't the way he wanted to live, although there was something relaxing and satisfying about such a life. Braxton wasn't quite sure how to respond, so he simply replied, "Okay." His face continued to remain contorted revealing his feelings of frustration, bewilderment, and contemplation.

Brynna looked back to the monitor, "Captain, can you arrange to get those buoys into places where we can monitor all hree of the populations we intend to contact? If they speak different languages, we can collect all of them simultaneously. Make sure they are programmed with the appropriate camouflage capabilities, and visual files would be helpful as well."

David responded promptly, "Of course, Commander. I'll send Lt. Ryder and Ensign Ryder down in the shuttle during the populations night cycle to drop them. Chief Holden can go with them as added security. Lt. Flint and Lt. Holden can help them pick some appropriate locations."

Marissa suddenly shivered visibly. Brynna looked at her quizzically. "Are you okay, Lieutenant?"

Marissa nodded. Jake snickered, and Marissa elbowed him.

Brynna cocked her head sideways and asked, "What am I missing?"

Marissa looked away as Jake answered for her. "She hates those buoys. She thinks they look like bugs."

The buoys had six legs, so they could clamp onto surfaces and were about the size of a large insect. It was surprising how much technology could be packed into such a small space. It contained an audiovisual recorder, a transmitter, a camouflage circuit, and a battery pack to power itself.

Most of the crew resided in an atmosphere-controlled environment, so insects were not very common. Jason and Laura were most accustomed to insects because their travels frequently took them to underdeveloped areas. Jason looked at Marissa and laughed. "You're not scared of a little bug, are you?" Jason put his hand on the table and made it crawl toward her. Laura slapped Jason's hand and yanked it off the table.

"Jason, stop it. Don't make fun of other people's fears."

"Oh, why not?" He started to put his hand back up on the table. Marissa sat there glaring at him.

Laura gave the ultimate response. "Because if you don't leave her alone, I'll tell them what you're afraid of."

Jason's face sobered and he quietly pulled his hand back off the table. Thane grinned, looked at Jake and whispered, "That must be some fear."

Jake nodded, "Yeah, he backed off pretty quickly."

Brynna felt like the crew could use a good laugh, but not at the expense of another crew member. The Commander reined them in to finish their plans.

●●

Once they reached the planet, they put the ship in an orbit matching the day and night cycle of the area where they intended to land. The Captain matched the duty roster to the planetary schedule as closely as possible.

Marissa, Lexi, Thane, and Aulani reviewed the demographic and geographic data they collected to determine the best places to plant the data collection buoys. The buoys needed to be positioned where they could pick up conversations and record activity without being found or inadvertently destroyed.

The nomads were easy to target because they lived in tent type dwellings on the ground. A buoy could be placed on a tent pole where it could hear and see a great deal of uninterrupted activity. The shuttle was put on stealth mode to reduce the chances of being seen. Thane put it down on a hill just outside the encampment. Aulani set the targeting computers to hit a tent pole near the center of the camp. Once she identified her target, the computer made the appropriate trajectory computations and fired the buoy. The buoys were fired like a bullet from a gun and attached to the first thing it hit. One had to be extremely cautious when planting them. If a human being were to cross the path of the buoy and be hit, the buoy would attach to the individual's skin or clothing. If it attached to the skin, the person it hit would undoubtedly notice. They might believe it to be an insect since it would cause pain, but it would be difficult to locate due to the camouflage abilities.

The hives were constructed so that storage areas and animal pens were on the outer rings and the residences and public gathering areas were further inside. There were walkways winding inward and upward. The crew chose a couple of outdoor walkways that seemed wider and well-traveled to plant buoys in the walls. Since they were open areas, the shuttle could also fire them from a safe distance.

Positioning buoys to monitor the cave dwellers was not as easy. They would have to land the shuttle and go in on foot to place he buoys inside the caves. Thane put the shuttle down outside of he caves as close as he dared. He kept watch on the scanners while Aulani and Jake headed toward the caves. There were several caves in the side of this mountain, which were guarded. Jake and Aulani carried Tri-EMPs programming the projectiles for stun. They stunned the guards at the base of the caves and then moved inward using their portable scanners as guides to get them to what appeared to be a public, but currently deserted, area of the caves. Aulani planted two buoys, and the two of them quietly slipped back out of the caves, retrieving their projectiles from the unconscious guards.

As they were heading back to the shuttle, a guard outside another cave entrance above them saw them leave. He shouted something at them. As soon as they knew they had been seen, Jake hit his comm unit to alert Thane, grabbed Aulani's hand and took off running toward the shuttle. Thane powered up the craft and moved closer to their position. As soon as they got close on the scanners, he popped the hatch so they could board quickly. Aulani and Jake could hear several people shouting and chasing after them. Aulani had to fight the urge to turn around and see how close they were getting. Her head knew doing so would only slow her escape. Her gut didn't particularly want to listen to reason. Having Jake beside her, forcing her to keep moving forward, helped to keep her wits about her. Jake put Aulani in front of him and kept yelling, "GO! GO! GO! Keep moving! Don't turn around!"

Aulani reached the shuttle and scrambled through the hatch. Jake was right behind her. She heard Jake give a grunt of pain when he hit the floor of the shuttle. She hollered to Thane, 'We're in. Go!"

Aulani turned around to help Jake close the hatch and saw him struggling to move. She pulled the hatch closed while watching him and asking, "Jake what's wrong?"

Jake was still struggling to move. He looked up at her. 'Something hit me. My back, I can't feel..." His speech was slurred, and he was very quickly losing the ability to move. His arm had been under him as he tried to push himself up, but as he lost control of his limbs, he fell face down on the deck.

It was then Aulani saw a dart in Jake's back. It wasn't near his spine, so she quickly and carefully removed it. "Thane, Jake's been hit with a poison dart. We have to get him back to the ship and fast."

In a moment, the shuttle lurched as Thane accelerated his trajectory. Aulani grabbed the emergency medical kit and scanned Jake. Thane heard the high pitched whine of the scanner. In a moment he asked, "Is it bad?"

Aulani shook her head and said, "I don't know. I can't be sure. He needs the Doc." Aulani carefully picked the dart up and placed it in a specimen container.

Thane contacted the ship. Cheyenne was on communications and Jason was at the helm. Jason saw Thane's aggressive piloting and called the Captain to the bridge. By the time the Captain stepped foot onto the bridge, Cheyenne had established communication with Thane.

"Report, Lt. Commander." David barked. Jason reported the shuttle was coming in hot and Thane was on the comm channel. David ordered Jason to make sure the shuttle bay was ready to receive the shuttle as he moved over to the comm station to hear Thane. "What's happening, Lieutenant?"

"Jake got hit with some sort of poison dart. He's alive, but he's lost consciousness. Before he lost consciousness, he was having trouble moving or feeling his extremities. Aulani is tending to him as best she can."

The Captain promptly responded, "Understood. I'll have the Doc waiting on you as soon as you land. As soon as Jake is settled in the Med Bay, report to the bridge."

"Yes, Captain."

The Captain took Jason's place at the helm and then asked Cheyenne to wake Brynna. Minutes later the shuttle landed, and the bay was re-pressurized. Jason bolted through the bay doors with his med-kit in hand as soon as the airlock allowed him to. By this time, Jake was barely breathing. The Doc gave him a neural stimulant. Jason and Thane loaded Jake onto a stretcher and moved him to the Med Bay.

Stepping onto the bridge, Brynna reported to the Captain. David brought her up to speed on the situation. He asked Brynna to get an update from Dr. Adams then wake Marissa and inform her of her husband's condition.

Brynna started to follow his orders then stopped and asked, "Are you sure you don't want to do this yourself?"

David paused for a brief second before answering. "When you talk to the Doc, if Jake's not going to make it, then come back up here to relieve me at the helm. If I show up at Marissa's door, she'll know it's bad news. I don't want to scare her without reason."

Brynna nodded, "Yes sir." The Commander followed his instructions and headed down to the Med Bay. She passed Thane in the hallway who simply gave her a polite nod as he headed to the bridge. She expected the doctor to be working feverishly over his patient. Instead, she found him quietly scanning the mysterious dart.

Jason glanced up at her when she entered and recognized the confused look on her face. "It's okay. He's stable for now."

"Is he going to be okay?"

"I'm checking the poison on the dart tip to be sure there are no surprises, but it appears to be meant to tranquilize large animals. The dose was a little strong for Jake's system, but the neural stimulant I gave him seems to have counter-acted it."

"Oh, good. I'm going to go wake Marissa and tell her what's happened."

Jason looked back at her, "You might want to just let her sleep. He's going to be out of it for a while, and there isn't anything she can do for him."

"I know she can't do anything for him, but she needs to be here when he wakes up. Just give her a bed beside him so she can get more sleep."

"Yes, ma'am."

When Brynna woke Marissa her first questions were, "What's wrong? Is Jake okay?"

Brynna told her what happened and took her to him. Standing at Jake's side, holding his hand, Marissa was on the verge of tears until Jake started to snore. His snoring made it clear to everyone he was going to be fine and provided some comic relief. Jason put Marissa on the bed next to Jake. He also offered her a sedative, in case Jake's snoring was too much to handle. Once Brynna was sure Marissa was all right, she returned to the bridge. Thane and Aulani had just finished briefing the Captain on what happened on the surface. The Captain assured them they made the right choices and sent them to get some sleep. The Captain finished Jason's shift at the helm.

The next morning there was plenty to talk about at the breakfast table. Jake woke up around lunchtime feeling as good as new. Dr. Adams gave him a clean bill of health and returned him to active duty. Later that day Thane and Aulani thanked Jake for saving Aulani. The doctor had told them if the dart had hit Aulani, she might not have made it because of the strength of the dose. It wasn't something David wanted to happen, but it did help repair the rifts between Jake and the rest of the crew. Jake was now appreciated for the brave man he was.

The next few days were mostly for data collection from the buoys. The crew had their standard supplies prepped shortly after leaving Galat III. They couldn't do very much until the computer had collected sufficient information for the language translation files. This gave them time to unwind from their experience on Galat III and clear their heads. What they experienced on Galat was not particularly traumatic, but it was one of those times that spooks a person. The crew took advantage of the time to relax and "play" a bit. They played several games of Zone, some got caught up on pleasure reading, and some spent time doing nothing but looking at the stars. Jake and Thane even played a game of Zone together without an incident. David made a trip through the public areas of the ship surveying the general state of the ship and crew. Hearing the sounds of laughter and relaxation, he breathed a sigh of relief. It was good to get back to normal.

After three days, the buoys had collected enough of the languages of the inhabitants to have reasonably complete files. There might still be some gaps, but the computer would continue to add to the files as the crew interacted with the population. The crew met again to go over the new data. Besides the language files, they now had some cultural information.

The cave dwellers were hunters and gatherers as well as traders. They were the ones who had traded with off-worlders for the precious tetrabradium. They mined iron ore and other metals which they in turn traded, along with animal skins to the nomads and hive dwellers. The cave dwellers were accustomed to difficult terrain and lived in a dimly lit environment, so they were more active at night. They were more likely to conduct an attack in the late evenings if their neighbors were unfortunate enough to provoke them.

The nomads hunted game and frequently stole whatever else they needed. They traded with the cave dwellers, but they stole from the hive dwellers. The cave dwellers were fierce warriors, so neither population wanted to cross them.

There were two hive cities in close proximity to each other. The hive dwellers were predominantly farmers ruled by an overlord. They were warlike, but it was driven by their need to defend their crops and their workers from the nomads.

The harvest season was nearly upon them, and this was the most volatile time of the year. The two populations were in close proximity to each other and had been for a while, so tensions were building. The nomads were preparing for the herds they followed to move again and needed to stock up on grain and hunting supplies such as spear and arrowheads. Once the crops were pulled into the hive, it would be difficult to get them out again. The population in the hives was becoming more and more fed up with being attacked year after year. Emotions were coming to a head, and things were about to get ugly.

From the information gathered by the buoys, there were no particular taboos or gender restraints. There was a hierarchy that had to be respected among all three populations. All three populations had a ruling caste, a working caste, and a slave population. Each of the three populations conveniently spoke the same language minus a few small inflection differences.

A council of the strongest warriors governed the caves, and the strongest council warrior ruled the council. He also ruled over the biggest caves with the best yield of ore. His caves had the best of the workers and slaves. It was considered an honor to work for him.

Elders governed the nomads. The elders were considered wise although there were occasional rifts between the rashness of the young able warriors and the more cautious elders. The nomads didn't have much use for slaves themselves, but as they would pass through an area and raid the fields, they would capture workers and force them to help the group move out of the area.

Once they reached the next area, they would trade the slaves for supplies in the new location. Some of them kept an occasional personal slave.

The hives were ruled by the wealthy and powerful. It was not the strongest or the oldest. They also had a ruling council of other wealthy and influential families. The middle class consisted of tradesmen who were blacksmiths, glass makers, and other trades. The lower class was the agricultural workers and manual laborers, as well as the slaves.

The crew, having received this new information, was nearly ready to start their new mission. They had practiced their self-defense techniques, their supplies were prepped and ready to go, and now their translators were up to date. The crew got a good night's sleep in order to be ready for landing the next morning.

THE PRICE OF PEACE

Brynna's plan was very different this time. The ship landed in the morning as usual, but first it flew slowly over the caves, then the nomads encampment and finally over the two hive cities before landing roughly between all of the populations. The crew had been advised the populations may or may not respond immediately. Lexi felt they might observe them from a distance for a short period of time.

After the ship landed, the crew set up an area between the landing gear under the belly of the ship with tables and chairs. There was plenty of room to stand up and walk around under the ship between the landing struts. Brynna anticipated using the area to meet with the locals. The ship itself could provide shade, and no one had to conquer their fear enough to go inside the ship. It kept things open and above board.

Laura and Jason started doing surveys of the vegetation that might be useful for food or medicines. Jake and Marissa went with them for extra security. The Captain kept one person watching the scanners at all times to monitor for anyone approaching.

The Cave Dwellers were the first to send a scouting party. Ten figures were spotted on the ship's scanners approaching through a forest at the base of the mountain where the caves were located. Only three people emerged from the woods. The other seven people stayed at the edge of the forest just out of sight of the ship. Cheyenne was monitoring the ship's scanners and watching for movement from the individuals at the edge of the woods. Thane and Lazaro were on board the shuttle ready to take off and defend the ship and its crew if necessary. Brynna, David, Lexi, and Braxton were under the ship awaiting the arrival of their visitors. As the three visitors drew closer to the ship, the crew saw two men and one woman approaching. They could also see the group were well armed for residents of this planet. The three carried knives, darts like the one that had hit Jake and blow guns to launch the darts through. They also carried hefty spears. When Cheyenne did further scans, she could tell the ones hiding in the woods were also carrying bows and arrows. However, bows and arrows were not carried by the three approaching. It was not a weapon easily used in close quarters, but it was the weapon of choice for someone at a distance.

Before Jason left to explore the flora and fauna, he drew up syringes of antidote for the poison darts. He administered one to each crew member as a precaution. When the three visitors showed up on the scanners, David contacted Jason. David asked him to stay close by, just in case.

Before the three walked under the ship, they stopped and asked if they were permitted to come closer. Brynna stood up and invited the three visitors to join them. The three moved closer slowly. Their attention was drawn to Brynna's talking bracelet. Brynna promptly explained the translators to the three visitors. The three still looked wary and uncomfortable. Brynna introduced herself and the three other crew members with her. Their guests identified themselves as the Akamu people. The male who seemed to be in charge was named Adan. His companions were Vesta, the female of the group, and Manton.

Adan had many questions for the crew but was cautious in his inquiries. "Did you come from the stars?"

Brynna took a strong, decisive lead as Lexi had suggested and answered Adan's questions. "Yes, we came from the stars."

Adan again cautiously ventured, "Are you gods or were you sent by the gods?"

Brynna didn't crack a smile even though she found such a notion humorous. "No, we are not gods. We were not sent by any gods. We have traveled very far, and we have never seen any gods.

"Why are you here?"

Brynna was waiting for this opening. "We represent a group of worlds who have joined together to form one ruling government known as the Commonwealth. We share our resources for the common good of all the worlds that are part of the Commonwealth. We have come to your world to invite you to join our alliance. We would like to begin our relationship with this world by trading for some supplies."

Lexi had been seated beside Brynna. She got up while Brynna was talking and brought a pitcher of water to the table along with several glasses. Lexi poured a glass of water for each one and set them down in front of each person seated at the table.

The three visitors watched Lexi carefully. Vesta started to take a drink of her water. As Vesta reached for her glass, Lexi sat down again next to Brynna and picked up her own glass to take a drink. Vesta slammed her drink down on the table and stood up quickly. The other men stood as well. David and Braxton were instantly on their guard, but they did not make a move toward the others. They waited for Brynna to get the situation under control. Brynna stood slowly. The three were giving angry looks at Lexi who was now unsure as to whether she should stand or stay seated. Before Brynna could react, Vesta began shouting angrily at her.

"We do not sit and eat or drink at the same table with slaves! You have insulted us!"

Brynna spoke kindly, but firmly to the three. "We do not mean to insult you. Lexi is not my slave. She is one of my advisers. We have no slaves at all. Our machines do most things for us, so we do not need slaves. Our ways are different from yours. It is not our intent to insult you. Please look on us as you would a child who needs to be trained. We aren't children, but we also are not trained in your ways."

Vesta still stood there scowling at Lexi. Lexi now stood and stared back at Vesta. Adan watched the two women for a second then turned back to Brynna. "We are sorry for the misunderstanding. We will continue with our meeting." Adan sat down, and Manton followed suit.

Vesta slowly sat down still eyeing Lexi. Lexi timed retaking her seat to match Vesta's. David and Braxton relaxed.

Adan tried to put the incident behind them by pushing the conversation back on track. "What is it you wish to trade?"

Brynna picked up a small container about the size of a loaf of bread and set it on the table. "We need a mineral that we have heard you possess. We only need enough to fill this container."

In order to introduce them to the data module that would later be left with them, Brynna placed one on the table before the arrival of their guests. She reached over, touched the module, and said, "Show me a picture of tetrabradium." The data module complied by displaying several full-color three-dimensional holograms of the element above the module. "This is what the mineral we seek looks like. We have no material goods to trade for the item, but we can trade certain services which I think you will find to be more than adequate compensation."

Manton inserted himself into the conversation rather abruptly, "What sort of services?" As soon as he said it, he looked over at Lexi.

The incident with Lexi kept Brynna focused on any new attention given to the lieutenant. Brynna said nothing to Manton about his glance at Lexi and answered his question. "We have a doctor who can care for anyone who needs medical attention. I have several advisers who can introduce new technologies to you, which may increase your productivity. I understand you have been trading with others for the mineral we seek. You may be able to increase your yield so you can make better trades. Along with the knowledge we offer, we will leave one of these…" Brynna had to pause and reconsider her words. Some things just don't translate well to less advanced societies. After carefully rethinking her words she continued, "This device has a record of knowledge. Some of our knowledge and technology can stay with you after we have left. All you have to do is ask it a question, and it can give you what information it has."

Adan looked down at it then asked Brynna, "What kind of questions can you ask it?"

Brynna took her glass of water and poured a couple drops on top of the recorder then touched the activation panel and asked, "What is this liquid and is it safe to drink?"

The data module shined a brief scanning light over the drops then replied. "This liquid is water, and it is safe to drink." The module paused for a moment then went inactive again. The three did not appear very impressed yet, so Brynna held out her hand and asked if she could use one of the darts the three of them carried on their belts. Adan picked one up and handed it to her carefully. Brynna placed the dart on the data module. "How can I increase the distance and effectiveness of this dart?" The data module scanned the dart and offered several technologically appropriate improvements to the design. It projected a three-dimensional holographic projection of an improved dart.

Vesta shifted her attention off Lexi and became visibly interested at the new dart floating above the device in front of her. She reached out to touch the new dart only to have her hand pass right through it. Vesta jumped up and gasped. She examined her hand carefully to be sure it was still intact, then looked back at the dart, which was equally as intact as it had been. Looking vexed, she snapped at Brynna, "What good are darts that can be seen, but not touched?"

Brynna was careful not to show any sign of amusement. "I'm sorry, this device can only show you pictures of these things. It is only a guide. You have to look at the guide and make them yourselves."

"You mentioned you wish us to join your Commonwealth. What will this mean? Do we have to join you in the skies?" Adan knew Vesta was very uncomfortable, so he wanted to keep the conversation moving.

"Each world who joins the Commonwealth must meet certain requirements. The worlds that do not meet these requirements are helped by the Commonwealth until they achieve the required levels. You do not have to leave this world if that is your desire. All the people of this world would need to be united in their agreement to join the Commonwealth. You can each maintain your own governments, but you would need to be at peace with each other. In return, this device can contact the Commonwealth to request help as needed. If you were to have a particularly long hard winter or a drought and were facing starvation, rather than turn against your neighbors, you could call the Commonwealth. We could bring food or water from other worlds that have a surplus."

Adan looked concerned. "You seem to be offering a lot and asking very little in return. What is the true cost of this arrangement?"

Brynna smiled and nodded. "You are a wise man. You are right to ask. We ask for your loyalty to the Commonwealth as your ruling body, but there is little here we need other than your loyalty. The Commonwealth does have enemies, and they have moved into the worlds like yours who have a short reach. They also seek your loyalty. They are trying to get a foothold in the Commonwealth's territory. They are attacking us in our weakest areas, so we are trying to fortify our weak areas as any good soldier would."

Manton now joined Vesta's state of being offended. "Do you consider us weak?"

Brynna moved quickly to correct the misconception. "No, we consider the Akamu strong. That is why we seek an alliance with you. It is the Commonwealth's weaknesses we seek to correct. Our needs are for allies on this world. We may come and ask for more ore from time to time, but all we really want is for you to let us know if our enemy comes here, be advanced scouts for us. Perhaps we do offer more than what loyalty is worth, but we can move you more quickly to become an advanced society and a more useful ally. Yes, we have selfish motives, but our arrangement is beneficial to both your people and ours. I do not believe we ask more than you can give."

Adan sat there thinking for a moment before speaking. "Why are worlds like ours so important?"

Brynna was a skilled strategist and had no trouble explaining their importance to Adan. "It only takes one voice to stir others to chaos. If someone takes a child and teaches him ideas contrary to what you believe, when he reaches manhood, those ideas will stay with him, and he will spread those ideas to others. Worlds like yours have little contact with others, but if the ideas are planted now, then when you are ready to reach the stars, those ideas will begin to infiltrate the other worlds. It is a slow progression, but it could, in time, take down the Commonwealth."

Adan found her candor appealing, so he didn't hesitate to ask his next question. "What makes the Commonwealth better than your enemy?"

Brynna didn't even blink at his question. "Ultimately that is a decision you have to make. We have approached you openly, but our enemy works subversively. We do not even know where he comes from, where his homeworld is, and we are familiar with all the worlds in these stars."

"What if we decline to join your Commonwealth?" Again, Adan did not hesitate. He watched Brynna carefully for signs of anger, fear, or deception.

Brynna confidently countered. "If you side with our enemy, the Commonwealth will treat you the same as the enemy. If you simply do not wish to choose sides, we would still like to trade our services for the ore we need, and we will leave the data module here with you to use if you wish to contact us. The decision is yours. I do not know what the Commonwealth will do when they find our enemy. We have had no open confrontations with him."

Adan had one more question. "Who is your enemy?"

"Pateras El Liontari and his son Arni Sotaeras Liontari." Brynna and the other crew members watched each person carefully for signs of recognition. Their faces remained blank at the mention of the Liontaris.

Adan noticed the increased attention they were receiving and answered carefully. "I have not heard of these you have mentioned. I will make inquiries among my people. I suggest you also ask the Sorley and the Kimbra. We will talk to our leader about your proposal. What will you do if he refuses to have any dealings with you at all? What if he refuses your gifts?"

Brynna maintained her demeanor. "We will offer the same things to the Sorley and the Kimbra whether you accept or decline. If all of you reject us, we will leave. We will report back to the Commonwealth. I assume your world will continue to be watched for the presence of the Liontaris. We will not cause you any harm, whatever you choose. If the Sorley and the Kimbra accept our offers and you do not, that would put them ahead of you in their development because we will leave a data module with each of them."

"So, you plan to pit us against each other?" Adan asked.

"As we understand it, you are already working against each other. We would prefer each of the populations on this world be at peace. The Commonwealth has been at peace for hundreds of years. This is why this new enemy is disturbing to us. We already planned to offer the same things to all three populations. One other thing we can offer is our assistance to establish a peace treaty between you and the Sorley and the Kimbra. Would this be of some value to you?"

"Perhaps. We will talk to our leader." Adan stood up to depart. "Is there anything else?"

"No, that is our offer. The choice is yours. When will you return to give us an answer?"

"We will return in a few days." With that Adan and his two companions departed.

The crew watched them get to the tree line before they began discussing the meeting. Brynna asked each one how they thought it went. Lexi was the first one to give her input. "I was definitely worried when I served them the glasses of water and they got offended. I think you handled it well, Commander. It was hard to get a reading on them though. I think they will take us up on our offers, if for no other reason than to keep the others from getting ahead of them."

Braxton also replied, "They did seem a little touchy. I definitely got uptight when they got offended. Lexi's right, you did a great job with that one, Commander."

Brynna smiled slightly, "Thanks. It took a second to sort it out. We know they respect strength; Lexi, I am glad you stood up to Vesta."

Lexi laughed, "I may have given the appearance of strength, but I was NOT feeling it."

Brynna looked at David who seemed distracted. "David, you haven't offered any input. What's on your mind?"

David had been looking at his comm unit's display. He looked up to answer her question. "I don't think they are sold on the idea. They left two men to watch us just beyond the tree line."

Brynna didn't seem overly concerned. "Then they will see me keep my word and offer this arrangement to the other two populations. I'm not surprised they are cautious because I came very close to threatening them."

"Threatening them with what? We don't know what the Commonwealth's plans are for these worlds. Do we?" Lexi looked at Brynna then back at David. She was really hoping one of them could answer her question.

David looked at Lexi, "I have not been given any information about the Commonwealth's intentions."

Lexi opened her mouth to address the obvious omissions from the Captain's statement until she felt Brynna's hand on her arm. The look on Brynna's face said, "Don't go there." Lexi wanted to ask why she shouldn't pursue this, but both the Captain and the Commander seemed to be in agreement. Braxton said nothing but was intently watching the exchanges. Through all of it, his gut told him he wasn't going to like the answers to these questions.

A few minutes later, the Surf-Ve returned. David instructed them to pull into the cargo bay before unloading. No one questioned him at the time, but once the vehicle was secure, Jake inquired about it. David filled him in about the two men watching them from the trees. He assured Jake he did not feel threatened, but he didn't want to reveal too much information too quickly. So far, the visitors did not know how many crew members there were, and the Captain preferred to keep it that way. Jake was not opposed either.

A couple of hours later, Cheyenne reported two groups approaching the ship from two different directions. One group appeared to be coming from the direction of the hive cities located east of the ship. According to the scanners, four men were riding in a carriage drawn by four horse-like animals. The animals looked like a cross between a llama and a horse. They were built like a workhorse with a long thick coat similar to the llama to protect them during the long cold winters. Four other men riding on horseback accompanied the carriage. The second group was coming from the south. There were ten men on horseback. Brynna surmised the second group was nomads or Sorley.

The Kimbra, or hive dwellers, were going to arrive first. Knowing what they did about the rivalries, Brynna and David were concerned about possible altercations. David and Brynna agreed Jake, Marissa, Jason, and Laura should join them for this meeting. As the carriage pulled up beside the ship, Brynna walked out to greet the newcomers. Jake and David followed her but kept a discreet distance behind her. When the carriage stopped, two men were sitting outside the carriage. One was the driver, and the other appeared to be both a servant and a guard. He was heavily armed, and when the carriage came to a stop, he glanced around at the crew then jumped down to open the door of the carriage. Two men on horseback were posted in front of the carriage and two behind it. Each man stayed on his horse. Two men stepped out of the carriage. Brynna stepped forward to greet them.

"Greetings. I am Brynna Alexander. I am the Commander of a Peace Mission from a group of worlds known as the Commonwealth." The men looked skeptically at her bracelet. "I do not speak your language, so I must use this device to assist me. It will translate what I say so you can understand, and it will tell me what you say. Is this acceptable to you?" Brynna pointed to the translator on her wrist, which started to speak as soon as she finished speaking.

The two men looked at each other a little warily then nodded slightly indicating each one was willing to go along with it for now. Lexi thought it looked more like they weren't willing to show weakness in front of each other. No one on this planet was accustomed to computers, technology, or anything more than simple machines. The idea of a bracelet talking was undoubtedly more disconcerting to this culture as it was on Galat III.

Brynna invited the two men to sit down at the table with her, Lexi, Jason, and Laura. The two men came and sat down with her, but the servant guard stood behind the two men and watched the other crewmen who were standing. Two of the horsemen decided to dismount so they could observe what was going on under the ship better. They remained at the edges of the ship, but they also watched the crew members who were not seated at the table.

Once they were seated, one of the men looked at Brynna and asked, "Are we to speak to you or to your bracelet?"

"You may speak to me. I can adjust the bracelet if it does not hear you well enough. The bracelet is nothing more than a tool. I can set it to speak only in my ear or to speak out loud. It cannot speak in your ears, but I thought it would be best to start out by setting it to speak out loud. Is this still acceptable to you?

The men looked at each other again. The second man had yet to say anything, but he nodded to the first man. The first man leaned over closer to Brynna's arm to say, "Yes, that is acceptable." Although he was looking at her, he was clearly talking "into" the bracelet. Her arms had been resting on the table in front of her with her hands clasped together. Brynna tried to discreetly pull her arms back so that her bracelet would not be the focus of attention.

Brynna introduced herself again and the rest of the crew that was present, including the ones acting as security guards. The two men then introduced themselves. The man who had done all the speaking introduced himself first, "My name is Cashel. I am the Lord Master of the Kimbra city Primus, and this is my brother."

The second man then introduced himself, "I am Medwin. I am the Lord Master of the Kimbra city, Corvan. Why are you here?"

Cashel seemed slightly embarrassed by his brother's bluntness. "What my brother would like to know is, are you seeking to make some sort of trade?"

"Before we get started, I think perhaps we should wait for the others." Brynna motioned toward the south. Cashel and Medwin stood up and looked in the general direction Brynna indicated. Medwin looked back at Brynna and demanded, "Who are you expecting?"

Brynna tried to reassure the two men. "We have sought to speak to you, the Sorley and the Akamu. We are on a mission of peace. We have already spoken to the Akamu because they arrived first. The Sorley are on their way and should be here in a few minutes."

Cashel whispered something quietly to Medwin who in turn sent their "guard" back to the carriage along with the four horsemen. The carriage moved behind some trees on the far side of the ship. Cashel turned back to Brynna and told her in a rather odd tone of voice, "We would not want to frighten the Sorley with our presence." The translators could not adequately translate someone's tone of voice. It could place emphasis on specific words if the speaker did so, but sometimes one had to glean what they could from personal observation.

Brynna felt she needed to try and diffuse the situation before anything even got started. "I understand you, the Sorley and the Akamu have had some difficulties. We would like to help you settle these problems if you will allow us to help. While you are here, you are under our protection. We will give the same guarantee to the others who come here."

Medwin, although somewhat reserved wasn't afraid to speak his mind. "Your people are armed only with knives? How

171

can you protect us with so little weaponry? I thought those of you who came from the stars had better weapons than that."

Brynna kept her reply purposely vague. "We do have more than knives. We have chosen to keep our weapons in less noticeable places."

Cashel was less sharp in his response, "Why do you hide your weapons? Why do you have so many female leaders and guards?"

"All of my people have been fully trained in defense tactics. We are being careful about displaying our weapons because they are extremely dangerous, and we don't want to cause any accidents. We don't intend harm to anyone, but we are quite capable of doing so if the need should arise." Brynna let this serve as a warning to the Kimbra they should not underestimate the crew and left the crew's motivation for defense unknown. The Kimbra were left to wonder what "need" might arise.

While they waited on the Sorley to arrive, Brynna offered the two men some refreshments. She was careful not to have anyone serve the men this time, but simply invited them to help themselves. Presently, the Sorley came within sight and headed straight toward the ship. Their pace increased abruptly as they neared. Some of the riders rode straight up to the ship while the others moved around to the back. Cashel and Medwin started to get up from the table, but Brynna motioned for them to remain seated. She then got up and moved to the edge of the ship. David stayed close behind her. Brynna looked at the horsemen nearest her and boldly asked, "Which of you leads the Sorley? I would like to speak with you. We mean you no harm. These men are under our protection, and your leader is given the same protection."

One of the men near Brynna drew his sword. The others followed his lead, except for one. Jake moved his hand to his more advanced weapons. David placed his hand on his knife.

Thane was sitting at the controls of the shuttle watching his scanner closely. His muscles tensed ready to take off the second he was needed.

When Lexi saw the men react as they did except for the one, she whispered into her comm unit. The one man who had not drawn a sword held the reigns of his horse in one hand and a small crossbow in the other, although he wasn't pointing it at anyone yet. Brynna looked back at Lexi who nodded then she looked back at the man with the crossbow. She walked over to him and grabbed the horse's bridle. "We invited you here to make an honest trade. Why do you test us like this?"

The horses, feeling the anxiety of their riders, danced back and forth, occasionally rearing, ready to bolt as soon as a command was given. The ship was too low for the riders to come underneath it while still on their horses. It also appeared to have the horses slightly spooked. The man who had been the first to draw his sword looked at the man with the crossbow. Brynna still held the horse's bridle firmly. The man hung his crossbow back on his saddle and carefully dismounted. He took the reins and led the horse to a third horseman near him. The third man had to sheath his sword in order to take the reins of the horse from his leader.

The man, who had drawn his sword first, sheathed his weapon, dismounted, and tied his horse to the saddle of the leader's horse. The other men also put their swords away. The leader walked up to Brynna and grabbed her arm. David moved quickly to Brynna's side. He was ready to take this man down fast and hard if he tried to hurt Brynna. Brynna raised her free arm to stop David. The man wasn't hurting her arm. He was merely looking at her comm unit and translator. The man saw David's response and sensed their relationship. He released Brynna's arm more gently than he had grabbed it initially. Still watching David, the man finally spoke, "How is it you can speak from your arm, but your arm has no mouth?"

Brynna breathed a sigh of relief. She explained the use and function of the translators to him as she had with their other two guests. She invited him and his men to join them. She knew he wouldn't invite all of his men in to join them, but she offered nonetheless. The man and his companion joined her under the ship leaving his men spread around the ship watching them closely. Brynna could tell the tension levels were coming down because the horses were also settling down.

Brynna introduced herself, the crew, and her other guests although she was fairly certain they were already acquainted. The leader then introduced himself and his companion. "I am Tharen of the Sorley, and this is Jager. My father is Kasen. He is the leader of the Sorley. You are strangers here. How did you know I was the leader? Did they tell you?" He asked pointing at the Kimbra delegation.

Brynna smiled, "No, they only arrived minutes before you did. I determined you were the leader for several reasons. You appeared ready to defend yourself, you did not draw your sword, and the others did not attack us. I interpreted that to mean they were waiting on you to attack."

"You mentioned several reasons."

"Your companion, Jager, looked to you for guidance. You also did not act like a follower, but a leader."

"Perhaps I should work on my skills as a follower then." Tharen tried not to smile, but his mouth still twitched ever so slightly. Brynna said nothing but smiled and looked away. Jager frowned. Lexi, observing his behavior, determined it was his job to protect Tharen and for him to be named as the one to betray Tharen's identity was not amusing to him. Lexi got up from the table and moved away to pass the information to Brynna via the comm system so only she could hear it. Brynna was in the process of offering her newest guests refreshments when Lexi started speaking to her through the comm unit in her ear. Brynna took a long slow sip of water so she could concentrate on Lexi's message.

"Brynna, I think Jager is considered Tharen's protector whether by his own choice or by design, I don't know, but you basically just said he's incompetent. You need to do something to restore his ego and trust."

Brynna whispered a quiet, "got it." She set her glass down, thought for a second before she began to speak again. "Tharen, I assume you will one day be the leader of the Sorley?"

"Yes, that is correct."

"I think you will be a wise leader then. It was a wise choice to have Jager conceal your identity when you approached. He must be a brave warrior and a good friend to take on such a great responsibility. If we had meant to harm you, he might have been the one harmed instead of you."

Tharen smiled. Jager was indeed a good friend. They had grown up together as best friends. Tharen knew Brynna was trying to make amends for her earlier mistake. Jager had the type of personality that caused him to brood over things for hours or even days. His ego could also over-inflate quickly. "Yes, Jager is a fine warrior, and he would give his life to save mine, but he doesn't hide his thoughts very well."

Jager had started to smile as Brynna spoke. The two saw him sit up straighter in his chair, he pulled his shoulders back, stuck his chest out and flexed his muscles. After Tharen's last comment, Jager's ego deflated just a little. Brynna and Tharen had both said basically the same things, but a friend can get away with saying things a stranger can't. Jager no longer appeared embarrassed or angry.

Brynna looked at all her guests and said, "Shall we begin?" Each man seemed to be ready to have his curiosity satisfied. Brynna repeated the offer she had given to the Akamu for technological advancements in exchange for an alliance. She omitted the agreement with the Akamu to trade for ore. When Brynna finished asking for their loyalty to the Commonwealth, she watched their faces for a reaction. Cashel and Medwin looked at each other. There seemed to be a mixture of emotions crossing their faces. Medwin finally spoke up. "You want us to turn control of our cities over to this Commonwealth?" He was on the verge of anger.

Brynna quickly countered, "No, absolutely not. Each society will maintain its autonomy. We seek to have you as allies. No one will be stationed here. We will only come here periodically to trade for supplies and to offer any help you may need. This is a harsh world. If famine or disease were to strike, who would be able to help you? We want each of your civilizations to be at peace with each other because the Commonwealth is an advocate of peace. We also want to know about our one enemy. He demands you become his allies or worse yet, his puppets. We have met followers of Pateras Liontari. His son told us anyone who does not choose to follow him will face destruction. The Commonwealth is not in the business of causing destruction. It is our goal to save people from his tyranny."

Each of the delegates looked at each other thoughtfully. Cashel was the next to speak. "We will consider your offer and let you know what we decide." With that, he stood up and walked to the north end of the ship where he signaled his carriage to return.

When the Sorley saw the carriage and the four horsemen headed their way, they became concerned.

Brynna stood up and called out, "Tharen, please do not be concerned, they are only here to protect Cashel and Medwin. Move your men aside and they will not harm anyone."

Jager advised his leader. "Tharen, this is our chance. We can take the leaders of the two cities here and now. If we take their leaders, we can own their cities."

Brynna pulled a knife from her belt and plunged the blade tip into the table neatly between two of Jager's fingers. Jager gave a startled look down at his hand then looked at Brynna. Brynna shook her head and said, "I can't allow that, gentlemen." Jager slowly and cautiously pulled his hand off the table.

Tharen did not want to appear weak, but he knew he could not fight both the Kimbra and the ship's crew. Brynna, seeing his dilemma, touched her comm unit and said, "Lt Ryder, I think we need a warning demonstration."

Thane powered the shuttle up and flew it in a tight circle above the ship firing a few brief laser blasts onto the ground around them. The carriage and horsemen slowed their approach. Several of the horses reared, but fortunately none of the riders were thrown. Tharen looked at Jager, "This is not the right time or place. There will be another time and place. Order the men to ride south, and you hold our horses on the south side of the ship. I will be there momentarily.

Cashel and Medwin were temporarily immobilized with fear when the shuttle started firing. They wanted to signal their carriage to hasten its approach but were now afraid to move. Jake walked over to them and motioned the carriage and horsemen to continue their advance.

Tharen's men moved about a hundred yards south of the ship, but they waited there to make sure Tharen and Jager were coming. Brynna signaled Thane to back off a little. Tharen looked at Brynna and scowled, "If this is what you mean by peace, I am not sure we want any part of it."

"I could not let you harm each other. I also have not harmed any of you. I promised you both protection, and I keep my promises. If your party rides south then heads east to try and catch them, we will not stop you. As long as either of you are within sight of this ship, you are in neutral territory. So far you have had nothing, but small skirmishes, do you really want open war?"

Tharen looked at her long and hard. He knew she was right but didn't want to admit it. He stood there with her until the Kimbra delegation was on its way before he turned to leave. He had stayed in place because he knew his men would not pursue the Kimbra and leave him at Brynna's mercy. He also knew his men would be angry because they had been stopped from grabbing the Kimbra delegation. He looked at Brynna again and said, "You know this puts me in an awkward position."

"I know it does. Perhaps the promise of better hunting weapons will placate your men. We promise to do what we can to make things easier for your people."

"I hope so." Tharen turned to go again but stopped one more time. "By the way, did you hit where you were aiming with that knife?" He asked and nodded at the knife still lodged in the table.

Brynna looked at him in all seriousness and said, "Absolutely." Jager, who was standing close enough to hear the exchange, felt some of the color drain from his face.

Brynna knew Tharen had stayed with her to "keep the peace," but she did not thank him for it. If she had, it would have put him in a more difficult position than he had already stated. She did hope he knew she was grateful. Perhaps there would be another opportunity to tell him later.

Once all their visitors were safely away, Thane landed the shuttle, and the crew moved back inside the ship. The crew again met in the dining hall. This time the Captain routed the scanners from the bridge into the dining hall, so no one had to remain on lookout on the bridge. Brynna didn't need to go over the details of the meetings with the crewmen. Most had been linked in on the comm units, which were also linked to the translators. Brynna just wanted to know how the others interpreted the meetings. It seemed everyone agreed the tension between the three populations was a little high. Lexi advised waiting a day or two then sending a party to visit each location casually. Everyone seemed to like the idea. It gave them all a chance to acclimate to the planet, more time to research flora and fauna, and some free time to socialize. Jake did warn everyone not to wander off alone.

Two days later the crew was still waiting for their answers from the three populations. They decided the next morning they would send a party out to visit the Akamu. The Captain and Commander agreed the crew should just relax and enjoy themselves for the evening. The computer was programmed to monitor the area and send an alarm to the Captain if anyone other than the crew came within five hundred yards of the ship. Jake and Marissa volunteered to watch the extended range scanners until they went to sleep that night. Jake directed the feed to their quarters where he and Marissa planned to spend the evening. Marissa prepared dinner while Jake practiced a form of self-defense focusing on balance and poise.

MISSING IN ACTION

It was a pleasant summer evening, and the calm atmosphere seemed to carry with it a sense of serenity and romance. Marissa prepared a quiet candlelight dinner from ship's rations, a few semi-fresh vegetables left from Galat. It was the best she could do under the circumstances. Thane and Aulani decided to play Zone with Jason and Laura. Lazaro and Cheyenne chose to get some fresh air and exercise by running laps around the outside of the ship. David and Brynna went up to the shuttle bay, opened the doors, and lay down on the top of the *Evangeline* to watch the sunset and the stars come out.

Lexi wanted to go for a walk, so Braxton went with her. It was still light out when they started to walk toward a nearby stream. The Akamu scouts were watching them from the northwest, the Kimbra were to the East, and the Sorley were to the south, so they felt heading southwest was the safest direction to go. The stream wound its way through a thin line of trees. When they got to it, the two sat down and talked quietly for a few minutes. Lexi got up and took her boots off, rolled up her pant legs and stepped into the icy water. The stream was fed from a mountain spring, so it stayed cold all year long. As soon as she stepped into it, she gasped and exclaimed, "Oh this is COLD!"

Braxton laughed at her and shook his head. "Then get out of the water, silly woman."

Lexi cupped her hands together, bent over and scooped up some of the cold water and held it close to her mouth. "Do you suppose it's safe to drink?" She asked while looking at Braxton with a mischievous look on her face.

Braxton had been reclining against a tree just relaxing, but now he sat upright and responded rather emphatically, "NO. Don't you dare drink that! We have a mission tomorrow and you can't afford to be in the Med Bay."

Lexi, still grinning said, "So you really think I shouldn't drink it?"

Braxton repeated his answer with less alarm, but more concern, "No. Get rid of it."

Lexi smiled and said, "Okay, if you say so." With that, she promptly threw the handful of water at him. Not very much of it hit him, but the threat was enough to stir him to action.

Braxton rolled away from her and onto his feet and began to chase her. "You're going to regret that." He hollered.

Braxton jumped into the water without even removing his shoes, he solidly splashed Lexi. Lexi squealed, kicked more water at him and ran onto the opposite bank. She lost her balance on a slippery rock and fell trying to get up the embankment. Braxton got in one more good dousing before reaching out to help her stand up again. Once she regained her footing, she started to run from him again, but this time he was ready for her. Braxton grabbed her arm and pulled her back to him. He wrapped his arms around her and kissed her. She returned the kiss, pulled back and looked to the west. "We're missing the sunset." She quietly reminded him.

He moved around behind her, so he could watch the sunset over her shoulder and wrapped his arms around her waist. They stood there watching the sun disappear below the horizon. They had very few moments like this since they had met. It was nice to just relax and enjoy each other's company and the scenery. Once it finally started getting dark, they decided they better head back to the ship. Braxton waded back through the water, but Lexi looked like she was trying to tiptoe through it. She was starting to get a little cool now that the sun had gone down, and her clothes were wet. When Lexi got to the other side, she sat down to put her boots back on and took one last look at the horizon. The moon was large and full, casting a lot of light on the ground, or so she thought.

When Lexi decided she had looked at the sky long enough, she stood up to walk with Braxton back to the ship. Braxton smiled at her. He loved watching her be happy. When she neared Braxton, he asked, "Are you ready to head back?"

She smiled at him and said as she turned to brush her clothes off, "As soon as I get cleaned up a little."

Lexi turned around just in time to see Vesta hit Braxton on the back of the head. Lexi screamed, "Braxton!" She tried to reach for him to break his fall, but someone grabbed her from behind. Lexi, realizing the gravity of her situation, decided it was past time to call for help and reached for her comm bracelet. She was too late. Whoever had grabbed her from behind jabbed a dart into her shoulder. She began to feel heavy and sleepy. She tried to speak, but she couldn't make any words come out of her mouth. In a moment, she felt herself being thrown over a shoulder... then she was unconscious.

Three hours later Jake was ready to get some sleep, but he didn't want to lie down until all the crew had checked in. Everyone except Braxton and Lexi was accounted for. Marissa was ready to go to bed and getting annoyed when Jake wouldn't shut down the computer and join her. "Jake, what's taking so long? We need to get some rest. It's late."

"Braxton and Lexi haven't checked in yet."

"Maybe they just went straight to their cabin and forgot."

"I doubt it, but I wouldn't want to bother them if that's the case."

"So just track their comm units, if they're on board, they just forgot."

Jake mulled over her suggestion then touched the computer controls and spoke the command, "Computer, locate Braxton Flint and Lexi Flint."

Presently a map of the area outside the ship displayed on his screen, which instantly sent up a red flag in Jake's mind. The map revealed a distance much further than the five hundred yards the crew was supposed to be from the ship. The map showed Braxton right at five hundred yards southwest of the *Evangeline* and stationary. Lexi's comm unit displayed about three miles northwest of the ship. Without hesitating, Jake hailed the Captain.

David and Brynna were already asleep when Jake's hail came through. David had to clear his head for a second before responding to Jake. His instinct was to chastise Jake for waking him up, but he knew Jake wouldn't disturb him without a good reason. David rubbed his face briefly then answered the call, "Captain here, what's wrong chief?"

Jake reported what he had just found out to the Captain. The Captain then inquired, "Did you try to hail them?"

"No, sir, I wanted to inform you first. I'm not sure we should try and hail Lexi because she isn't where she's supposed to be. Scans show she's in the Akamu caves. I think we need to go after Braxton and find out what's happened. I did a scan of the terrain around Braxton. It's accessible by either Surf-Ve or shuttle. I suggest the shuttle so we can get a better look around before getting in the middle of something."

David thought for a second then issued orders he really didn't want to issue, but it was for the best. "Good call chief. Wake the crew. Take Jason, Laura, Cheyenne, and the Commander in the shuttle to locate Braxton and get him back here. I want Lazaro, Thane, Marissa, and Aulani to their stations. I will join them on the bridge shortly."

David wanted to be out on the ground himself, but he knew he needed to stay with the ship and make command decisions. He also didn't want to send others out into danger, especially not his wife. As uncomfortable as it was, his decision was the correct one. "Jake, after you get Braxton back, we'll decide how to proceed in getting Lexi back."

"Yes sir," Jake replied and didn't question him. When Jake disconnected the call, he saw Marissa standing in the doorway watching him.

"What's wrong?" She asked. He quickly brought her up to speed then told her to report to her duty station. She looked almost numb but quickly returned to the bedroom to change clothes and do as she was instructed.

Jake punched the ship-wide comm unit and spoke into it, "Attention all hands, attention all hands, Lt. Commander Dominick, Lt. Ryder, Ensign Ryder, report to your duty stations immediately. Lt. Commander Adams, Lt. Adams, and Ensign Dominick report to the shuttle bay immediately with search and rescue gear and full weapons complement."

The message was put on a repeating cycle until each crewman responded. Jake saw no reason to put the call out to

Marissa or Brynna. He knew the Captain would tell Brynna and he had already told Marissa. It was a tiny assumption, but a reasonably safe one. Once everyone reached his or her appropriate locations, Jake briefed the shuttle crew, and the Captain briefed the ship's crew.

With the shuttle on its way, David had Aulani start trying to hail Braxton. He had Marissa track the location of the comm units for all the crew who had just left the ship as well as Lexi and Braxton. Aulani continued trying to hail Braxton. Presently, Braxton's comm unit was activated. Aulani could hear what sounded like labored breathing inter-mixed with moaning and groaning. As soon as Aulani heard it, she turned to face the Captain. "Captain, his unit is active, and I think I hear him moving around."

Aulani had the sound coming through her earpiece so she could pay attention to it and block out the other bridge noises. When she got through on Braxton's comm unit, she switched it to the bridge speakers. David activated his comm unit to see if he could further encourage Braxton to respond. "Lt. Commander Flint, what is your situation?" The crew heard another moan and more shuffling noises. David knew he was probably injured and didn't want to be cruel, but he needed to know what the crew was walking into. "Commander Flint, Report! Commander Flint, Report!" The Captain paused waiting for a response for what seemed like an eternity.

Finally, slowly, Braxton was able to respond. "I'm here...ohhh... my head... Lexi?"

Although they couldn't see him, the crew knew he was struggling to pull himself together. It was agonizing for them to hear him and not be able to help him. David wanted to keep him communicating so he muted the comm unit for a second and told Aulani to keep the shuttle updated on Braxton's status. David unmuted the comm unit and spoke to Braxton again. "Lt Commander Flint, the shuttle is on its way to you. What is your situation?"

Braxton didn't respond as quickly, so the Captain repeated himself in a firmer tone. Braxton again struggled for words, "My head... hurts. Something hit me... Lexi? Captain, I... I can't see very well. Lexi isn't answering... I can't see her. I think I hear the shuttle." His words were starting to come to him.

David still didn't want to tell him Lexi wasn't there to hear him call her. The Captain thought the Adrenalin rush induced by trying to find her would help him more than knowing she was not there to find.

In another few seconds, David could hear the crew reach Braxton's side. David shut off the comm line between himself and Braxton and turned his attention toward locating Lexi. "Marissa, are you still tracking Lexi's comm unit?"

"Yes sir, it's stationary in the Akamu caves, and it shows she's still wearing it because I still have a heart rate registering. It matches the record we have on file although the rate is much slower than normal. It indicates she's unconscious." Marissa was trying to sound matter of fact, but her voice cracked just a little when she reported to the Captain.

David knew everyone needed to stay focused, so he barked orders as though he had not heard the crack in her voice. "Keep track of each comm unit. Lt. Ryder, watch the scanner for any movement among the local population. Ensign, has the ground team reported in yet?"

Thane hastily acknowledged the order then carried it out. Ensign Ryder reported back to the Captain, "Yes sir, I have the Commander for you, sir."

The Captain pushed the button on his console to connect to Brynna, "Report Commander."

"Captain, Lt. Commander Flint appears to have a concussion. He's disoriented and doesn't know what happened. He said he and Lexi were about to return to the ship when he got hit from behind. There is no one else here. I do see several sets of footprints, but they disappear at the water's edge. What are your orders, sir?"

"Get the Lt. Commander back here to the Med Bay. The Lieutenant's comm unit shows she's alive. If they were going to hurt her, I doubt they would carry her all the way back to the caves first."

"Yes sir."

As soon as David got off the comms with Brynna, he turned back to Aulani, "Can you monitor and record from her comm unit without anyone near her knowing?"

Aulani nodded, "Yes sir."

"Then do it. I want to know who took her and what they intend to do with her."

Aulani got right on her task. She was careful to shut off the indicator lights first when she tapped into the bracelet's comm unit, so if it were visible, her actions wouldn't be detected. As she was working Aulani began to realize the crew had become like family to her, and a quiet nagging worry was filling her heart and mind. One of the things they covered when she was in training was if you let your emotions take over, you would be of no use to your crewmates. With that thought in mind, she shook off the feelings, which were trying to slowly overtake her, and forced herself to concentrate on the job at hand. Aulani wasn't focused on David, but he saw her hands start trembling. Before he could say anything, he saw her shake her head, then both her hands, and start back to work with an air of determination. David smiled slightly. Aulani was just an Ensign, but he was sure she would move up in the ranks quickly.

Aulani made the connection to Lexi's comm unit but wasn't picking up very many sounds. The sounds she did pick up were distorted. She tried boosting the gain as much as she could, but she still had trouble making anything out. She turned to report back to the Captain. "Captain, I have Lexi's comm unit, but I really can't make much out."

The Captain looked back at her, "Let's hear it." Aulani pushed a button on her console. Suddenly they could hear Lexi breathing and a blur of voices. The four bridge crew members listened for a moment.

Thane furrowed his brow, "It sounds like she's inside the caves. Do you hear how the voices are overlapping? They're echoing off the walls."

Marissa pointed at the layout on her scanner, "That's where her comm unit is showing up. It's deep inside the Akamu caves."

David looked back at Aulani, "Can you clean that sound up any and narrow in on the voices?"

"I'll try sir." Aulani continued to work on it. Suddenly she heard footsteps and voices coming in quite clearly.

The first voice said, "Here she is." The voice sounded like Manton's voice.

The second voice they did not recognize. "What have you done? These people have sought to become our allies, and now you take one of them captive. They have weapons far more advanced than ours. You know they could destroy us easily."

Manton's voice came through again, "She's just their slave. I have a plan. They'll never know she's here."

The second voice spoke again, "But Manton, why did you take her?"

"She's strong. She's already a slave, even though they deny it, and she looks a lot like Vesta. Maybe if they do discover she's here, we can offer them more ore for her."

"Take her back!"

"Tarin, no! Please! She's perfect for us! After she has borne children for us, the gods will be pleased when we offer them such a fine sacrifice. Vesta and I have agreed on her. We have not found a woman yet we agreed on. Don't do this!"

There was a long silence and what sounded like someone pacing.

"All right Manton, you and Vesta may keep her for now. How did you get Vesta to agree to this?"

"She looks enough like Vesta; her children will appear to be Vesta's children. I also had to agree to allow Vesta to give her slave markings. After the marking ceremony, we will take her bloody clothing and her weapons and leave them near the Sorley encampment. They will think the Sorley took her."

The voices started to become fainter and were accompanied by fading footsteps. Tarin's voiced continued as they moved out of range of the comm unit, "That's a shame, she has such a pleasing face. You must keep her hidden until we know they think the Sorley took her. Make sure neither Vesta nor you harm her in any way until..." The rest of the conversation faded.

Except for the sound of Lexi's breathing coming through the speakers, there was dead silence on the bridge. Aulani looked at Thane then Marissa and finally the Captain. David noticed the tremor in her hand was back, and the color in her face was pale.

She was seeking some comfort and reassurance from her husband first, her friend second and ultimately her Captain. Knowing her need and the crew's needs at this unstable juncture, the Captain took decisive action. "Ensign, keep monitoring her comm unit and let me know if anything changes. It didn't sound like they were going to do anything to her tonight, but I don't want to take any chances. Also, Braxton does not need to hear that conversation. Restrict his access to it. For now, we know they want her alive. Understood?"

"Yes sir."

"Lt. Holden, keep an eye on those signals. If there is any unusual movement, let me know. Are the Akamu scouts still watching us?"

"Yes sir."

"Okay, good. Let me know if they move away from their current location. Lt. Ryder and Lt. Holden use the scanners to try to get a map of those caverns. Start with Lexi's current position and work your way out in concentric circles. I want to know every route in and out of that cave."

"Sir, could you have the shuttle make a slow pass over the caves and scan them. It'll give us better readings. The tetrabradium makes some of our readings sketchy, and they might be able to fill in some of the gaps."

David hesitated to approve the request. If they did the fly by, would the Akamu think they were just randomly looking for Lexi, or would the Akamu realize they knew where she was? If they tipped their hand, it could put Lexi in more danger. David decided on a variation of Thane's request. "Have the shuttle land here. It can drop Lt. Commander Flint and the doc off in the Med Bay, then send it to fly over the Sorley, then the Akamu. Don't stay too long over the Akamu but have them scan as best they can then head east to make a pass over the hive cities before coming back here."

"Sir?" Thane wasn't sure he understood the plan.

David furrowed his brow and looked at Thane. He didn't want to explain himself, but if Thane didn't understand the plan, it might not work. "Lieutenant, I don't want them to know that we know where she is. We still have two spies out beyond the tree line who can report back to their leaders. They need to think we're looking at all three populations."

As an afterthought, David added, "Also map out the area to see if we can get the Surf-Ve in there."

Thane gave instructions for landing to the shuttle as it took off from retrieving Braxton. David asked Brynna to leave the shuttle and join him on the bridge. Brynna wanted to stay on the shuttle and start the rescue mission, but she knew she would be ill-prepared at this point, so she complied with David's request. Waiting was always the hardest part of a crisis.

David filled Brynna in on their status. Lexi's rescue was his responsibility, although Brynna's visibility was crucial to the success of the mission. There was still a chance of a successful mission. After he brought Brynna up to speed, they began to discuss the rescue operation. This was a difficult discussion because Lexi was Brynna's closest adviser and the security chief was piloting the shuttle at the moment.

"Are we going after her as soon as the shuttle returns?" What Brynna really wanted to say was, "We are going after the shuttle returns, aren't we?"

"I don't think we should go until morning. When I say morning though, I'm talking about sunrise."

Brynna clenched her jaw until she could respond appropriately to him. "Why wait that long?" She kept her voice calm and her sentences short. She was both angry and worried. She was angry with the people who hurt Braxton and took Lexi, but also, she was worried about Lexi's safety.

"First of all, from what we heard through the comm unit, they aren't going to hurt her, especially not tonight. Second, I think if we give them a chance to relax, they won't do anything rash and neither will we. If we rush in there too quickly, Lexi could get hurt. I'd like to go in on a diplomatic mission to bargain for her release. These people aren't morning people, it will throw them off their game if we go right at sun up."

Brynna opened her mouth to object, but David held up his hand to stop her. He went on to explain himself. "If they won't concede, I want a backup plan to get her by whatever force is necessary. We've told them we're here on a mission of peace, so I don't want our first action or reaction to be one of violence."

David and Brynna continued their discussion in David's office. Brynna took a seat at the table when they first walked in, but could not remain in her chair. She stood up and began to pace. Finally, she turned back to David, "I understand. I don't want to wait until morning to go after her, and I don't want to take 'No' for an answer, but I do see your point."

"This is what we trained for. We knew there would be difficulties. We can't let our emotions take over. We have a job to do."

Brynna sighed. "I know. I agree with you. I will support you with whatever decisions you make." She paused a minute then David her heard say something that was a cross between an ironic laugh and a moment of discovery.

David looked at her quizzically, "What is it?"

She shook her head. "I think I felt safer on Galat in the presence of our known enemy." David gave a wry smile and nodded. Brynna took a deep breath then sat back down. "So how do we convince them to give us our crewman back?"

David looked at her and the coldness he had been feeling softened just a little. He knew he was going to have to direct the crew's energy toward the tasks at hand and away from their emotions. He hoped Lexi could do the same for herself. David then redirected his own thoughts and energies, "The Akamu have a tactical advantage in those caves. They are used to the darkness, they are patient people, and they have access to an abundance of ore. There is also some volcanic activity inside those caves, so forging weapons has to be easy for them." Brynna wasn't sure where he was headed with this, but she continued to listen. "They can be warlike, but they apparently have some fears about us. They accept us as being powerful. I think we need to demonstrate our power in a non-threatening manner and let them choose to do the right thing."

"How do you propose to do that?"

"We tell them what we know, but not how we know it."

Brynna shook her head. "Just what is it we know? You told me approximately where in the caves she's located and what they were planning to do to her, but I fail to see how that helps us."

"I think we need to walk in and ask why Manton and Vesta kidnapped Lexi and why they have chosen to insult us like this."

"Insult? How is this an insult?"

"They called Lexi a slave. You clearly told them she was not and that we have no slaves. They have called you a liar, and by taking Lexi, they have shown themselves to be thieves, not warriors."

Brynna thought for a moment. "That could work, or it could start a brawl."

"It could, but from what I could tell their leader is a wise man. I think he will listen to reason."

"What is the back-up plan?"

"I want Jake to lead a team into the caves using night vision viewers and full tactical gear including deflectors. Thane can take them in via shuttle and lay down cover fire to aid their entrance and escape."

"Who do you want on the extraction team?"

"I want to wait and see how Braxton is doing to make the final determination. If he still needs medical care, that cuts our options down by two. I want Marissa riding as copilot and weapons support in the shuttle. I think Lazaro and Aulani should accompany Jake. I want Braxton and Jason with us if possible and Laura as a medical back-up in the shuttle."

"Are you sure you want five people to go in to meet with Tarin? That seems like a show of force."

"If we have to leave some of them outside, that's what we'll do, but I want them to see the look in Braxton's eyes."

"Are you really going to play a sympathy card on a warrior?"

"No, I expect him to be angry, not afraid or worried. That's what I want them to see."

Brynna just blinked at him a couple times uncertain of what to say. David saw the expression on her face and with a straight face said, "It's a guy thing." Brynna furrowed her brow, puckered her lips, and decided she didn't want to understand it any better.

After the shuttle returned, David and Brynna briefed the crew on their plans. They expected Jake to raise some sort of objection. Other than a couple questions, he complied completely with the plan. Thane was full of objections this time. Jake knew tactical operations, and he knew if they went into those caves hot, they would meet lots of resistance and even if the crew survived,

Lexi might not. Thane wanted to move in on them immediately. The Captain put down Thane's objections quickly and decisively.

Jason reported Braxton's condition was stable and with a couple more hours of treatment his concussion would be healed. He would probably still suffer from fatigue and slight headaches for another day or so, but he would be fit for duty in time for them to leave for the caves in the morning. David left two of the tactical crew on duty to watch for any activity and ordered everyone to get some sleep. He asked the doctor to give anyone who thought they might need it something light to help them sleep. When they were to get up in the early morning, the two tactical crewmen would swap out with two others to get some sleep. David and Brynna went to bed leaving Thane in command with strict orders to wake them if anything happened. David and Brynna had a device in their quarters operating on self-hypnosis and white noise principles to help them sleep. They didn't want to be under the influence of medications at a time like this, but they knew they would not be able to sleep without help. Now that a plan was in place, the crew was able to get some rest. It wasn't the best rest, but it was enough for now.

A couple of hours later, Lexi started to wake up. She felt heavy, and her mouth was dry and tasted terrible. She tried to close her mouth and realized she couldn't. She was gagged. She felt stiff and sore. She tried to move around and discovered her hands were bound behind her and her feet were also bound. She lifted her head to look around but couldn't see anything. Had they put a blindfold on her? She felt herself blink twice. No, she wasn't blindfolded, she was just in someplace so dark she couldn't see, or she been blinded by something. The darkness was so thick she could almost taste it. She heard a few sounds that seemed to be echoing around her. She could hear water dripping and what was probably somebody snoring.

Why was she awake? When Jake was hit with the poison dart, he had slept the whole night. It was still pitch dark outside, or was it? How long had she been asleep? Doc had given them all an antidote to the poison darts, maybe some of that was still in her system. She didn't have any idea. The cobwebs started to clear from her mind and she realized she was lying on some type of bedding. It felt like a cot and a couple blankets. At this point, she was faced with several immediate dilemmas. She had to assume she was in the caves because of the darkness and the echoing sounds. Trying to scream for help would probably only bring her captors and not anyone willing to help her. Not to mention, with a gag in her mouth, she wouldn't be able to get much sound out. If she tried to move from her current location without any light, she could run into something or fall off a ledge.

Memories of how she had gotten here started coming back to the forefront of her mind. Braxton was hurt! Had they killed him? Did the crew find him? Was he a prisoner too? Lexi felt a wave of panic rise up in her. She tried to resist but was finding it more and more difficult with each passing second. She decided to try something… anything. She threw her legs off the side of the cot, which helped her sit upright. Thankfully the ceiling was far enough away her head didn't hit it when she sat up. As she got upright, her feet found the floor. That was encouraging. She still had no idea which direction was the way out. There was a flashlight on her bracelet, but it wouldn't be a whole lot of help behind her and with her feet bound. She finally had an answer to her dilemma. Her first task was to get her feet untied. She lay back down on her cot and bent her knees up so her feet were just within reach of her hands. She was so stiff from being bound and carried over Manton's shoulder; it took a couple minutes for her to get into position to try and loosen the ropes on her ankles.

Before she had much of a chance to work on the knot at her ankles, she saw a hint of light and heard a scraping sound. Someone was coming toward her. Should she pretend to be asleep still or take this chance to review her surroundings? She decided to fake sleep and try to get a look around if she could when the individual turned to leave. Lexi moved her feet away from her hands into a more neutral position. Even with her eyes closed, Lexi could tell there was more light around her. She remained perfectly motionless. The raspy voice of an aged man softly spoke to her. "I know you not sleeping."

Lexi wasn't going to respond no matter what, but the words were in broken Intergalactic Standard. She had not expected anyone on this planet to speak in any recognizable language. It caught her off guard, and she opened her eyes to look at the man standing in front of her. The man had advanced age carved into his face and was stooped over from bone decalcification. The man brought a lantern into the room, which cast a small amount of light on her surroundings. The room was not much bigger than a walk-in closet. The ground was a mixture of rock and sand, it was unevenly shaped, and the walls were smooth stone. Her captors were using two large rocks to close off the entrance to her "cell." The man sat down on the edge of her cot. Lexi's heart started to race as the man got close to her. What did he want with her?

"I not hurt you. I keep you safe." The man told her. He helped her into a sitting position. "I bring you water. I take this off you. If you scream, they know you wake. You no scream?"

Lexi nodded slowly. As soon as the gag was out of her mouth, she wiggled her jaw around then closed her mouth. The man picked up a bag from his waistband and opened it. He held it up to her lips, so she could drink the water. She was so dry that she drank too quickly at first and choked. The man pulled the bag away until she caught her breath, then he allowed her to drink more. Once she had quenched her thirst and caught her breath again, she had a million questions and wanted answers.

"Who are you? Why have you brought me here? Where is my husband? Is Braxton all right? Did you hurt him? If you've hurt him..."

The old man pressed two of his fingers against her lips. He spoke slowly and softly. "I not bring you here. I sent here to protect you. You no talk about me to anyone. The Akamu not know I am here. Your man is fine. Your people get him. You listen. You not try to escape. No matter what they say, they not harm you. I not allow it. Your job not done. You stay calm and no try to escape. You not see me, but I not leave you. I must put gag back in your mouth."

"Wait, who are you? What is your name? Who sent you?" The old man put his fingers up to his own lips to silence her and then put the gag back into her mouth. She tried to object, but for an old man, he was fast, sure, and strong. He picked up his lantern and looked back at her. "My name Gabe. Stay here, your people come soon."

With that he left, taking the only light with him. Lexi heard him pushing the rocks back into place and thought if she could get free of the ropes, she could push those rocks out of her way. She struggled to pull her feet back up behind her. She could reach the ropes, but she had to do some major twisting to reach the knot. Unfortunately, her hands were swollen from having her circulation restricted, and she had trouble getting and keeping a grip on the knot. Between the fatigue, the darkness and still having the drug in her system Lexi dosed off again when she stopped to rest from trying to untie her feet.

Thane and Aulani's watch was nearly over when Aulani noticed Lexi's heart rate speed up. She immediately alerted Thane. Thane had her put the audio input from Lexi's comm unit back through the main speakers on the bridge. They heard noises indicating movement and then detected a significant rise in Lexi's heart rate. Someone was apparently in the room with her and Lexi appeared to be reacting with fear. Her heart dropped back down to a normal rate as they heard her swallow and cough. After they heard her stop drinking, they heard her ask several questions. Someone was with her. She was speaking in Intergalactic Standard. Thane and Aulani wondered if she was dazed and confused. No one on this planet knew their language. There was a period of silence, and then Lexi was asking her visitor to identify himself, or herself. There was no reply only the sound of Lexi trying to say something else but being cut off abruptly. In another few seconds, they heard the sounds of movement and a scraping sound, then nothing, but the sounds of Lexi moving around. In a few more minutes, it appeared she had either gone to sleep or passed out again. Thane and Aulani sat there in silence after the noise stopped until Aulani took the sound off the speakers. Thane had not ordered her to turn the sound off. Under the tension of the situation, he gave Aulani a startled scowl for turning it off.

Aulani gave him a sullen, "Sorry. Scans indicate she's not conscious."

Thane's scowl faded. He knew she was right. There was no reason to continue listening right now. Thane looked back at Aulani quizzically, "Who was she talking to and why was she speaking in I.S.?"

Aulani looked somewhat puzzled. "Maybe she was confused?"

Thane shook his head, "I don't think so. It sounded like someone was giving her a drink. Someone was definitely there, but maybe she was confused enough to use I.S."

"Are you going to wake the Captain?"

"No, nothing relevant has happened. I'll fill him in when he wakes up. He needs to get as much sleep as he can, right now."

In another hour, David and Brynna were up and getting ready to depart. They grabbed a basic breakfast, which consisted of coffee and meal replacement bars. Thane filled the Captain in on what had transpired earlier with Lexi. Jake and Marissa took Thane and Aulani's place on watch so they could get some sleep. David didn't expect to need them immediately. It would take the initial team nearly an hour to get to the caves. The only route available to them was a winding wagon trail made by the inhabitants. The shuttle could get them there in just a couple minutes, but that would cause too much concern. If they ended up in an emergency, they were to wake Thane and Aulani and leave them with the ship. Jake was to bring the rest of the crew with him to provide whatever support was necessary. Since the Surf-Ve was not going to be there for an hour, Jake let the rest of the crew sleep for most of that hour.

When Jason woke Braxton that morning, there were lots of questions, namely he wanted to know where his wife was and if she was okay. Jason told him briefly she was alive and well, but that was all he knew. The Captain would have to fill him in on the rest.

David gave Jake some last-minute orders. He didn't want to lose contact with Lexi. If it looked like she was going to lose her comm unit, or they were going to try and move her deeper into the caves, Jake should move in quickly.

According to their scans, the caves ran very deeply into the mountain. The mountain was a fairly dormant volcano. There were a couple of fissures at the top emitting a small, but steady flow of steam, but there was no sign of anything threatening. The scans revealed no pressure points building.

Once the diplomatic team boarded the Surf-Ve, Cheyenne drove while David and Brynna brought Braxton up to speed. They left a couple key pieces of information out because, at this point, Braxton didn't need to know. David wanted Braxton angry, not fearful and distracted. Jason had already told David if Lexi were disfigured in some way, he should be able to repair any physical damage although the emotional scars would be permanent. David saw no reason to worry Braxton any more than he already was.

The Captain and Commander told Braxton he needed to let them handle the negotiations, but he wasn't to be afraid to show his anger. Braxton was not in the mood to play political games. David assured him, they weren't going to take "No," for an answer. He also encouraged Braxton to go with his feelings of anger.

When the crew arrived at the main entrance to the caves, the sun had just crested over the horizon. The guards posted at the entrances along the side of the mountain had been up all night and were ready for some sleep. When the crew pulled up, it gave them a second wind. David approached the nearest guard and told him plainly via his translator, "We need to see Tarin immediately." The guard was not quite sure how to react. David was used to the confusion his bracelet caused and was frequently amused by it, but not today. David had not given an order to the guard, nor had he asked a question. The guard expected either, not the statement of a "need." After a brief moment of being flustered, the guard called to another guard above him and passed the message to him. The guard disappeared inside. The first guard stayed in front of David and watched him and the rest of the crew who were still seated in the Surf-Ve anxiously.

As word began to spread inside the caves, curious onlookers started poking their heads out of the caves to look at the large, horse-less wagon. They also wanted to see the odd clothing of the crew. Several bleary-eyed children gathered several hundred feet above them until one of the guards chased them back inside. In a few minutes, the guard who had taken the message inside came back and spoke to the guard standing nearest to David. David's translator didn't pick up the comment, but he wasn't worried about it. The guard approached David and glanced nervously down at David's bracelet. Instead of passing the message along he simply motioned for David to follow him. David, in turn, motioned for the others to accompany him. The guard saw the other four crewmen following and stopped. He motioned for them to stay where they were. David stepped between the guard and his crew. "I told you we needed to see Tarin. Did you give him the wrong message?" The guard was still afraid to speak. He looked down at David's bracelet again and shook his head. "The bracelet will not harm you. You are obviously a strong warrior. You have nothing to fear from a piece of jewelry, and surely you have more than five guards to protect your leader. Why do you hesitate to obey your leader?"

David touched several nerves with the guard. His words suggested the warrior might be incompetent or even ignorant. A warrior was not supposed to be afraid and certainly not afraid of a piece of jewelry. He also indicated the guard would be disobeying orders if he didn't take the entire group in to see his leader. The guard called to several of the others to accompany them into the caves. David had no intention of starting an altercation, so he wasn't worried about the extra guards… for now.

Lexi woke up to someone shaking her and speaking harshly. As her eyes started to focus, she saw Manton and Vesta. They untied her hands and pointed to her bracelet. Lexi massaged her wrists and hands briefly then turned on her translator. Vesta removed the gag from her mouth and Lexi promptly asked, "Why have you brought me here? What do you want?"

Vesta slapped Lexi across the face and shouted at her, "Do not speak until you have been spoken to, Slave." A wave of anger welled up inside her. She started to respond but thought better of it since her feet were still bound. Vesta threw some clothing at Lexi and ordered her to change her clothes.

Manton carried in a bucket, so she could relieve herself, a bowl of water for her to clean herself up and some bread and cheese to eat. If Lexi had not been in such a foul mood, she might have found it amusing they were serving their new "slave." After Vesta gave Lexi her instructions, she left the room. Manton untied her feet and turned to leave the room also. Lexi took the opportunity to kick his feet out from under him. Manton landed on his knees then rolled toward the door before he stood up again. In the same instant, he pulled a dagger from his belt and had it pointed at Lexi's throat. He grabbed Lexi by the hair and forced her onto her knees. The pain in her scalp caused her to want to grab her head, but she knew it was a bad tactical move. She forced her hands to reach out to the hand holding the dagger to try to push it away from her. This move was making Manton nervous. He had less control of his dagger. It was still pointed at her throat, but if she moved suddenly, it could cause any number of unwanted outcomes. Manton pulled her head back away from the dagger then threw her to the ground. Lexi tried to roll to regain her footing. Manton was ready for her this time. He planted his foot quickly and firmly on her back. Leaning over he placed the dagger again next to her neck. "You ever try to strike me again and I will beat you until you beg for mercy, Slave. Take your clothes off and place them and your shoes by the door. Put on the clothing Vesta gave you. If you cannot follow my orders, I will cut your clothes off you myself. You may keep your bracelet until you learn our language."

Manton took his foot off her and moved toward the door, but this time he didn't turn his back on her. As soon as he was gone Lexi felt tears start to roll down her face. No matter how hard she tried, she couldn't force them to stop. She was tired, sore, scared, angry, frustrated, and alone. Suddenly she remembered Gabe's words, "I not leave you." As soon as the words entered her mind, a sense of comfort washed over her. She wasn't sure why, because he had also said he wouldn't allow them to hurt her. Her face was still stinging from Vesta's slap and her scalp hurt from Manton grabbing her hair. She felt a couple new bruises from being thrown to the ground. Gabe did tell her not to try and escape. Maybe this had been his way of trying to protect her. In either case, she decided it would be best to comply until the Captain got her out of this mess. She certainly didn't want Manton to come back and change her outfit for her. She changed quickly, washed up a bit, and ate the food they had left for her. The rebellious nature in her didn't want to do any of it, especially not eat their food. You never eat your enemy's food, but she knew if she got the chance to escape she would need her strength. After she finished eating she tried her best to move the stones by the entrance. She couldn't budge either of them. How had Gabe moved them? She used the lantern Manton and Vesta had left behind to thoroughly explore her surroundings, looking for anything that could be used as a weapon. There was nothing, not even a rock or stone. Lexi took a chance and activated her comm unit to try and reach the ship. She wasn't sure how far away she was and what the mineral content might be in the caverns.

"*Evangeline*, this is Lexi, are you receiving me?"

There were several seconds of silence; then she heard Jake's voice. "Lexi, this is Jake. We are receiving you. The Captain is near you trying to negotiate your release so sit tight for now. We've been monitoring you since last night. Are you all right?"

Before Lexi could respond, she heard noises at the door. She whispered quickly and quietly, "I'm fine for now. Someone's coming." She switched the comm unit back into translation mode. Lexi sat there on the edge of her cot to wait for whatever came next. She didn't want to give up her clothes. The outfit they had given her was a plain dingy tunic that came almost down to her knees. It didn't have a hem or a collar or even sleeves. The material was somewhat thick and heavy which was a plus; otherwise, Lexi would have gotten cold quickly. She especially didn't like the idea of giving up her boots. She would be better able to defend herself with her boots on.

Vesta started to come into her cell, but Manton called her back. She could hear them talking softly. Manton came back in, threw Lexi down on the cot, and rolled her onto her stomach. He pulled her arms behind her and started to tie her up again. Lexi called out for Manton to stop. She begged him to tie her hands in front of her. Manton stopped. Lexi rolled slightly so she could see his face. Tears were running down her face again. "Please." She sobbed. "If you must tie my hands, can you please tie them in front of me? I can't use my translator if it's behind me." Manton considered her request. His face still showed reluctance. Lexi offered one more plea, "I won't try to escape again. I give you my word. I'm not strong enough to move the stones from the door, and I won't attack you or Vesta. Please leave my hands in front of me. Please." Lexi wasn't as distraught as she appeared to be, but she knew if she appeared to be giving up, he might drop his guard. Manton relented, but he warned her not to break her word, or she would regret it. Manton finished tying her hands in front of her then got up to leave. He reached down to pick up her clothing on his way out.

Lexi sat back up and asked Manton, "May I please ask a question?" Manton stopped in the doorway holding her clothing. He looked back over his shoulder and nodded. Lexi stood up and asked, "Why did you bring me here?"

Manton looked down for a moment as though he were embarrassed or ashamed then his demeanor changed to one of confidence. "Vesta cannot have children. You are going to bear my children for her, and you will be her personal slave until we no longer have need of you. We have promised the gods to return you to them if they will give us children through you."

Lexi felt a wave of panic well up inside her. She quickly quashed the wave by reminding herself the Captain was nearby trying to get her back. She tried to regain a small amount of control. "I can't give you children. The Commonwealth has prevented us from having children for two years."

Manton turned around to face her. "That will be too bad for you then. As long as you are bearing children, we will keep you alive. If you are not with child by this time next year, we will sacrifice you to the gods. Maybe then they will allow Vesta to have a child."

Manton turned to leave. As he closed the stone door, Lexi shouted at him, "There are no gods. They are a myth. They won't help you."

Lexi lay down on her cot and began to cry for real this time. This was the one thing all women feared. Lexi rolled over to face the wall when she suddenly heard Gabe's voice repeating what he had said to her earlier, "No matter what they say, they not harm you. I not allow it. Your job not done. You stay calm and no try to escape. You not see me, but I not leave you." Lexi rolled over to look at him. She had not heard the door open, which was surprising because it was not a quiet thing to move those rocks. Gabe wasn't there. She was still entirely alone in her cell. Lexi didn't know if she was remembering what he said or if she had really heard his voice. In either case, it interrupted her thoughts and gave her a chance to realize this wasn't the time for self-pity. She was an officer in the Commonwealth Interstellar Force and needed to act like one. She dried her tears and washed her face again, then contacted the ship to find out what was happening.

Jake was relieved to hear from her again because when she had shut her comm unit off earlier, it blocked them from listening temporarily. They were putting in the reactivation sequence, but it had not been completed yet. Jake filled her in on the Captain's plan. Lexi smiled to herself. The Captain may not have a degree in psychology, but he did have a good set of people skills. It seemed to come naturally to him. Lexi felt a degree of pride rising up in her although she knew she wasn't responsible for the Captain's abilities. She was at the very least proud to serve under him.

Lexi started reviewing possible scenarios in her mind to see if there was anything she could add to the plan. At Jake's request, Lexi set her comm unit to transmit and to translate audibly and locked it in place. She also turned off all visible screen notifications and lights so it would appear inactive. Lexi was extremely grateful she was able to convince Manton to tie her hands in front of her this time instead of behind her. Jake gave her one last consolation, "Lexi, we know why they took you, and if things... well, let me just say, I know when to stop monitoring."

Lexi knew he was trying to make sure she had a certain amount of dignity if Manton carried out his intentions. Lexi remained quiet for a moment considering the impact of his words then responded, "Thanks, Jake."

Once outside her cell, Vesta cornered Manton. "Why did you send me away from the slave's cell?"

Manton tried to brush her off. "I just wanted to make sure she was tied up again."

Vesta wasn't going to be put off so easily. She knew something was bothering him. "Do you think I am incapable of tying up a slave? Why did you want her tied up again anyway? She can't move those stones to get away."

Manton scowled at her. He knew she wouldn't accept anything, but the full reason. He had never been any good at keeping his thoughts and feelings from his mate. Somehow, she seemed to always see into his very soul. He also knew if he didn't convince her, she might make a costly mistake with Lexi and allow her to escape. "I think they may have been telling the truth about the woman not being a slave."

"What do you mean? She served us, and her own people."

"When I untied her, she attacked me. I just didn't want her to hurt you."

"A seasoned slave will sometimes fight to get back to her own master."

Manton shook his head. "It wasn't like that. She fights like a trained warrior. She knocked me off my feet."

Manton could see anger welling up in Vesta. Vesta started past him. "I'll make her pay for that."

Manton grabbed her arm and stopped her. "Tarin said not to touch her. They have advanced weapons, if we harm her and Tarin tries to return her to them, they could destroy us for hurting her."

Vesta glared at him for a minute then jerked her arm from his grasp and turned away from the cell. In doing so, she managed to run straight into a child who was running through the passage. The child bounced off her landing on his backside. Vesta glowered at him, then seeing the stunned look on the child's face her mood softened. She reached down, helped him to his feet and brushed the dirt off his backside. "Where are you going in such a hurry? You know you aren't supposed to run in the passages."

"I was going to get my sister. I saw the Sky People come into the caves to see Tarin." The boy trotted on down the passage and turned toward his family's dwelling area.

Vesta and Manton looked at each other debating what to do. Manton finally said, "They may just be looking for her. There is no way they could know she's here. We should go to greet our guests. We were part of the greeting party so it would raise questions if we didn't show up."

Vesta nodded, "You're probably right." They made their way to one of the larger open caverns where their gatherings were held. Vesta was silent for most of the walk, but just before they entered, she spoke one more time. "Manton, I don't want to give her up. I want to give you children."

Manton reached up and caressed her cheek and said, "I know. We'll find a way to fix this." The two tried to look nonchalant as they entered the cavern.

The cavern was large and open with a cathedral type ceiling. Several fissures were opening to the outsides allowing light to enter and smoke from torches and cooking fires to escape. David entered the cavern first followed by Brynna, Cheyenne,

Braxton, and finally Jason. It took several seconds for their eyes to adjust to the darkness. Despite the vented ceiling, the air was still smoky, and the crew's eyes burned. They reflexively coughed until they grew accustomed to the thick air. Leading them to the center of the room, the guard told them to wait. People began gathering in from all sides. The cavern had entrances and exits on several levels. In the center of the cavern, seats were strategically placed around a fire ring. The two largest were side by side, and as the seats progressed around the circle, they became smaller and less ornate.

David saw Manton and Vesta enter and take their places near the larger seats in the circle. A couple other men entered and took seats further around the circle. Jake piped into David and Brynna's earpieces and let them know he had talked to Lexi. David discreetly thanked Jake for the update. It wasn't easy because although Jake could talk to the Captain without anyone else knowing, the Captain had to verbalize his responses. In a moment, a man followed by a woman and Adan entered the cavern and took their places in the circle. The man took the largest chair, and the woman took the second largest which was to his right. Adan took the chair to the left.

As yet, they had not officially met Tarin, but David and Brynna knew from their previous meeting with the Akamu, Tarin was the leader of the Akamu people. The crew also knew of his involvement with Lexi's abduction. He hadn't taken part in it, but he hadn't done anything to correct the situation.

David and the rest of the crew were standing several yards outside the ring housing of the ruling body of the Akamu. Once everyone was seated Tarin nodded to the guard to bring David and the others to the opposite end of the ring. David and the others entered the ring. There were four large rectangular rocks at the end of the ring where David and the others entered, presumably for sitting on. Since there were five crew members, someone would have to stand. The guard motioned for them to be seated then he stepped a discreet, but ready distance away from the circle. David stood directly between two of the rocks. Brynna and Cheyenne sat to his right and Braxton and Jason to his left. The Captain didn't want to transgress against any cultural taboos or cause any ill will by displaying an angry stance, but he wasn't sure it was going to make much difference at this point. He also thought perhaps if he and Brynna gave a "good cop" vs. "bad cop" routine it would provide the Akamu a way out of this difficult situation. David quietly relayed his intentions through the comm unit, bypassing the translation of course.

Adan began the dialogue by welcoming them and introducing them to Tarin. Tarin took over once he had been introduced. "Welcome to our home. This is my chief adviser and my wife Gaia, she is also an able warrior. You already know Adan, Manton, and Vesta. These others are also able warriors and advisers to me, Caius, Iresh, and Akish." Tarin looked at David. Since David had chosen his strategy, he started glaring at Tarin and taking on a more defiant posture. Tarin was not comfortable with David. He had been told Brynna led negotiations, so he looked to her to continue. "I know you are unfamiliar with our customs, so I will overlook your mistakes, but it is not customary for guards to be present within the ring of leadership. If you could send your guard outside the ring, we can talk."

Brynna wasn't terribly comfortable with the "good cop" routine, so she was a bit hesitant. She glanced at David who looked down at her and nodded. Brynna looked back at Tarin and tried to look confused. "Whom are you referring to? We didn't bring any guards."

Tarin was not amused. He wanted David out of his direct line of sight. "The guard who stands at your side."

Brynna looked back at David. This time David didn't return her glance, but he continued to glare at Tarin. Brynna took a deep breath then looked back at Tarin. "I'm sorry Tarin, but this is not a guard. This is my commanding officer and my mate. He commands our ship and is responsible for the safety of all our crew members."

Tarin leaned over to Adan and whispered something. Adan looked lost and confused. He nervously glanced back at the crew and whispered something back to Tarin. Tarin looked back at the crew but was angry this time. "Why have you lied to my people?"

Brynna replied to him. "We have not lied to you. Our ship has two teams on board, one is a diplomatic team, and the other team runs the ship. Each team provides support to the other. My team helps pilot the ship, and his team provides support to my diplomatic missions. Ultimately, my husband, Captain David Alexander has the final say for both teams, but we work together."

"I see. Why does he appear to be angry?"

David stepped forward one step, which was enough to bring Tarin's guard closer to the circle. Tactically the odds were not good despite their superior weapons, so David didn't want to start anything, but he did want to make his point. "I am angry because I have a small crew. There are exactly six men and six women who have been carefully selected because of their specific skills to go on this mission. I am angry because you have allowed two of your people to interfere in these negotiations by taking one of our most trusted advisers and the wife of this crew member," David pointed at Braxton who stood up, "to be a slave. I am also angry because you have allowed two of your people to call us liars and have shown yourselves to be thieves."

By this time Tarin was angry and was now on his feet. Adan was confused because he knew nothing about Lexi. Manton and Vesta were scared, but since Tarin was on his feet, they stood as well. The rest of the ruling council joined Tarin slowly. The council members were all equally confused about what was transpiring. Brynna stood up and moved in front of David turning her back to the council. She appeared to be quietly calming him down and coaxing him to sit in her seat. He slowly sat down. Braxton remained standing until Brynna spoke softly to him. Once the two men were again seated, Brynna turned to face Tarin. "May we discuss this calmly?"

Tarin, still glaring at David, retorted. "He called us thieves and liars. If he would like to apologize, I will consider it."

"Tarin, he will gladly apologize... once Manton and Vesta return our crew member to us. She cannot bear children for them. Our mission is a long one, and our ship is small, so the Commonwealth has taken steps to prevent any of us from having children. She cannot help them."

Tarin's glare moved from David to Manton and Vesta. Brynna continued, "When your party came to our ship the other day, they mistakenly thought Lexi was a slave because she served drinks to them. I told them, we do not have slaves. By taking her to be a slave, Manton and Vesta have called us liars. We are the ones who have been insulted. Return her to her husband and the matter will be forgotten. We can continue our negotiations."

Tarin looked back at Brynna. "Why do you believe your crew member is here? The Sorley are notorious for taking slaves. What few slaves we have, we bought from the Sorley."

Brynna hoped she could pull this next part off. "Our ship is capable of seeing movements from a great distance. You put two men at the edge of the trees by our ship the day your people came to talk to us. They have remained there watching our people ever since. We know Lexi is being held in a cavern in that direction... and why." Brynna pointed in the general direction of Lexi's cell. "We also know, you were told she is there, Tarin. You wisely told them not to harm her, for which we are very grateful."

Tarin got up from his seat again and paced back and forth. David stood slowly. His posture was no longer defiant. He took a couple steps toward Tarin and spoke kindly. "Tarin, look at your wife." Gaia had been silent the whole time. She was not sure how to take this sudden attention by these impertinent outsiders. Tarin looked at her as David requested. She was a beautiful woman and a good warrior. She had given him five strong children. He was proud to have such a good woman. David gave him a moment to gaze at his wife before he continued to speak. "I can tell by the way you look at her, you care very deeply for her. Braxton looks on his wife the same way, and he hurts very badly right now. How much would you hurt if the Sorley had taken Gaia? What would you do to get her back if she were taken from you?"

Tarin turned around abruptly to look at David. Was David threatening his wife? The look on David's face was not threatening at all. It showed only care and concern. Tarin returned to his seat. "Wait outside. I need to talk to my council alone."

David searched his eyes for some sign of what the leader was thinking. He couldn't see anything, except a blank stare. David nodded at the crew to move to the exit. The crew stepped away as ordered. As they moved back outside, the sun blinded them again for a few seconds. David contacted Jake to let him know their progress. Jake asked if he should head in to pull Lexi out. David had him wait for now. He didn't think they were done with their negotiations. The Captain also asked Jason if he had been able to get any scans of Manton or Vesta. If they could find out what was wrong with them, the Doc might be able to correct it so they could have children of their own instead of using a surrogate. Jason had been too far away for the scanner to pick up sufficient information. His scanner basically picked up their heart rates and very little else.

Once the crew was gone, the council began to discuss what had just happened. Adan and the others were angry at the accusations and started to express themselves. Tarin let them blow off steam for a minute then he held up his hand for silence. Adan defied Tarin's call for silence, "How can you sit there and ignore their insults? They have insulted you, Manton and Vesta. Manton, how can you and Vesta sit there and say nothing?" Then it dawned in on Adan. Manton and Vesta were guilty. They had taken Lexi, and Tarin knew about it. Adan looked at Manton and Vesta, guilt was written blatantly across their faces. Adan looked back at Tarin, "They did this, didn't they? You knew about it too."

Tarin stood up and looked at his wife and mulled over David's words. He then looked at Adan and the other council members. "Yes, Manton and Vesta have the woman. They told me about it late last night. They have given an oath to the gods to sacrifice her to them once she gives them children."

Adan's face went pale. "We can never tell them she is here then. They cannot break an oath to the gods. We will all suffer for it if they do."

Tarin glowered at him, "They KNOW she's here already. If we don't give her to them, we will suffer their wrath, if we do we will suffer the wrath of the gods."

"Which is worse?" Caius had been quiet until now.

Iresh answered him, "Both are powerful. We will suffer no matter what."

Akish stood up angrily and looked at Manton and Vesta, "What have you done to us?"

Gaia spoke softly, "Tarin, I think we should give them their slave back then decide how best to appease the gods. The Sky People can bring their wrath here and now. The gods may forgive us for the rashness of Manton and Vesta's actions."

Caius added, "I agree, give them their slave back."

Manton looking down at the ground said, "She's no slave. She is trained as a warrior."

Tarin looked at Manton even angrier than before. "You took a warrior as a slave? There is no greater insult. Did you think the gods would reward you for such a sacrifice by giving you my place of leadership?"

It was Manton's turn to pale. "No, Tarin, I didn't know until this morning. I untied her, and she attacked me with the skill of a warrior. I overpowered her, but she is a trained warrior. I didn't mean to bring destruction on our people. I'm sorry."

"It is settled then. We will return her to her people then we will find a way to appease the gods." Tarin said with an air of finality.

Vesta jumped to her feet, "No! You can't do this to us."

Tarin turned to face her. He walked directly up to her and spoke, "I suggest you adjust your tone or I will appease the gods by giving them you and Manton. It would be well deserved and a proper atonement for my part in this travesty."

Vesta bowed her head to show her submission to his leadership and said softly, "My apologies Tarin. I am sorry for my transgressions."

Tarin moved away from her, "You are forgiven. Leave my sight while I decide how to appease the gods. Vesta retreated hastily.

Manton quietly spoke in his wife's defense, "Tarin, please don't be too harsh with her. She just wants to bear a child so badly."

Tarin cast a harsh glance in his direction but said nothing. Manton sat down quietly. Tarin sat down again having the look of a man who was beaten. "So how do we appease the gods? They were promised a sacrifice and the sacrifice of a strong woman at that. Do we have any other slaves that might meet the criteria of the sacrifice?"

Iresh looked at Manton, "No, all our slaves are old and weak. We need to buy new slaves. I still like the idea of sacrificing Vesta and Manton." Manton and Iresh glared at each other.

After several more minutes of arguing, Gaia spoke up again. "Perhaps the Sky People can help. They have been many places and seen many things. Maybe they know what will please the gods."

Manton spoke up again, "The woman we have, said there are no gods."

Caius countered, "I don't think it would hurt anything to ask them. They have offered to help us. Let them demonstrate their ability to help now."

A murmur of approval moved around the circle. Tarin seeing a consensus said, "So be it. Bring the Sky People back in."

When the crew came back in, they found a fifth rock so all of them could sit this time. Animal skins had been placed on the stones to pad their seats. Cheyenne gave the skins a skittish glance then looked over at Brynna. Brynna gave her a look that said, "Sit!" Cheyenne sat, gingerly, on the edge of the pelt-covered rock. David and Brynna immediately noticed Vesta's absence. They hoped it meant she was retrieving Lexi.

Tarin addressed David, Brynna, and Braxton. "I wish to apologize to you. We do have your crew member. Manton and Vesta acted rashly in their desire to have children. We will return her to you unharmed, but we ask for your help in return."

The crew felt relieved. Brynna took a deep breath, glanced at David then replied, "Thank you. We would be glad to help you. What do you need help with?"

Tarin explained to the crew his people feared the wrath of the gods for releasing their sacrifice back to the crew. Brynna wasn't sure what to say. David was just as unsure. Brynna finally decided on an appropriate response. "I have been to many worlds and have not seen any gods, so I have little knowledge on the matter, but perhaps I can offer a possible solution. If I understand you correctly, Manton and Vesta offered Lexi to the gods, if the gods would first give them children. The gods have not yet given them children, so your gods have not fulfilled the contract. Therefore, no breach has occurred. I do not think your gods could be angry if they were supposed to fulfill their part first. I may be able to offer Manton and Vesta another alternative. Our doctor may be able to find out why they have been unable to have children and heal them. They will need to come back to our ship for a little while, but we promise no harm will come to them."

Tarin looked at Manton. Manton looked like he was afraid to hope for this possibility. Tarin finally responded. "You are a wise woman. Your answer has merit. If we sacrifice Lexi to you, the Sky People, then it is only fitting you be the ones to give Manton and Vesta children. I will give Manton and Vesta to do with as you please. They have harmed you, and if you wish to give them to gods of the skies, or if you wish to heal them and return them to us, their fate is in your hands."

While Tarin was speaking, Jake hailed the Captain privately. As soon as his message was complete, David stood up quickly and asked, "What is Vesta doing with Lexi? Where is she taking her?"

Tarin had a blank look on his face. He glanced over at Vesta's empty seat. He had ordered her out of the room, but he had not recalled her. Tarin looked at Manton. Manton knew what Tarin was thinking, and he also suspected what Vesta was doing. Manton suddenly felt and looked terrified.

Tarin stood up, still focusing his attention on Manton, "What is Vesta doing with the woman?"

Manton looked down at the ground then back up at Tarin, "I am afraid she is going to sacrifice her in hopes the gods will allow her to bear children herself instead of through a slave. I'm sorry Tarin. I didn't think she would go this far."

After Vesta was ordered to leave the council chamber, she felt angry and disgraced. She headed back to her own cavern, but as she neared the cell holding Lexi, she decided the gods were causing her to suffer for her lack of faith. She should have sacrificed Lexi to them immediately. The two stones blocking the doorway to Lexi's chamber were held in place by wooden braces like a wheel chock. The stones were heavy, but they rolled easily when the chocks were removed. Vesta moved them out of the way and entered Lexi's cell. Lexi was sitting on her cot when she heard Vesta coming in. Lexi saw the murderous look on her face. She didn't want to give Vesta a reason to attack her, so she kept her questions to herself. She was hoping the angry look meant Vesta was being forced to let her go. Vesta picked up the rope that had previously tied Lexi's feet. When Vesta wrapped it around the ropes on Lexi's wrists like a tether line, Lexi got scared.

The frightened lieutenant decided to risk speaking. "I promised Manton I wouldn't try to escape. Vesta, what are you doing?" Surprisingly, Vesta didn't strike her. She did pick up the gag and tied it tightly back in her mouth. Lexi tried to object. She decided maybe it was time to fight back. As soon as she resisted, Vesta pulled a blade from her waistband. She held it to Lexi's throat and said, "If you fight me, I will kill you here and then give your body to the mountain gods, or you can live to walk to meet them."

Lexi decided to walk. Every minute she could stay alive meant another minute the Captain and Jake would have to rescue her. She did her best to slow Vesta down. She knew Jake had been listening to everything.

Jake had heard and was watching the location of her comm unit move further inward, deep into the depths of the mountain. Their scans had detected a couple of lava pools deep under the mountain. This seemed to be their intended destination. Jake passed on the information to the Captain as quickly as he could and continued to give him updates as he had them. He also gave Lexi a quick private message to let her know the Captain was on his way.

As soon as the council knew where the two women were headed, Tarin sounded an alarm meant to clear the passages of all unnecessary traffic. It was a horn of sorts, and the sound resonated deep into the mountain passages. The only problem with it was Vesta heard it too. She knew it was being blown because of her. Lexi didn't know exactly what it meant, but when Vesta picked up their pace abruptly, she figured it out.

Lexi waited for a few more steps then purposefully tripped and landed on the ground. It would only buy her a few seconds, but every little bit would help. Vesta pulled Lexi to her feet and decided to push her forward using the tip of her dagger as an incentive instead of pulling her by the rope. Lexi gathered the slack in her tether up into her hands for whatever use she might decide on later. With Vesta's blade at her back, Lexi couldn't do much to slow down. While she walked, Lexi managed to tie the end of the rope into a slipknot. She wasn't sure when and where she could use the rope, but she was ready should the moment present itself.

●●●

Once Tarin blew the horn, he led David and the crew deep into the mountain passages. Jake warned David this could be a trap. David told Jake not to risk any other lives if it was a trap.

Jake was to take the ship and leave if they didn't return by nightfall. Tarin's council members went with the crew. They made good time moving through the caverns. Tarin advised David to intersperse his people with his own. The crew was unfamiliar with the caverns. Tarin's people knew when to duck under a low ceiling and where to watch their footing. David agreed they could move faster this way.

As Vesta and Lexi reached an open area deep in the mountain, they could hear the distant echoes of runners approaching. This area was much warmer than the rest of the caves. Lexi soon saw why. Vesta pushed Lexi near a ledge. As she looked over the edge, she saw a pool of lava about fifty feet below her bubbling and steaming.

Vesta called out to the "god of the mountain." "Mountain gods, I bring you a fine gift, a strong young slave. Now grant me my greatest desire." As Vesta prayed to the god of the mountain, Lexi was able to work the gag out of her mouth. Vesta pushed her closer to the edge.

Lexi stopped walking voluntarily even with the dagger pressing against her. She turned to face Vesta, "There are no gods in this mountain! They cannot help you because they aren't real. Our doctor might be able to help you." Vesta held her dagger in her right hand and pulled her arm across her body intending to backhand Lexi with the hilt of the dagger. Lexi poised to protect herself, but the search party reached the cavern just before Vesta could strike Lexi. Vesta decided a different course of action was required. She lowered her dagger causing Lexi to lower her guard and look toward the ones coming into the cavern. Vesta was waiting for just this very thing. She grabbed Lexi by her hair and pulled her directly in front of her holding the dagger to Lexi's throat.

Tarin was the first one into the cavern. "Vesta! Release the woman! She is a warrior of the Sky People, not a slave. The Sky People have promised to help you have children and keep the gods from being angry with us."

"No, Tarin, I promised the gods a sacrifice. This is my last chance."

"No, Vesta, release her or I will run you through myself, and you will never have children."

Vesta was slowly inching the two of them closer to the ledge. The Akamu warriors, David, and Braxton moved into a semi-circle around the two women.

Braxton moved in closer to them and began to plead with Vesta. "Please give me my wife. We would like to have children someday ourselves."

Vesta adjusted her grip on Lexi and pulled more tightly on her hair. She pointed the dagger toward Braxton and shouted angrily, "She said she couldn't have children!"

Braxton looked around helplessly. It was the truth, and he doubted he could lie convincingly to her.

Jason stepped forward. "That is true, to a degree, but she can have children later. Before we left, the Commonwealth..." Birth control was not an easy concept for such a backward society. After pausing to phrase things carefully, Jason began again, "The Commonwealth gave us medicines to prevent us from having children for the next two years. We have other medicines to reverse the process if we want children before that time. I can probably help you to have children with Manton. Let me try, please."

Vesta thought about his words. She had moved her dagger to face Jason. Finally, she spoke, "You aren't sure you can help. I know the gods can." Vesta started moving her dagger back toward Lexi. Lexi chose this as her moment to toss her slipknot over the dagger, which slid all the way down to Vesta's wrist. In trying to shake it off, Lexi elbowed Vesta in the ribs. Vesta released her grip on Lexi's hair. Lexi grabbed the hand holding the dagger then backed Vesta into a large stalagmite. The two women lost their footing. Both went over the ledge, one on either side of the stalagmite. Lexi heard Braxton cry out her name. She heard the Captain and the two women cry out.

Vesta heard Manton call out her name. Lexi looked to her side and saw Vesta suspended by the tether she had tied the slipknot in. The tightness of the rope on Vesta's wrist caused her to drop her dagger. The two of them were balanced against each other around the stalagmite on the ledge. Although Vesta was hanging by her one arm, she was determined to rid herself of Lexi. She pulled another small knife from her belt and tried to reach Lexi's bonds to cut the ropes off her. Lexi pulled a foot up and kicked Vesta squarely in the stomach causing her to drop the knife. A half second later, Braxton and Tarin's faces appeared over the ledge. They each grabbed one of Lexi's arms to pull her up. Vesta looked up to see Manton and David trying to pull her up. Vesta looked up at Manton with tears in her eyes. "Please, just cut the rope and let me go to the mountain gods. I cannot live if I cannot give you children."

Manton reached his hand out to her and said, "And I cannot live without you. Give me your hand. We cannot face the judgment of the mountain gods until we have paid for the crimes we have committed. Tarin has agreed to turn us over to the Sky People to face their justice. We must face it with honor like a true warrior. Please give me your hand."

Tarin and Braxton were waiting on Vesta to give her free hand to Manton because if they attempted to pull Lexi up, it would cause Vesta to fall further down. No matter how distraught she was, Vesta would not dishonor the warrior's code. She lifted her free hand up and grabbed onto Manton's arm. The others held onto the four men's legs to give them a longer reach and greater stability. Together they pulled the two women to safety. Once Lexi was lifted onto the ledge, Tarin handed his knife to Braxton so he could cut her bonds. Tarin had two reasons for not cutting her bonds himself. One, it was only fitting a husband be responsible for saving his wife and two, Lexi had been through enough. He didn't want her to think he might harm her further. David did exactly the opposite. He pulled his own knife and cut the rope from Vesta's wrist. It was his way of saying her life belongs to him now.

While Jason scanned Lexi for injuries, Tarin approached David cautiously. "I have returned her to you. Will you still help us?"

"I am a warrior and a man of my word. Let us see what we can do to help Manton and Vesta, and we will return them to you unharmed along with all the other help we can give you."

"If you do as you say, you will have our loyalty as requested."

Lexi wanted to thank Tarin for helping to save her life. Braxton still had his arm around her. He escorted her to Tarin and introduced him to her. "Tarin, I am grateful you saved my life."

Tarin bowed his head and apologized to her. "Please forgive me for allowing this to happen to you. When Manton told me what he had done last night, I should have returned you to your people immediately. I'm glad Vesta did not harm you."

"What's going to happen to them?"

"I have turned them over to your Captain to deal with as he pleases."

The others had already made their way into the passages except for David, Jason, and Gaia. Tarin pointed toward the passage he had used when they arrived, "This is the best way out."

Lexi started to head that direction then stopped again, "Is there any chance?" She stopped speaking for a moment. She felt a little foolish for asking. Tarin looked at her puzzled. He wondered if the machine on her wrist was broken because her question made no sense to him. "Is there any chance for what?"

"Is there any chance I could get my clothes back?"

Tarin looked at Gaia. Gaia smiled. Apparently, even women from the skies were particular about their clothes. Gaia told Tarin, "I will see if Manton and Vesta still have them and return them to her."

Lexi smiled, "Thanks. I really liked that outfit." Lexi had been wearing civilian clothes and not her uniform. It was her favorite outfit. She had been in a relaxed and romantic mood the previous evening, and the outfit had suited her mood perfectly. It was both comfortable and attractive which was a rare combination in women's clothing. Gaia headed quickly through the passages to find Manton and Vesta.

Adan led the entire group through the winding passages straight outside. He didn't think they needed to stop back in the meeting hall and he was reasonably certain the Sky People wanted to get back to their own home. Once outside, David ordered

Manton and Vesta into the back of the Surf-Ve. Cheyenne got into the driver's seat, and Brynna took the co-pilot's chair. The others sat in the middle seats of the vehicle. David put himself and Jason between Lexi and her captors as a safety barrier. He didn't expect any trouble, but he also wasn't going to risk it.

Just before they started up the engine to leave Gaia came running out to them with Lexi's clothes in hand. As Gaia handed them to Lexi, tears began to well up in her eyes. It wasn't the clothes that brought Lexi to tears. The return of her clothing represented the end of a frightening event in her life. She had been running on Adrenalin and holding back the majority of her emotions since the point where her clothing had been taken away from her. Now the fear and the anger came flooding back. Braxton held her tightly and kept assuring her everything was okay now. His heart began to break seeing her so upset. Jason moved to give her a sedative. Lexi promptly refused it. "No, Jason, I don't want it. I just need to cry for a while. I'll be all right. Just leave me alone for now."

David and Brynna promised to send a party back to Tarin to work with the Akamu and complete their negotiations. David wanted time to work with Manton and Vesta to earn their trust before sending them back home. Tarin agreed and apologized again to David. Tarin also wished blessings from his gods on David and his crew. David cordially thanked him. Although he had no confidence in those blessings, he knew Tarin did.

Once back at the ship, everyone hugged Lexi and welcomed her back. Lexi was happy for the warm welcome because it helped to dry her tears. After a thorough exam by Dr. Adams, Lexi was able to go back to her quarters and be alone. The first thing she wanted to do was take a hot bath and get rid of that awful tunic. Braxton brought her a hot meal from the dining hall. She ate every bite, despite having eaten the bread and cheese earlier that morning. She was sore and bruised from her ordeal, but because of the tranquilizer they used on her, she had slept well. She wasn't sleepy at all. She decided the next thing she wanted to do was go to the gym and punch the life out of a punching bag.

Jake happened to be escorting his prisoners to the Med Bay, and they saw Lexi taking her vengeance out on the punching bag.

Jake, looking at Manton and Vesta said, "Be glad she's not taking her frustrations out on you." He took a small amount of pleasure in the wide-eyed looks appearing on both their faces.

Jake brought the couple into the Med Bay where Jason set them up on scanning beds to do a full body scan. Manton and Vesta knew their fate was in the hands of the ship's crew and they deserved whatever happened to them. They were also afraid of the Sky People. These people had great power at their disposal. They also had strange ideas, so the couple had no idea what to expect. Fear of the unknown could be the worst of all fears. Jake stood guard at the door while Jason got the couple settled on the scanning beds. The material was strange to them. It was thin material similar to what they sometimes purchased from the Kimbra. The surface beneath was unlike anything they had ever known. It was like the bags they carried water in except it didn't flow like water. The mattress was made of a gel substance making it easier for the scanner to read. Jason got Vesta settled first.

Vesta had said very little after the incident in the cavern. Manton was extremely concerned, as she had never been so quiet. She was definitely the type to speak her mind. After Jason got the scan started on Vesta, he turned to work on Manton. Manton reached up and grabbed his arm. Seeing him move suddenly Jake moved forward and placed his hand on a weapon. Manton relaxed his grip on the doctor's arm. Jason waived Jake off when he saw the worry in Manton's eyes. Jason made sure his translator was on before speaking, "Everything's okay. I'm not going to hurt you or your wife. I'm trying to help you."

Manton glanced over at Vesta who was staring at the ceiling. "What is your Captain going to do with us? Let him do whatever he wants to me, but please don't hurt my wife."

Jason assured him again, "None of us are going to hurt you unless it is in self-defense. I don't know what the Captain's plans are, but he only means to do what is right for all concerned. He isn't going to harm either of you."

Jake moved back to his position by the door and quietly notified the Captain of the incident. The incident wasn't the real issue, but the fear the couple carried could cause them to react badly. David told Jake he would handle it.

The captain walked into the gym to discuss the matter with Lexi. He wanted the couple to stay with them and work alongside the crew to learn from them. He planned to send them back to the Akamu, hopefully with new ideas. He didn't, however, want to put Lexi in an uncomfortable position. Lexi was uncomfortable having them around her. She knew she needed to face her fear. The Captain's idea was a good one. She agreed to let them stay on the ship but asked him to give her a couple days before requiring her to interact with them. David agreed to her terms and assured her they would be locked in their quarters at night and kept under close supervision during the day. David thanked her for her cooperation. He also insisted she tell him if things got to be too much for her. Lexi assured him she would. David turned to leave the gym. Lexi was bent over while still trying to catch her breath from her workout. She looked up and called to David as he started out the door, "Captain."

David stopped and turned to look at her. Lexi brushed a couple stray hairs out of her face while still trying to catch her breath. She finally stood upright and said. "Captain, thanks for coming for me."

David took a few steps back toward her. He wanted to word his response carefully. Logically his crew was already at a bare minimum, and no one was expendable. He needed everyone, but that wasn't why he went after her so aggressively. "You're welcome. There's no way I could have done anything else. You aren't just a crucial part of this crew. This crew is family."

He said things just the way he should have because tears began to fall down Lexi's face again. David wasn't sure about hugging female crew members, but he couldn't leave her crying. He gave a firm, but quick hug then excused himself to get back to work. Braxton passed him on the way out. David was glad to see him.

"Oh good, Braxton, you're here just in time. Your wife needs a hug. I'm afraid I made her cry again." David made a hasty exit without giving Braxton time to ask any questions. Braxton went on in to check on Lexi.

Lexi smiled when Braxton walked in which confused him even more. "The Captain said he came after me because we were family. It wasn't just because it was his job."

Braxton cocked his head to the side, "Is that how he made you cry?" Lexi nodded. She grabbed Braxton and hugged him tightly. Braxton gladly returned her affection.

David headed into the Med Bay to have a talk with Manton and Vesta. He assured them he had no intention of harming them. He told them they were going to stay with the ship as long as they remained on their world to learn about the Commonwealth. The goal was for the couple to share their knowledge with their own people after the crew was gone. Manton and Vesta looked confused. Manton spoke up, "But this is a position of honor and esteem. We don't deserve such an honor."

David shook his head, "This is a difficult job, a job for someone extremely determined. You two appear to have determination. You are going to have to teach everyone how to work out his or her problems through negotiations instead of force. Do you think you can do that?"

Manton and Vesta both nodded. Vesta finally spoke, "I don't know if we will be good at this task, but we will try."

MISSING IN ACTION

THE SORLEY

The next morning at breakfast, David had Jake bring their "guests" to the dining hall to join them. Jake wasn't sure what he would find when he went to escort them to breakfast. The couple was not used to the sophisticated facilities on the ship. Jake had to introduce them to the furniture, light and heat controls, and the bathroom facilities.

Before the couple was brought in for breakfast, David checked in with Jason quietly about the couple's fertility problem. Jason was evasive in his response, but David persisted. Jason finally gave him the information he was looking for.

"Look, Captain, I took care of their problem and even gave them a head start."

"What do you mean? What was wrong – in layman's terms, not medical jargon?"

"In some societies, a woman may be considered a failure if she doesn't bear children, but if a man doesn't produce children, he is worse than that. He's a laughing stock, a joke. He's no longer taken seriously at anything he does. A woman can still succeed at other things, but it's over for a man if it's discovered he's the one with the problem."

"Are you saying Vesta was fine, but Manton was the one with the problem?"

Jason was watching carefully to see if anyone else was close enough to hear him. He wanted to be careful to protect his patients' privacy. "Yes, it was. I repaired the damage and gave Vesta a head start."

"So she's already...?"

"Yes, but she doesn't know it yet."

"Why didn't you tell her?"

"It's better if she finds out on her own."

"Are you going to tell them what was wrong?

Jason shook his head. "No, I just told them I found the problem, used some medical jargon they wouldn't understand, and she would be able to have children now."

Jason saw Jake walk in with the couple, so he went from talking in hushed tones to not talking at all. David decided he had heard everything he needed to hear and went over to greet the couple. After introducing them to the food dispensers, he brought them over to sit with Brynna. Jake had delivered food to them in their quarters yesterday, so this was new to them.

Jake went over and sat with Lexi and Braxton. He had developed a bit of a bond with Lexi since she had been counseling him on his anger management issues. He had spent so much time keeping an eye on their new guests, he thought they might appreciate time away from him. Jake also wanted to make sure Lexi was all right. He knew she had to be uncomfortable with the couple's presence on the ship. Marissa joined her husband at the table. Thane and Aulani sat at the third table with Cheyenne and Lazaro. Jason and Laura joined the Captain's table.

After the group was finished eating, Brynna stood up to address the crew. "Could I have everyone's attention?" The crew stopped their casual conversations and turned their chairs to face her. Brynna walked casually over to refill her coffee, while she continued to talk to the crew. "We have reached an agreement with the Akamu. I want to send Cheyenne and Braxton back in to work on projects to improve their mining operations, as well as ways to improve their living conditions in general. I'm sure breathing in smoke all the time can't be good for them."

Aulani had given Manton and Vesta comm units and translators. The devices had only the most basic of functions. They didn't want to give the couple too much to deal with at one time. Aulani showed them how to work the units for both communications and translation. There was also a lockout feature, but only Jake, Aulani, and the Command staff were authorized to use it.

Brynna looked at Cheyenne and Braxton. "Can the two of you handle that?" Braxton didn't look happy and looked like he really wanted to say something. She watched him closely to see if the look on his face would change to one of acceptance. It didn't. "Lt. Commander, is there a problem?"

Braxton glanced at the visiting Akamu couple. He knew if he spoke, they would understand him, so he guarded his words. "After what their people did to Lexi and to me, I'm not comfortable going there. I'm also not comfortable having them here."

Brynna didn't want to sound callous, but she needed him to do this. It wasn't just the task she needed, but she needed the Akamu to see a demonstration of their benevolence and forgiveness. He and Lexi were the best suited for that task. "Lt. Commander, the Akamu did not attack you and Lexi, the ones who did are sitting here with us. Their purpose for being here with us is to learn the art of negotiation in the face of difficulties. I can send you and Cheyenne or Lazaro and Lexi. Which would you prefer?"

Braxton's face went from distaste to shock and disbelief. He stammered. "You -You- can't expect Lexi to go back in there."

Brynna looked at Lexi. Lexi didn't seem overjoyed at the prospect, but her face didn't show nearly the amount of emotion that Braxton was expressing. For a split second, she thought maybe sending Lexi in wasn't a half bad idea. "No, I am not expecting her to go back in there unless she chooses to. I am asking you if you're going to be able to do your job?" She had started to say, "THE job" and decided to change the emphasis. Braxton was silent.

Lexi looked up, "Commander, let us both go."

Braxton's head whipped around so fast, Lexi thought he was going to give himself whiplash. "WHAT? No way! You can't go back in there!"

Lexi looked at Braxton and placed her hand on his. "I need to do this. Brynna's right. The Akamu didn't do this to me. They did," she said looking at Manton and Vesta. "I am afraid, and the only way to get over it is to face it. It will also help seal our agreement if the ones who were wronged can go back in and offer the friendship we want."

Braxton now wished he had just agreed to go in and had kept his mouth shut. He looked at Lexi, then Brynna, then the

Captain. He felt helpless. He didn't want to put Lexi through that, but he certainly couldn't appeal to the Captain to overrule the Commander.

Brynna really wasn't sure about sending Lexi back into the caves, so she gave them a choice. "Here are your options. Lexi, I really don't expect you to go back in there. I can send Jake, Marissa, Braxton, and Cheyenne in, or if you really want to, you can take Cheyenne's place on the team. I can send Lazaro in Braxton's place. You can let me know what you decide. I want to leave a second team here at the ship and a third team to visit the Sorley. Team Two will be Jason, Laura, Thane, and Aulani. Team Three will be me, David, Lazaro, either Cheyenne or Lexi, and Manton and Vesta.

Manton and Vesta had been sitting quietly with their heads down and not looking at anyone. They appeared to be embarrassed by the reminder of what they had done. When they heard their names come up, they looked up in disbelief. During their breakfast, they had not said anything other than answering questions that were put to them directly. When they heard their names, they immediately had several questions pop into their heads, but they didn't know if they should ask them or not. They also weren't sure what the proper procedures were here with the Sky People. Despite the Captain's reassurances, they still assumed they were either prisoners or slaves. Although their stay had not been unpleasant, they kept expecting their punishment to come, and so far, it had not. They thought maybe it would come now. The waiting seemed worse than any punishment they had imagined thus far.

Brynna made a mental note to address the confusion on the faces of Manton and Vesta and proceeded on with her briefing. "Team Two, I want you here in case we get visitors and to be ready to assist if either of the other two teams gets into trouble. Team Three, we are going to visit the Sorley. I want to see how their deliberations are going and to make sure they aren't worried about our fly-by last night."

Thane had been leaning back against the wall in his chair with his arms folded across his chest just listening. At this point, he halfway raised one hand and asked, "Commander, why are we worried about the Sorley and not the Kimbra?"

"I'm not really all that worried, but the Sorley are nomadic and can pick up and move easily if they get spooked. The Kimbra will just lock down their city and peek out of their windows if they get spooked. It's better to let them just peek out their windows until they see we aren't doing anything to them."

Several of the crew members laughed softly at the thought of the Kimbra peeking out their windows at them. Thane smiled, "Okay so if they don't lock down the city, and they come here to just ask why we're buzzing their cities, you want someone here to answer the door. Got it."

Another ripple of laughter made its way through the room. Brynna smiled and said, "Yes, Thane, I need you to stay home and answer the door. Any other questions?"

No one seemed to have any, except Vesta and Manton. Brynna gave the crew a second to think of any, then she looked at Manton and Vesta. "Do you have questions?"

Manton, having seen Thane's raised hand, stood up and while looking down at the floor also gave a half-raised hand and said, "Forgive me, but yes, we do have questions."

Brynna thought about dismissing the rest of the crew to allow them to prepare themselves and dealing with Manton's questions personally, but she decided the entire crew needed to know what they might be dealing with. Brynna looked at Manton. The man looked scared to death. "Manton, Vesta, you may ask as many questions as you need to and don't be afraid. Please sit down and make yourself comfortable. You are, for the time being, part of this crew, an equal not a servant. Don't be afraid to talk, ask questions, or look at us. We do expect you to follow our orders, but I expect the same from the other crewmen. Do you understand?"

Manton and Vesta raised their heads slowly, halfway expecting to be slapped down for doing so. Manton sat back down in his chair and slowly asked, "What is it you expect us to do on this Team Three? We are not trained as servants, but we will do our best to serve you. We are trained as warriors if you need us to serve as protectors, this we can do well."

Brynna tried not to smile too much as she replied. "That is a good question. The Captain and I expect you to listen and learn about the art of negotiation, about the Commonwealth, and we also expect you to help us avoid any cultural taboos."

Manton still looked a little confused. Brynna coaxed him to ask whatever was on his mind. "I do not know what you mean by cultural taboos."

Apparently, the words were translatable, but the concept didn't make it. Brynna thought for a moment about how to explain the concept. She remembered the incident where Vesta had assumed Lexi was a slave and had gotten angry when she sat down to eat and drink with them. She explained to sit and eat with a slave would be a taboo, but only to certain cultures because the Commonwealth doesn't have slaves. Brynna also explained they would need to watch and learn from the crew so the two of them could see possible infractions before they occurred. The look of confusion began to disappear from Manton's face. They were going to be protectors, but not quite in the way he had initially thought.

They were protecting the crew from having bad manners. Manton had not understood the laughter earlier but had a laugh of his own when he realized what his new job was.

Brynna looked back at Lexi and Braxton who had been whispering tersely back and forth. Braxton looked annoyed, and Lexi appeared to be "at peace."

"Braxton, Lexi, what decision have you reached?"

Braxton spoke up, "She's going, and so am I."

Since the ship only had one Surf-Ve, Team One used it to get to the Akamu caves. It was smaller than the shuttle and could get closer and into tighter locations. Team Three used the shuttle since the Sorley were out in the open. They did have to be cautious about frightening the herds grazing out in the fields and causing them to stampede. The two teams were ready to go in a matter of minutes.

Brynna took a moment to ask Manton and Vesta if they needed the other team to bring any of their personal belongings back to them. She doubted they were in a fastidious routine of bathing and changing clothes, but she hoped they at least owned more than the one outfit they were wearing. The couple denied needing anything, but Brynna asked the other team to request any additional clothing anyway. She could have given them clothing from the ship's stores, but she didn't want anyone to mistake them for crew members. She also figured the couple would not be comfortable in such strange clothing.

Brynna did one last check with Lexi to be sure she was going to be all right with her choice to go visit the Akamu. She admitted being a little nervous but insisted she would rather do that than be around Manton and Vesta. Brynna gave one last instruction to the team. "Make sure Tarin knows Manton and Vesta will be returned to them. Tell him we are teaching them about our ways and they are also serving as guides for us and teaching us about the ways of those who live here. When we return them to him, he should welcome them back as advisers and Commonwealth ambassadors."

Lexi nodded but looked annoyed. "Commander, that's an awfully important role to set them up in considering what they did to me, and to Braxton. It seems like you're rewarding bad behavior."

Brynna was not trained as a psychologist like Lexi, but she knew Lexi needed to express her emotions and get them out in the open. Knowing this, Brynna deliberately provoked Lexi, "So what do you think should be done to them? A firm tongue lashing or maybe I should have smacked their hands?"

Lexi got angry and glared at her Commander but held her tongue. She still respected Brynna and her rank, so she tried to stifle her feelings. Brynna didn't want her to stifle, so she pressed her even further. "Go ahead, speak your mind. Don't be afraid of this." Brynna covered the rank insignia on her uniform with her hand. It was a Commonwealth soldier's way of taking things "off the record." Her tone was quite harsh. Lexi still didn't say anything, so Brynna pushed just a little harder. "I guess you would rather we put restraints on them and sell them as slaves to the Kimbra or Sorley. Maybe you would prefer to just execute them. After all, Vesta tried to do that to you. You want us to become savages like them? Give up the enlightened ways of the Commonwealth?" By this time, Lexi was beginning to tremble in anger. Brynna pulled a knife from her belt and offered it hilt first to Lexi and a set of binding restraints. "So, what's it going to be? How do you want them punished?"

Lexi turned away from Brynna. Her anger gave way to tears. "Please, put those away." She whispered and leaned against the nearest wall.

"What do you think should happen to them, Lexi?" Brynna's tone was softer now.

Lexi, tears running down her face, turned to Brynna. She had only been crying off and on for about one day, but it was getting old. Lexi finally managed to answer Brynna although it wasn't much of an answer. "I don't know. It just feels like they aren't paying for their crimes. Do you know what they tried to do to me?" Lexi knew the question was irrelevant because Brynna knew.

Brynna looked at her, "Yes, I know what they tried to do. They wanted desperately to have a baby, and they did the only things they could. They chose an action considered acceptable in their society. So, what should their punishment be?"

Lexi took a couple steps away again. She looked down at her hands. She wasn't sure if she had caught herself wringing her hands or symbolically washing them. "Abhorrent behavior is corrected through reeducation and relocation."

Brynna folded her arms across her chest. "That was a very nice, textbook answer. What do you think should be done to them?"

Lexi turned to face Brynna again. Her eyes were suddenly dark and cold. "I would love to see someone do to them exactly what was done to me and maybe a little more for good measure."

Brynna stood quietly, waiting for Lexi to connect all the dots. Lexi didn't seem quite ready to make that leap, so Brynna helped her out a little. "So how does it help their society, as a whole? They did nothing wrong by their own standards." She paused a moment. "They just wanted children."

Lexi began to cry again only this time it was a cry of resolve. She knew Brynna was right. She also knew Brynna had been manipulating her emotions on purpose. She knew she needed to deal with this so she could get her head back on straight. She was hoping to have more time to deal with it slowly.

Jake popped around the corner abruptly and hastily asked, "Are you two ready... to go?" Realizing he had walked into the middle of something, he backed out almost as hastily. "Um, we'll be outside when you're ready. Sorry for interrupting."

Lexi wiped her tears away. "I'm sorry, Commander. You're right. They already know they did wrong. They're also scared to death of us, but somehow, I just wanted to see them in more pain. I wanted them to feel as helpless as I felt."

Brynna put her hand on Lexi's shoulder. "You don't need me to tell you that your feelings are normal. It was pain and helplessness causing their behavior to begin with. We need to teach them, and their culture, to search for other solutions when they feel helpless and in pain. Can you handle going back into those caves?"

Lexi pushed her hair back away from her face, took a deep breath and blinked back the last couple of tears still trying to escape. "I think so. I hope so. I need to do this."

Brynna felt better about Lexi's skeptical answer than her more confident one earlier. Brynna gave Lexi a hug and sent her to take a minute to freshen up. When Brynna walked outside, David and Jake were talking casually. As soon as Brynna walked up David asked, "Everything okay?"

Brynna nodded, "I think so. Although, nothing's more dangerous than telling yourself you're okay when you aren't. I think she's okay though. Jake, stay close to her and Braxton."

Jake nodded, "Yes, ma'am."

A couple minutes later everyone, including Lexi, was ready to go. Team One headed for the caves in the Surf-Ve and Team Three headed south to the Sorley in the shuttle. The crew was so used to space flight and flying, they didn't remember their guests had never experienced such things. They forgot to warn the couple the shuttle was a flying vehicle. The couple had help getting buckled into their seats unaware of what was about to happen. The two thought it was just another carriage like the Surf-Ve or the Kimbra used, only without horses. When it took off into the air, Manton cried out and started jabbering excitedly. The startled crew looked back at him and Vesta. Vesta had a white-knuckled death grip on the arms of her chair and was pale as a ghost. Manton was frantically trying to unfasten his seat belt.

As soon as Lazaro realized what Manton was trying to do, he yelled, "Captain! Set it down!" Although captains are not accustomed to taking orders from their crew, a smart Captain listens when a subordinate gives an order in a crisis. David sat the shuttle down a mere hundred yards from the ship. The crew on the Surf-Ve saw the sudden landing. They stopped their departure and hailed the shuttle.

David climbed out of the pilot's seat and moved toward Manton and Vesta. He glanced back at Brynna, "Tell the Surf-Ve to standby. If we can't resolve this, we may need to change vehicles." Brynna did as she was instructed without giving any explanation. David asked Cheyenne to go to Vesta to offer her reassurance. Upon questioning them, David and Cheyenne realized the couple was overwhelmed and frightened by the new sensations. David assured them that although the sensations were new and different, they were perfectly safe. Manton continued to claw at his seat belt. He was shaking so badly he couldn't force his fingers to comply with his brain. Cheyenne seemed to be having better luck talking Vesta down than David was having with Manton. David finally decided to change his approach and become the hard-nosed Captain instead of the nurturing type. The look on his face transformed from a caring, compassionate look, to one of anger.

"I thought you were a warrior! Warriors don't show this kind of fear even if they feel fear! What are you afraid of? Is the warrior afraid he's going to die? You are nothing more than a scared child!"

David's speech was so convincing Cheyenne looked at him in shock. David unfastened Manton's seat belt and turned to walk away from him. "Go back to your cabin. If you are no better than this, I have no use for you!" David had to turn his back because Cheyenne's shocked look nearly caused him to burst out laughing. David understood Manton's fear, but he needed Manton to choose to get past it. The only way he could think of to push him was to challenge him and make him angry. He had unfastened Manton's seat belt to allow him a chance to no longer feel trapped. As David passed the shuttle door, he hit the release to open it.

Brynna had seen David's mouth flinch before he turned around and knew he was struggling to keep a straight face. She casually turned around to face the front of the shuttle so she couldn't see his face anymore. Lazaro saw the same thing and chose this moment to run a diagnostic on his scanner. Once David had his urge to laugh under control, he turned back around to face Manton. Manton was now standing angrily facing the captain. He shook his fist. "I am no child! I do not fear death!"

The two men stood there a moment glaring at each other. David finally spoke again. This time Manton's fear had subsided enough for David's words to get through to him. "Do you think I would put my life and my crew's lives in danger without reason? I told you I would not harm you. Are you again calling us liars? Are you cowards?"

Manton responded with less venom. "I am no coward." He was quiet for a moment then added. "I am sorry for the second insult. You have not lied to us. I will not make this mistake a third time."

David's voice and demeanor softened in turn. "I did not think you were a coward. I forgot all of this is new to you. Forgive me. I need you and Vesta to trust me. It is not my intention to put either of you in danger. I need the two of you on this mission. Can you trust me?"

Manton looked at Vesta who was still slightly pale but looking more relaxed. She gave him a slight nod. Manton looked back at David. "We will trust you." The warrior returned to his seat and managed to fasten his own seat belt this time. Vesta seemed to relax even more when Manton sat down. She seemed more afraid David and Manton were going to come to blows at any moment. She did not want to see her husband die in battle with the Sky People, but she also didn't know what would happen to her if Manton killed David in battle. The Sky People had strange ideas about things.

David punched the control to close the door then stepped closer to the couple. He wasn't sure how sensitive their translators were set, but he wanted to be sure they understood him. "Before we left the caves, your lives belonged to me. Tarin gave me the right to do what I pleased with you. If I had wanted to harm you, I would have killed you in the caves and left the Akamu to deal with your dead bodies. You are under my protection. Trust in that. You might also view this time with us like a child would. It's an adventure your Akamu friends won't get to have. Have some fun with it." David looked back and forth at the couple reading their expressions.

Manton settled back into his seat and took a deep breath. He nodded at the captain and repeated his earlier statement. "We will trust you, and we will try to have fun."

The look on his face was so strained David couldn't resist laughing any longer. He playfully patted Manton's shoulder and laughed. "You need to try harder my friend, try harder."

As David and Cheyenne moved back to their seats, Manton looked at Vesta in amazement. He didn't say anything, but she knew what the look meant. The leader of the Sky People had called him "friend."

David buckled himself back into his seat as Brynna hailed the Surf-Ve and told them to proceed with their mission. This time David did things more slowly and deliberately. He powered the shuttle up then called out, "Here we go." He kept his movements as smooth as he could. Brynna kept looking back periodically to check on the couple. They still seemed nervous, but certainly nothing like before.

When the shuttle got near the Sorley encampment, they made a higher altitude pass to locate the best place to land. The entire flight, including the incident with Manton and Vesta, only took twelve minutes. The shuttle landed within sight of the encampment. The crew climbed out slowly. Cheyenne gave Manton and Vesta a quick drink of water. Their episode of panic had caused them to be extremely thirsty. Brynna gave some last-minute instructions while they waited for the Sorley to send out a greeting party. "Manton, stay near David and warn him if you see anything we need to be aware of. Vesta you stay with Cheyenne. We don't want them to think this is an invasion or something, so we are going to move slowly and wait for a proper invitation. Any last-minute questions?" No one appeared to have any.

Within a minute Tharen and Jager and several other warriors on horseback had surrounded the shuttle and crew. An older man resembling Tharen was on the horse directly in front of them. Brynna stepped forward and introduced herself. "My name is Brynna Alexander. I am the Commander of this mission. We come in peace. We would like to visit with you and your people and get to know you." The man continued to stare at her. He had been told about the crew's translators so when Brynna's bracelet started speaking to him, he barely gave it a glance. Brynna figured he was trying to size her up and determine whether her motives were genuine or not. Since he was refusing to speak to her or identify himself, Brynna decided to take matters into her own hands. "You must be Kasen, leader of the Sorley. Your son Tharen is a wise man and a fine warrior. I assume he gets these traits from you. May we visit with you?"

Kasen looked at Manton and Vesta. "Why have you brought Akamu warriors with you?"

Brynna didn't flinch or hesitate. "We are not knowledgeable about the customs of your people. We unintentionally caused insult to the Akamu delegation. We now have an alliance with the Akamu and thought it wise to have a guide and adviser to prevent other insults. These two are here to teach us and to learn from us. They are not here as warriors. They carry no weapons except a knife each to protect themselves if necessary."

Kasen was not convinced. He motioned for one of his men to check the two Akamu out. Brynna casually touched her comm unit and quietly instructed the couple to let the Sorley check them out. Jake had not wanted to allow the couple to have any weapons, but Brynna wasn't comfortable allowing them on the mission without them. They were viewed as warriors, but if a warrior showed up without weapons, she wasn't sure how it would be perceived. A warrior without a weapon might be regarded as a disgrace. Once Kasen verified what Brynna had said, he decided they weren't a threat. He still wanted nothing to do with them. He pulled at his horse's reigns and turned to leave. "Leave here. You have nothing we need."

Brynna called after him, "Perhaps I was wrong about Tharen. He must have gotten his skills from his mother." Kasen yanked hard on the reigns again. His horse reared and turned abruptly back toward Brynna. In about three sharp jumps the horse reached the commander. In a flash, Kasen was off his horse. He drew a knife and was holding it across Brynna's throat. When

David saw Kasen's horse rear and turn, he grabbed for one of his own weapons and started to move to Brynna's defense.

Manton grabbed his arm to stop him. He quietly told David, "As long as she doesn't draw her weapon, he will not harm her." David knew a lot was riding on Manton's supposition. If he didn't trust Manton's advice, it could get Brynna killed. If he did listen and Manton was wrong, it could still get her killed. David knew they were surrounded and would take serious casualties if Brynna didn't defuse the situation. He had little choice but to trust Manton's advice. He stood there helplessly watching her.

Brynna stood there, face to face with Kasen, not backing down in spite of the knife poised at her throat. Kasen shouted angrily at her, "Why do you test me?"

Brynna kept her eyes locked firmly on Kasen's, "Why do you fear me?"

Kasen sneered at her, "I don't fear you." He slowly began to lower his knife. "I see you don't fear me either." Brynna had been forcing herself to concentrate on Kasen's eyes and not the knife he was holding at her throat. Her heart began to pound so hard she was sure everyone could see it and count the beats through her uniform. It was so loud in her ears she barely heard Manton's advice to David not to pull a weapon. Mentally she started kicking herself for calling Tharen a mama's boy to his father. She decided it wasn't her smartest move, but now she was stuck with it.

Kasen put his knife away but remained no more than an arm's length from Brynna. He repeated his question. "Why are you testing my patience?"

Brynna finally blinked and took a deep breath. "We have sought to gain an alliance with this world, and you did not seem inclined to even listen to our proposal. We have a lot to offer and ask little in return. I offered my admiration of your son's skills, and you were not impressed. What would you have done to get my attention?"

"I would have presented you with gifts and treated you to a feast of fine foods."

Brynna smiled. "I'm afraid the food we have would not qualify as a feast or fine foods. We do offer gifts, but not the tangible kind. We offer knowledge. Perhaps, you can offer the fine feast, and we will offer you our knowledge."

Kasen turned away from her and mounted his horse. He looked down from his perch and studied her again. He finally spoke, "So be it." He reached his hand down to offer her a lift up onto the horse with him. Brynna grabbed his arm and swung her leg up over the horse. Tharen moved over to David and offered his hand to him. David climbed up quickly behind Tharen. Tharen knew David and Brynna were somehow romantically involved. He moved quickly to David for that very reason. He didn't want David to make a foolish move on Brynna's behalf. Tharen moved his horse in a close formation near Kasen and Brynna. David recognized Tharen's actions for what they were and was grateful. The other riders, in turn, each picked up a crew member. Cheyenne's eyes sparkled as one of the riders pulled her effortlessly up onto the horse. She had seen horses before but had never ridden one. She had always admired them and was overjoyed at this chance to ride one. Lazaro was less enthusiastic. He much preferred machines to animals. Machines were more predictable. The Akamu didn't keep horses, so Manton and Vesta had no practical knowledge about the animals, but they weren't afraid of them. David and Brynna had ridden horses a time or two before, but they were far from knowledgeable horsemen.

It only took a minute to get into the village. There had appeared to be approximately fifty huts in the encampment arranged in a circle around a large canopy. The sidewalls of the tent were rolled up along the edges. As they reached the canopy, the horses were reined to a stop. The ship's crew was helped down from their mounts. Once they dismounted, the riders came off their own steeds more quickly than their passengers had. After Brynna and David dismounted, David walked over to her and grabbed her elbow firmly and pulled her aside. "Do you have to antagonize every one of our potential allies?"

Brynna looked at him sharply. She studied his eyes for a moment before answering. "Is it my husband who is asking or my captain?"

David felt himself start to get angry at her question then realized why. His grip on her arm relaxed. "Some of both. Your captain wants you to be careful and not get yourself killed. Your husband..." His hand slid from her elbow down to her hand and gripped it gently. "Your husband says, please be careful and don't get yourself killed."

Brynna smiled and squeezed his hand. She sensed it was about ninety percent husband and ten percent captain taking issue with her actions. "Please let both gentlemen know I'm being careful, and I promise not to get myself killed." She winked at him and then pulled away to start her negotiations.

Kasen moved over under the canopy and sat down on a blanket on the ground. Tharen escorted the crew under the canopy and invited them to sit on other blankets on the ground. Tharen, Jager, and several others sat down with them. There was a fire pit located in the center of the canopy area, and a flap cut into the canopy above it to let the smoke out. No fire was burning, but warm ashes still smoldered in the pit.

Once everyone was seated, Kasen started the conversation. "My son Tharen tells me you want to establish an alliance with the Sorley."

Brynna nodded, "Yes, we want an alliance with you, as well as the Akamu and the Kimbra. You are one of the three major powers on this world. Your influence is extensive, and we thought you would be a worthy ally."

Kasen gave her an icy stare. He wondered if her words were meant to flatter him into dropping his guard or if it were her genuine opinion. She had not been overly generous with her compliment. If she had been, he would have thrown them out instantly. Kasen despised false flattery. He stood up and walked to the edge of the canopy and looked out for a moment. He turned around and looked at Brynna and gave his blunt opinion. "I don't know you. I don't know what you value or what is important to you. I don't know if I can trust you."

Brynna found his candor refreshing. "You're right. You don't know us any more than we know you. We know some basic information about your people, but whether you are trustworthy or not, well, let's just say we may be optimistic. We are choosing to trust you even though we don't really know you."

"The Sorley do not give their loyalty lightly. From what my son has told me, you have little to lose by trusting us. We have much greater risks in trusting you. Tharen mentioned your enemy.

If your enemy is so powerful, what are we risking by taking your side instead of his?"

Brynna shifted her position on the ground until she was resting on her knees. Since Kasen had stood and started moving around, Brynna had difficulty facing him. He had been blunt with her, and she returned the favor. "I don't know what you would be risking from the enemy. I do know what you would be risking as our enemy. Our enemy has taken over the minds and wills of some of our own people. Our leaders had no choice, but to execute them. We did everything we could to protect them. We tried reeducation, medications, and solitary confinement, even bribery. Nothing convinced them to return their loyalty to the Commonwealth. I've seen some of the interrogations. It was like they wanted to choose the Commonwealth but couldn't. Something was stopping them. The enemy has never made an outward open attack on the Commonwealth. He is moving his forces slowly and quietly into place. The Commonwealth has rarely sanctioned executions. We don't believe in such things. I don't know what the enemy believes in. I am happy to share as much information as you require to get to know us, but the risk is still yours. I can't help you know the enemy. I can only help you get to know us. How can we show you what kind of people we are?"

Kasen walked over and squatted down in front of the fire pit. Picking up a nearby stick he started poking at the smoldering ashes and uncovering the hot coals. He stared at the ashes and coals for a few minutes. Finally, he looked up at her, "The only way to get to know who you are is to spend time with you and your people. We will have several competitions. Only when metal is tested by fire can you know how strong it is."

Brynna looked cautiously at David then at Kasen. She was watching for some hint as to his intentions. She decided Tharen and Jager would be the better ones to watch as she responded. They were young and less able to conceal their emotions. "Let me make sure I understand. You will agree to our alliance if we will compete with you in some sort of competitions? What type of competitions?"

Watching Tharen and Jager wasn't as helpful as she had hoped, because the only thing she could determine from watching them is they were as clueless as she was. Tharen abruptly stood up and approached his father and whispered something to him. Kasen looked up at Brynna, "Wait here." He then walked away from the group with Tharen following quickly behind him.

Brynna took advantage of his absence. She switched her translator offline for a moment and looked at David. "What do you think?"

David was skeptical. "I don't think he would risk his people's lives without a good reason. He either is very confident in his people, or it is just a healthy competition. Ask a few more questions to be sure without showing fear. I think he just wants to learn about our character."

Brynna nodded then looked at Vesta and Cheyenne. She turned her translator back on so Vesta and Manton could understand, but only transmitted into their earpieces. Their opinions were the same as David's although Manton and Vesta encouraged extra caution. They knew Kasen from personal experience and knew he was a hard man. He believed in swift and harsh justice and was a man of his word.

Tharen had pulled his father outside to find out what his plans were. He knew his father was up to something and he was also concerned at the display of power he had seen from the shuttle a few days ago. "Father, what are you doing? These people have great power at their disposal. They could destroy this camp in a matter of minutes."

Kasen looked sternly at his son, "Yet they don't come here displaying their power. They hide it. What else do they hide? I only want to find out what kind of people they truly are."

Tharen eyed him. "And you aren't up to something that's going to backfire on us?"

Kasen put his hand on his son's shoulder. "I have no intention of harming the Sky People although I do intend to throw a few surprises their way. I trust I will have your full support. I only want to know how they handle themselves. Can I count on you?"

Tharen was hesitant to agree. He had seen his father in action, and he had seen the shuttles lasers. He knew his father was keeping something from him. Tharen agreed, but with reservation, "I will support you so long as no harm comes to the Sky People."

"Then let's get back in there and get this done."

The two walked back in and took their places again. Kasen looked at Brynna still maintaining a stern demeanor he asked, "So will you join us in competition?"

Brynna responded positively, but cautiously. "We'd be glad to try, but your competitions are unknown to us. What would be involved and if we do participate will you agree to join us as allies?"

Kasen practiced his unique ability to be blunt. "No."

Brynna looked sideways at David. "No? Then why should we join your competition?"

"The competition will be a series of events we use for training our warriors. If you win enough events to win the competition, I will discuss your alliance."

Brynna took a deep breath. "So, if we win your competition, we get a definite maybe."

Kasen nodded. "We will leave you alone to discuss this among yourselves. The choice is yours. You may join us, or you may leave."

As the men got up to leave, Brynna stood up to ask one more question. "I have one more question. Are all of my people to participate?" Kasen nodded and started to leave again. "Including the Akamu?"

Kasen turned again to face her. "The Akamu have no business in this."

Brynna took a step forward. "The Akamu have already agreed to be our allies, and these two are part of our crew as long as we remain on this world. We are not familiar with your ways or your competitions. Can you allow them to help us?"

Kasen gave a firm, "No." He attempted to walk away again, but not without Brynna baiting him.

"So, you prefer to take advantage of our ignorance? Or are you afraid the Akamu would give us an unfair advantage over your warriors?"

Kasen stopped dead in his tracks and walked back over to Brynna. David shifted his position until he was kneeling instead of sitting. It was a position making it easy for him to stand up quickly if he needed to. David saw the anger in Kasen's eyes. This was twice she had pushed his buttons. Kasen saw David's move in his peripheral vision. He stopped right in front of Brynna and kept his hands down at his sides. He knew if he moved toward his knife again, David would be on him in a second. Kasen took a deep breath and looked away for a second then looked back at her. "As you wish. They may compete as Sky People." He turned and walked briskly out of the tent followed closely by his companions. After they were a discreet distance away from the canopy, Kasen started giving orders to his men. He was confident the Sky People would agree to the competition.

After Kasen left the tent, David gave Brynna a look that said, "Again?!"

She gave him an equally meaningful look that said, "I got this."

Lazaro broke the tension by saying, "So what are we going to do? Are we participating?"

Brynna turned to Manton and Vesta, "Would you be willing to participate with us?"

Manton and Vesta looked confused. "You asked Kasen if we could be part of the games. Why are you asking us? I thought it was already decided."

Brynna smiled at the couple. "We consider you as part of our crew while we are here, but after we leave you will still remain on this world. I want you to be a part of this, but not if it causes you problems after we leave. I had to ask Kasen for permission for you to participate, but the choice is yours in this case."

Manton and Vesta looked at each other having an unspoken conversation of their own. They again bowed their heads in shame and Manton gave their answer to Brynna, "We have much to atone for and we will gladly do whatever we can to help your mission succeed. We will give this competition our best."

Brynna was on the verge of getting excited. "Let's do this then."

Kasen sent Tharen to wait near the canopy for the crew's answer. When it appeared they had come to a decision, he moved to the edge of the canopy. "May I join you?"

Brynna turned and invited him in. He approached the crew and asked, "Have you reached a decision?"

Brynna responded, "Do you know of any reason why we should decline?"

Tharen was caught off guard by her question. He looked around nervously. He finally shook his head and responded. "His intentions with the competition are straightforward. He believes a lot can be learned from the way a person reacts during competition. He will be watching both the competitors and those who are just watching."

Brynna eyed him. "And...?"

Tharen gave her a vague blank look. "And what?"

She knew there was something else he wasn't saying. "What else do we need to watch out for?"

Tharen's posture changed. He stood more erect and appeared indignant. "Am I your ally?"

Brynna spoke softly. "You are a wise man. I wanted to tell you I appreciated your wisdom and restraint when we met at the ship. I hope you will be our ally, but I would hate to make a bad impression on your father. I thought you might be able to warn us if he were planning something that could cause harm to us or to our mission."

Tharen frowned. "I don't know what he has planned, but he does have something in mind. He wants to truly test your character. Just don't do anything rash."

Brynna smiled. "Thank you, Tharen. Please tell your father we will accept his challenge. Will it begin today, or should we return another day?"

"It will start in a few minutes." The young man turned and left as abruptly as his father had.

Brynna took a moment to check in with the other two teams. Lexi reported being nervous going in, but she had settled down once she got busy in the caves. She indicated Braxton seemed settled, and Jake hadn't started any fights. Braxton was giving the Akamu several engineering improvement suggestions including using geothermic heat, sanitation, and venting smoke from cooking fires. Jake was instructing on defense tactics for the caves, weapons modifications, and personal self-defense.

Team Two reported no activity from the Kimbra other than routine farming activity. Brynna didn't like Team Two sitting around doing nothing, but she couldn't lead three separate missions simultaneously. She had to accept it and hoped they enjoyed a day of light duty.

A few minutes later the Sorley leaders returned to the canopy. Kasen explained the rules of the day. Each first-place winner's team would receive three points, second place would be awarded two points, and third place one point. The Sky People could enter as many people in each event as they wanted, and the Sorley would match the number of participants. Kasen would allow the Sky People to decline to participate in one event if they determined it would be too dangerous or difficult. He did have one stipulation. If the Akamu were entered in an event at least one of the Sky People must also participate in that event. Brynna had already decided on that point anyway. She didn't want it to look like the Akamu were fighting their battles for them. Once Kasen laid down the rules he asked if the crew had any questions.

Brynna did have one other caveat. "If a task is new to us, can our people be allowed a few minutes to practice before the competition begins? I doubt a few minutes will compare to the years of experience your people have invested." Brynna now wished she had brought Jake and Thane instead of Lazaro and Cheyenne because they were the better athletes. Oh well, she was just going to have to do the best she could with the crew she had.

Kasen agreed to her request. If they felt the need to practice first, he doubted they would best his warriors.

Now that everyone was in agreement, they headed to the edge of the encampment to begin the competition. The first event was knife throwing. The crew had some experience in this area although they were by no means experts. Brynna entered the whole group in this event including the Akamu couple. The crew did avail themselves of the chance to get in some practice throws. On the first round Brynna, Cheyenne, and Lazaro were defeated. David and the Akamu couple made it into round two. Manton was knocked out in the second round by less than half an inch. The third round decided the winners. Of the Sorley; Tharen, Jager, and Gervas, another of the ruling council, all competed. Tharen took first place. Brynna had the feeling Jager was the better shot, but he always seemed to falter under the stress of the moment. Brynna wondered if the stress was in trying not to look better than the leader's son. Vesta took second place when Jager's shot went too wide. David surprised himself and took third place. He had experience at knife throwing but was by no means proficient. Kasen was serving as judge and overseer of the games, so he did not participate although David and Brynna were sure he was quite capable at these games.

The next event was a spear-throwing contest. Everyone again participated, but Brynna, Cheyenne, Lazaro, and Vesta were knocked out in the first round. David and Manton made it to the second round. David's muscles, although strong, were unaccustomed to launching pointed sticks over long distances. He made a mental note to practice this particular skill. Since their missions were going to routinely involve societies on this evolutionary level, it seemed a worthwhile skill to have. David was eliminated in this round, and only Manton advanced from their team. This contest not only included distance, but also accuracy. They didn't want to know who could propel their spear the farthest. You had to hit a target, and the spear had to stay lodged in the target. David was eliminated when his last throw hit the target but bounced off without penetrating it. The targets were three target dummies held up off the ground by wooden posts. The dummies were cloth stuffed tightly with straw in the rough shape of a human. The dummies had a trunk, head, two stubby arms, and two stubby legs. You received higher points for hits on the head and trunk and fewer points for the arms and legs. As the contest progressed, the difficulty was increased by changing the distance to the target. Round two the goals were to hit only the center dummy. If you hit the ones on either side, you would lose points. The last round had the dummy attached to a framework being pulled by a horse. Manton took third place.

Even though David had been eliminated in the previous round, he wanted very much to try his hand at this round. He asked if he could try this one just for fun after the winners had been determined. Tharen smiled at David's enthusiasm and had the rider make another pass for him. Kasen watched from a strategic distance. He was curious about this stranger's attempt.

David found the appropriate place on the spear to keep it properly balanced, waited for the rider to get to the most advantageous spot, and for the wind to be at his back before launching the spear. The spear soared serenely through the air. It just missed its target. The spear landed and dug into the framework holding the target. Several of the Sorley warriors smiled and nodded. Tharen congratulated David on an excellent try. Kasen turned and walked away so the crew would not see him smile. He admired David's spirit.

After these first two contests, Kasen had food and water brought out to the participants. Brynna noticed the men and women who brought the food out had what appeared to be deliberate scarring on their faces or arms. Brynna asked Manton and Vesta what it indicated. Manton and Vesta appeared reluctant to talk about it. Manton finally answered Brynna. "It means they are slaves. If one is particularly attractive and the owner wishes to keep them attractive, he may scar their arms instead of the face. It makes a runaway slave easy to find."

Brynna felt a wave of anger, sympathy, and nausea wash over her. "And this is what you would have done to Lexi?"

Vesta looked away, one silent tear ran down her face. Manton bowed his head and meekly replied. "I am sorry, but yes, we would have if Tarin had not stopped us."

Brynna stood up and walked away from the couple. It was one thing to accept cultural differences. It was something entirely different to have a cultural difference thrust upon one of their own. Brynna did not intend to force them to remake their culture, but to think Lexi might have been hurt by it was beyond belief. Vesta knew Brynna was upset. She went to Brynna's side. "Commander, please forgive us. I was jealous of Lexi. I didn't want her to bear my husband's children. I wanted to be able to do that. I knew it was the only way we could have children and I hated her for it. I wanted to do whatever I could to hurt her. This was my fault. Please, please forgive us."

Brynna listened quietly to Vesta. Finally, she turned to her to answer. "It's not just Lexi I am upset about. This is one of the things we want to teach this world. Everyone has the right to choose his or her own destiny. No one should be a slave. No one should be stolen away from their friends and family and forced to serve another. They don't deserve to have their bodies carved up like a piece of meat. Suppose you and Manton do have children and a raiding party comes through and snatches your child. How would you feel if your child was taken to a far city and their face scarred?"

Vesta's face clouded with anger as she considered the scenario Brynna presented. "I would hunt them down and kill them all."

Brynna nodded. "When you buy a slave or trade for a slave, you are bartering for someone's child or sister or brother or mother or father. You saw how angry Braxton was at losing Lexi. How do you think Manton would feel if you were taken?"

Vesta meekly responded, "I understand, but Manton and I can't stop this alone."

"I know. That is why this mission is so important. The Sorley are the key to stopping slavery on the entire planet, uh world." Brynna was so infused with emotion, she forgot to keep her vocabulary on the appropriate level.

"I understand why you are upset. Manton and I will do all we can to help you." Vesta stood there strong and firm, ready to do whatever was asked of her.

Brynna reached over and gave her arm an appreciative squeeze. "Thank you. I thank both of you."

Kasen called for the rest period to end and the next event to begin. Brynna saw the setup. She realized what the next event was and smiled. David saw her smile and looked at her quizzically. "What's so amusing?"

Since David and Brynna hadn't known each other very long, and the time they had spent socializing was in between long, arduous training sessions. There was a lot they hadn't yet learned about each other. "Archery is a hobby of mine."

David grinned, "Really? How come you never told me?" He admired a woman who knew how to handle a weapon.

Brynna smiled at him. "I'm sure there are a lot of things I haven't gotten around to telling you yet."

David slipped an arm around her waist and pulled her closer to him whispering, "Oh really? Like what?"

Brynna gave him a flirtatious grin and pulled away from him, "I guess you'll just have to wait and see." David smiled and shook his head as she walked away. He wondered how he had been so fortunate to have a woman like her.

Kasen explained the rules for this event. The targets were the same dummies as the spear-throwing contest. Kasen didn't say anything about hitting a moving target like round three of the spear-throwing contest. Brynna asked David if he thought this was a possibility. David nodded, "I suppose it is. Why?"

Brynna frowned. "I've never tried to hit a moving target."

David answered somewhat smugly, "We'll just have to win the event before it gets to that point."

Brynna shook her head. "Oh, is that all?" The crew took the practice shots Kasen granted them.

In round one, Cheyenne and Lazaro were eliminated as well as four of the Sorley. In round two David and the two remaining Sorley were eliminated leaving Brynna, Manton, and Vesta as the top three contenders. Kasen gave them the option of finishing the contest to see who would take first, second, and third place. Brynna was glad to say she would take third place, and Manton and Vesta could fight it out for first and second. David thought they should go ahead and play it out. Manton shook his head and said, "Vesta can out-shoot me with a bow. I can best her with the spear. We have practiced together for years."

Brynna gave their answer to Kasen. "I hope you won't be disappointed if we don't choose to go to the next round. I have never shot at a moving target, and Manton and Vesta know each other's strengths. Perhaps you can give me a chance to see how I would do on another occasion. I don't want to waste your time or ours on a contest to tell us what we already know."

Kasen nodded thoughtfully. "You present valid arguments for your decision. I am curious to see how you would do, but it can wait, as you say, for another time."

Kasen moved on to the next contest. It was a simple foot race. There wouldn't be any disqualifying events just the top three runners. The course appeared to be about a quarter of a mile. It was two wide laps around the camp. After the first lap, it was clear who was accustomed to running and who wasn't. The entire ship's crew was well trained in running, but so were the Sorley. The Akamu could travel long distances at a steady pace, but they were not runners. The caves were not conducive to running at all.

Lazaro came in first. Running was one of his hobbies, and Cheyenne took second. Running was one of the things that had attracted Lazaro and Cheyenne to each other. Tharen took third, but he worked hard for it, just narrowly staying ahead of David.

Kasen did not look amused at the race results. Each team's score was displayed by a rope with colored pieces of fabric tied to the rope indicating the score. David glanced at the score and saw why. The ship's crew was up by six points. He and Brynna weren't in a hurry to say they were a sure thing to win because the next event was a horse race. Even the Akamu were not seasoned horsemen. Tharen and Jager gave the crew and the Akamu an abbreviated lesson in horseback riding. Before they took the horses for a practice run, David pulled Brynna aside. "Brynna, I don't think Lazaro, Cheyenne, or Vesta should participate in this event."

Brynna glanced over at the three he mentioned. "What are your reasons?" She didn't totally object, but she wanted to know what he was thinking. David hesitated a moment. "Lazaro and Cheyenne have NO experience with horses, and I don't want to risk an accident. I also don't like the fact we are several points ahead, and apparently, neither does Kasen. Have you seen the looks on his face recently?"

"I have noticed he isn't looking happy. Why not Vesta?"

"It's too risky for her."

"What do you mean by that? She's a capable warrior."

"Jason didn't tell you?"

"Tell me what, David?"

"She's pregnant, but she doesn't know it yet."

"Oh, that would have been good information to have before now. So, what excuse do we give Vesta for not letting her participate?"

David looked at the three of them for a minute and said, "Tell her we're concerned for the crew's safety if we win this event and we want her to watch out for them, just in case."

Brynna nodded, "Okay, I'll go along with that. Is there anything else I need to know?" Her voice revealed a certain amount of frustration, or maybe annoyance.

David shook his head, "No, I don't think so. Sorry. I didn't realize you didn't know."

Brynna turned and walked toward the rest of the crew who were still getting pointers from Tharen and Jager. "Tharen, David, and I have decided only three of my people are going to participate in this event. My people are not accustomed to animals, and I am choosing only the most experienced to enter."

Tharen nodded his understanding and started to walk away. "I will inform my father we only need three riders and six horses.

Jager jumped in to ask, "Which three will be riding?" Tharen gave Jager a look of consternation.

Brynna caught a sideways view of Tharen's face. If Tharen was concerned, perhaps she should be. She wasn't sure it was going to make much difference since it was only a matter of minutes before the chosen riders would mount their horses. Brynna gave Jager the answer he requested, then she decided to test him. "Will each rider get to choose their own horses?"

Jager looked at Tharen then back at Brynna, "I... uh... I will ask Kasen." Brynna watched the two men as they walked away. Tharen and Jager seemed to be arguing about something. The two men stopped arguing, then headed to talk to Kasen. The argument appeared to continue, and Tharen walked away angrily.

David walked up behind Brynna. Noticing her intent gaze, he asked, "What's got your attention?"

Before she could answer, Cheyenne, Lazaro, and Vesta were also at her side. "Commander, why do you want us to sit this one out?"

Brynna looked at Lazaro and back at David. She decided to answer both questions at once. "Something strange is going on, and I don't want to put us all in jeopardy. Kasen, Jager, and Tharen are having some sort of disagreement pertaining to this last event. I want the three of you to keep alert to your surroundings and give us a shout if you see anything suspicious. Vesta, I want you to help them get back to the shuttle if it looks like they are in danger. If you can't make it back, get word to the ship and get out of the village.

Understood?"

Each one in turn, including David, replied, "Yes, Commander."

Cheyenne made a pouty face. "I was really hoping to get a chance to ride the horses again."

Lazaro smiled and shook his head, "That's my wife, lover of all things fuzzy and furry."

David couldn't resist the obvious opening, "So why did she fall for you? You're not fuzzy or furry. And you're fast losing what you got on top there."

Lazaro scowled at the captain. If it had been anyone else, he would have given him a playful punch in the arm, but he wasn't about to do that to the captain. He kept his response verbal and highly sarcastic, "Ha – Ha, very funny."

David had seen Lazaro's arm flinch instinctively and then stop. He understood the hesitation, and under other circumstances, he knew he would have gotten punched. He was glad Lazaro respected him and his rank, but a part of him missed the opportunity to goof off and just be himself instead of being "The captain." David laughed and said, "You walked into that one, Lazaro."

David, Brynna, and Manton approached Kasen to get the information for the next event. Jager had conveyed Brynna's question about choosing their own horses. Kasen had ten horses brought out for the riders to choose from. He instructed his own riders to choose a horse that wasn't one of their own to ride. Brynna was trying to mitigate the "home court advantage" at least a little bit. She also didn't want the crew to be given the oldest sickest steeds the Sorley had. By asking the question she was letting Kasen know she was no fool. She didn't really know much about horses, but she didn't want Kasen to know that. Brynna was given the chance to choose first. She slowly walked past each horse and touched each one gently either on the side of its face or the crest of its neck. Each horse took her touch calmly. The tenth pulled away from her. It neighed, danced, and jumped. Brynna grabbed the horse's bridle and patted him gently.

David stood there watching, thinking, "Not that one, please not that one."

The horse seemed to calm down when Brynna asserted herself with the bridle. She looked into the horse's eyes, and she felt it relax. She looked at Kasen, "I choose this one."

Kasen smiled. "Are you certain? This horse is newly broken and very spirited."

David silently shook his head. Brynna was going to get herself killed. The horses were already saddled, so Brynna nimbly hoisted herself onto the horse, made a quick lap around a nearby tree, and rode back over toward Kasen. She rode straight at him, then reined the horse in hard and stopped abruptly causing a cloud of dust to rise up around her. Kasen stood there refusing to show fear, but several of the people standing near him made hasty retreats. Brynna looked down from her perch, smiled, and said, "Yes, I'm certain."

Tharen chose a horse next, then Manton, Jager, David, and finally Gervas.

The course consisted of three laps around the camp. Part of each lap included riding around two trees about a hundred yards from the edge of the camp and about a hundred yards apart from each other. The finish line wasn't a "line" at all, but the riders would go from the second tree to a post at the starting line and grab a flag from the post. There were three flags, and only the top three could get a flag. This method did have its drawbacks in cases of a tie. Sometimes a fight would break out.

The riders lined up at the starting line. To start, the riders would be standing on the ground in front of their horses. A flag with a rock attached would be thrown into the air. As soon as it hit the ground, the riders would mount and head around the assigned course. This being the final event created an air of excitement. It seemed the entire Sorley population had turned out to watch. Some climbed the hills around the encampment and were watching from the outside of the course where they had a higher vantage point. A few young people climbed into two of the trees, which were part of the riding course. The slaves were even standing around watching the excitement. As the starter moved up to start the race, a hush fell over the crowd. There was a surreal silence as the flag was launched into the air and it lasted until the rock brought the flag crashing into the ground and a cheer erupted from the crowd.

As the rock hit, the riders leaped onto their horses and took off. Brynna had chosen her animal wisely. This horse was young and ready to prove himself to his rivals. Brynna also weighed less than any of her opponents, so she didn't weigh her horse down. She wasn't an accomplished rider, but the horse understood the competition. Brynna took an early lead, but Tharen and Jager were close behind her. David and Manton were close together, but not very far behind Tharen and Jager. Gervas had apparently underestimated his rivals. He didn't seem to understand their resolve outweighed their inexperience. After the first lap around the track, Tharen's expertise began to win out over Brynna. He matched her as they went around the second tree, and he was able to keep pace with her throughout the second lap. As they neared the trees at the end of the second lap, Tharen got ahead of her, and Jager managed to get alongside her. By this time Gervas had gotten his head in the game and had passed David and Manton. David was coming in last place but was pushing hard. All of the riders were still fairly close together.

On the third lap, both the horses and their riders began to tire, and the gaps were more spread out. Tharen had pulled solidly ahead of Brynna. Jager was keeping pace with her in what seemed like an almost deliberate manner. Brynna couldn't be sure, but it seemed like there were a couple of opportunities for him to get past her and he didn't. It was enough to make her push harder to put some distance between her and Jager. David pushed his horse harder and passed Gervas and Manton again. He didn't like being so far from Brynna, and Jager's riding didn't look right to him either.

As Brynna and Jager reached the first tree on the final lap, Jager pulled a small blow dart gun from his tunic. He blew a dart hitting the backside of Brynna's horse. The horse whinnied painfully and reared. When Brynna heard the horse whinny, she braced for it to rear and managed to stay mounted. She wasn't prepared however for it to buck. When the horse bucked, it sent Brynna flying head first over the horse's head. Brynna made a valiant effort to tuck and roll, but it wasn't enough to prevent injury. She was able to protect her head from the initial impact but landed on her shoulder. A searing pain ran through her arm and shoulder causing her to lose the ability to stay tucked. Her body flattened out, and she rolled a couple more times. Her head hit a rock somewhere along her trajectory causing more intense pain then unconsciousness. Tharen was too far ahead at this point to see what happened and made his way for the finish line. Jager dodged the angry horse and kept moving toward finishing the race. He glanced nervously at Brynna's unmoving body but pressed onward. David seeing what happened rode immediately to Brynna's aid. Manton knew the importance of winning the race, but when he saw David abandon the competition, he chose to follow his example. Gervas took advantage of the opportunity and rode on to get third place.

The crowd was roaring with excitement as their champions rode in. Vesta, Cheyenne, and Lazaro stood in shock for a moment after seeing Brynna fall. In a second, they realized David would need a scanner and a med-kit to tend to Brynna. Lazaro grabbed Vesta's arm and told her he needed to get to the shuttle to pick up a med kit immediately. Vesta grabbed one of the two horses not chosen by the riders and mounted it. She offered Lazaro a hand up and the two raced off toward the shuttle. Cheyenne headed for the spot where Brynna had fallen.

Tharen was enjoying the satisfaction of winning and the adulation of his people. He turned expecting to see Brynna and Jager rejoicing for second and third places. When he didn't see any of the Sky People, he glanced back along the race route to see Brynna's horse running loose, bucking and kicking. Then he saw David and Manton kneeling on the ground by Brynna and Cheyenne running toward them. Tharen turned his horse and raced toward Cheyenne. He rode up beside her and offered her his arm to ride behind him. Cheyenne hesitated, but the look on his face showed genuine concern and a hint of anger. She took his arm and he pulled her up onto the horse like she weighed nothing at all. She guessed it was a result of the anger he was feeling. Tharen took her out to the others, helped her dismount, and then dismounted himself.

When David reached Brynna, he kept thinking, "She's finally done it. She's gotten herself killed. I should have stopped her. I should have put my foot down. Uncle Rob was right. I'm too soft and it's gotten her killed." David was immensely relieved when he got to her side and saw her breathing. He grabbed her hand and checked for a pulse on her wrist. "Brynna? Brynna! Can you hear me?" Her pulse was fast but strong. When she heard him call her name, Brynna tried to respond, but she was having trouble making her body do what she wanted. David gently turned her head to see her face and repeated his question. "Brynna, can you hear me?" This time she managed at least a groan.

Manton reached David's side, "How can I help?" David and his entire crew were trained as field medics. As much as he wanted to gather her up into his arms and hold her, he knew that was the wrong thing to do. David forced himself to focus. He told Manton to check her arms and legs for broken bones. David reached around and felt Brynna's scalp, looking for injuries. He found a knot on her head the size of a large egg. He kept her head in straight alignment with her body in the event she had a spine injury and checked her for broken ribs and any immediate signs of internal bleeding. He knew a slow bleed would be harder to detect and wished he had a medical scanner.

By this time Tharen and Cheyenne had reached them. Cheyenne came down off her horse and asked how Brynna was. David looked up at Cheyenne. "I don't know for sure. I need a scanner." Cheyenne told the captain, Lazaro, and Vesta had taken a horse to the shuttle to get the Med Kit. Manton looked up at David with his hands on Brynna's left arm and shoulder. The translator told David that Manton reported Brynna's arm was missing. David looked down at Brynna and back at Manton. "I don't understand. Your words didn't come through right."

Manton thought for a second and tried again. This time it came through as "Her shoulder is broken."

David checked the shoulder for himself. He finally determined it was dislocated, but hopefully not broken. Between David and Manton both pressing on her shoulder, Brynna began to moan. David looked toward the shuttle to see how close Lazaro was with the Med Kit. The shuttle was on the far side of the camp and not visible from their position.

David looked up to see Tharen standing there looking quite concerned. "Did you come to see if your friend did a good job?" Tharen looked at David while the translator did its job.

When the message came through, Tharen gave David a shocked look and asked, "What do you mean?"

David stood up. "I saw Jager with some sort of dart gun. He was trying to fix the race, and it worked. Your team won. Are you happy now?"

Jager realized his friend was no longer in the safety of the crowd and rode his horse out to Tharen and the others. When Tharen saw Jager approach, he ordered him to retrieve Brynna's horse and bring it to him immediately. Tharen knew Jager shouldn't be near David right now. As soon as Jager was otherwise occupied, Tharen knelt beside Brynna and David. "I'm sorry. I didn't know what my father was planning. How can I help?"

David wasn't sure if he believed Tharen or not, but the young man seemed sincere. "Can you get her some water and we'll need a stretcher to carry her back on?"

Tharen picked up a canteen from his saddle and handed it to David. "I will bring a stretcher back momentarily.

Tharen rode back toward the camp and ordered a stretcher and some able-bodied men to carry it out to David. He also called for the camp's healer. The healer went to get his own medicine bag. He told Tharen to bring Brynna to the meeting tent.

Vesta and Lazaro made record time in getting to the shuttle and back. Lazaro brought the kit and opened it up to start working on Brynna. David tried to take it from him, but Lazaro refused to hand it over. "Captain, this is your wife, not your crewman. Be her husband right now and let me be the medic."

David knew Lazaro was right. It took all his strength not to argue and fight back. David told Lazaro what they already had determined about her injuries then moved back out of his way. Lazaro used the scanner to go over Brynna more in-depth. Cheyenne contacted the ship and asked Thane to get the Doc standing by. The scans were relayed through the comm units back to the *Evangeline*. Jason was reviewing the data as it came through. Brynna began to stir. Her first words were quite succinct and to the point. "Ow, that hurts."

Lazaro looked down at her and asked, "What hurts?" David nearly pushed Lazaro out of the way to get to Brynna's side again. David had been on Brynna's right side. Lazaro moved to her left and continued scanning. "Tell me where you hurt."

Brynna looked over at Lazaro, "a little bit of everything hurts, but mostly my head, my shoulder and... ow... my right ankle." Lazaro relayed the information to Jason. Jason continued to direct Lazaro on areas to scan and in what order he wanted them scanned.

David carefully picked up Brynna's right hand and squeezed it. "I told you to be careful." Brynna wasn't in any condition to give an appropriate retort.

Brynna looked around at the group standing or kneeling around her. She was having difficulty getting her eyes to focus.

"What happened?"

David gave a terse reply, "Your horse threw you."

Brynna's response was almost comical, "Why?"

David wasn't sure if Brynna was ready for that information. Looking slightly confused by her question David asked, "What do you mean, 'Why'?"

Brynna's response was again almost comical, "I thought we had an understanding."

David was getting more confused by the moment. "Who had an understanding?"

"The horse and I had an understanding."

Manton quickly handed the water canteen to David. David gave him a grateful look and offered Brynna a drink. The two men, upon hearing Brynna's strange comments thought she was delirious. Lazaro cautioned David to only give her small sips. David looked hesitant. "Why?"

Lazaro sat there staring for a moment before answering. "Doc says Brynna has a concussion and may be nauseated." David had not connected his comm unit into their conversation, so Lazaro was hearing the Doc talk to him, but David wasn't hearing any of it. He was suddenly annoyed with himself for overlooking such an obvious step in staying connected. David connected his comm unit. He wasn't about to miss anything else. Brynna started moving around and tried to work her way into a sitting position, but her shoulder was fairly useless right now. David told her to lie still. Lazaro finished his scans and waited on the doctor's instructions. Jason reported Brynna's tuck and roll had been reasonably successful. She had no broken bones or internal bleeding. She just had the concussion, dislocated shoulder, a sprained ankle, and numerous bruises, cuts, and scrapes. Lazaro gave Brynna a couple of injections to treat nausea, pain, swelling, and to fight off possible infection from the cuts and scrapes. The doc did instruct them to get her back to the ship as soon as they could so he could do more precise treatments, but he assured them she was going to live.

Tharen and several other young men arrived with a stretcher. They carefully helped her onto it and gently carried her back to camp. Jager had now captured the escaped horse and brought it back to Tharen as instructed. Tharen took the reins from Jager and sent him to help the other men carry Brynna back to camp. Tharen tied the horse to the tree and carefully examined it. Lazaro started to follow Brynna and the others back to camp until he saw what Tharen was doing. Lazaro took his scanner and scanned the horse for anomalies. Since the horse was covered in a woolly coat, the mark from the dart was harder to find, but the scanner made finding the source of the irritation quick and easy. David, seeing Lazaro had not followed them, turned to locate him. He told Brynna he would be back in a minute. Brynna watched him walk away and wondered what he was looking into. He found Lazaro and Tharen discussing what had been done to the horse. David told the two men he had seen Jager pull a blow dart gun out and use it. Tharen warned David not to accuse Kasen directly of cheating, although he was most certainly the instigator. David made no promises, but he understood.

The men took Brynna back to the pavilion where the camp healer began to examine her. David told Tharen not to bother. They would take Brynna back to their ship, and their own healer would care for her. Kasen looked at David and then at Brynna. "So you wish to admit defeat?"

David looked back at Kasen. "What do you mean by that? The score is tied. We haven't lost. I need to get my wife back to our healer. Her injuries need to be treated."

Kasen shook his head, "You may take her back with your people if you wish, or you may stay to break the tie. If you leave, you admit defeat. Our healer can fix her shoulder and bandage her cuts and scrapes unless you do not trust our healer or our help. You have asked for our trust and loyalty. Do you not trust us to care for your wife? We may not have your magical devices, but we can handle her simple injuries. I have had the same injury to my shoulder before, and the healer has healed it."

David had a lot more questions. "Why are you insisting on this?

"Once a tournament has begun, no one may leave without admitting defeat. You do not strike me as one who gives up so easily." Kasen looked like he was daring David to react.

"Just let me get my wife back to the ship, and I'll finish this myself."

Kasen was unyielding. "You may leave if you wish, but if you do the tournament is over and so are the negotiations."

David was equally unyielding. "I'm not afraid to admit defeat, but the loss would be yours. You would lose more by not entering into an alliance with us."

The Sorley healer was still trying to examine Brynna. Brynna gently pushed him aside for a moment and struggled to sit up. The healer helped ease her into a sitting position. The healer had a good bedside manner. Brynna could tell he cared about his patients.

Brynna had been listening to the conversation between Kasen and David. Once she got upright she called out, "David, may I speak to you for a moment?"

David looked vexed. He knew she was about to side with Kasen. He moved to her side and knelt in front of her. He turned his translator off and then helped her turn hers off.

"David, my injuries are not life-threatening. I don't have to go back right now. Let their healer tend to me. He seems to be competent and caring. I doubt they would do anything to harm me, and if I get worse, we can always leave later and admit defeat. Lazaro gave me something for pain, so I really feel much better.

David shook his head and started to say no when he heard Jason's voice in his ear. "Captain, Brynna is correct about her situation. The treatments I could give are purely cosmetic and symptomatic except for the concussion, but she should be fine for another few hours."

David was looking vexed again. He had forgotten to turn his comm unit off this time. "Thank you for your assessment, Jason." His tone said, "You aren't helping."

Jason gave a quick and concise reply, "I just wanted you to have the facts, sir. Jason out." Jason cut communication from his end.

Brynna had heard Jason as well. "Captain, we are so close. Please let me stay. I'll be fine, really."

David looked at her when she called him captain. "You don't play fair."

Brynna smiled, "I know."

"There's something you don't know though."

"What is it?"

David glanced over at Kasen and Jager. "We think Kasen tried to fix the horse race. Jager fired a dart at your horse causing it to throw you. You said you doubted they would hurt you, but they did hurt you. Tharen warned me not to confront Kasen directly, but he probably instructed Jager to do it."

"Do you have proof?"

"Yes, but I am not sure it would convince them. Our scanners may not be considered acceptable evidence. There is a mark on the horse, but it isn't enough proof."

"Does Jager still have evidence on him?"

"I don't know. What do you want me to do? If I accuse him on his home turf, it puts us at a severe disadvantage."

Brynna looked over at Kasen who was idly talking with Tharen and Jager. "Can we ask Tharen's advice?"

"You want to pit him against his father?!"

"No, but he seems genuinely upset over these circumstances. He'll probably be honest with us, and he may help us get on his father's good side."

David nodded. "All right, I'll ask Kasen if he will allow Tharen to advise us." David stood up and turned toward Kasen. As he walked closer to the three men, he reached down and turned his translator back on. Seeing David approach, the three men stopped their conversation and turned to face him. David chose his words very cautiously. "Kasen, may we consult with Tharen on how to proceed. You have trained your son well, and he has shown himself to be a wise man. We need good counsel from a Sorley perspective."

Kasen looked like he was close to getting angry. "Do you think you can turn my son against me? Do the Akamu not provide you with adequate counsel?"

David was quick to reply, "By no means are we trying to turn him against you. We're trying to do just the opposite. The Akamu are good advisers, but would you consider them to be experts in Sorley government or law?"

Kasen huffed and looked away, so David continued. "We want nothing more than to gain your trust and to be your allies.

Who would know best how to win your favor, but your own son? If you sought to impress me who would you ask to advise you?"

Kasen stared at David for a moment then laughed loudly. "You seem to have a great deal of wisdom as well. I don't know why you need advice. Your choices seem rather obvious to me, but if you think he can help you then let him advise you. We will leave you to talk in private." Kasen sent the slaves away and took Jager and the healer with him.

Tharen and David walked back over to Brynna. Lazaro, Cheyenne, Manton, and Vesta came in closer. Tharen looked at Brynna, "You seem to like putting me in awkward positions."

Brynna smiled apologetically. "I'm sorry Tharen. In the short amount of time we've known you, you have proven to be trustworthy. I hope it's not too awkward for you."

"What is it you need?" The man seemed slightly disturbed by his predicament.

David took the lead in the discussion. "You told me not to openly accuse your father of sabotaging the race, so I can't ask him why he did it. I don't know what sort of reaction he expects from us. I assume he is trying to find out more about us by judging our actions in difficult situations. Do you know what he's doing?"

Tharen's solemn visage was equivalent to his next statement. "You're asking me to betray my father."

David frowned. "No, Tharen, I'm sorry. That is not what I meant to do." David paced for a moment trying to phrase his question more appropriately.

Cheyenne, the resident expert in linguistics, came to the captain's rescue "Captain, may I?" David nodded. Cheyenne proceeded to address Tharen. "What does your father value? Honesty? Physical strength? Bravery? Defense of one's family? Military strength? Wealth? Diplomacy? Respect?"

David smiled and walked back over to Tharen who seemed to be more at ease now. "Yes! That's it! That's what I need to know."

Tharen wasn't uneasy about answering this question. "My father values all of these things. He also values knowledge, openness, and familiarity. He trades with the same people and follows the same routes. He doesn't like change."

Lazaro snickered and shook his head. "A nomad that doesn't like change? That's an oxymoron if I ever heard one." Lazaro's translator beeped at him. Either the Sorley didn't have a word for "oxymoron," or it was used so rarely it wasn't in the language file.

Tharen looked puzzled when the translation was incomplete. Lazaro tried to think of a way to reword his statement, but he came up empty. He finally just waved his hand as if he could erase what he had said. "Just forget it. I can't explain it. It's not important anyway."

David was slightly annoyed at Lazaro's verbal detour. He chose, however, to ignore it and move on. "What would be of greatest importance to him?"

Tharen contemplated his answer carefully before answering, "I would say defense of one's family, honesty, and respect."

David looked over at Brynna. "I guess I need to honestly and respectfully defend my family."

"You still can't accuse him in front of his people. If he chooses to admit what he has done, that would be acceptable." Tharen liked these people for some reason and wanted to keep them out of trouble with his father.

Brynna still needed more information. "Tharen, what is this last event?"

Tharen's eyes grew distant. "Hand to hand combat... probably against me."

"Are there weapons involved?"

"For tournament combat, we each get a helmet and a staff with cloth wrapped around each end to give us some protection. We would still be expected to give our best efforts, which is what I will do if I am called upon to fight you."

David put his suggested course of action out for the others to consider. "So, if I tell Kasen I'm not comfortable finishing the tournament because Jager cheated..."

Tharen's eyes cut back to David sharply. "If you accuse Jager and my father doesn't intervene, Jager can take my place in the match to defend his honor."

Tharen's guarded statement got David's attention. "Is this a problem?"

Tharen nodded. "If you challenge Jager, the weapons will be real, and Jager can fight until he is defeated or gets satisfaction."

Brynna looked crosswise at David. "What do you mean by satisfaction?

Tharen appeared to be struggling for words. "Satisfaction means... satisfaction. He will fight until your captain retracts his accusation or begs for mercy. He may be satisfied by simply giving you a sound beating, or if he is angered enough... he could... kill you."

Brynna was already a bit pale from her fall, but she turned another shade lighter when she heard Tharen's explanation. "David, we could just ignore the so-called insult, say nothing and just finish the tournament."

Tharen nodded. "My father will not be pleased if you defeat me, but it's better than fighting Jager. Jager can be a formidable opponent. He is strong, fast, and he has a bad temper. I suggest you follow the advice of your woman."

"What if I render him unable to fight, but still alive?"

"Then a second would take his place. Take my advice and finish the competition by fighting me. We can make it look good, and no one else gets hurt. I will throw the fight, so my father is honor bound to discuss the alliance with you. This is the best way."

"And what will you tell your father about our need for advice?"

"I can dodge his questions until after the tournament, and then privately tell him the truth. He can't take offense if you choose to ignore this incident."

David looked at Brynna, "What does it say to Kasen if we just let this go? Will he consider us and the Commonwealth weak?"

Brynna winced, her pain medications were starting to wear off and with her shoulder still out of place every movement hurt. "David, I can't be sure I am thinking clearly right now, but I do know I don't want to risk you getting hurt. I'm sure their healer can take care of my shoulder and bandage my wounds, but..." Brynna seemed to lose her train of thought. "I need to lay back down." Lazaro helped her lie down and gave her another dose of pain medication.

The group moved away from Brynna. They continued talking in low voices. David kept questioning Tharen. "What does your father expect us to do?"

Tharen shook his head, "I don't really know. I think he really wants to know what you are capable of. Just do what you think is best. That will tell him what he wants to know."

David considered Tharen's words. Getting this agreement in place was the main goal, but that wouldn't happen if they didn't win the competition, and that wasn't a sure thing even then. Kasen was apparently trying to provoke the team so ignoring it probably wouldn't help matters at all. Kasen had been yanking their chains from the beginning. David decided it was time to yank Kasen's chain a little. He turned to face Tharen. "Forgive me for putting you in a bad position, but this is what I have to do. Please tell your father we appreciate his hospitality, but under the circumstances, we cannot finish this competition. We do not admit defeat. We will gladly finish this if he so desires, but not here and now."

Tharen looked surprised. "You know that's going to make him angry, but you're doing it anyway? Do I tell him you know what Jager did?"

"Absolutely. I have nothing to hide from Kasen."

"Are you sure you want to do this?"

"It all ends the same way, Tharen. Your father is going to force a conflict, so it doesn't matter what I do. This way he has to show his hand first."

Tharen looked at David's hands, which were clearly visible and empty. "I don't understand? Show his hands?"

David realized the idiom wasn't translating accurately. They had been warned in their training months ago, about using such phrases, but sometimes those things just slipped out naturally. "Sorry Tharen, it refers to a game of both chance and skill. The skill is in maneuvering an opponent's perceptions. To show one's hand means to show what you actually have and what your intentions were." The translators weren't programmed to include alerts about idioms. The Sorley didn't have paper, so card games and their intricacies were unknown to them.

Tharen looked a little less confused. "So, it isn't about his hands at all. It is about his intentions."

"Right. Just thank your father for his hospitality but tell him we are leaving. We will not bother him any longer." David motioned for Manton, Lazaro, and Vesta to grab the corners of Brynna's stretcher and the group started walking toward the shuttle.

Tharen headed quickly to his father's dwelling and conveyed David's message. Tharen knew his father would not react well, and he was right. Kasen grabbed Tharen's clothes with both fists and pulled him forward until the two were in each other's faces. "Just what advice did you give him?"

Tharen looked his father straight in the eye and answered honestly. "I advised him to finish the tournament and say nothing about Jager sabotaging the race."

Kasen's face got redder. "You told him what I did!!!"

Tharen grabbed his father's fist and firmly yanked them off his clothes. "No! I didn't! I didn't have to! Captain Alexander saw Jager fire the dart at the horse. He also knew you were behind it. He's no fool."

Kasen stormed out. Tharen heard him get on his horse and ride off in the direction the crew was headed. He also heard Kasen call out to several men to come with him. Tharen decided he should follow them as well. He ran outside, grabbed his horse, and brought up the rear. Kasen circled around and caught up to the crew as they were nearing the edge of the encampment. He and his men surrounded the crew. Kasen got down off his horse and brusquely made his way over to David. David motioned for Cheyenne to take over his corner of Brynna's stretcher while he moved to meet Kasen. He only advanced a couple of steps before he was face to face with Kasen.

"I thought you were unafraid to admit defeat, yet you try to leave so you do not have to admit defeat to my face."

"Perhaps you would like to discuss this privately."

"I do not hide things from my people. Tharen said he advised you to complete the tournament. Why did you choose not to follow his advice?"

"As you wish. I suspect that wasn't all Tharen told you. I chose not to take his advice because my priority is the safety of my people. I can't be sure they will be safe if we complete this tournament. I don't need your help to complete our mission. It will take longer and be more work, but I can accomplish what I need without you."

Kasen weighed his words carefully. "I can assure you, we do not mean your people any harm. If you participate in the final event, win or lose you are under my protection."

"Would we be protected like Brynna was during the horse race?"

Kasen glared at David. "And just what are you implying?"

David snapped back at Kasen, "You know exactly what I am implying. Do you want me to say it? You want to lock me into a position and force my hand? Is that it? I'd love to sit down and talk about this, but if you want me to fight you, or Tharen, or Jager, just say it outright. Stop toying with us."

Kasen stepped back. He wasn't sure how to handle the young captain's response. His tone and demeanor eased just a little. "Admit defeat, and you may leave, or stay and finish the tournament. It's that simple."

"I'll tell you how simple it is. If I admit defeat, I will explain why we were defeated and not just to you, but to the Kimbra and the Akamu. Do you want this information spread halfway across your world?"

Kasen realized at this point, his men would suspect he had kept something from them. "Perhaps you are right. We should return to the meeting tent and sit down and talk about this. You seem to believe I have harmed you in some way. The healer can attend to your woman's injuries while we talk. Would this be acceptable to you? Your safety and that of your people is assured."

David stared at Kasen for another moment. He was sizing him up and making sure Kasen didn't underestimate him. David finally gave him a verbal response other than a stare laden with testosterone. "Fine. Let's get this settled." David backed away and pointed the crew back toward the tent they had just left. Kasen motioned for his men to take over carrying Brynna's stretcher.

Once back in the tent, David and Lazaro watched the healer, known as Darda, as he tended to Brynna's injuries. Darda started on her shoulder first. He was apparently a good healer and had an excellent bedside manner. He told Brynna what he was about to do every step of the way. Before he attempted to put her shoulder back into socket, he looked up at David and Lazaro. "If you have medicines for pain, you may want to give them to her now. This process is short and quick, and she will feel much better once I am done, but it will hurt when I do it." Darda had seen them give her injections earlier and recognized they were for pain. Lazaro gave her another dose of medication, with Jason's remotely approved blessing. Jason wasn't happy at all; they weren't bringing her back for him to treat Brynna. He did instruct Lazaro to also give her a muscle relaxer.

Now that Brynna was sufficiently medicated, Darda had David hold her right hand and instructed David to smile at Brynna. David looked confused. Darda simply said, "I need her to relax. You can help her with that. Focus her attention on you, not on her injuries."

David knelt beside Brynna. He grasped her hand gently and kissed it. With his left hand, David caressed her head. With all the medications in her system, Brynna's speech was no longer inhibited. "Oh, David, your bedside manner is horrible."

David looked confused. He looked back and forth between Brynna, Darda, and Lazaro. "What did I do?"

Brynna settled back and closed her eyes so she wouldn't see his face. "The look on your face says you think I'm dying. I'm not dying, David." David again looked up at Lazaro and Darda. He was feeling helpless. Darda scowled at him. He was already slowly pulling at Brynna's arm to stretch the muscles and couldn't concentrate on anything else.

Lazaro glanced down at Brynna, who was wincing periodically at the pain of having her muscles pulled and stretched. "She's right, sir."

Still glancing around David asked, "So what should I be doing, cracking jokes?"

Lazaro quickly responded, "Sure."

The translation of David's facetious question reached Darda a second later who gave a similar affirmative response. David looked back at Brynna's closed eyes and gave it his best effort. "Brynna, I have a problem."

Brynna's eyes fluttered open, and she looked over at David. "What is it? I'm not really dying, am I?"

David reassured her, "No, that's not it at all. My problem is... well, I don't know how to say this, but I'm not a comedian."

Brynna just stopped and looked at him for a moment, then burst out laughing. Darda chose that moment to slide her shoulder back into place. Brynna stopped laughing. "Ahh. Owww!" She took a deep breath then relaxed again. "That feels better." Lazaro smiled and looked away. David's humor was subtle but deeply effective.

David didn't want Brynna to know his difficulty smiling at her was unrelated to her injuries, but to the ones he knew he would potentially get in the upcoming match. Brynna had made her wishes clear earlier. He also knew he was going to have to disregard those same wishes. David quietly instructed Lazaro to give Brynna something to help her sleep. Brynna was now accustomed to Lazaro giving her injections, so she didn't stop him or question him, but when she saw the look on David's face, she knew. She grabbed Lazaro's hand, "What did you give me?"

Lazaro didn't realize the implications of what he was giving her or why she reacted so strongly. "I – I just gave you something to help you rest."

Brynna was already starting to fade, "Don't do...that...again."

Lazaro looked up at David, "Did I do something wrong?"

David shook his head. "You did as you were ordered."

Lazaro gave a bewildered look at David, "Did you do something wrong?"

David took a deep breath and walked toward Kasen. Lazaro heard David say "probably," under his breath.

"Kasen, before we begin, may I ask a favor?"

There was no longer any sign of anger on Kasen's face. "What is it?"

"Allow my crew to return to our ship so Brynna can rest comfortably in her own bed. Manton and I will stay here and finish this. The shuttle can return and pick us up after Brynna is settled, and we are done here."

"Why is this so important to you?"

David answered very candidly, "If things don't go well for me here, Brynna needs to be ready to take command of the ship. She doesn't need to have a bad memory clouding her judgment."

Kasen still showed no signs of anger. This time he showed a hint of compassion. "As you wish. I will have four of my warriors carry her to your ship, outside our camp."

"I need to give one of my men some instructions, then we can begin." Kasen nodded his approval to David. Kasen turned to give instructions to his own men.

David walked back over to his crew and began barking out instructions. "Manton, I want you to stay here with me. Lazaro, take Brynna, Cheyenne, and Vesta back to the ship. Bring Jason and Thane back here to pick us up after Brynna has been attended to. Brynna is not to be brought back here under any circumstances. If I don't make it back, she's in command. Finish the mission without the Sorley's help. Understand?"

Lazaro responded with a prompt and somber, "Yes, Captain."

Cheyenne's eyes got wide, and her response was more of a question, "Captain?"

David looked at her, knowing she was suddenly scared. "Ensign, I am not planning on dying, but sometimes things don't work out like we plan. I need to know everything is handled. Do you understand my orders?"

Cheyenne, still looking scared answered, "Yes sir."

David then drove his point home, "Will you obey my orders?" Cheyenne was too stunned to speak. Of all his crew members, Cheyenne was the youngest, least experienced, and the most emotional. David pushed again this time more forcefully, "ENSIGN, are you going to obey my orders?"

Shaken out of her daze by his tone, Cheyenne responded, "Yes, Captain."

The captain looked at Vesta. Before he could ask, she responded. Vesta had surprisingly picked up a little of their language already and responded in Intergalactic Standard, "Yes, Captain."

David smiled at her response. There was a little bit of an accent in her response, but he had no trouble understanding her words or her intentions. "Okay, everybody get moving. Lazaro, don't let the Commander bully you into turning the shuttle around if she wakes up. My orders are for the good of the entire crew, and they stand until you know for certain I am no longer alive. Got it?"

Lazaro nodded, "Yes sir." He checked to see how long it had been since he had given her the sedative. He really didn't want to fight that battle. He wanted to be sure they were back on the ship before she woke up.

David watched as the crew walked down the path toward the shuttle, then he turned to face Kasen. David took his place sitting on the ground opposite Kasen. "Let's get started."

Kasen motioned for his other advisers to take their places. Tharen, Jager, and Gervas took their seats. Slaves brought in food and water to each of them. David knew he best refresh while he had the chance. He and Manton ate a meager, yet well-balanced amount of food. Kasen finally started the discussion. "You seem to think we have wronged you in some way. Please explain what you think has happened to you."

David kept his attention focused on Kasen. "Our society believes in fairness, keeping competition honorable and straightforward. We do not change the rules in the middle of a competition, nor do we have different sets of rules for different competitors. All competitors have access to all the rules of an event before it happens. Cheating is not permissible. It brings dishonor to the competition."

Kasen still seemed surprisingly calm. "State your grievance."

David kept his gaze on Kasen and very calmly and carefully stated his grievance as requested. "Whether you are aware or involved, I do not know for certain, but I do know Jager blew a dart into Brynna's horse causing it to throw her. I demand satisfaction. Brynna would have probably placed in the top three of the horse race, meaning we would have won the competition. He has caused her to be injured, and she could have been killed. I witnessed him blow the dart, our scanner found the irritant in the horse's system. The mark was found on the horse's backside."

Jager started to jump up exuding righteous indignation, despite his guilt. Kasen had instructed him to react as though he were offended. Tharen grabbed Jager's arm to keep him seated. It was still improper for him to interrupt the proceeding. Tharen also hoped, by holding Jager back his father would admit his complicity in the process.

Kasen looked over at Jager, "What do you have to say?"

Jager jumped to his feet. "I have been accused of bringing dishonor on myself and my people. I demand satisfaction!"

Tharen gave a subtle nod to David. David stood up and calmly claimed, "You cannot demand satisfaction. I have already demanded it."

Jager looked at Kasen, unsure of what to say next. Kasen looked at David and the corner of his mouth twitched as though he were trying to stop himself from smiling. "Do you know what you are asking when you demand satisfaction?"

David nodded at Kasen and kept one eye on Jager. "I do."

"And what will bring you satisfaction?"

"Confession of guilt by anyone involved or Jager's blood on my hands."

Jager looked back and forth from David to Kasen. This wasn't how it was supposed to go. Jager wasn't afraid to fight, but if he accepted David's challenge he had no way out except to admit his guilt. If Jager had been the one to demand satisfaction, he could have quit at any time.

"Jager, I assume you would rather accept this challenge than admit guilt?" It sounded more like an instruction than a question. Jager and Kasen appeared to pass unspoken words between them.

Kasen stood up, grasped the wrists of David and Jager and held them up. "It is my decision that these two shall compete in mortal combat until satisfaction is achieved. This combat shall also decide the winner of today's competition. He who wins, wins all. Prepare the circle."

Several men took off for the edge of the encampment where the other events had been held. Kasen told the two men it would take a few minutes to prepare the circle. He instructed the men to spend this time preparing themselves to fight and to meet their gods.

Tharen walked over and spoke to David quietly. "Well played, Captain. Are you prepared to kill my best friend?"

David looked over at Jager who was watching him just as closely. Looking at Tharen, David candidly replied, "I hope it doesn't get that far, but I'm not going to let him kill me."

Tharen studied David carefully, "You've never killed before, have you?"

David returned Tharen's gaze. "The Commonwealth wouldn't put anyone in command of one of their ships if they hadn't killed before. I've killed in combat. It's not something I want to repeat." Tharen didn't appear satisfied. David knew he shouldn't be. The kills David made were using a long-range laser, and he barely saw the faces of those he killed, let alone see the life drain from their eyes. Hand-to-hand combat was different. If it came down to it, he would have to look Jager in the eye and still kill him. The Commonwealth Tenets protected life. He had been raised to protect life, and now he was at a point where he might have to take one or have his own life taken. He really hoped Kasen or Jager would value life more than protecting a lie.

Before Tharen walked over to talk to Jager, he needed to let everyone know where his loyalties were. Tharen whispered to David and waited for the translation to reach him. "Sorry about this." David wasn't sure what to expect, but he understood the gist of what was about to happen. Tharen shoved David, then landed a right cross on David's left cheek. David, being marginally ready, was able to mitigate the full impact of the blow. Tharen did manage to bust the corner of David's lip and drew blood. Tharen shouted at David, "You used my advice against me! Jager will make you regret this!" David calmly wiped the blood from the corner of his mouth and glared at Tharen. He decided to say nothing. Tharen walked on over to Jager and appeared to be giving him encouragement.

Manton, feeling lost looked at David. "Am I supposed to be your second?" David shook his head. "No, I don't want it to come to that. I want to win or lose on my own."

Manton shook his head. "What is gained by your death?"

David shook his head, "Not much is gained by my death, but killing Jager doesn't help anything either. If I die, Kasen can't be trusted, and the mission needs to move on to other areas."

Manton didn't look any less confused. "So, what is gained by fighting Jager?"

David shook his head and started to wonder himself if this was going to be a worthwhile venture. "Hopefully, the truth." David realized if he fell and were unable to continue to fight Manton might voluntarily take his place as his second. "Manton, you are NOT to take my place, no matter what. If the crew gets here before this is over, they are not to take my place either. Make sure they know those are my orders. Understand?"

Manton followed his wife's precedent earlier and answered in Intergalactic Standard. "Yes, Captain."

David laughed. He found it very amusing the first words the Akamu learned were "Yes, Captain." He expected them to be able to say something more like "hello," "where can I get some food?" or "where's the bathroom?" David slapped Manton lightly on the back. "You are a good man, Manton. If I fall, just make sure my body gets back to the ship." David wasn't sure why he was concerned about the disposition of his own body. If he died, it wasn't like he would need it anymore.

A call was heard being passed from a distance toward the meeting tent. Upon hearing the call come in, Kasen stood up and announced, "The circle is ready. Let us go."

David and Manton joined the group heading to the edge of the camp. By this time the sun was setting, and the air was starting to cool. The sunset was going to be beautiful, although no one was currently interested in watching it. David would have enjoyed the colorful display, and he observed as much of it as he could. He and Brynna's work was so intense they enjoyed doing the simplest of pleasures to relax. When they reached the edge of the encampment, David saw a large circle had been plowed up by horses. The freshly plowed ground had one narrow walkway into the center of the circle, which was also untouched by the plows. The area closest to the inner circle was being piled up with logs and tree branches. David assumed they were creating a barrier to keep the two fighters contained. The two men were brought before a row of pikes. Since Jager had been challenged, he had the option of choosing his staff first, but Kasen encouraged Jager to let David go first. David went through and picked a staff, which seemed sturdy and made of newer, greener wood. After David chose his pike, he moved onto the walkway. He turned to Kasen, "Are there any rules I need to know about?"

Kasen turned to answer David. "In order to win the tournament, you must defeat Jager. To achieve satisfaction, Jager must confess the truth, and you must believe him, or you must kill him. If he is injured and unable to continue or confess, you must defeat his second. Tharen is his second. You must stay inside the circle until the matter is decided. There are no other rules. You can stop short of killing if you so desire by announcing you have achieved satisfaction. Be warned though, if you leave your opponent alive they may demand satisfaction for the humiliation you caused them. If you need a respite, you must convince your opponent to take one as well. Do you understand these rules? There can be no cheating because nothing is prohibited."

David gripped his staff firmly. "I understand." He had been sipping on his canteen of water. He took the last sip and tossed it to Manton along with his jacket.

Kasen had one last question for David, "Do you have a second?"

Kasen expected David would name Manton as his second, but without flinching David firmly said, "No, I don't."

"As you wish." Kasen stepped closer to David and quietly told him, "Stay alive, and we will definitely have some things to discuss." He then turned and went to talk to Jager. The two spoke quietly for a moment. David hoped he was assuring Jager he would set the record straight before things went too far.

David entered the circle and moved to the far side of it. While he waited on Jager, he practiced with the staff to get the feel of it. It was exactly how Tharen had described it. It had been sharpened to a point on one end but was blunt on the other. Jager moved into the circle, only he stayed closer to the center. Jager didn't appear to be ready to start combat, but David knew if Jager was staying toward the center of the circle, there must be a reason. He noticed a heavy, oily smell around him. He suddenly realized the unusually wide area carved out of the ground wasn't just overzealous plowing. David moved away from the edge just in time to see torches being thrown into the piles around the circle. The fire spread quickly around the circle. As the ring became engulfed in flames, Jager's posture went from a casual warm-up stance to a stance of battle readiness. He eyed David cautiously.

David gathered it was up to him to make the first move. Jager did not strike David as being shy or reserved in his battle strategies. David had sized him up as having an aggressive fighting style the first time he met him. David and Jager circled each other for a moment, and David raised the blunt end of his staff for a quick short swing toward Jager's head, which Jager easily blocked. The crowd around them gave a loud shout when the first contact was made. David again made a straight on jab toward Jager's face, which was blocked again. This time Jager followed his block with the blunt end of his staff, catching David's back just below his shoulder blade. David had left himself open for the blow to test Jager out. It was a safe way to test him because a blow there, although not comfortable for David, was relatively harmless. Jager didn't have room to take a broad swing and pick up any momentum, but taking the obvious opening gave David insight into Jager's mindset and fighting style.

Now that the door was open for Jager, he wasted no time. He swung at David's head, and when David ducked the blow, Jager spun all the way around to increase his momentum and came in low with his next blow. David jumped back to avoid the impact but lost his balance in his haste and landed on his back. Jager wasted no time and attempted to land a blow while David was down. David blocked Jager's staff, but Jager put his weight on the staff to keep himself steady as he pulled his foot back and gave David a sturdy kick in the ribs. Despite the new pain in his ribs, David was able to throw Jager off balance and roll to his feet. Before David could get turned around to face Jager, he could hear Jager coming up behind him. David took a chance and shoved the blunt end of his staff straight behind him. His gamble paid off as he felt his staff make contact with Jager's abdomen. David knew it wouldn't take him but a second to counter again, so the young captain turned around quickly to face his opponent. He chose not to move in quickly, but to take a second to regain his bearings and catch his breath. David hoped this strategy would cause Jager to wear himself out quicker. Jager stabbed at David with the sharp end of his staff then tried to follow through with the same move he had hit David with earlier. David was ready for it this time and rolled away from it. He managed to get a glancing blow in across Jager's temple.

The blow angered Jager. He somehow had the impression Sky People were weak because they depended on their machines to do all their work for them. Jager did get the impression David's fighting style was similar to Tharen's. Jager did not like this feeling. It felt like fighting Tharen only more violently. Jager moved on David with many short, fast blows. David blocked as many as he could, as fast as he could, but he wasn't able to stop them all. He felt a blow land on the same ribs Jager kicked earlier. Only this time he felt a sickening crunch. David attempted to retreat to catch his breath and get his bearings, but Jager didn't relent. He struck David's staff and sent it flying to the other side of the circle. David knew he didn't stand a chance against Jager without that staff. He dodged the next two swings. He tried to work his way to the spot where his staff had landed, but Jager kept his path blocked.

Jager swung at David a third time without making contact, but before Jager could return his staff to a neutral blocking position, David launched himself at Jager and began to punch him repeatedly. In the ensuing scuffle, the two rolled and tumbled back and forth in the circle. David tried to wrestle Jager's staff out of his hands. The two continued to wrestle and came dangerously close to the fire ring. Jager forced the staff over a nearby flame. The burn from the flame forced David to release his grip on the staff, but not before he threw Jager off him. David and Jager continued to wrestle. David landed several blows, but he could not knock the staff from Jager's hands.

David ended up face down with Jager sitting on him pulling his staff hard against David's throat. The pressure on his neck and throat became so intense, David felt himself losing consciousness. Jager felt David's body going limp. As his body collapsed, Jager kept a firm grip on his throat. David was sure this was the end. Just before he lost consciousness, he heard a voice tell him, "Get up and finish this. We have work to do. I'm not done with you yet. Get up NOW." David was confused by who else was in the ring. Jager released his hold on David's throat. He got up slowly and backed away from David. Jager knew he had stopped just short of ending

David's life, but he also knew he was guilty of what David had accused him of. He couldn't in good conscience kill him.

David opened his eyes to see Jager leaving the circle. If he completely exited the circle, it would be over. David's hand found a rock, which he threw as hard as he could at Jager. It wasn't large enough to do any real damage, but David was sure it stung. While Jager assessed the damage done by the rock and David's renewed attack, David managed to reach his staff again. He used Jager's moment of hesitation to catch his breath and clear his head. He wished he could clear the pain as well. Jager advanced toward him again and shook his head. He shouted at David, "Why didn't you just stay down and let me walk away? You're just going to get yourself hurt worse." Thankfully, Jager gave the translator time to catch up before taking any other action although David's resilience angered him and waiting on the translation just added fuel to the fire. Jager was an honorable man and wanted David to hear his warning. He didn't want to harm him.

David didn't waste his breath trying to answer. Every breath hurt. David let his thoughts jump back to his combat training classes. Suddenly his moves came from rote memory, he attacked Jager with precision and skill he didn't remember having. He felt so incredibly focused nothing distracted him. The next thing he knew, Jager was lying on the ground unconscious. When Jager ceased fighting, David backed away from him and looked outside the ring until his eyes found Kasen. He seriously hoped Kasen would now confess to the actions that led up to this.

Captain Alexander was not so lucky. Two men walked in unarmed and carried Jager out. As soon as they cleared the path, Tharen stepped onto it and entered the circle carrying a staff of his own choosing. David wiped the sweat from his brow and face. The dirt and sweat were causing his eyes to sting. As soon as Tharen entered, David said, "You've got to be kidding. I don't suppose I could get a canteen of water before starting over."

Tharen nodded for Manton to toss David a canteen. Manton had refilled both canteens from a nearby barrel. He tossed one to David over the flames that were beginning to die down. The oil had burned off and only the wood remained. The added heat had not made this fight any easier. David took several large swigs of the water then poured some of the water over his face and head.

He pulled his shirt off to wipe the excess water from his face. Taking two more quick swallows, he tossed the canteen along with his shirt back to Manton. David knew Tharen did not have to agree to the brief respite, but he appreciated it very much. This wasn't the time or place to express his appreciation.

After the canteen was tossed away, Tharen assumed a battle posture. David was less enthusiastic but rejoined the fight and attempted to focus his mind, as it had been moments earlier. Tharen took on an aggressive but calculating fighting style. David felt like he was fighting himself because Tharen seemed to anticipate his moves. Tharen was leading with the sharp end of the staff more than the blunt end. David's training had not really covered weapons like spears, which was what this really was. He was comfortable fighting against a staff, a sword or knife, but this pike had the length of a spear, a sharp point, but hefty like a staff. Tharen's strategy was paying off. Tharen managed to draw blood from David's arm, thigh, and chest. They were all just grazes.

David knew, no matter how Tharen felt about him and his mission, he would have to fight genuinely. He doubted Tharen would carry it too far, but he also wouldn't let David off easily. David managed to get a lucky blow into Tharen's thigh. Instinctively, David backed off to give Tharen a chance to recover. Tharen took full advantage of David's hesitation and came back at him with renewed vigor. David managed to get his focus back but didn't like the results of using the sharp end of the staff. They traded blows equally for a few minutes until Tharen landed another blow just above the ribs Jager had already hit and probably broken. David felt a similar sensation to the new ribs. He knew his time was running out in this fight. He was going to have to make some quick and decisive moves to end this once and for all. He just needed to somehow rattle or distract Tharen.

As if in answer to a prayer, the shuttle flew over the circle looking for a better place to land. Tharen caught himself watching the shuttle instead of David. David didn't hesitate. He knocked Tharen's staff from his hands then hit him behind the knees, which put him on the ground. David put one foot firmly on Tharen's chest and held the point at his throat. Tharen lay very still. If David slipped, it could be fatal for him. David looked up at Kasen to see if he would relent his position. Jager was now conscious and sitting on the ground. He looked up at Kasen, who didn't return his look. He seemed to be waiting for something.

Receiving no input from Kasen, Jager jumped up and shouted.

"I confess. I tampered with the race. I am guilty. You have your satisfaction. Release him."

Kasen still did not take his eyes off David. David didn't understand what Kasen was waiting on. David shouted back to Jager, "You did not do this alone. Who else was involved? Speak now, or I will destroy him." Jager stood up beside Kasen. The crowd was on their feet yelling loudly. David could see the crew running toward the circle. There would be no satisfaction in killing Tharen. He watched Kasen to see if he would stop him. David's eyes locked on Tharen's. David gave a brief, quick glance to the right. Tharen nodded. David pulled his foot off Tharen's chest and then reared back to land the final blow. As the spike came back down, Tharen twisted to his left. The point landed in the dirt narrowly missing Tharen.

Tharen looked up at David gratefully. He was afraid to move but knowing David was not going to harm him, he allowed himself to relax. His arms had been poised ready to react if the opportunity presented itself. He laid his head back down on the ground and let his arms and legs go limp. He wasn't trying to play dead, but for those outside the circle, it appeared David had killed Tharen. His intention had been to test Kasen to see how far Kasen would let things go. He expected that if it appeared Tharen were dead, Kasen would confess. It didn't happen as David expected.

David looked up at the Sorley Leader. His posture indicated he had yelled to stop David but was not heard because of the roar of the crowd around them. He was now standing there in shock. Suddenly Kasen was moving. He grabbed two of the pikes from the ground and headed toward David with murder in his eyes. David looked down at Tharen and realized what he was thinking. He held up his hands to get Kasen to stop and listen to him. The crowd was shouting so loudly and angrily David couldn't be heard. He moved toward Kasen in order to be heard. His broken ribs and exhausted condition slowed his movement down. He had used his last bit of strength to plunge the staff into the ground. David tried to pull his staff free, but he couldn't dislodge it. Tharen was no longer in a direct line of sight from Kasen's new position. He had cut his jab so close. Tharen's clothing had been caught by the point of the staff and pinned to the ground. He thought if he could free Tharen, Kasen would stop his murderous advance. Kasen, still on the path into the circle, took his first staff and threw it at David. It was a narrow miss. David saw the pike land just inside the fire ring and thought he might be able to retrieve it. He thought he could use it to protect himself until he could make Kasen understand Tharen was still alive. Between the fire ring and his grief-stricken anger, Kasen could not see Tharen moving on the ground trying to free himself from the pike. David reached for the pike lodged in the fire. It was firmly planted in a log that was still intact. The fire was so hot David couldn't stay close enough to dislodge it.

By this time, Kasen was nearly on top of David. Kasen took the second staff and struck David across the side of the head. David tried to move toward Tharen so Kasen would see he was still alive. Kasen plunged the pike into David's calf. David cried out in pain but still struggled to move toward Tharen. Kasen pulled the pike out of David's calf and moved backward. He struck David with the blunt end again. David saw stars after the first blow, but now he saw darkness. He knew if Tharen didn't get Kasen's attention, it would all be over in a moment.

Kasen backed away from David far enough to throw the pike. David's vision started to clear. He wondered why Kasen kept throwing the pike instead of simply running him through. What David didn't know was retribution after a bout like this was forbidden, and it was merely a loophole. If Kasen's hands were on the weapon, Kasen would be guilty of a heinous crime, but if the pike were flying through the air, he would be considered blameless. David could see well enough now to see Kasen lean back to launch the weapon at him. He also saw Tharen get free of his pinned clothing and race toward David. Kasen launched the weapon at David who was no longer in any position to move. Tharen cried out and dove for the pike. He tried to block it with his hand but missed. The pike lodged in the left side of his chest, very near his heart. Kasen's face went from anger to surprise and relief as his eyes focused on Tharen then fear and horror as he saw the staff lodge in Tharen's chest. The complete transition took about half a second, but as David watched, it felt like the whole thing was moving in slow motion. He saw every expression with amazing clarity. Kasen immediately ran to Tharen's side and lifted his head off the ground. Tharen was still conscious but struggling to breathe and trying not to succumb to the pain. Kasen now had a stricken look on his face. David struggled to his knees and motioned for Jason to come into the ring. Thane, Lazaro, and Manton followed close behind. Tharen's eyes were already glazed as he began to go into shock. Kasen looked down at his son and begged his forgiveness and apologized repeatedly.

Jason got to Tharen's side and began scanning him. Jason wanted to check on David, but he knew Tharen's injuries were far more serious. Jason looked up at David.

"I think I can save him, but I have to get him back to the infirmary right now."

David looked at Kasen, "This time, will you let my healer help you?" Kasen nodded. He was too paralyzed with grief over what he had done to speak. Jason gave Tharen a couple injections to stabilize him until he could get him back to the ship. He drew his laser and cut the staff off close to Tharen's body then secured it to keep it from moving during the trip. Thane, Jager, and two warriors carried Tharen out to the shuttle. Manton helped David back to the shuttle. The angry crowd followed. Kasen wanted to board the shuttle and go with Tharen, but he feared his people would riot. The captain also realized the potential problems especially if all of them left. It would appear they had kidnapped the ruling body of the Sorley. David stopped short of getting on the shuttle. Thane had the shuttle powered up and ready to go. Kasen stayed outside the shuttle. David looked back at the angry mob. Jager was on the shuttle at Tharen's side. Jason looked up and saw David and Kasen standing outside the shuttle. "Get in, we have to get moving!"

Kasen looked at Tharen then at his people. "I can't go. I need to stay with my people."

David's compassion for the man outweighed his desire to go home and get in his own bed. "Kasen, you go. I will stay as a hostage until the two of you return."

Kasen was partially relieved at the suggestion, but still concerned. Manton again followed the captain's lead. "I will stay as well."

Kasen called for Gervas and Jager. The two men came to his side. Kasen motioned for silence. The people quieted down. He shouted loudly for all to hear. "My people, I have caused my own son harm. It is not the fault of the Sky People. They are graciously trying to heal my son and return him to us. I am going to accompany my son to the home of the Sky People. Gervas and Jager will rule until I return. Listen to them. They are wiser men than I am. The leader of the Sky People will stay here to ensure my safe return. If I do not return within three days, his life is forfeit. Tonight, you will pray to the gods for my son's life. Cleanse yourselves and pray!"

Jason, hearing what David had planned, objected strenuously. "Captain, you need treatment too."

David shook his head. "Get Tharen taken care of and get back here as soon as possible. Then you can treat me." Lazaro, now quite used to being a medic, grabbed the spare med kit and jumped off the shuttle. Kasen was guided to a seat near Tharen and assisted in getting buckled up. David and the others moved away from the shuttle as it powered up to lift off. David hit his comm unit and hoped after the beating he had taken, it was still working. It was.

"Captain Alexander to the *Evangeline*, please respond."

Aulani answered, "Captain, this is the *Evangeline*, go ahead."

"What is the status of the crew?"

"Team One has just returned from the caves, Jake is on his way to the bridge. Brynna has been moved back to your cabin and is still sleeping. Laura is keeping an eye on her. Are you on your way back, sir?"

"Negative, Ensign. The shuttle is coming in hot. They have a critical patient on board who needs urgent treatment. It's Tharen, the son of the Sorley Leader, Kasen. Kasen is with his son. Lt. Commander Dominick and Manton are here with me. We will stay here until Kasen comes back to the village. The Sorley population is on the edge of declaring war on us, so we're staying here to keep the peace. Let Brynna know I'm okay, I'm a little banged up, and a couple broken ribs, but I'll be fine. Pass that information on to Jake."

Jake had come onto the bridge while Aulani was reporting to the captain. "I'm here sir, I caught it all. What are the security risks?"

"Kasen and Tharen are not security risks unless Tharen doesn't make it. The risk would be out here with us if we can't contain the situation. I think everything will be fine here but keep an eye on the scanners. Lt. Commander Flint is in charge until Commander Alexander is considered medically fit to return to duty."

"Sir? I thought you would be in command remotely?"

"Negative, I am not medically fit for duty anymore."

"Sir, how bad is your physical condition?"

David tried to take a deep breath, but it hurt to breathe, and he ended up coughing which hurt even more. Once he caught his breath, he answered Jake. "I'm not critical chief, but I will need treatment soon. Lazaro stayed behind to take care of me. I assume he will have me sedated shortly."

"I'm sorry sir, but I have one more question. If you're supposed to be keeping the peace out there, can you do that and be sedated at the same time?"

David was extremely tired and on the verge of being both cranky and slaphappy, but he held it in for a moment longer. "Chief, we're hostages. Kasen left two of his men in charge, and it's their job to keep the peace. If Tharen doesn't make it, or Kasen doesn't return within three days, my life is forfeit. Just get Tharen and Kasen back here as soon as Tharen is able to travel."

"Yes sir. Let us know if we need to find a way to pull you out."

"That will be Lt. Commander Dominick's call."

"Understood, Captain. Get some rest, sir. Evangeline out."

David had his left arm across Manton's shoulders for support while he walked. Lazaro was on his right. "Commander, I don't remember agreeing to forfeit my life if Kasen doesn't return. Do you remember me making that agreement? Manton, do you remember me agreeing to that?"

Lazaro shook his head, "No, Captain, but I was gone for a while."

Manton had a contemplative look on his face. "Captain, I think he said that to satisfy his people. I think he trusts your people enough to know he will be back well before that is an issue."

David laughed, "That must be it. He's going to kill me because he trusts me. Ow. Hey, Dr. Lazaro, I think my Adrenalin is wearing off."

Lazaro reached into the med kit and pulled out a dose of medication. He gave David a quick injection. "I guess it was a good thing you took yourself out of command for tonight."

Jager and Gervas got the three men settled in the meeting tent to sleep. The two men made sure their guests had plenty of food, water, and bedding. They unrolled the sides of the tent to give them warmth and privacy. Lazaro did what he could to treat David's injuries and then gave him something to help him sleep. Jager set guards outside the tent on all sides, mostly for the crew's protection. It also let the general population know the crew wasn't going anywhere.

Lazaro pushed David to eat a little bit before he settled down to sleep. When Lazaro scanned him, it confirmed David's broken ribs.

He had numerous bruises, cuts, scrapes, a couple burns, and an ugly stab wound in his calf. The scan also revealed a nasty concussion from blows to the head. Lazaro followed the scanners instructions for treating David the best that he could. As David tried to get comfortable, he looked over at the crew who were sitting around softly talking. They were trying to be quiet and let the captain rest. David was very drowsy from exhaustion, pain medications, and sedatives, but he did want to convey one more message prior to sleeping. "Lazaro, Manton, I just want to tell you, um, to thank you for your help. You probably saved my life today. Um, tell Brynna I had to get some, some sleep. Thanks for yelling at me, Manton. Jager almost had me... I." David's speech was slurred, and his thoughts were jumbled. "If you hadn't yelled..." With that, David was asleep.

Manton gave a puzzled look toward Lazaro. Lazaro thought perhaps the translator didn't understand David's ramblings. "I think he means whatever you said to him gave him the motivation to keep fighting."

The look on Manton's face didn't get any less puzzled. "I didn't say anything to him."

Now it was Lazaro's time to be puzzled. "Well, maybe it will make more sense in the morning."

Manton thought a minute and then laughed. "I need to find out what I said that was so inspiring. I might want to say it again sometime."

Lazaro joined his laughter. "That's a good idea. Maybe I could use it sometime too. Let's get some sleep. I think we could all use the rest now. We have no idea what tomorrow holds."

THE SORELY

THE SORELY RESOLUTION

The shuttle trip back to the ship was quick and easy. As soon as the shuttle landed, Jake and Braxton were waiting to get the young Sorley warrior to the infirmary. Vesta was a fast learner and went to Kasen's aid. She helped him get unbuckled. As soon as he was free, he quickly grabbed one corner of the stretcher to carry his son. Thane, Jake, and Braxton carried the other three corners. Jason led the way to the infirmary. Laura was already there waiting on them. She had the room prepped for the anticipated surgical procedure. Laura was a botanist by preference, but she was also trained as a nurse and field medic. She was accustomed to assisting her husband in these situations. Most couples didn't work well together, but they seemed to have an affinity for it.

The four men brought the stretcher in and moved Tharen into a bed in the Med Bay. Lexi and Cheyenne had been assisting Laura in getting things prepared. Jason and Laura were ready to start working on Tharen. Jason asked Lexi to escort Kasen from the room. Thane and Vesta had already left. Braxton and Jake were waiting by the door. Lexi approached Kasen. "Kasen, I am Lexi. I am an adviser to the captain. We need to leave this room so the doctor can work."

Kasen adamantly refused to leave. "I will not leave my son in the hands of my enemies. I will stay and stand watch."

Vesta and Lazaro had told the crew earlier the captain was staying behind to fight one of the warriors. Lexi looked back at Tharen. "Did the captain do that to him?"

Kasen winced, "No, I did it. I was trying to kill your captain because I thought he killed my son. Tharen jumped in between your captain and the pike. He was protecting your captain."

Lexi looked at Tharen again then back at Kasen. Jason was waiting as patiently as he could for Kasen to leave the room, but Lexi could see his patience was wearing thin. Lexi tried again to reason with Kasen. "Your son saved our captain's life, and our captain stayed behind refusing medical care so Tharen's life might be saved. How does that make us enemies? Do you really think our doctor would dishonor his captain's sacrifice? The doctor does not consider Tharen his enemy. Since the captain put Tharen's importance over his own, we all value Tharen's importance. The doctor needs us to leave so he can focus entirely on Tharen. If the doctor isn't focused on Tharen, he could unintentionally cause worse harm. We are just going down the hall. There is a way we can stand watch from another room. Please, this is what is best for Tharen." Kasen realized if they truly wanted Tharen dead, they simply had to leave him back at the camp and do nothing. The truth was, Kasen didn't want to leave his son's side because he felt guilty. Kasen indicated his consent with a brief sullen nod.

Braxton and Jake led Kasen to the dining hall. Lexi followed him out. When they reached the dining hall, Braxton instructed both Lexi and Jake to see to the man's needs, but not to let him have free run of the ship. The first thing Lexi did was turn the video surveillance on so Kasen could see what was happening with Tharen. She did manipulate the angle, so he could see Tharen's face and the monitor indicating his vital signs but obscured the details of the surgery as they worked. Cheyenne stayed in the room helping with the surgery.

Kasen looked at the computer screen, then looked at the wall behind him. It appeared he was torn between panic, confusion, and anger. Lexi looked at Jake, "Get Vesta in here, now!" Jake hailed her on the comm unit. Jake wasn't about to leave Lexi alone with Kasen. Vesta was getting used to the advanced technology but having Jake's voice suddenly in her ear without his presence was still unnerving to her. Hearing the tension in his voice, she shook off the eerie feeling and made her way quickly to the dining hall. When she arrived, it was just in time to find Kasen ranting about the computer screen.

"This window is trickery. My son is behind us. This window is in front of us. This cannot show me my son."

Lexi was having trouble bringing her explanation of video cameras down to his level. She looked helplessly at Vesta. "Can you think of a way to explain how we can see Tharen from in here?"

Vesta thought for a moment then told Kasen. "These people have many eyes and windows. They can see places where we cannot, but they are not deceiving you. Let me show you." Vesta walked over to a drawer and picked up a shiny reflective spoon. She held one up in front of Kasen. "Can you see your own reflection in the metal?" Kasen nodded. Vesta moved around behind him and held the spoon up so he could see her reflection. "I am not in front of you now, but you can see my image in the spoon can you not?" Kasen nodded again. "I do not know how all these things work, but this window is not hard for me to believe." Vesta turned to Jake, "Can you go into that room and let him see you then come back in here?" Jake was hesitant, but Kasen seemed to be more settled. Jake agreed and headed down the hall. He popped briefly into the infirmary, apologized to the Doc for interrupting, got in the camera's line of sight, waved, then quickly headed back to the dining hall.

Cheyenne, Laura, and Jason gave each other confused looks. Laura laughed and said, "I don't even want to know what that was about."

When Jake returned, Kasen was now seated and intently staring at the computer screen. He was rocking and muttering a phrase repeatedly. Lexi got close enough to pick up a translation. The translation was of a prayer to one of the Sorley deities. Lexi asked Vesta if she would mind staying with them in the dining hall for a while. She was still unnerved by Vesta's presence, but she had to admit the woman had been helpful with Kasen. Lexi picked up a datapad to work on a report of the work she had done with the Akamu during the day and made herself a note to add Vesta's valuable assistance to her report. Jake took up a position near Lexi. He knew she was still uneasy about her recent ordeal. Jake also wanted to keep a close eye on Kasen and the surgery. He wanted as much warning as possible if the surgery didn't go well, so he sat where he had a good vantage point of everything.

Vesta was not quite sure what was expected of her, except to help keep Kasen calm. She decided to sit beside him and pray to her gods as well. She hoped they could hear her so far from the caves. She began to whisper phrases similar to the ones Kasen was using except she called the name of other deities.

The two were not being particularly noisy, but it was distracting for Lexi. Lexi thought about leaving Kasen in Jake's care for a little while but decided if something happened, she would be needed quickly. Jake saw her frustration and decided to strike up a conversation. "That was a good explanation Vesta gave Kasen, wasn't it?"

Lexi looked up at Jake who as now sitting at the corner of her table. He was keeping his eyes on the screen while he talked to her. Lexi didn't want to "disturb" the prayers in the room, so she answered softly. "Yes, it was. I was surprised. It was a very rudimentary explanation, but it was on target."

Jake nodded in agreement. "This is going to be an interesting debrief when this mission is over. We've got the Commander on Medical Leave in her cabin, the captain taking himself off active duty because he's injured and should be in the Med Bay himself. The Doc is doing major surgery on a chieftain's son who was trying to stop the chieftain from killing the captain. We're also depending on the help of a local warrior to explain a computer screen."

Lexi smiled. "You're right. It's going to be an interesting meeting. I can't wait to hear the specifics. Do you think the captain's okay?"

Marissa wandered in to get something to eat. After getting her food, she started to sit down by Jake, but when she saw the surgery going on in the background and heard the mantras, she decided to go back to her cabin to eat. She gave Jake a quick peck on the cheek and told him she would see him later. Jake smelled her food and realized he was hungry. It had been at least six hours since he had eaten, maybe eight. Jake got a plate of food for himself and Lexi, then sat down beside her to eat. He had not forgotten her question. "I talked to the captain."

Lexi motioned for Jake to wait a moment. She went to the dispensers and ordered a couple of bowls of soup and some bread with cheese, then slid one of the tables in front of Kasen and Vesta and placed the food on the tables in front of them. She also poured glasses of water for them. Kasen took his eyes off the monitor for a moment. He thanked Lexi for the food but declined to eat it. "I cannot eat until my son is out of danger. The gods must know his life is more important than mine."

Vesta chose to abstain with him. Lexi told them she understood, although in truth she really didn't. She did understand that sometimes people couldn't eat when they are upset, but a conscious decision not to eat was odd. Lexi told the couple it was there whenever they wanted, and it could be reheated if necessary.

Lexi sat back down with her plate and started her conversation and her meal over again. "What were you saying about the captain?"

Jake continued in between bites. "I talked to him just before the shuttle returned. He was exhausted, in pain, and his thought processes were slow, but they were still on target. He's going to need some recuperation time, but he'll be fine. Were you planning on going back to the caves tomorrow?"

Lexi shrugged. "I told the Akamu we would be back, but I wasn't sure if we would be back tomorrow or not. I guess it depends on how things go tonight."

"You're probably right."

The two ate quietly for a few minutes when they heard Jason announce, "The pike is out. I still have a lot of repair work to do, but so far so good. It missed his heart, but he does have a collapsed lung. It nicked an artery and broke just one rib, although the one rib is broken badly."

Kasen turned to Lexi and Jake. "What does this mean? Will my son live?"

Lexi stopped eating and moved around in front of Kasen so he wouldn't have to turn his back to the computer screen. "It means the pike was removed without causing his death, but there is more work to be done. The most dangerous part is over, and his chances for surviving just got better. Does that answer your question?"

Kasen nodded. "I believe so." Lexi looked down at his bowl of soup. "Do you think your gods would let you eat yet?"

Kasen looked at the bowl. He was indeed hungry, and it smelled good too. But he didn't want to risk his son's life. "Not yet."

An hour or so later, Jason finished up the surgery. He left Laura to get Tharen cleaned up and tucked into bed. Jason walked into the dining hall to give Kasen an update on Tharen's condition. As Jason entered the room, Kasen and the others stood up to face the doctor. Jason had not done this much intense medical care in quite some time. He appeared fatigued when he walked into the room. Jake prepared himself for a bad reaction from Kasen if the news wasn't good. Kasen wasn't sure if the look on Jason's face was fatigue or distress. He steeled himself for the worst. "My son… is he…?"

Jason realized his face was not reflecting the good news he was bringing, but the exhaustion he felt. He forced the muscles in his face to relax. "Tharen is going to be fine. He will need to rest for a few days, but he will be back to normal soon enough." Relief flooded across the faces of everyone in the room. Kasen knelt on one knee before the doctor and bowed his head. "I am most grateful to you for saving my son from my own foolishness. The gods have given you a great gift, healer. What can I do to repay the debt I now owe you?"

Jason reached down and took Kasen's elbow to pull him back to his feet. "You don't owe me anything. I am a healer. It is what I have chosen to do with my life. I would appreciate it if you would sit down with our delegation and strongly consider our proposal."

"It will be done. Your people have proven yourselves as worthy allies and dangerous enemies. I would be foolish to do otherwise. May I see my son?"

Jason nodded. "Laura is getting him settled in. He's going to be asleep for the rest of tonight. Let's get something to eat then I will take you to see him. There is a bed in there so you can sleep near him tonight. I will stay in there as well in case he needs anything else."

Kasen again bowed his head. "You are a wise man and a kind man. Thank you. Thank you for saving my son."

Jason stepped over to the counter to get something to eat. Lexi offered to reheat Kasen's soup for him. This time he gladly accepted her offer, and once he sat down to eat it, he consumed it as though he had not eaten for days. Vesta reheated her own food and ate quietly.

As soon as Jason had finished his meal, he walked over to the computer and tried to contact the captain. The captain's comm unit was off, which struck Jason as rather odd. Captains didn't generally turn their comms off even when they were considered off duty. Since he couldn't reach David, he hailed Lazaro instead. Lazaro answered, but it took a couple tries before he was awake enough to answer. "Lt. Commander Dominick here."

"Commander, this is Jason, I was just checking on the captain's condition, but he didn't answer. Why did he turn his comm unit off?"

Lazaro hesitated before answering. "His condition is stable. He needs further treatment, but he's all right for now. He turned off his comm unit because he's not in any shape to command. I guess he wanted to be sure he couldn't be put in a position to make any command decisions." Lazaro had only been asleep for less than an hour and was having trouble putting his thoughts together.

"What's the extent of his injuries?"

"He has a nasty concussion, several broken ribs, lots of cuts, scrapes, and bruises, and a couple second-degree burns. He's also physically exhausted. His electrolytes are totally off. I've treated him the best I can, but he needs to be in the infirmary. How's Tharen?"

"Tharen's going to be fine. He should be ready to travel in the morning. I want to watch him for a few hours to make sure there aren't any complications. Can I send Thane out to get the captain?"

"No. Absolutely not. The captain's last orders were to get Tharen back here before he would allow us to take him back in. I'm not about to go against his last order before taking himself off the duty roster. If you want to come out here and treat him, well, that's Braxton's call, but the captain's staying here."

"I have two patients here that I don't want to leave alone tonight. Are you sure he's stable?"

"Yes, Doc, he's stable for now. I promise I'll keep an eye on him."

"As you wish Mr. Dominick. I'll go along with it for the moment, but you contact me immediately if there are any complications."

"Doc, don't worry. I have the scanner set to wake me up if anything changes, and right now the captain is resting pretty well. I'll call you, I promise."

"All right Mr. Dominick. I'll leave it with you. Get some rest. I'll contact you in the morning. *Evangeline*, out."

Jason was tired and frustrated. He punched the button on the computer to close the communications link. His meal had taken the edge off his mood, but he was still frustrated. He had a patient who needed him, but there wasn't anything he could do about it. It only served to add to his frustration that it was the most important person on the ship. David wasn't the type to consider himself to be the most important person, but Jason felt he was.

Jason got up and moved back over to the table where Kasen was just finishing his food. Kasen stood up as the doctor reached the table. "May we see my son now?"

Jason nodded and smiled. Although he wasn't in the best of moods, he liked giving family members good news. The two walked back down the hall to the infirmary. Jake followed them out, leaving Lexi and Vesta alone in the dining hall.

Vesta seemed to be just as uncomfortable as Lexi. Lexi stood up to leave the room, and Vesta went back to finishing her food.

When Lexi got to the door, she stopped. She turned around and started to speak. Vesta looked up from her bowl. Lexi walked over in front of her. "Thank you for your help today. You've done a great job helping us with the Sorley." Lexi would much rather have stayed by the door to tell her that, but the translator probably wouldn't have picked it up. It was hard enough for her to admit such a thing, but to have to get so close to Vesta made it harder. Despite their rough beginnings, Lexi knew she should push past it, accept Vesta, and forgive her. She was trying. Maybe by the time they left this world, she'd be past it. When the translation made it through to Vesta, Lexi thought she saw Vesta almost tear up. Lexi turned to go. Suddenly Vesta grabbed her arm. Lexi froze. A fight or flight response nearly overtook her. Logically she knew Vesta would not even attempt to harm her, but the emotions still lingered. Lexi looked back at Vesta.

"Thank you for saying so." Vesta looked like there was more to be said but wasn't sure how. She released Lexi's arm and went back to eating her food. Lexi breathed a sigh of relief and left the room.

Jason escorted Kasen to Tharen's bedside. He cautioned Kasen while they were in route, the medication would keep Tharen asleep for the night. Jason didn't want Kasen to be concerned when his son would not wake up. Kasen sat at his son's bedside for several minutes listening to the slow, steady rhythm of his breathing. He touched Tharen's hand. It was warm, not hot with fever or cold from shock, or blood loss. When he laid Tharen's hand down on the bed, he noticed a lack of bandages on his son's chest. Jason was still standing close by to answer any questions Kasen might have. He saw Kasen reach up and pull back the covers from Tharen's chest. Jason stepped forward. Kasen touched the sight of the wound he had caused then looked at Jason. "I don't understand. Where is the wound?"

Jason had forgotten to take into account the expectation of scar tissue. "Our treatments repair all of the damage including scars. The skin is still weak, and it will take time for it to be strong again, but it will look like his own skin."

Kasen touched the place where the wound had been one more time then pulled the covers back up over Tharen. "You have my eternal gratitude for saving the life of my son, and it appears you have done excellent work as a healer."

Jason thanked Kasen for the compliment then told him he could sleep in the patient bed next to Tharen. Jason pointed at a third bed in the room. "I'll sleep over here if you or Tharen need anything during the night." Jason also directed Kasen to the adjoining bathroom and gave him instructions on operating the sink, shower, and toilet. It ended up being a rather amusing tour. Explaining modern plumbing to underdeveloped cultures was always an adventure.

Jake, who had been standing on the sidelines, decided he was no longer needed and slipped out quietly. Jason did notice that Jake locked the door as he left

Jason instructed Laura to stay in the seating area of the Commander's quarters for the night just as a precaution. After checking on the Commander, Laura lay down on the sofa and pulled a blanket around her.

Braxton set up a rotation of crew members to take turns acting as a watch commander. If anything were to happen, they would notify him at once. He kept the shifts short because it had already been a long day, and tomorrow didn't look to be any better. Now, they were shorthanded.

The crew aboard the *Evangeline* was settling down to finally get some rest, as well as the three in the Sorley village. It looked as though things were going to be resolved. Several of the Sorley warriors were still upset about the events of the day and were not inclined to follow Kasen's last orders.

Once Brynna's anesthesia wore off early that morning her wrath over David's last orders became apparent as well. She woke up about an hour before sunrise and wondered where David was. She didn't remember all the events leading up to this point, at least not immediately. Brynna felt stiff and groggy. She vaguely remembered being thrown from her horse. She decided a shower should be first on her agenda. As the hot water poured over her body, the stiffness began to fade, and her thoughts cleared. She started remembering the discussion about whether to finish the competition. Then she remembered the look on David's face as Lazaro had given her something to make her sleep. It had been a look of guilt! Suddenly she realized what he had done. So where was he now?

Brynna abruptly shut off the water and quickly dried off. She got dressed and headed into the seating area of her quarters where she saw Laurel sleeping on her couch. Brynna didn't want to wake her, so she headed out into the corridor and tried to hail David. Her call failed to connect to his comm unit. Brynna decided to check the infirmary. If David had been in hand-to-hand combat, there was a chance he was injured. Brynna thought to herself; if he wasn't hurt she might have to hurt him for drugging her. Brynna entered the medical bay and was confused to see Tharen and

Kasen. She turned to head to the bridge and saw Jason just getting out of the spare bed.

Jason glanced at the display over Tharen's bed before turning his attention to Brynna. He picked up a portable scanner and motioned for her to step back out into the corridor. Once in the hall, Jason proceeded to scan her. "How are you feeling this morning? Any pain, headache, dizziness, or blurred vision?"

Brynna's mood was hovering somewhere between worry and concern for David, and being angry at what he had done to her. She hesitated before answering his question. She was more focused on wanting to know what happened after she left the Sorley village. The doctor mistook her hesitation as a lack of focus. "Are you having trouble concentrating or focusing?

Realizing he wasn't going to let this go, Brynna forced herself to let him do his job. "I was feeling stiff and groggy, but a shower helped clear that up. I just need to know what happened last night and where the captain is. I would also like to know why Tharen and Kasen are in our Med Bay."

The doctor continued his scanning without answering her. Brynna was fast losing patience. "Doctor, I need some answers."

The doctor shut off his scanner. "All right commander, you are hereby cleared to return to duty. I suggest you get your answers from Lt. Commander Flint. The captain suffered some minor injuries, so he took himself off-duty. Lt. Commander Flint is the Commander in charge."

"What sort of injuries? Where is the captain?"

The doctor really didn't want to get into this with the Commander. He didn't like the situation any more than she did, but he knew the medical information should come from him. "The captain suffered several broken ribs, a concussion, a puncture wound to his calf, and several minor cuts, scrapes, bruises, and second-degree burns. There were no life-threatening injuries, just painful ones. I suggest you talk to the Lt. Commander to get the full report." The doctor was carefully dodging telling her the captain wasn't on the ship and his injuries hadn't been treated yet.

Brynna hadn't picked up on the doctor's omission as yet, but she wasn't done getting information from him. "What about Tharen? Why is he here and what is his condition?" The monitor had been operational over Tharen's bed, but the one over Kasen was off.

The doctor took a deep breath and answered carefully. "Tharen is stable. He took a spear to the chest and nearly died. I was able to treat him in time, and before you ask, no, David didn't do it. Tharen is going to be fine. He'll be weak for a few days. Now please talk to Braxton. I need to check on my patient."

Brynna headed to the bridge. Aulani was very much a morning person and volunteered to take the early morning duty shift, so she was alone on the bridge. Brynna walked in and found her running several programs at once. She was actively monitoring the crew members who were not on the ship, watching the scanners for movement in the surrounding areas and had a program running to update the translation files. She was also working on the report she would eventually file about their time here on the planet. Brynna hated to interrupt such ambition, but she needed answers. "Ensign, I need a report of everything that happened since yesterday evening when I returned from the Sorley encampment."

Aulani was caught slightly off-guard. "Uh, yes, ma'am. Has the doctor cleared you for duty yet ma'am?"

Brynna was not the type to get angry easily, but she was getting there quickly. Something disconcerting had definitely happened. David's absence and unanswered comm unit, the look on his face when Lazaro sedated her, the doctor, and Aulani dodging her questions were all starting to add up. Brynna took a deep breath and was about to answer her with all the calm she could muster when Braxton stepped onto the bridge. He had already checked the doctor's log to see if Brynna was cleared for duty, so he was prepared to face her. He was carrying a cup of coffee and a data pad. "Good morning Commander. Are you ready to get report and assume command?"

"Yes, I am. Jason cleared me for duty, and I need some answers now."

Braxton nodded. "I assumed you would. Let's step into the captain's office and I'll bring you up to speed." The two headed into the office and sat down. Braxton calmly brought the Commander up to date on the events of the evening. He gave special emphasis to the captain's orders and the captain's refusal to return until Kasen and Tharen were brought back to the Sorley village. After he finished updating the Commander, he relinquished command. "Commander, I return command to you."

Brynna responded flatly and routinely, "I accept command." She sat in her chair with a sullen look on her face.

She sat there without saying anything for so long Braxton was getting concerned. "Do you have any orders, Commander?"

Before she could respond, Aulani hailed them. "Commander, I'm getting some peculiar activity in the Sorley encampment." The two returned quickly to the bridge. Aulani had a scanner image of the Sorley encampment. The image showed a significant number of heat signatures amassing on the eastern side of the encampment.

Brynna looked at the image then looked back at Braxton. "You said the captain and Kasen were afraid of retaliation by his people, right?"

Braxton nodded, "Yes, that's why the captain insisted on staying behind. He was afraid of a riot last night. He thought it would diffuse the situation if he stayed."

Brynna instantly set aside her feelings and got down to business. "Have Thane prep the shuttle for immediate take off. Get me Jason now, and wake the rest of the crew."

Malek, Damar, and Tolem sat around the fire in Malek's tent grumbling and complaining about the day's events. They had followed Kasen's instructions to cleanse themselves, to a small degree. They had completed the ceremonial washing of their bodies, or at least had their slaves do it for them, refused to eat their evening meal, and said a brief prayer to their gods. Now they sat around drowning their sorrows and getting intoxicated with a drink made from one of the local plants. The more they drank, the angrier they became. The three men finally fell into a drunken stupor and slept for a few hours, but the minute they were conscious, they began to drink again.

As the sun rose, their anger came to a head. Malek had a slave whose daily responsibilities started with rolling up the sides of the tent. Once the tent walls were rolled up, others who were passing by could hear the ongoing conversation. A crowd began to gather, Damar took advantage of the gathering by formally addressing the spectators.

"My friends, these Sky People have brought us nothing, but trouble. They have tried to force us into an alliance with them. They tried to embarrass our leaders by beating us at our own games. When that failed, they resorted to trickery and sorcery."

A murmur ran through the crowd. There were looks of shock, confusion, and disbelief exchanged. One disbelieving man questioned Damar, "Sorcery? What sorcery?"

Tolem stood up to back his friends claim. "It's true. How else could you explain what happened? He tricked Kasen into killing his own son."

Another man hollered out another objection. "Tharen wasn't dead when they left here."

Malek rose to add his voice to his two friends. "No, he was not dead yet, but he probably is by now. That was the intention of the Sky People. I was there when we first encountered the Sky People. I saw their captain's woman embarrass Tharen and Jager. She nearly stabbed Jager and held the two of them captive while the Kimbra were allowed to escape. I think they wanted Kasen to kill Tharen, but his pike missed its mark. Kasen is a strong man and a strong leader. His willpower prevented him from killing his son."

The crowd was not yet convinced. "So why did Kasen go with them?"

Damar took the tale back from his two friends. "Kasen was overwhelmed by his own grief and the sorcery. He didn't know his own mind. They were able to convince Kasen they could save his son. We saw the wound. It was near the heart. If Tharen lives, it is more evil sorcery."

Malek added to Damar's explanation. "If they can save Tharen, then Kasen will be indebted to the Sky People and be forced into an alliance with them."

Someone shouted, "So what do we do?"

Tolem answered. "We make them pay for what they have done to us. Kasen is a good man and a good leader. It is our responsibility to support and protect him when he cannot take care of himself. We are his people. He would do whatever it takes to take care of us would he not?"

A murmur of approval rippled through the ever-growing crowd. Gervas happened to pass by about that time and heard what was happening. He stood and listened for a few minutes then headed for the meeting tent.

Tolem continued his dissertation. "Tharen was to one day become the leader of our people. Tharen is a good man like his father. Now that the Sky People have him, they will cast a spell on him to gain his loyalty. We must stop them. We have their leader here among us. If we destroy him, the Sky People will know we are not weak and cannot be toyed with. If we kill their people, they will leave this world and never return. It will break their evil spells and release Kasen and Tharen from their control."

The crowd shouted their approval again. One last reluctant voice called out from the crowd, "Kasen told us to wait three days. Can't we just kill them in three days like he told us to?"

Malek jumped back in with a hasty response. "Because in three days, the spell will be complete, and we will be unable to break it. We HAVE to act NOW to stop them." Each man's voice had gotten louder and more excited and angry as they spoke. The crowd only served to fuel their fear and anger.

Damar started a chant to ensure the crowd would help rid the encampment of this dangerous sorcery. "Death to the Sky Wizards!" Once the chant was in full chorus, Damar and his companions picked up weapons and headed toward the center of the camp.

Once Gervas was out of sight of the crowd, he took off running. He found Jager about to enter the tent. He quickly told Jager what was happening on the east side of the camp. The two men went inside the tent and woke their three visitors. Gervas repeated his observations to them as hastily as he could. Jager told the three men, "We have to get you out of here."

David managed to get to his feet. "Jager, get them to safety. I'm really the one they want, and I'm not in any shape to run." Lazaro grabbed his med kit and pulled out a syringe. He gave David a strong dose of a painkiller, and then lifted one of David's arms onto his own shoulder. David objected. "What are you doing? You and Manton need to go without me. That's an order Lt. Commander."

Lazaro motioned for Manton to take David's other arm. "With all due respect, Captain, you took yourself off-duty for medical incapacity. Until you're cleared by the doc, you can't give orders... sir."

David looked vexed. Lazaro anticipated hearing more about this later, but there wasn't time now. Lazaro looked at Jager, "Let's go."

Jager and Gervas lifted the west wall of the tent, which was on the opposite side from the entrance. Jager and Gervas were not sure how the two guards at the door would respond to the approaching mob, so they decided to leave them in place without telling them about their departure. After they were outside the tent walls, Jager instructed them to head to the west side of the camp and to stay one row of tents off the main path. Jager and Gervas stayed on the inside of the tent and went back out the entrance talking casually about arranging for food for their guests. They wanted to make sure the guards didn't tip off the angry mob. Gervas sent slaves to place food and water in the tent but ordered them not to speak to anyone. After the slaves headed off to complete their task, Gervas grabbed some food and tossed it quickly into a sack. Jager went to grab some horses.

As the three crewmen made their way down the path, Lazaro hit his comm unit to contact the ship. Aulani answered. He then heard her call out to someone else, "Commander, I have Lazaro on comms."

Brynna didn't waste any time, "Put him through!" As soon as the channel was open, Brynna asked, "Lt. Commander what is your status?"

"Commander, we are headed toward the west side of the encampment. We have an angry mob headed our way. The captain's injuries are preventing us from moving very quickly. Jager and Gervas are trying to help us get away. We could use some help!"

"We're already getting the shuttle ready for launch. We should be in the air in the next two minutes. Do what you can to hang on until we get there."

"Understood, Commander." The crew kept moving as fast as they could. Each step jarred the captain's ribs causing increased pain despite the medications. He tried walking as much as he could on his injured leg, but the pressure, movement, and swelling made each step harder. It wasn't long until his breathing became labored. Taking deep breaths hurt. Fluid was building up in his lungs causing him to cough each time he took a deep breath. It was becoming a vicious downward spiral.

Behind them, they began to hear yells of anger. Manton heard and understood their shouts immediately, but the translators couldn't pick up the distant speech. Manton relayed what he heard to the translators. "They know we are missing. They are spreading out to search for us."

The captain, accustomed to making command decisions, issued more orders. "Let's move a little more north. We're..." He took a deep breath and coughed then winced. "We're still in a line of sight from the meeting tent, but nearly to the outskirts of the encampment. Once we clear the camp, there's no place to hide. We'll be out in the open. Jager and Gervas shouldn't..." The captain took another breath and coughed again. "They shouldn't have trouble finding us if we're just a little off target."

This time Lazaro didn't argue. They made the course adjustment and got to the edge of the camp without being spotted. Their pursuers were getting closer, so the three ducked into a tent. They gently put the captain down on a bed inside the tent to rest. Lazaro stood ready with his Tri-EMP set on level one. Manton stood ready to jump out and flag down Jager and Gervas as soon as he spotted them. The captain had handed his weapon to Manton before the last tournament match with strict instructions not to use it. Now he programmed it and showed Manton how to use it.

As they waited, they could hear the angry voices drawing closer. They also heard the voices of two women approaching. The women stopped right outside the tent entrance. By the tone and inflection, it sounded like they were closing their conversation and going their separate ways. One voice moved further away as it answered. Suddenly one of the women stepped into the tent. Manton reacted quickly. He grabbed her and covered her mouth with his hand. David, in a loud whisper, instructed Manton not to hurt her. Manton spoke softly to the woman who appeared terrified. She nodded in response to his whispered instructions. Manton slowly took his hand off her mouth and sat her down on the floor in front of the captain. Manton asked her what her name was.

"Kainda," she replied softly.

Manton didn't feel what he was about to say, but he knew she had to believe him for the safety of the group. Manton allowed a coldness to come over himself. "Kainda, if you make one sound or do anything to let the others know where we are, we will mark you as a slave. As long as you are quiet and remain still, we will not harm you. Do you understand?" The frightened young woman nodded. Manton pulled a knife from his belt and handed it to the captain. David wasn't happy about this, but he understood why Manton had done it. David took the knife and roughly grabbed the woman by her hair. He kept her facing away from him because he didn't want her to see the compassion he felt showing on his face.

He wasn't sure scaring women to death was in his job description. Lazaro stood there and tried not to look shocked. He was now having second thoughts about signing onto this mission. This was their "goodwill" mission? Tears quietly began to run down Kainda's face. When David saw them, he lowered the knife, so it was no longer the only thing she would see. He loosened his grip on her hair. Her breathing slowed down.

Without warning, another young woman near Kainda's age suddenly appeared in the tent entrance. It only took the woman a half second to size up the situation and run screaming from the tent.

Kainda, afraid her friend's reaction would yield unfortunate consequences for herself, tried to call out to stop her friend. "Winda, no!" Kainda began to cry again.

David released his grip on her. Unless he truly planned on harming her, it was now pointless to hold her. David stuck the knife in his waistband, lifted the woman's chin with his hand gently and said, "I'm very sorry for scaring you." The translators were going directly into their earpieces and were not audible to anyone, but the crew. David hoped she would still understand. He only had a second to convince her of his sorrow. She was still crying, but her shaking seemed to diminish slightly. Maybe she had understood. Manton and Lazaro knew they could no longer stay here. They helped the captain to his feet and headed back out into the open. There were men every direction, though none were particularly close to them.

David pointed to the edge of the camp. "Head straight out to open ground. We can't even duck into another tent now." The men moved as fast as they could while holding the captain up. They hadn't gotten very far when they saw Jager and Gervas coming with the horses, but the two were still several hundred yards away. Manton heard a shout from behind them. "They found us."

Lazaro and the captain didn't really need him to relay that particular point. They understood it without help. They altered their route toward the two men on horseback. The men behind them were going to catch them before they reached the horses. David jerked away from the two men and hit the ground. They turned to pick him up. David looked at Lazaro, "You and Manton get to safety, when the shuttle gets here you can attempt a rescue, but don't risk any more of the crew!"

Lazaro started to object. "But, Captain..."

"That's an order Lt. Commander. Go! NOW!"

Manton didn't have to wait for the translation to understand the captain. He grabbed Lazaro's arm and they ran full force toward the horses. Jager and Gervas brought two spare horses. When the two parties met, Lazaro and Manton mounted the spare horses. Lazaro turned his horse back toward where they had left the captain. The angry crowd already had him surrounded.

Lazaro started to push his horse toward the captain, but Jager grabbed his bridle. "It's too late. If you try it, you'll only get yourself captured or killed. We need to get you back to your ship and bring Kasen back. He's the only one who might be able to stop this."

David stayed on his knees but turned to face the approaching mob. He took the knife from his belt and tossed it onto the ground a few feet from him and raised his hands to indicate his surrender. Several men surrounded him pointing spears and knives at him. David watched as two of the men started to go after Lazaro and Manton. One of the men knew they wouldn't get there in time and called them back. David knew he was the object of their anger. He just hoped they would keep him alive until the crew could rescue him. The crowd around him got larger and angrier. The captain had set his translator to only verbalize his words. Anything they said to him would go only into his ear-piece. He suspected his technology would only add fuel to the fire.

Lazaro took one last look at his captain and turned his horse to ride the direction he expected the shuttle to come from. They had to ride past the angry mob, but they kept just out of range of their weapons. Lazaro wasn't looking forward to reporting back to the Commander. As soon as they were far enough away for the mob to lose interest in them, Lazaro reported in.

Malek, Damar, and Tolem were so drunk they weren't moving as fast as the crowd they had stirred up. They were some of the last ones to reach the captain. Damar walked up to the captain and looked at his tired face. A little piece of Damar felt pity for the captain. Damar's own feelings of sympathy made him even angrier. He reasoned the captain must be putting some sort of spell on him. He backhanded the young captain.

Malek grabbed the captain's hands and bound them behind him. He and Tolem grabbed each of his arms and dragged him back to the fire circle. The men dropped him in the center of the circle. They gave orders to rebuild the fire circle and to gather large stones. Damar looked down at David who was trying to catch his breath. "You thought you could manipulate us and take control of our minds. You were wrong. We are stronger than you. Where is your sorcery now? Where are your poisonous words? Now, sorcerer, you will be stoned to death for the harm you have done to us."

David looked up at him. "I'm just a man. I'm not a sorcerer. Don't I even get a trial or any last words?"

"So, you can try to cast more spells on us?"

David managed to get back on his knees. "Don't I have the right to prove my innocence, or are you that afraid of me?"

Damar punched David in the mouth. "I do not fear you, but your guilt has already been decided. I suggest you pray to your gods before you die. I can only imagine what the gods will do to you for tricking Kasen into killing his own son."

Damar started to walk away. David had one last retort. It wasn't one he believed in, but he knew it would put more pressure on Damar. "And what will your gods do to a man who gets drunk, disobeys his leader, and kills an innocent man who was the guest of his leader? Kasen gave me his word we were under his protection. What will your gods do to you?" David had smelled the alcohol on the three men and knew they were drunk. He made a little bit of an assumption that drinking was forbidden when one was supposed to be cleansing themselves and praying. In this case, his assumption was accurate.

Damar's anger consumed him. He drew his knife intending to kill David on the spot. Tolem, who was standing quietly beside Damar, grabbed Damar's arm to stop him from killing David.

David locked eyes with Damar. "Come on, finish it!"

Tolem held Damar's arm even more tightly. "He's baiting you. He knows if you kill him alone, Kasen and the gods can seek vengeance. What can Kasen or the gods do if the people choose to kill him? They will know it is the will of the people."

David could see the wheels turning in Damar's head, and despite his pain and trouble breathing David laughed at Damar. Damar sheathed his knife, turned, and walked quickly away. Tolem glared at David for a moment before following Damar out of the circle.

David sat there thinking. He was waiting for death or rescue, whichever came first. Here he was being accused of taking over the minds of unsuspecting people. Their mission was to stop Pateras El Liontari from doing exactly that. He laughed at the irony. This really wasn't a laughing occasion, but what else was he going to do? At least if he didn't make it back to the ship, then he wouldn't have to face Brynna's wrath. He laughed to himself again. The realization he might never see her beautiful face again began to hit him. He looked up and searched the skies for the shuttle. It was nowhere to be seen. Was it his imagination, or was this pile of brush higher than it had been during his combat the previous night? David got to his feet. No, it was definitely not his imagination. It also seemed closer, and this time they blocked the entrance to the circle. Soon they were dousing the wood and brush with oil, the smell was stronger than before. David realized they weren't taking any chances. Between the heat of the sun, the heat of the fire, and the fact he had very little room to maneuver, his chances for survival were small. Several men moved forward to light the fire ring. David suddenly felt very alone. He began wishing he did have a god to pray to. Some Divine intervention would be helpful about now.

The fire was now burning all the way around the ring. David searched the sky again for the shuttle. The crowd began to shout angrily at him. He watched as they each started picking up rocks. The fire got so large and intense, David knew he was going to have trouble seeing the rocks in time to dodge them. He also realized they might have trouble aiming them at him as well. David decided it was in his best interest to make himself as small a target as possible and stay near the highest part of the fire. He moved as quickly as he could into the spot that looked like the most protected. He was sweating profusely already because of the heat, and he knew he would start getting first and second degree burns fairly quickly.

Seeing him move, the crowd began throwing their rocks. Their anger had the best of them. Their aim was off. So far not one made contact. It was getting much harder for him to breathe. The smoke and heat caused him to cough even more. David thought if he could get close enough to the fire, he might be able to burn the ropes off his wrists.

As the fire started to spread around the ring, Malek and the others could see David was trying to conceal himself behind the wall of flames. "See how this sneaky coward tries to hide. He can't even face death with honor. Kill the sorcerer!" The crowd hurled numerous rocks. The more the rocks failed to hit their target, the angrier they became. The crowd was persistent in their attempts to hurt the leader of the Sky People.

Without warning, a bright, white light filled the fire ring. For a minute the crowd couldn't see anything. Once their eyes began to adjust they could make out the silhouettes of two men. One woman cried out, "The gods are angry with us." Damar who was standing right next to the woman felt a knot form in his stomach. He remembered David's taunt about his disobedience and the wrath of the gods. Tolem looked at Damar then back at the two figures in the ring. He wasn't sure how to interpret what he was seeing. His head was starting to hurt from a developing hangover, which didn't help matters in any way.

David took a deep breath. The air entering his lungs was cool, crisp, and clean. It felt so good that he took a couple more breaths. He wasn't sure where the air had come from, but he was happy to have it. Refreshed, David started to move again closer to the fire. Suddenly a hand on his shoulder stopped him. Someone was untying the rope from his wrists. David tried to stand up and turn around. He wanted to see who was helping him. His rescuer helped him to his feet, and as he did, David felt the pain from his numerous injuries disappear. David turned around and felt the blood drain from his face. It was Arni.

Captain Alexander was accustomed to dealing in facts. These events defied the facts. David had been alone in a circle of fire with no way in or out. Arni came from a world without space travel, and this was a different planet. How could he be here? "Arni?"

Arni smiled, "Yes, it's me. No, you aren't hallucinating."

David touched the place where his broken ribs had been. There was no pain, and the ribs were firmly in place. He reached down and touched the calf Kasen had stabbed with his pike. His pants were still torn, but the calf was perfectly healed. David suddenly had a thousand questions. His first thought was concerning the incoming rocks, but he realized none were coming. It was as though time were frozen outside the circle. He took advantage of the lull and quickly started asking some of his questions. "Why are you here? How did you get here? Why are you helping me? Why did you heal me?"

Arni smiled again. "You definitely have a lot of questions. First, you needed me, and you didn't want to die alone. Second, I got here the same way I get most places. My father brings me. I healed you for several reasons. You have a job to do, and you can't get it done with those injuries. I don't like it when my people hurt. I want your trust. Just so you know, these people don't know me or my father. They cannot help you find us."

The young captain's emotions were in turmoil. "We are looking for your father to stop him. We're trying to destroy his plans. Yet you still came to my rescue, why?"

"My father has plans for you and your crew. My father wants to stop the chaos and destruction Luciano Hale is causing. We'd like your help."

"Chaos and destruction Executor Hale is causing? The Executor is trying to unite this galaxy, so everyone is equal and at peace. Your father is the one trying to cause chaos. Does this mean you and your father are going to take over our minds?"

Arni shook his head. "No, it has to be your choice to help us. My father doesn't force anyone to do anything they don't want to do. Even if you choose to follow my father, you can walk away from him at any time."

David scowled, "But what about the people the Executor had to execute?"

A sad look crossed Arni's face. "The Executor knew they were a threat to him and him alone. Luciano gave them a choice to swear loyalty to him and the Commonwealth or die. They chose willingly to follow my father. They were not forced in any way. Luciano is responsible for that tragedy and many others." Arni looked up. "It's time for me to go. Your shuttle has arrived. None of the rocks will reach you."

"Wait! How did you know I didn't want to die alone?"

Arni smiled again. "The same way I know you wished you had a god to pray to. I know your thoughts. You might want to wait in the center of the ring. It's cooler over there, and as I said before, their rocks won't reach you. If you wish to talk with me again, just call my name. I will come to wherever you are."

David looked at the center of the ring, and when he looked back at Arni, the man was nowhere to be seen. For some strange reason, David trusted Arni. He walked to the center of the ring. Rocks were again flying past him, but none hit him.

In a second the light was gone. David was alone in the center of the circle. The crowd continued to throw stones, but it was if the wind had been taken out of their sails. Some were now afraid their gods were angry. Others were afraid David was a god. A few were still throwing stones because they were afraid of him.

The shuttle flew overhead and landed on the south side of the fire ring. The men on horseback came riding in from the north, straight through the camp at full gallop. Normally, this was frowned on, but they felt justified under the circumstances and took extra precautions to avoid the few remaining pedestrians.

Malek had not, as yet, lost his momentum or his misguided purpose. He grabbed two stones and began to try inciting the crowd again. "STONE ALL THE SKY PEOPLE!" Malek headed toward the shuttle. A few of the crowd followed him, rocks in hand. The four men on horseback slowed down when they reached the crowd, but as soon as they saw Malek's intentions, they turned their horses to the outside edge of the crowd. Lazaro and Manton looked over at David in the center of the circle. David waved them on indicating he was fine. Lazaro took off after Jager and Gervas. The men pushed their horses as fast as they could go, trying to intercept Malek and the others before they reached the shuttle.

The shuttle door opened. Jake and Brynna were the first two to exit the shuttle with weapons in hand. Jake also had his portable deflector shield on his wrist and ready to activate if needed. Kasen was the next to emerge from the shuttle and step onto the ground between Jake and Brynna. Malek was now close enough to start throwing his rocks. He shouted again. "FREE KASEN! KILL THE SKY PEOPLE!!" Malek launched his first two rocks.

Jake activated his deflector and stepped in front of Kasen and Brynna. The rocks easily bounced off the shield. Jake and Brynna didn't even appear flustered. Due to Malek's inebriated state, his aim was off, and one of the rocks hit the shield right in front of Kasen's face. If the shield hadn't been there, Kasen would have been hit. Seeing Malek's failed strike, the group following Malek froze. They didn't know whether to give up or continue trying to save their leader. The four men on horseback reached Malek. Jager and Gervas had their spears pointed at Malek mere inches from his neck. Manton and Lazaro weren't carrying spears. The two resorted to holding the man and his followers at bay with the Tri-EMPs they were carrying. None of the locals had seen a Tri-EMP before so although they didn't know what it did, they knew enough to fear it

The crowd behind Malek gasped. Malek could not see what the startled crowd was seeing. His focus was on the spears pointed at his throat, and the horses blocked his line of sight. Malek heard the crowd behind him begin shouting, "Tharen! Tharen lives!"

Tharen had his left arm across Jason's shoulders and was walking slowly away from the shuttle. Jason wanted to bring Tharen back on a stretcher, but Kasen and Tharen both insisted he should walk even if it wasn't entirely under his own power.

Jager and Gervas were just as happy to see Tharen. Malek took advantage of the distraction and took off running. Manton was not so distracted. He pointed the Tri-EMP at Malek and fired. When the captain programmed it and handed it to him, Manton didn't really know what it would do, only that it wouldn't kill anyone. The projectile hit Malek squarely in the back. His body wrenched violently once then he dropped to the ground. Jager and Gervas looked at Malek then back at Manton.

Gervas finally asked, "Did you kill him?"

Manton looked down at the weapon then back at Malek. "No, I don't think so."

The two rode over to Malek's limp body and checked for signs of life. Jager shouted back to the others, "He's still alive!"

Manton looked at Lazaro and smiled, "I think I like this weapon." Lazaro laughed. Jager and Gervas tied Malek's hands behind him, then threw him across one of the saddles to carry him back.

Kasen wasn't happy about what his people had done in his absence. He started walking toward the fire ring. Jake and Brynna followed him closely. Jager and Gervas walked on opposing sides leading their horses. Tharen and Jason followed slowly behind them. Manton and Lazaro dismounted and led their horses like Jager and Gervas were doing. Thane and Lexi stayed with the shuttle, just in case.

As they got to the still burning fire ring, Kasen turned to Jake. "It will take some time to get your captain out of there. We will have to cover the fire with dirt to put it out."

Jake grinned. "I might be able to help with that." He pulled a small object from his belt about the size and shape of an egg. He made a couple adjustments to it then looked up. "Everybody stand back! Captain! Move Back!" As soon as everyone was clear, Jake tossed the "egg" into the fire. Three seconds later there was a loud pop and a flash of light. An eight-foot section of the fire went out in a matter of seconds. The "egg" worked on principles similar to the deflector shield. It had an initial burst of power from an internal battery releasing an energy field covering the fire and blocking oxygen from getting to the fire. The field would continue to draw energy from the heat of the fire until the fire was suppressed entirely. It didn't, however, do anything about the remaining heat.

There were numerous large smooth flat rocks and logs strategically placed around the ring for spectators to sit or stand on. Jason helped Tharen to sit on one near Kasen. The doctor was anxious to evaluate the captain for himself and get him back to the ship for treatment. Once a portion of the fire was out Jason was ready to go through the opening. Jake pulled him back. "Slow down, Doc. The fire may be out, but that spot is still too hot to cross."

Dr. Adams wasn't about to let that stop him. He had waited all night to get to his patient, and he was not happy about waiting any longer. While Jake looked around to find a way to get the captain the rest of the way out of the circle, David walked over to the edge of the hole in the wall of fire. Jason got as close as he dared. "Captain, how are you doing?"

David was feeling excellent, but he didn't know how to explain it to the others. "I'm doing surprisingly well. Jake! Can you reconfigure your deflector, so I can cross on the shield?"

Jake looked at the hole and then at his deflector and thought for a moment. Lazaro walked over to Jake. The two began to adjust the controls. In a few moments, Jake looked up and shook his head. "Sir it won't reach far enough, but the doc could come through to you. He'll have to jump the last little bit."

David shook his head. "If the doc can get in, I should be able to get out." Jake objected, "Sir, you can't make the distance with broken ribs and a bum leg."

David put his hands on his hips and looked down at the ground. He knew he had to tell them something, but he doubted anyone would believe him. He looked around for a moment then decided to use his captain's authority to his advantage. "Gentlemen! I can't explain it right now, but I am not injured in any way. I am perfectly healthy. My leg is fine, and my ribs are not broken. Are we clear on that point?"

The crew, including Brynna, looked at each other. This was more than just a little confusing. Jason looked at Lazaro, "Just how much pain medication did you give him?"

Lazaro looked at David and then at the Doc. "I gave the prescribed dosages. I swear, it was correct. I checked and double checked it."

The captain saw they weren't accepting his word for it. "All right Doc, come on in here and check me out yourself." As soon as he spoke, the captain saw the concern on Jason's face relax. Jake knelt as close to the smoldering debris as he dared. He instructed Manton and Lazaro to stand on either side of the opening in case one of them lost their balance. Jason got a running start. The shield was flattened as much as they could get it, but it still had a distinct curve. Jason would have to run and jump over the leading edge, stepping onto the inside of the shield, then propel himself over the far edge, and across the last few feet of the fire ring. It was like jumping into and out of a giant bowl. Jason made it in easily. He did a thorough scan and found nothing wrong with David. He physically pressed on all David's ribs, examined his leg and his head, and found nothing but dirt and torn clothing.

He turned off his translator and David's and quietly asked him. "What's going on? I saw Lazaro's readings. They were yours, and they weren't good."

David put his hands back on his hips again. "You're right. I was badly in need of medical care, but I got medical care while you were on your way. I can't tell you who did it or how right now, but I will during our debriefing. Am I clear to get out of this circle now? It's really hot in here."

Jason looked more concerned than before he had entered the ring. He turned his head toward Jake but kept his eyes locked on David's. "Jake! I'm coming out!" Presently Jake replied, "Okay, I'm ready when you are." Jason moved away from the entrance and got a running start again only he tripped on the edge of the shield and took an unplanned tumble into the bowl. The only thing hurt was his dignity. Jason got back out of the shield in a slightly less dignified manner, then turned to assist the Captain in his exit.

As David prepared to make his escape from the fire ring, Jake grinned and looked at his captain. "Sir! You'll need to take a flying leap, sir."

The captain scowled at the grinning security chief. "You've been waiting a long time to say that. Haven't you, Chief?"

Jake continued to grin. "I'm not sure what you mean, sir."

David mumbled under his breath, "Yeah, right."

David backed up as far as he dared and ran for the opening. He planted his feet, leaped into the air and over the hot ground, launching himself head first. He put his arms down in front and somersaulted through the shield. He neatly rolled forward onto his feet. Jason quietly walked past David and muttered, "Show off."

David grinned and whispered back, "I'm the captain. It's in my contract. I have to look good."

Jason quickly retorted. "Have you looked in the mirror lately?"

David frowned. Aside from splashing a little water on his face last night, he had not had a bath or shower since yesterday morning. He rubbed his face and felt a heavy layer of razor stubble. Looking down at himself, he saw dirt, dust, dried blood, and sweat stains. He imagined he must look pretty rough. He doubted he smelled very good either.

David looked up and saw Brynna standing near Kasen. She was trying to focus on what Kasen was dealing with, but her attention was clearly divided as she kept glancing toward David. David decided it was time to face the music. He walked over to Brynna and Kasen. Before he reached them, he stopped to speak to Tharen. "Tharen, how are you feeling?"

Tharen gave David a small smile. "I'm weak and sore, but I'm alive. Thank you for sending me back to your ship. I owe you my life."

David sat down beside Tharen. "I think we're even. If you hadn't jumped in front of me, I would be dead. I'm very thankful the doctor was able to help you."

Tharen looked David up and down then cocked his head sideways. "I don't understand something though. What happened to your injuries? I know you were badly hurt. Did your doctor come and heal you in the night?"

David shook his head. "No, the doctor never left your side last night. I know another man who is a healer. He came this morning and healed me. I'm surprised he came and healed me because he's my sworn enemy. I don't understand why he did it, but I am healed... at least until my wife gets ahold of me." David looked past Tharen at Brynna as she stole another look toward him.

Tharen turned around just in time to see her avert her eyes. Tharen smiled again weakly. "I think she needs to spend at least a moment in your arms. She is a strong woman. The gods have blessed you with a fine woman. Go to her now. She's waited long enough, and I think perhaps you have as well."

David smiled at Tharen and stood up. "Thank you for saving my life. You are a good man, and you'll make a good leader of these people someday."

David walked up behind Brynna. He gently reached up and put his hand on her shoulder. "Brynna?"

Brynna turned around slowly. She was almost afraid to look at him. She was trying to be a proper Commander and keep her emotions in check. Her emotions included anger, fear, relief, joy, and excitement. She was angry he had drugged her and sent her back to the ship, as well as over-riding her plan to let the Sorley go as unnecessary to their plan. Her fear stemmed from thinking he might have died, and she might never see him again. Her relief, joy, and excitement were all related to knowing he was alive and well. She was also curious as to why he was well despite the reports she had received. Curiosity was the least prominent of her feelings at the moment. David's gentle touch, the welcoming look in his eyes and the soft, warm way he spoke her name was enough to tear down the walls around her emotions. Brynna jumped quickly into his arms, and silent tears began to flow down her cheeks. David wrapped his arms tightly around her. He whispered quietly to her.

Aulani was still monitoring comms back on the ship and realized David had forgotten to turn his unit off. His whispers were reaching everyone's ears who had an ear-piece. She quickly muted his transmitter.

In a couple minutes, the two relaxed their grips on each other. Brynna wiped the tears from her own eyes. David gave her hand a quick squeeze then said, "We need to talk more later, but we have work to do right now." Brynna nodded. She gave David a quick kiss on the cheek and turned to talk to Kasen.

●●

Kasen had been busy ferreting out Malek's co-conspirators. He now had Malek, Tolem, and Damar on their knees in front of him. Kasen stepped up onto one of the tallest stones to address the crowd. He was angry. He looked like he would rather punish the three men quickly and finally at that very moment. Kasen, despite his explosive personality, knew there was a time and a place for restraint. Punishing the three men would only stir up feelings of discontent among his people. Kasen stood on the stone and looked slowly across the crowd. The people gathered in as close as they could to hear him speak. He took special care to make eye contact with as many as he could before he began to speak.

"This is truly a sad day for me. I asked you to cleanse yourselves and pray to the gods for my son's life. I asked you to wait three days for my return. I asked you to look to Jager and Gervas in my absence for guidance. The leader of the Sky People offered his life in exchange for my son. You have disgraced me as a leader. You could not follow my simple instructions. Why? Why did you do this?"

Kasen's people had varied reactions, although most were ashamed by their actions. Some looked at each other hoping somebody had an answer for Kasen. Others looked down at the ground, and others looked at Malek and his companions. Kasen waited. He wanted them to challenge him. He needed to know what they were afraid of and put their fears to rest. A voice finally spoke from the crowd, "They told us the Sky People killed Tharen!"

Kasen turned around and waved at Tharen to stand. Jason and Manton helped Tharen stand and step up onto the stone he had been sitting on. "As you can see for yourselves, Tharen is very much alive. If he had died by the hands of the Sky People, I would have ordered their deaths last night. I would not have gotten into their Sky boat and flown away with them. Do you take me for a fool? I left to see to his care. They were able to save his life. If we had stayed here, he would have died. We do not have the medicines and tools that they have. Perhaps you failed to see last night, I was the one who injured my own son. Tharen was trying to save the life of the leader of the Sky People, and I hit him with my spear. This was my fault, not theirs." Kasen waved at the crew. Tharen stepped back down with help and sat back down on the stone. Jager handed him a canteen of water, which he gladly accepted. Kasen continued. "This was not the only reason you defied me. Speak!"

Another voice spoke up, "The Sky People are sorcerers." Voice after voice began to erupt from the crowd.

"They cast a spell on you!"

"They are trying to force us to be their allies."

"They cast spells on you and Tharen."

"They're trying to control us."

Kasen raised his hands for silence. "Why do you think they cast a spell on me? What makes you think they control me?"

There was silence again. No one seemed to have an answer. Finally, a woman standing nearby pointed at the three troublemakers and spoke, "They told us you were under a spell." The woman had slave markings etched in her face and arms. It took a lot of boldness for a slave to speak out in public.

Upon hearing her voice, Malek looked up and turned three different shades of red. It was his own slave Auryon, who spoke and condemned him. He gave her a look that spoke volumes, but she didn't back down. She saw this moment as the perfect time to be rid of her cruel master once and for all.

Kasen looked down at her. As much as he knew she spoke the truth, Kasen could not accept her words alone. He knew her motivation was to get back at her master. Kasen again looked to the crowd and made it easy for them. "Does this woman speak the truth?" Gervas started to speak up, but Tharen shook his head at him. If Gervas spoke up, he might be accused of siding with the Sky People and being under their influence.

Another voice spoke up, "The slave speaks the truth." Several other voices echoed in agreement. The crowd, sensing a way to get out of Kasen's line of fire, began to point fingers at the three men condemning them loudly.

Kasen again called for silence. "Do you trust this slave to speak the truth for you?" There were several uncomfortable murmurs of approval. The crowd decided if this went badly, they were more than willing to let a slave bear the brunt of Kasen's anger.

Kasen looked at the slave. "Woman step forward." Auryon felt her heart beginning to pound. She really didn't want this much attention. She had just hoped to get the crowd to lay blame where it needed to go. Kasen looked down at the woman. "What is your name?"

The woman stood in front of Kasen to answer but made sure she didn't make eye contact with him. "My name is Auryon."

Kasen instructed her to stand on a stone near him and face the crowd. By this time, she was nearly frightened to death.

Kasen stepped down and stood directly in her line of sight. He gave instructions loud enough for everyone around to hear. "Auryon, you will speak to the crowd and tell them exactly what you heard and saw. Do not exaggerate or embellish the story. Simply speak the truth. Do you understand? You will only suffer consequences if you lie."

Auryon acknowledged her instructions and told the crowd how the three men made only a halfhearted attempt at cleansing themselves and praying. She told them about spending most of the night fetching alcoholic beverages for the three men. She expounded on how the crowd grew as they heard the three grumbling and complaining.

Once she finished recounting her tale of the events, Kasen stepped back onto his own platform and asked again. "Has this woman spoken the truth?"

The crowd was silent. They had been implicated in Auryon's testimony, as well as the three troublemakers.

Kasen decided to make it easy for them again. "If she has lied then sit down on the ground. If she has spoken the truth remain standing. If you have no knowledge of what she has said, kneel, but do not sit."

A few in the crowd got on their knees, but no one sat down. Most remained standing. Kasen helped Auryon down from her perch and quietly gave her instructions. "Go now to your master's tent and collect whatever you can consider yours. You will not be returning to his household." Auryon's hands had broken out in a cold sweat while she spoke, but now they began to warm up. At Kasen's instructions, she was immediately relieved. She quietly moved through the crowd to follow his instructions. She didn't know where she would end up, but it had to be better than Malek's household.

As soon as the woman was on her way, Kasen walked over to the three men on their knees. He looked out at the crowd, "So you would choose to have three drunken men to rule over you?"

The crowd looked around at each other confused by this new line of thought. One voice responded, "No, Kasen, you are our leader! We follow you!"

Kasen walked back and forth in front of the crowd. "I gave you instructions, and you disobeyed them. Instead, you followed these drunkards. Which of them have you voted to be your new leader? I need to know so I can challenge him for control of my people."

The three men on the ground looked up. Each man suddenly looked scared. This sort of challenge only resulted in death or getting banished from the encampment. Staying in the area meant trying to find someone who would take them in like the Akamu and facing the winter. It was a frightening thought for the warm weather nomads. They couldn't stay anywhere near the encampment, because their lives would be forfeit if they were found.

Damar finally had enough courage to speak. "Great Leader Kasen, we do not challenge your authority over us. We were too drunk because of grief. We feared for you and the life of your son. We didn't know what we were doing. Forgive us! Please, we thought they meant our great leader harm. We sought only to protect you!"

Tolem quickly jumped in. "Mighty Kasen, Damar speaks the truth. The liquor confused our senses. We sought only to serve you and Tharen. We made a grave mistake. Please forgive us."

Kasen looked at Malek who still had not spoken. He wasn't even looking up. Malek was still brooding over what his slave had done. Kasen knew Malek was a quiet instigator by nature. He would start a ball rolling then sit back and watch it gain momentum. Kasen had to push Malek harder to get his confession. "Malek, you have said nothing. Were your friends and your slave lying, or did they speak the truth?" Malek remained silent.

"Answer, or I will take this as your challenge for control of the Sorley."

Malek finally looked up. "I do not challenge you, Kasen. You are my leader. I follow you."

Kasen wasn't happy with his response yet. "So Tolem and Damar have spoken the truth?"

Malek looked back down at the ground. "Yes, they spoke the truth." His voice was so low that only a few heard him. Kasen jerked him up and turned him around to face the crowd. "You disobeyed my orders, challenged my authority, caused my people to disobey me, and you think your little whimper will appease me?! Speak! You wanted the people to hear you before. Make sure they hear you now!"

Malek lifted his head and looked at the crowd and spoke loudly. "Tolem and Damar speak the truth. We sought only to protect you from the Sky People. We did wrong, but only because we serve you as our leader. We were drunk and not thinking clearly. We are sorry for our transgressions against you, Kasen. We ask you and the people to forgive us. Allow us to show our loyalty to you, Great Leader."

Kasen pushed him one step further, "Your slave, Auryon was speaking the truth?"

Malek looked over at Kasen like he was about to throw up. He knew he had no choice, but to answer. "Auryon spoke the truth!" The words made him sick to his stomach. Kasen sent Malek back to his place beside Damar and Tolem.

Kasen had to accomplish two more things. He had to somehow prove he wasn't under the spell of the Sky People and to confess his guilt in the horse race. Kasen paced back and forth, considering his next words carefully. The crew stayed back out of the way and tried to show little interest in Kasen's business. Finally, Kasen had the three men stand. Their hands had been tied behind them. Kasen freed the men from their bonds and face the crowd. "You thought the Sky People were controlling me. Why? What convinced you I did not know my own mind?"

Now that Malek's hands were free, his confidence returned. "They manipulated you into harming Tharen then healed him, so you would be grateful to them for saving him. You would never have harmed Tharen on your own. They had to be responsible.

319

Their leader tricked you into believing he had killed Tharen himself. He must have forced Tharen to throw himself in front of your pike."

Kasen decided it was time for a full confession. "The only one who is guilty of manipulation is ME!"

The crowd looked confused. The three men displayed equal befuddlement. Kasen continued before any of them had time to object. "The Sky People are strangers to me. I had never met them before yesterday. I did not know what sort of men they were. I did not know if they could be trusted. I wanted to learn more about them, so I forced them to participate in the games. Much can be learned from watching how athletes compete. They did not cheat. They worked hard at winning but did not get angry when they lost. They gave up their opportunity to win in order to care for their wounded comrade. They were gracious while winning, and while losing. Their actions were honorable, but I was not convinced. Another true test of a man's character is to back him into a corner and see how he reacts. I decided to test the Sky People even more." Kasen turned to face the crew. "Jager, I gave you a command before the race. What did I order you to do?"

Jager stepped forward and swallowed hard. Kasen nodded to him. "Speak the truth and hold nothing back."

"You ordered me to hit one of the Sky People's horses with a dart to cause it to throw its rider."

Kasen picked up again. "I ordered the race to be fixed. I cheated the Sky People out of an easy victory. They continued to act honorably. Tharen! Did the Sky People know I cheated?"

Tharen stood where he was. "Yes, they did. We found the mark on the horse from the dart and their leader, Captain David saw Jager blow the dart." Tharen remained standing until he knew Kasen was done asking him questions.

Kasen went on again. "The Sky People tried to leave quietly, knowing I had cheated them. I did not allow it. I pushed them until they finally pushed back. I pushed until I put my son's life at risk. I did this. They asked for an alliance. They did not demand one. The only sorcery here is mine."

Malek spoke up one last time. "Their leader must be a sorcerer. He was badly injured, and now he is whole again. We saw his sorcery in the fire ring. A great white light filled the ring, and a second man appeared in the ring with him." Malek looked at Damar and Tolem. "Tell him. You saw it too."

Damar and Tolem looked at each other. They had seen the same thing, but they interpreted it differently. Damar finally spoke. "We saw the bright light and one of the gods appeared inside the fire ring to save the leader of the Sky People." Tolem voiced his agreement with Damar's explanation.

Malek looked at the two like they had each lost their minds. Several people in the crowd began to shout out affirmation of Damar's description of the events. Malek finally lost the rest of his fight. His hangover was starting to move in and take over. He just wanted to go back to his tent, pull the flaps down, and sleep.

Kasen looked around at the crowd who were still claiming the gods were responsible for David's good health. He looked back at David who had no real explanation. David just shrugged his shoulders. The rest of the crew was also looking to David for an explanation. Kasen finally spoke again.

"I have done wrong to the Sky People. They have proven to have the favor of the gods. I ask you, my people, for forgiveness because I have put you in danger of angering the gods. Can you forgive me?"

Kasen got down on his knees and bowed his head. There was silence for a moment as his words sunk in. The crowd, one by one, began to shout their various responses of approval. Even Malek, Damar, and Tolem gave Kasen their forgiveness.

Kasen thanked his people and vowed he would never make this mistake again. Next, he apologized loudly to the gods for his offenses and asked for their forgiveness. He apologized to Tharen and Jager and finally, he apologized to the ship's crew, especially to David and Brynna.

Kasen punished Malek, Damar, and Tolem by confining them to their tents for ten days with nothing but bread and water. He also admonished them to think twice before ever indulging in alcohol outside of the appropriate celebration times. The three men were glad to return to their tents by this time. Although they swore to abstain from drinking, Kasen doubted they would live up to it.

Kasen ordered a feast to honor the gods for their benevolence. While the feast was being prepared, he sat down with Brynna and worked out the alliance with the Commonwealth. He was feeling very generous and didn't hesitate on any of the points. He also agreed to allow them to arbitrate a peace agreement with the Kimbra. Brynna sent Thane and Lexi back to the ship to pick up the Sorley data module. They also brought most of the crew back to join the feast. Two crewmen remained behind on the ship. The day proved to be rather enjoyable. The crew finally climbed aboard the shuttle to head back to the ship as the sun was setting. There were repeated apologies passed back and forth again, but as they left, the crew felt as though the mission was a success. David wasn't sure if the cost was worth it, but he was glad they finally succeeded.

Once the crew got back to the ship, David started issuing orders. Jason and Brynna politely reminded him that he had not been cleared for active duty yet. David objected strenuously. "I'm fine, and I have work to do."

Jason insisted. "Captain, you can let the Commander handle it for now, but I am required by regulations to clear you before you return to duty. And Captain, pardon me for saying so, but you very definitely had broken bones this morning, and now you don't. I need to know how that happened without appropriate medical treatment. I have the equipment here capable of mending bones, but you weren't here. Brynna can come along to find out what your orders are, but this has to be done. If you don't want to do it tonight, you could wait and do it in the morning."

Jason knew David wasn't about to wait until morning to get cleared for duty. The entire crew was watching to see how he would react. He knew once they found out the truth about what happened, he would be under even more scrutiny. David tried to maintain nonchalance about the regulatory requirement, but he was genuinely feeling annoyed and inconvenienced. "Let's get it over with tonight. I have too much to do to let this wait until morning." Jason and Brynna promptly escorted him to the Med Bay for a full checkup.

David continued to give orders, but where Brynna was concerned he phrased them carefully. His orders were more of a strong suggestion rather than a straight order. Brynna made a couple minor adjustments to his orders and passed them onto the crew as though they were her own.

Jason scanned David all the way down to a cellular level and found him to be perfectly healthy. There were no signs of burns, broken bones, no cuts, scrapes or bruises. After the ordeal of that morning, David should have had at least signs of smoke inhalation, burns, and dehydration. Jason didn't find even one small sign of any of it. Finally, after Jason ran every test he could think of, he simply started asking questions. Brynna stayed right by David's side because she wanted answers too.

"Captain, what happened to you out there? Your test results don't show any indication there was ever anything wrong with you at all. I need an explanation."

The Captain hopped down from the exam table. "Does this mean I'm cleared for duty?"

Jason shook his head. "Not until I get some satisfactory answers. I can't vouch for your mental stability yet."

David gave Jason and Brynna a wry smile. "I was hoping to wait and explain everything one time at the debriefing." He looked at the Doctor. "I get the feeling even if I could put you off until morning, I wouldn't in a million years be able to put her off, so you might as well hear it together."

David sat back down and took a deep breath. This wasn't going to be easy to explain. Brynna had been patient all day long, but her patience was running out. "David! Spill it already!"

David decided bluntness was best. "It was Arni." He gave his words a moment to sink in before elaborating. "I was tied up and put in the center of the fire ring alone. They set the ring on fire. I tried to move over to the largest part of the blaze and stay low so the crowd couldn't hit me with the rocks. I wasn't in any shape to do any ducking or dodging. It was so hot and smoky, and I was having trouble breathing. I really thought I was a dead man. Arni just showed up out of nowhere. He untied my hands and healed my wounds like he did the boy on Galat. I wasn't hallucinating, and he hasn't taken over my mind. I am still loyal to the Commonwealth. I plan on giving a full report in the debriefing tomorrow morning."

Jason and Brynna just looked at each other for a moment. David knew they had doubts about his mind and his loyalties. "We have a mission to complete, and I'd really like to get back down to business. Can you clear me for duty?"

Jason paced for a moment. He looked back at David. "Here's the deal. First of all, I have to notify the Security Chief about what you just told me. Second, I want you to get a good night's rest. If I don't see anything overnight that concerns me, my log will reflect that you are automatically cleared for duty at 0700 hours tomorrow morning. Do you have a problem with that?"

David sighed. "I was actually feeling pretty good, so I was going to be the night shift watch commander. I thought everyone else might need the rest tonight."

"I think Braxton can handle it for one more night, especially now that everyone is safely back in the ship and there is nothing pressing tonight," Brynna volunteered.

David agreed to their conditions and plan. It was annoying, but he knew it was necessary. He also hoped to have the "captain's prerogative" excuse to fall back on to keep him out of too much trouble with Brynna. He couldn't use that excuse if he wasn't currently "Captain."

After Jason released the Captain, David and Brynna headed back to their cabin. Brynna sent out the final orders for the evening, and the two started getting ready for bed. David took a nice long hot shower. He had so much dirt and soot on him, he thought he might never get clean. The two said very little until they crawled into bed. Then, it started.

"David, why did you have Lazaro drug me?"

David's brow wrinkled, and he pressed his lips together tightly. He turned around in the bed so he could face her. "Brynna, you were not in any shape to make command decisions, and I didn't want you to be worried. You needed medical treatment and rest."

"Did you drug me just to keep me quiet?"

David reached over and grasped her hand. "No. I could have simply ordered you back to the ship and removed you from active duty if I just wanted you to be quiet. I didn't want you to be worried about me."

The two spent the next two hours talking, arguing, venting, shedding a few tears, and giving each other heartfelt apologies. Ultimately, they made up and snuggled together in each other's arms. Before drifting off to sleep, David asked one more question. "Is this why you moved the time of the debriefing two hours later than when I wanted it scheduled in the morning?"

Brynna didn't move or open her eyes, but simply responded, "Absolutely."

●●

The next morning everyone reported his or her activities and observations for the previous day. The captain made sure everyone was on the same page before they moved on to the next step in their mission. Once all reports had been given, David gave his. He told the crew Arni healed his wounds and denied having any contact with the people on this planet. David also told them what Arni said about needing them to stop the Supreme Executor, but not forcing them. He didn't mention to anyone Arni's knowledge of David's thoughts about his impending death. That part was just a little too personal and it showed weakness. It wasn't something a captain needed to show without an excellent reason.

Manton and Vesta were confused by the mention of Arni. Finally, they interrupted the conversation to ask. "Who is this Arni?"

The room became silent for a moment then Brynna picked up the conversation. "He is the enemy we've been looking for. As part of our alliance, if Arni Liontari or Pateras El Liontari were to show up here, your people have agreed to notify us immediately."

The couple's confusion was not mitigated in the slightest. Vesta scowled. "Your enemy healed you? Why would he do that? If he is capable of such benevolence, why is he your enemy?"

"I don't know what their exact strategy is, but I think they want us to drop our guard. The Liontaris know we are hunting them now. They are looking to get a foot in the door of the Commonwealth. They are our enemies because they have chosen to be our enemies. They possess the minds of their followers causing them to reject the Commonwealth. The Commonwealth wants peace and unity among all worlds and all people. The Liontaris are trying to destroy all the good the Commonwealth has done." Brynna had questions of her own at this point, but that was the best answer she could offer. Since David told them about Arni's claim that the Supreme Executor was guilty of atrocities of his own, she definitely had questions. Unfortunately, only Arni could answer those questions.

Manton and Vesta assured the crew they had never seen or heard of anyone with this sort of power, not even in the stories from the other populations on the planet. The couple was still confused by this recent turn of events, but so were the rest of the crew. Manton and Vesta vowed that no matter what sort of trickery they saw, they would let the Commonwealth know the instant Arni showed up again.

David also beat Jake to the punch. "As soon as we leave Medoris, I will contact home base and ask for further instructions on how to handle any future run-ins with Arni. I don't think we need to leave yet, because I don't think Pateras has a foothold here. I also get the feeling this ship and crew are his targets, not the population of this planet. If that is the case, it won't matter where we are. We may as well complete our mission so we will have the allies if we need them."

"Captain, if we are his targets, this could give us a unique opportunity to catch him." Braxton suggested.

David nodded. "That thought crossed my mind, which is why I want to contact CIF headquarters. Our orders were very specific, and I don't want to stray from them without permission from higher up."

Jake was trying not to appear overzealous, but it was obvious when he relaxed after David's comment. Their discussion about Jake's fanatical enthusiasm made a difference, but Jake was still going to be Jake. At least David didn't feel like he was about to be shot in the back, at least not today.

THE KIMBRA

The crew finished the debriefing, and David turned the meeting over to Brynna to discuss the next portion of the debrief: The Kimbra.

Brynna went back to their previous plan of splitting the crew into three teams. The first team would stay with the ship, the second team would return to the Akamu caves, and the third team would head to the Kimbra cities.

Brynna planned on Team One consisting of Jason, Laura, Thane, and Aulani. Before the crew left the Sorley encampment, Brynna invited Kasen to send any of his people who needed medical care beyond the Sorley healer's capabilities to the ship for Jason to treat. Jason invited their healer to come and observe. Jason was very tactful with his invitation to avoid offending the camp's only medical person. The Sorley population trusted their healer. If the people saw the healer trusting Jason, they would hopefully trust him too. Jason and Laura would handle the medical side of things. Aulani and Thane would act as support personnel for them and the rest of the ship's crew.

Team Two would go back to the Akamu caves and continue making improvements to the caves. Braxton had been teaching the Akamu how to improve ventilation in the caves without sacrificing heat. He was also working on improvements to lighting and sanitation. The Akamu agreed to stop owning slaves. Lexi was working with slave owners, the Akamu ruling council, and the slaves to find the best way to transition the slaves back into normal human relationships. Jake and Marissa were the support personnel on Team Two. Jake would continue to help the Akamu improve their defenses and teach self-defense tactics. Lexi asked the couple to spend as much time teaching the slave population self-defense as they could spare. Slaves were generally expected to be weak and powerless. Lexi wanted to empower them so that after the crew was gone, they wouldn't be subjugated again. Lexi was also going to invite the Akamu to bring the sick, injured, and scarred to Jason the next day. Brynna didn't want half of the planet's population hitting Jason at once.

Team Three would head to the Kimbra cities to meet with their leaders and try to build an alliance. Before the teams could get underway, the Sorley healer was waiting outside with a long line of people awaiting medical care. The healer even brought the slave population, so their markings could be removed and their skin reconstructed. If they no longer looked like slaves, their freedom would be easier to guarantee.

Upon seeing the crowd outside the ship, Brynna quickly dismissed the meeting and sent the teams on their way. Thane took care of crowd control, while the Surf-Ve and shuttle were pulled out of the docking bays. The teams boarded their respective vessels and got moving. Manton and Vesta boarded the shuttle with Team Three to visit the Kimbra.

The shuttle flew toward the two cities and made a figure eight around them looking for a good place to land. Lazaro wanted to put the shuttle down between the two cities, but the fields were covered with crops. He finally put down on the east side of the fields in a rocky area located an almost equal distance from the two cities. Once on the ground, the crew was greeted by several men guarding the fields. The men were carrying crossbows, knives, and swords. The greeting was not as friendly as the crew would have liked. The presence of the two Akamu warriors seemed to keep them from doing anything rash.

Manton took the role of interpreter since he now wore an earpiece like the rest of the crew. It reduced the fear factor of having a "talking bracelet." Manton greeted the men and assured them the crew was not there to steal the crops or to take slaves. Manton's explanation to the guards gave Brynna a solid piece of information she could use in her negotiations. Manton informed the guards they were there to talk to Cashel and Medwin. The guards sent a messenger to each city, but they stayed close by and watched the crew closely.

David and Brynna stood around with the others chatting about nothing in particular. Brynna headed back into the shuttle and sat down. When she didn't come back out in a couple minutes, David went in to check on her. When he found her just sitting there, he was instantly concerned. "Are you okay?"

Brynna opened her eyes, "Sure. I'm just a little tired. Why?"

David moved to the seat next to her. He picked up her hand and gave it a gentle squeeze. "You haven't pushed yourself too hard, too fast have you? Or maybe I should ask if I'm pushing you too hard too fast. You just don't seem like yourself."

Brynna smiled at David and squeezed his hand in return. "I think maybe we could have all used a day to recoup, but we didn't really leave ourselves an opening."

David's injuries had been much worse than Brynna's, but Arni cured more than the broken bones and the other injuries. His cure went all the way to a cellular level. Arni cured the exhaustion, the dehydration, and even electrolyte and chemical imbalances. Jason treated Brynna's injuries to a similar degree, but it usually took a few days to feel normal again. David looked down at the ground then back at Brynna. He felt like because Arni had healed him, he had somehow cheated to get ahead. Lexi would have considered it "survivors guilt."

David held both her hands in his. "If you need to sit this one out, I can take this one."

Brynna lifted her head off the headrest. "David, I'm fine. I'm a little drained. I just thought it would be prudent to conserve my energy. What else is bothering you?"

David squeezed her hands again. "I just don't think it's fair that I'm fine and you're still not feeling well. This part is your job. I'm supposed to be a glorified security guard."

Brynna leaned forward and kissed his forehead. "Personally, if you're my security detail, I'm really glad you don't feel like I do."

David looked up and smiled. "You are such a diplomat." Brynna grinned back at him.

Lazaro stepped to the doorway of the shuttle. He was trying to give the couple sufficient privacy, while still interrupting them with news. "Captain, Commander, we've got company coming." The two stood up and walked back outside.

Cashel sent a delegate out to speak for him. "My name is Jabre. The Lord Master Cashel has sent me to find out why you have come here. He has said he would return to you when he has made his decision regarding your proposal."

Brynna spoke directly to Manton and did not acknowledge Jabre directly. "Tell the delegate, Jabre, I have news regarding our relations with the Sorley and the Akamu for the Lord Master Cashel. I wish to share this information with him and the Lord Master Medwin. We also came to admire the fantastic construction work that has gone into building his fine city. I have other things I would like to discuss with the two Lord Masters if they can find the time to meet with us."

Manton relayed her words to the delegate. The delegate smiled and nodded. "I will be glad to give your messages to the Lord Master."

Brynna thanked Jabre and said nothing else. Jabre stood there waiting on Brynna to speak, and Brynna turned her back and started talking to Cheyenne or so it appeared. She spoke out loud while facing Cheyenne, but she was actually transmitting to Manton. "Manton, I am not going to give this delegate any further information. I want to speak only to the Lord Masters. I may have to appear offended that we have been treated so badly. Make sure you relay only the words I give directly to you. If you understand walk over to the rest of us."

Manton still felt strange hearing words in his ears without someone speaking right next to him. He did as he was instructed.

After an awkward silence, Jabre called out to Manton. "Akamu, what news of the Akamu and the Sorley do the Sky People want me to tell the Lord Master?"

Manton looked back at him then he looked at Brynna and asked, "What shall I tell him?"

Brynna looked over at Jabre. Her expression showed hints of annoyance. She looked at Manton, "Tell Jabre I have news for the Lord Master, and I will give the Lord Master the news when I see him. The news I have is for the Lord Masters only."

Manton passed the information yet again to Jabre who looked perturbed. Brynna heard him protest. In a moment, the translation came through. "The Lord Master sent me to talk to you. He expects me to tell him what you want."

Brynna whipped around and walked over to the man. She felt sorry for him, but she had no choice. Standing directly in front of him, Brynna kept her eyes on Jabre but spoke to Manton. "Manton, tell Jabre we are leaving. Tell him we are offended by the way we have been treated today and if the Lord Master wishes to speak with us, he can meet us at our ship in the west." Brynna turned around and motioned for the crew to start boarding the shuttle. Lazaro looked confused but complied. The others began to follow him.

Jabre reached out and grabbed Brynna's shoulder to stop her from leaving. Brynna spun around, grabbed his hand bent his thumb backward in one quick swift move. The man yelped and dropped to his knees. Brynna looked down at his frightened face. "How dare you touch me! Tell your Lord Master I am not a weakling to be toyed with. I can help him make peace with the Sorley, or I can let them wipe him out. I protected him from the Sorley, but I can remove my protection any time I want. Do you understand?" Manton passed her message on exactly as she said it. The precision and effectiveness of her defensive move gave Manton newfound respect for the Commander. Two of the men who had been guarding the fields were still standing close by. The two men looked at each other. Jabre was not a small man, but Brynna had quickly and easily put him on his knees. They weren't sure whether to move to his rescue or stand their ground. Brynna made the decision for them when she released his hand. Jabre grabbed his aching hand and massaged it. His face was pale in comparison to what it had been earlier. Brynna looked at Manton and gave him one last message to pass along. "Tell him I will forgive his impertinence and consider his transgression atoned for. He doesn't need to tell his Master about it, and I will not mention it either."

Brynna and the crew boarded the shuttle and took off. The crew watched out the windows and saw the nearby guards checking on Jabre and escorting him back toward the city. Brynna shook her head. "I hate being like that. I'm trying to raise their standards, but I end up lowering mine."

Cheyenne agreed. "With these primitive cultures, you have to do that sometimes, so they can relate to you. It's sad, but it's true."

●●

When the shuttle was picked up on the ship's scanners, Thane hailed them. "*Evangeline* to shuttle. Is there a problem?"

Brynna picked up comms to answer. "Shuttle to *Evangeline*. Negative, we're fine, but we are returning to base. We're going to have to wait the Kimbra out." Thane acknowledged their intentions and made preparations for them to land.

Before they landed, Brynna made some basic assignments. "Everybody, help Jason and Thane out with our guests. They're probably going to need food and water, as well as other sanitation and hygiene issues. There seems to be a large number of people needing attention down there. If you aren't needed, then take some personal time."

Upon landing, everyone scattered to see what he or she could do to help. While Lazaro got the shuttle buttoned up, David pulled Brynna aside. "Brynna, I think you need to take some downtime yourself." Brynna started a long list of objections. David quickly cut her off. "Brynna, we can handle this. You need to be ready when the Kimbra get here. They don't need to see any weakness in you."

"They won't, David. I'm fine. I'll take it easy until they get here." Brynna interjected.

"Brynna, I can make it an order if I have to and I know Jason will back me up."

Brynna's face flashed bright red. "You wouldn't dare. David, your injuries were far worse than mine. I don't see you taking any downtime."

"Jason said it himself, whatever technology Arni used to heal me worked all the way down to a cellular level. It's as though I was never injured in the first place. Jason doesn't have that ability. It's going to take a few days for you to get your strength back. Take a break. It's not going to hurt anything, and it will help you do a better job later. We need you to be on top of your game when we deal with the Kimbra. Brynna, please."

Tears began to run down her face. David was now officially confused. He wrapped his arms around her and pulled her close to him. He didn't know why she had started crying, but he did know the right prescription. "Brynna, what's wrong?"

Brynna buried her head in his shoulder and cried quietly for a few minutes. When she didn't answer, David simply held her tightly and stroked her hair. Her breathing finally slowed, and her tears subsided. She wiped her eyes and took a deep breath and finally spoke. "I'm sorry for such a pathetic display."

David cocked his head slightly. "No apology necessary, but I would like to know what caused it."

Brynna let go of him and stepped away. In a moment, she turned back around to face him. "Maybe you're right. Maybe I do need to get some rest." She started to turn and walk away.

"Brynna. Don't try and snow me like this. You don't cry easily. What else is going on?"

She stopped dead in her tracks. Still standing with her back to him, "It's nothing. I'm sure I'll see things much better after I get some rest." With that, she headed back to their quarters.

David wasn't about to give up so easily. He followed her into their quarters. "Brynna, I really need to know what's going on. If it's important enough to push you to tears, then it's important."

Brynna sat down on the bed. She looked up at David. Silent tears again started to roll slowly down her face. "David, I'm beginning to wonder if I can do this job. You had to take the lead on Galat because they didn't respect women in leadership. You had to take over when Lexi was kidnapped. You were the key one responsible for getting the Sorley to sign on. Now I'm having trouble facing the Kimbra because of exhaustion and having to be something I'm not. I didn't like bullying their messenger, but I felt like they wouldn't respect me if I didn't."

David stood there looking down at her, trying to process what she said. The wise young captain knelt in front of his new wife. Taking her hands in his, he laid her fears to rest. "Brynna, on Galat III, I was the visible front. You were the brains behind the mission. You did the planning and organizing. I followed your orders. When Lexi was kidnapped, that was a matter of crew protection, and it was unrelated to our negotiations. That was my job, not yours, although I think it helped your job. If you don't like being something you aren't, then make them respect you for who you are. Brynna, I couldn't do this job without you. The only reason the Sorley thing went forward is because I carried out your plan."

"No, David, we were leaving the Sorley encampment. You changed the plan."

David looked up at her and grinned just a little. "Actually, I stuck with plan A, instead of moving to plan B. They were both your plans, I just wasn't ready to give up on the first one."

Brynna had the urge to smile at him, but the urge was drowned by her other emotions. "David, you drugged me."

David's grin faded, so much for his attempt to cheer her up. "Brynna, I'm sorry. I promise I will never do that again. I just wanted to protect you. If I hadn't done it, you would have stayed through the rest of the tournament, and your life would have been at risk. Kasen might have killed you in retaliation for Tharen. I was doing my job in keeping my crew safe. That does include you, you know."

Brynna nodded. Her face still showed her doubts. David vacillated between being the hard-nosed captain and pushing her or being the warm caring attentive husband. He finally compromised with himself. "Brynna, I cannot do this job without you. You are a crucial part of this crew. Tell me one thing. If I had been the one injured in the horse race, what would you have done?"

The Commander thought carefully for a moment. "I don't know, David. I can't be sure what I would have done."

David stood up and walked around for a moment. "C'mon Commander, the captain is injured, and there is only one way to get the Sorley on board. What are you going to do? Are you going to push the mission forward without the Sorley? You said we could accomplish our goals without them, but it would be faster and easier with them. What would you have done?"

Brynna grimaced. "I suppose I would do the same thing you did, mostly."

"Mostly?"

Brynna gave him a venomous look. "I wouldn't have drugged the captain unless he was a danger to himself or others."

David responded sheepishly. "Yeah, I kinda picked up on that point several times. Brynna, you don't have any reason to doubt yourself. I suppose one of the reasons I drugged you was because I knew how strong you really are. I knew you would fight back. I needed to know you were safe, both as the captain and as your husband. I don't know if Kasen would have allowed us to leave, and I needed to have my second in command able to take over if things didn't go well for me. I'm fairly certain you would have made the same choices."

David sat down on the bed beside her and put his arm around her. Brynna snuggled up under his arm and wrapped her arms around him. Tears rolled down her face again. David looked at her sideways, "What are these tears for?"

Brynna looked up at him and smiled. "You always know the right things to say."

David gave her one more, firm hug and a gentle kiss. "Get some rest. You need to be ready when the Kimbra show up."

Brynna crawled under the covers. Looking up at David she smiled and said, "Yes, Captain."

David left their cabin and headed to the bridge. He thought about asking the doc to give Brynna another once over but decided to wait and see how she felt later. When he stepped onto the bridge, Thane and Aulani greeted him. "Captain, I was just about to contact you."

"What's up, Lieutenant?"

"Captain, we have at least thirty people outside, and they're still coming. We've set up latrines and water stations, but these people are going to need to eat soon. We don't have enough food to go around. What do you want me to do?"

David thought a moment. "Where are those herds the Sorley follow? How would you and Lazaro feel about going hunting?"

Thane's face brightened noticeably. "Really?"

Most of the crew had been raised in urban settings. They had read about hunting in their history lessons, but few had any hunting experience. Eating actual meat was also a rarity. The crew had been exposed to hunting for food in their survival basic course during their training. Some of the crew took to it better than others.

Upon seeing Thane's reaction, Aulani shook her head. "Eww, yuck." David and Thane laughed at her reaction. David and Thane enjoyed the survival course. The captain suggested they take Vesta and Manton with them.

Thane hailed Lazaro, who had just gotten the shuttle bay closed up. Lazaro responded to the hail. "Are you kidding? I just got the shuttle locked down." Lazaro grudgingly opened the shuttle bay again. Hunting wasn't something Lazaro looked forward to. Manton and Vesta were glad to join the hunt. Manton asked if he could use a Tri-EMP for hunting. Lazaro volunteered to fly the shuttle so Manton could use his Tri-EMP. The four took off shortly and headed toward the herds.

Less than two hours later, the shuttle returned hauling four of the large beasts. The crew hadn't seen the animals up close. The beasts were larger in real life than they appeared from a distance. They were lean like an antelope but had large muscle mass. As with most of the animal population on this planet, their fur was heavier than their off-world counterparts. Their horns were more akin to a buffalo or cow.

The shuttle contacted the ship, letting them know they were on their way back. David, with the help of the Sorley, had a roaring fire ready to roast the meat. As much as David hated to admit it, they were good at building fires. Several of the Sorley jumped in and got the animals skinned quickly and expertly. The skins were kept in usable condition.

Aulani checked the ship's inventory and found a few vegetables still being stored from Galat III, as well as some cheese. It wasn't much, but she brought them out to prepare. They still had no bread. It took some time for the meat to cook.

While the meat was cooking, Jager and Gervas rode up. David greeted them warmly. "Welcome to our home. What can we do for you?"

Jager got off his horse and greeted David with as much enthusiasm. "I am glad to see you are still doing well. Kasen sent us with some food for the people. He was afraid his people had not planned ahead."

David looked around at the crowd. He had not seen anyone eating anything. "I think Kasen is a wise man. I don't think anyone brought food."

Gervas walked up beside Jager. "It appears you are not without merit yourself. I see you have done well at hunting."

"I sent Thane, Lazaro, Manton, and Vesta hunting. They are the ones who did well."

"You are the one who sent them. It appears the gods favor you very much." Gervas replied.

David shrugged and politely defused his suggestion. "I can't speak for the gods. I don't believe I've met any, but I appreciate your help and Kasen's."

The crew, with the help of Jager and Gervas, got everyone seated and began handing out food. Brynna got up and came outside just in time to join in the feast. While everyone was eating, the Surf-Ve returned with the four who had been working with the Akamu. They weren't expected back so soon. Braxton reported to the Commander and captain that the Akamu were very independent and self-sufficient by nature. They were adjusting very quickly to the use of the data module and no longer needed the crew's input or supervision.

The Lt. Commander assured the Commander and the Captain the Akamu weren't pushing the crew away. "Captain, they were so proactive in their efforts we were just getting in the way. Jake stayed busier than the rest of us. Once they learned the data module could also teach hand-to-hand combat and defense strategies, then Jake was no longer needed. We might need to get them a second data module; there was a line to use the thing. Some of the women wanted to use it for cooking and sewing tips, but the warriors wanted to use it to make better weapons. Tarin was using it. If the kids ever find the gaming files, well, we could start a civil war among the Akamu." The captain found that possibility quite amusing. The new insights into the Akamu explained how Manton and Vesta had fit in so quickly and learned how to use basic ship's equipment so easily.

As the crowd was finishing their food, the crew started cleaning up. Aulani reported three riders coming in from the east.

By the time the riders reached them, Brynna, Jake, and David were there to greet them. Brynna immediately recognized the lead rider as Jabre, Cashel's messenger. Brynna decided to take David's advice to convince the locals to respect her for the person that she is. Brynna greeted the men warmly and invited them to have something to eat. The three men were nervous about being so heavily outnumbered by the Sorley citizens. Brynna reassured them they were safe and under her protection. David and Jake stayed close to the men as they availed themselves of the delicious smelling meal. Brynna sat down with the men to find out why they had come to the ship. Jabre was bringing a message from Cashel. "The Lord Master Cashel wishes to extend his apologies for how you were treated today. He also would like to invite you and your people to return tomorrow, and he will be glad to meet with you and show you around his city."

"Thank you Jabre, we would be honored to meet with the Lord Master Cashel," Brynna replied. "I hope we didn't offend the Lord Master by leaving today."

"No, Mistress Alexander. The Lord Master..."

"Jabre!" A woman's voice interrupted the messenger.

Upon hearing the woman's voice, Jabre instantly froze. His face a ghostly white, the man turned around slowly. Standing behind him was the Sorley slave, Auryon.

Jabre was now clearly shaking. He stood up then immediately knelt down in front of the woman. His voice quivered as he spoke, "My Lady, you – you are alive!" Tears began to pour down Jabre's face. "My Lady, forgive me. I am so sorry. I failed you!" Auryon reached down and cradled Jabre's face in her hands. Jabre reached up, grabbed her hands in his own and kissed them.

Jabre's two guards were not sitting at the same table with Jabre and the crew because it was considered a societal taboo. On seeing Jabre's strange behavior, the guards looked very disturbed. It was not acceptable for a man of Jabre's stature to kneel before a slave. Auryon had been a slave just long enough to feel uncomfortable having Jabre kneel at her feet. The woman tried to encourage him to stand. The harder she tried to get him off his knees, the harder he cried and tighter he clung to her. The longer it continued, the angrier the guards became. They stepped forward and began to push Auryon away from Jabre. They didn't know what power the woman had over him, but they speculated she must be a witch or sorceress.

Brynna signaled Lexi to escort Auryon inside the ship. Jabre sat there on the ground weeping bitterly. The guards didn't dare lay a hand on Jabre, but they didn't hesitate to touch Auryon and pull her away from him. Jabre seemed paralyzed with whatever sorrow had overtaken him. All the cleanup activities came to a grinding halt as the curious crowd stopped to watch the peculiar display of emotion.

Brynna encouraged Lexi to get some information about what just happened from Auryon. Brynna and David helped Jabre to his feet and escorted him away from the uncomfortable stares around him. They walked over to the stream Braxton and Lexi visited the night she was kidnapped. David and Brynna stepped over to a nearby tree to give the man some time to compose himself. A portion of the trunk ran low to the ground making it an ideal place to sit. Brynna had found a comfortable perch while David chose to merely lean against a more upright section of the tree.

Jabre knew they wanted an explanation, but he was having a difficult time getting his mouth to form the words. After sitting on the bank of the stream for what felt like an eternity, Jabre knelt at the edge of the water and washed his face. He finally stood up and slowly walked over to David and Brynna. Before he could speak, Brynna spoke first. "Jabre, you do not owe us any explanations. If there is anything we can do to help you, we will do what we can, but if this is private, then please keep it private."

As the translation came through, Jabre nodded his understanding. He took a deep breath. Looking directly at Brynna he slowly spoke. "You said you would say nothing to the Lord Master regarding my indiscretion this morning." He took another long deep breath. "Did you mean that?"

Brynna earnestly replied, "Of course I did. I do not want to embarrass or humiliate anyone purposely. I also never intend to lie or mislead anyone. I want others to know I can be trusted."

Jabre spent a great deal of time staring at the ground or off in the distance, but he brought his gaze back to her. "Thank you for your discretion. I will give you my trust in return. Mistress Auryon is the sister of the Lord Masters, Cashel and Medwin. We were overseeing the harvest several years ago when the Sorley attacked us. I tried to get her to safety. I failed. I was injured and nearly died. The Sorley took her away. It was my fault. I don't know why the Lord Masters allowed me to live. I should have been executed, or at least banished for my failure."

David and Brynna looked at each other. Surely this wasn't all there was to the story. Brynna looked back at Jabre and cautiously asked. "Is that all you wanted to share?"

Jabre took yet another deep breath. "There is more." He hung his head in shame. "If I tell you the rest, you must not tell anyone of the Kimbra people. I will certainly be punished if it is found out."

Brynna and David glanced at each other. This was getting into dangerous territory. Keeping information from the Kimbra leaders could interfere with their upcoming negotiations. It could also give new insight into the lives of the Kimbra. Brynna looked back at Jabre and assured him they would not speak of it to the Kimbra.

Jabre stared off into space again, and tears slipped down his cheeks as he began to speak quietly. "I fell in love with the Mistress Auryon. I do not understand why, but I believe she loved me as well. We are not of the same social station, and our relationship was never supposed to happen, at least not publicly. Her brothers arranged a marriage for her, and they were quite angry with her when she refused to marry the man they chose for her. She tried to stay out of their sight until they got over being angry. That is why she was out in the fields when the Sorley attacked. It's all my fault she was taken."

"Jabre, may I ask you a question?" Brynna queried. Jabre nodded. She proceeded with her question, "Who was Auryon supposed to marry?"

"They were arranging a marriage with one of the Sorley ruling council to bring peace between them and us. Tensions have been worse between us since this happened."

Brynna glanced at David. "Jabre, the Sorley have freed all their slaves. They are going to allow them to choose to continue living among their people as free citizens or escort them back to their homes."

Jabre's shoulders slumped, and the tears ran faster again. "She cannot come back to the Kimbra as one of the elite. She bears the markings of a slave. If her brothers take her in, she will have to live as a hermit hidden in their homes. She would not be free there. They would not treat her as a slave, but she would be a prisoner for her own protection."

Having numerous thoughts run through her mind at once, Brynna hesitated to respond. Finally, she asked Jabre, "What are your intentions, Jabre? What will you do if Auryon chooses to stay with the Sorley?"

Jabre's mind started racing. He had been so busy beating himself up again he failed to think about what to do next. "I – I don't know. I would gladly give my life for her. I will go wherever she goes if she will have me." A stricken look suddenly crossed his face. "What if she has found another? What if she blames me for the horrible things that happened to her? I don't know if I could bear that."

Brynna slid off the tree trunk. "Jabre, I am going to do everything I can to work this out for the best, for you and for Auryon, as well as the Kimbra and Sorley. I will say nothing of your relationship with Mistress Auryon or your outburst. You'll have to do something to contain your own guards. I suggest you talk to Auryon then return to your Lord Master as planned. Tell him his sister is alive and well and has been freed by the Sorley."

"Unless my Mistress sends me away, I will not leave her side ever again."

Brynna and David started back to the ship, "Then let's go talk with your Mistress. It might take a little work, but I think we can fix it, so you never have to leave her again."

The three walked hastily back to the ship. David glanced at the two guards who had walked over to the fire and were talking. They appeared to be uncomfortable around so many of their enemy. They also seemed uncomfortable being around so many slaves. David supposed they were behaving themselves, due to Jake and Thane's obvious presence and watchful eyes. The two appeared not to notice their return, which suited David and Brynna just fine.

Brynna escorted Jabre to the captain's office where Lexi was talking with Auryon. It appeared Auryon had also been crying. When Jabre walked in Auryon looked away from him. Jabre moved directly in front of her. He pulled up a chair and began to softly talk to her. Lexi walked over to the Commander and the captain. She wanted to give the couple a few minutes to talk while she updated the Commander.

"Commander, there's something you need to know."

"What is it, Lexi?"

"I strongly advised Auryon not to mention this to Jabre, but it wasn't his fault she was taken. They were set up by Medwin."

"What?! How?"

"Cashel and Medwin arranged a marriage between Auryon and Malek. Medwin was pushing it because he knew about her relationship with Jabre. He apparently strongly disapproved and was trying to use the marriage and alliance to break the two of them up."

"Malek? He was the hothead who caused all the unrest among the Sorley that nearly got me killed." David was not amused by this information. "She was supposed to be his wife, but ended up as his slave? How did that happen?"

Lexi kept her voice low. "Malek apparently got drunk one night and spilled his guts to Auryon. He was angry at her rejection. Medwin approached Malek and told him it was Jabre's fault Auryon refused him. He offered Malek a chance to get even with Jabre. He told Malek when and where to find Jabre. Medwin didn't care if Malek took him as a slave or killed him. He just wanted him gone. Malek led the raid as planned and discovered Auryon was with Jabre. He thought he killed Jabre then he took Auryon. He gave her the option of being his wife or his slave. She chose to be his slave. He was so angry at being rejected twice; he nearly killed her. The one thing she wasn't sure of was Cashel's involvement. If Jabre finds out what Medwin did, he will undoubtedly go after him."

Brynna smiled. David looked at her quizzically then realized what she was thinking. His face then mimicked hers. Lexi looked back and forth at the two of them. She knew something was going on. Finally, she asked. "Okay, what am I missing?"

Brynna explained her thoughts. "Kasen can force Malek to testify to his part and to Medwin's if necessary. We can use that as a bargaining chip to force Medwin to support the alliance. If we have to, we can expose everything that's happened. How do you think the Kimbra will react when they find out the raids are escalating because of their own leaders?"

Lexi's face brightened. "That's brilliant!"

Brynna's smile was replaced by knit eyebrows. "There's just one problem. We must convince Jabre to go back to Cashel as expected. He never wants to leave her side again."

Lexi grinned, "I got this." She turned and walked over to the couple who were coming to terms with their situations. Auryon was embarrassed by the scarring on her face and body. Although she was excited to see Jabre, she was afraid he would no longer want to see her because of her looks and her change in station. Jabre repeatedly assured her she was still the most beautiful woman he had ever seen, and he would never again leave her side.

Lexi, Brynna, and David sat down around the table with the couple. Lexi started the conversation cautiously. "Auryon, Jabre told the Commander he would never again leave your side. I think we should tell him a little bit about what you told me. It would help build an alliance between the Sorley and the Kimbra, as well as begin the process of freeing all the slaves. Will you allow me to talk to him?"

Jabre looked at Auryon, "What is it?"

Auryon felt trapped. If she said "yes," she wasn't sure just how much Lexi would say, but she didn't want Jabre to find out what her brother had done. If she said "no," Jabre would want to know why. Lexi laid her hand on Auryon's arm. "Trust me, please." Auryon was still hesitant. Lexi added one more incentive. "I think we can do this in a way that no one gets hurt." A look of relief crossed her face, and she finally consented. Lexi gave Auryon's arm a reassuring squeeze.

Lexi looked at Jabre who was holding tightly to Auryon's other hand. "Jabre, I need to ask for your help with something. What I am going to ask is going to be difficult for you, but it is going to help us create an alliance between the Sorley and the Kimbra."

Jabre interrupted. "I do not care about your alliance. I care only about Auryon's welfare."

Lexi nodded. "I understand, but the alliance will help Auryon. Whether she stays with the Kimbra or the Sorley, she may be viewed as a slave and won't be treated with the respect she deserves. If she remains with the Kimbra, your relationship will be forbidden. The Sorley have only known her as a slave. We can fix this, if you will help us."

Jabre asked somberly, "What do you need me to do?"

Lexi glanced at Auryon. "Someone sabotaged the peace between the Sorley and the Kimbra. We can find out who, but we need you to return to Cashel and tell him his sister has been found. She will be returned by the Sorley when they meet with him. You must remain calm and respond as though she is the missing Mistress, not the love of your life."

Jabre's face darkened. "Do you believe Cashel is responsible for sabotaging the peace?"

Lexi quickly countered. "We believe there are several people involved, and we intend to find out through our negotiations. Some of the information we have, Auryon brought from the Sorley. We believe when we get all parties together, the truth will come out. It is essential that you return to Cashel as normal."

"Why is it so important for me to return?"

Lexi hesitated, and Brynna quickly came to her rescue. "If we set up a defined set of circumstances, we expect a certain outcome. If someone strays from the outcome, they have a reason that is outside the circumstances we set up."

Jabre had a look on his face indicating he didn't have a clue what Brynna was talking about. David took the explanation a step further by putting it into context. "Let me give you an example. If I suspected a man of lying, and I say I have a device that will tell me who is lying, the man may run away or hide. He isn't running or hiding because I know the truth. He's hiding because he thinks I will find out. We believe we can find out who caused this harm to come to Auryon. We know some of the ones who are responsible, but we need to know everyone who was involved. If you return to Primus and learn about those responsible, you must not react. You cannot take any action against those responsible. You must get the information back to us, or it could compromise Auryon's safety."

Jabre's confusion appeared to resolve until David mentioned Auryon's safety. Jabre instantly became alarmed.

"Who would cause harm to Auryon? Why would anyone want to harm her?"

David calmly answered the man. "Since we don't know who is involved or why we don't know what they are capable of doing. They may not be capable of harming her at all. We just don't want to put her in danger. It may also be that they think she can identify them. If you proclaim for all to hear the Mistress is returning, someone may panic and do something rash. We will keep her here under our protection until we know the whole story and know she is safe."

Jabre looked mournfully at Auryon. "I cannot do this. I cannot leave your side again."

Auryon stroked his face gently. "Jabre, you must, or I will never be safe. Not with the Kimbra or the Sorley, and I do not want to live in the caves with the Akamu."

The muscles in Jabre's face began to flex as he set his jaw and gritted his teeth. Seeing his struggle, Auryon asked the crew if they could be alone for a few minutes. The crew got up to leave the two alone. Auryon grabbed Lexi's arm and whispered, "Thank you." Lexi smiled back at her then left the room.

In a few minutes, Jabre met them in the hallway. "You are sure she will be safe?"

Brynna nodded. "You have my word."

Jabre sighed, "Then I will do as you ask."

Brynna asked, "What are you going to tell your guards?"

"You want me to proclaim openly, the Mistress is returning, and this is where I will start. They do not know the Mistress because they were still young men when she was taken. I will tell them I failed her and was afraid she would demand my life when she returned. That they will understand."

Brynna smiled. "Thank you Jabre. You are a good man. By the way, I am sorry for the way I treated you this morning. I didn't mean to embarrass you."

"I am used to it. It is my lot in life."

David scowled. "Not anymore. You will be considered a great man of honor when this is over."

Jabre left the ship and joined his guards. The crew saw him give a brief explanation to them. He also warned them that, although she bore the markings of a slave, she could demand retribution against the two of them for pushing her away earlier. He advised them to treat her with respect in the future and suggested they apologize to her if they got a chance or stay out of her sight. He then quickly led them to retrieve their horses. The whole encounter took less than two minutes. Two minutes after that, they were no longer visible on the horizon. Auryon stepped just outside the ship to watch Jabre leave.

Once the men moved out of sight behind a line of trees, Jason came to get Auryon. Brynna told him the removal of her slave markings were going to play an integral part in their upcoming negotiations. Jason continued to work on into the evening. He managed to treat most of those who had come to him. The only ones who still needed treatment were those needing reconstruction of their skin to remove the slave markings. Once it got late, he and the crew told the ones remaining to get some sleep, and he would begin again in the morning. Jake organized the former slaves to take turns at a fire watch. There weren't enough beds on board the ship for the group, and the Sorley were accustomed to sleeping outdoors, so it seemed the best option. The weather was expected to be a little cool, but dry. It turned out to be a quiet night. The only ones who didn't get much sleep were Jabre and Auryon.

The next morning came too early for the weary crew. Brynna got with the crew over breakfast to reorganize the teams. Team One would stay at the ship and look out for the needs of their visitors. The Akamu were expected to send their sick and injured, as well as their former slaves to have markings removed. Team One would consist of Thane, Aulani, Jason, Laura, Jake, Marissa, and Vesta. The remaining crew members were on the second team. Team Two would go to visit the Kimbra. After breakfast, everyone got their days started. Team Two boarded the shuttle and took off. Team One found the Sorley eating the remains of their food from yesterday. Jason began running the people through the infirmary as quickly as he could. Jake, Vesta, and Thane decided they should go hunting again in preparation for today's visitors. They grabbed the Surf-Ve and took off for a quick hunting trip. Jason treated the last Sorley slave just in time to start treating the first of the Akamu. He sighed. It was going to be another long day.

The shuttle landed at the same place it had yesterday, but this time Cashel was ready for them. Two carriages were waiting for the crew when they landed. Jabre warmly greeted the crew while trying to maintain his professional poise. Jabre and a security detail escorted the crew into the city. The Lord Master Cashel maintained a large residence in the center of the city. The carriage dropped them at his doorstep. Jabre led the crew into the Lord Master's home. They entered a large, well-lit hall with a table at the center of the room and a stone fireplace across from it. The floor was covered with rugs made from animal skins. The table was round and set up with an array of food and drink. There were other benches and small tables along the walls. The candles and lanterns around the room made the room quite warm, although somewhat smoky. Some of the developments here on Medoris IV were much less advanced, and some were more advanced. It appeared their government and sociological development was very primal. Galat had a much better-developed system of government, but some of their technology was way behind Medoran skills. The Medorans were very well equipped to handle the long cold winters. They were good at food preservation and used glass and mirrors to improve lighting. Galat depended solely on candles and torches.

Jabre asked the crew to remain in the great hall while he informed the Lord Master of their presence. The crew milled around and carefully examined the architecture, structure, and technology. Braxton and Lazaro immediately found ways to improve ventilation and lighting without sacrificing heat. Sometimes it was more fun to watch them think than it was to do one's own job.

Moments later, Jabre returned and loudly announced the Lord Master Cashel of the Primus City and the Lord Master Medwin of the Corvan City. The room began to have a flurry of activity. Servants entered the room and began offering drinks to everyone. They also offered snacks of bread, fruit, and cheese. Cashel greeted his guests warmly, but Medwin stood quietly at his brother's side. Cashel invited the crew to join him around the table. He appeared eager to talk to them but held his tongue until the crew brought him their message.

Brynna began by granting the egocentric men all the pomp and circumstance they had come to expect. "Lord Master Cashel, Lord Master Medwin, I have come to give you what I consider to be much good news. The Commonwealth has reached an agreement with the Akamu and the Sorley. They are already learning new technologies and improving their societies even as we speak. You told us you would let us know when you had come to a decision. I thought it was important for you to know what the others have already decided. I also wanted to tell you the Sorley would like us to help your society and their society to achieve a peace agreement. The last thing I want to tell you about, I'm sure your servant Jabre has already told you. Your sister, Mistress Auryon, has been found alive and well. She remains at our ship with our people for her own protection. We have reason to believe her life may be in danger."

Brynna watched the faces of the two men carefully. David was watching them as well. Lexi was casually keeping her eyes on Jabre through all of this. Cashel listened anxiously and eagerly until he heard Auryon's life was in danger. Medwin's face never changed until Brynna's last sentence. He allowed himself one telling blink. From that point on, he took his cues from Cashel and mirrored his every response. Cashel's face grew very somber. He stood up from the table and went to stand in front of the roaring fire. Brynna waited calmly and quietly for him to respond.

In a moment, Cashel responded. "Clear the room!" He ordered with full authority. The crew wasn't sure if they were included in his order or not, but they followed Brynna's lead and stayed seated. The servants, however, did not hesitate and scampered away immediately.

Jabre did hesitate. Sometimes he was included in those types of orders, but sometimes he was not. Cashel looked at Jabre, and despite the fire in his eyes, he spoke more kindly to the man. "Jabre, I need you to go too, and close the doors."

Jabre looked at the crew then back at the Lord Master, "My Lord, I failed the Mistress once before, I cannot fail her again."

Cashel moved over beside Jabre and again spoke gently to him, "Jabre, I know what this means to you. We will see to her safety, but I must speak to the Sky People alone." Jabre did as he was told.

Once the two men were alone with the crew, Medwin jumped in first. "How do you know our sister's life is in danger? Who is she in danger from?"

Brynna looked at Medwin then at Cashel. "I am afraid, I can't give you that information. The same people who put Mistress Auryon in danger are the ones who endangered your peace agreement with the Sorley years ago. I believe this information should only be shared as part of a new peace agreement."

Cashel angrily threw his mug of ale across the room. "Are you using my sister to force us to the negotiating table with those snakes?"

Medwin was just as startled as the crew, but he snapped himself out of it and stood up quickly causing his chair to fall over backward. "You will return our sister at once! We will see to her safety ourselves."

Brynna stood up slowly looking back and forth at the two brothers, making sure her gaze didn't linger on the one she knew to be guilty. She purposely skewed the story with a different slant. "Someone betrayed her to the Sorley. Someone told Malek, where she would be the day she was taken."

Medwin looked alarmed. In his mind, he was thinking, "No, that isn't what happened!"

Cashel's temper cooled slightly. His mind became more focused on who this new enemy was. He thought for a moment then looked up at Brynna. "She has lived as Malek's wife all this time? She never got word to us that she was alive and well. Why have the Sorley continued to attack us then? Her marriage to Malek was supposed to bring peace. Who would do this?"

Brynna sat back down slowly. "I hate to tell you this, but she has not been Malek's wife. She has been his slave."

Cashel's temper flared again. He paced a moment and then slammed his fist down onto the table, causing the dishes closest to him to dance and fall. Through gritted teeth he asked, "Did – he – MARK – her?" Brynna didn't have to answer. He saw the answer on her face and slammed the table once again before turning his back on his visitors. Brynna suspected he was crying, but he didn't dare show it.

Medwin rushed to his brother's side. Brynna casually turned the volume up on her translator, which had been programmed to translate into the earpieces instead of audibly. She heard Medwin whisper to his brother, "She can come stay with me in my home. No one will have to see or know. I can care for her there. I will have clothes made special for her to keep her face hidden. I will forbid my slaves to ever speak of her under punishment of death. Please brother, we can do whatever it takes to get her back safely."

Cashel angrily looked at Medwin, "And have our sister live like a prisoner?"

Brynna waited for Cashel to turn back around. "I think my people can help you with this. Your sister won't have to be shunned as a slave, the truth can be found out, and peace can be made. I just need you to trust me and agree to our proposal. Kasen has already agreed to bring Malek to testify to what he knows, and your sister can testify to what she knows."

Medwin objected. "My sister cannot testify. If she is marked as a slave, her words are not considered relevant in any society."

Brynna looked at Cashel, "What if we kept her skin covered so no one could see the markings? Would that be acceptable? We can tell everyone she needs to hide her identity for her own safety."

Cashel nodded. "That may work. I will agree to it if Kasen agrees."

Medwin continued to balk. "Brother, we cannot do this. What if someone were to find out? We should just bring her home quietly and leave the Sorley out of this."

Cashel looked at Brynna, "Part of the agreement was to end slavery was it not?" Brynna nodded. "Perhaps this would be a good time to do so, if for no other reason than to save our sister. Medwin, I assume you are in agreement with me?"

"The people will revolt if they are forced to give up their slaves, Cashel. You know they will. Perhaps this is a step that should be taken slowly." Medwin spoke much more calmly this time and watched his brother's reaction carefully.

Cashel thought for what seemed like a painfully long time. Finally, he returned to his seat and offered Brynna a proposal of his own. "Our two cities have been trying to build a wall to keep out the slave traders and the migrating herds from trampling our crops. If your people can help us build the walls we need, we could call out all the slaves to help, and when the wall is done, we announce all slaves are now free. Medwin, what do you think? No one would dare revolt under those circumstances."

Medwin shook his head. "If word got out, everyone would withhold their slaves from finishing the walls.

Brynna glanced over at Braxton and Lazaro. "What would it take to finish their walls?" The two men looked at each other for a moment. Braxton looked back at Brynna, "If we can locate a good source of stone, the shuttles lasers could carve out large chunks of stone and haul the stones into place. We'd have to do a little research, but it could be done in a matter of days, at least most of it could."

"Days?" Both Cashel and Medwin were startled by this revelation, although the looks on their faces were quite contrasting. Cashel was pleasantly surprised. Medwin was not. The look on his face reflected fear.

Cashel looked at Medwin and proudly announced, "Then it is done! If you can help us build our walls, we will call out all slaves to help. At the end of the endeavor, we will announce that as a part of the peace agreement, and in return for your help with the walls, Medwin and I will free all slaves. We will agree never to participate in slave trade again. I do have one question though. What will be done with all those who are slaves?"

Brynna smiled. "We will give them the choice of what they want to do. If some choose to stay here with you; you must give them and us your word that they will receive the respect due any human being. We would also like you to make sure they have a decent place to live and allow them to work to earn a living in whatever way suits them. The Sorley have agreed to take in any who wish to travel back to their homelands, and they will also accept those who wish to live with them. The Akamu will accept their former citizens back, but they don't have room to take in very many people. They have agreed to do what they can."

Medwin, still hovering around the fireplace, walked back over to the table. "Brother, I think you should let me speak for myself and my city. Don't presume to know what I will and will not agree to."

Cashel's bewildered look gave way to annoyance. "Medwin, what has gotten into you today? We have always worked together in dealing with the Sorley and the Akamu. Why are you so against this? This will mean an end to fighting the Sorley. No more losing a third of our crops to their raids, no more of our citizens taken as slaves, and sending armed escorts every time we leave the city walls. We can use ALL our crops for ourselves instead of what we manage to keep away from predators. This is good for all of us. The only things we lose are a few slaves. I don't see why you are so upset."

Feeling everyone's eyes on him, Medwin began to realize his behavior was becoming suspect. He slowly relented. "Maybe I am just afraid of change. This is a lot to take in all at once, especially in light of getting Auryon home. We also don't know these people. Are they trustworthy?"

Brynna turned the tables immediately on Medwin. "How do we know if we help you build your wall, you will release your slaves as promised? We don't know if you're trustworthy either."

Medwin looked surprised anyone would question his integrity. "Fine. I will agree to your proposal if you first help us build our wall."

Cashel seemed pleased at the outcome. "When are we to receive this rock of knowledge?"

The translation came through, and Brynna looked down at her translator to be sure she understood it correctly. "Rock of knowledge?" She glanced over at Lexi.

Lexi's face suddenly lit up. "He's talking about the data module." The data module did resemble an odd sort of rock formation. It used a series of crystals on the top of the module for projection, and its case was made of a metallic alloy to ensure sturdiness. When Brynna understood what he was asking about, she quickly told him it would be ready when the two men came to meet with the Sorley. The data module was actually ready, but she didn't want to move too quickly. She told the two men it could be customized with information to suit their specific needs, and they would know more about how to prepare it once they saw more of the city's needs.

Medwin suddenly became concerned. "You want to see our weaknesses? Are you working with the Sorley and the Akamu to destroy us?" Cashel was quiet, but his concerns were clearly displayed across his face.

Brynna backpedaled quickly. "No, that isn't what I meant. I don't need to see your defenses or your troops. I was referring to things like how you heat your homes in the winter, how you store food to keep it from going bad, but nothing of military value." The two seemed to relax again. "Once you have the data module, we will show you how to use it, and you will have the same advantages the Akamu and Sorley have. It is not our desire to eliminate anyone or exalt one over another. In a few weeks, we'll be gone. We don't have a personal stake in your world. We seek only to have you grow into one large Commonwealth ally. We want to unite you all to the point of working together as one world, not several societies. Show us whatever you wish, and don't show us whatever you don't trust us to see. These two gentlemen will need to see the areas where you are building your walls though. We cannot help build your wall without seeing it."

Medwin and Cashel seemed to relax. They agreed to move forward with the alliance. They proudly took the crew on a tour of their city. It was clear they felt far superior to the Akamu who lived in "holes in the ground" and the Sorley who lived in tents. At the end of the day, they treated the crew to a luxurious dinner and entertainment in a great hall down in the bowels of the second hive. As the night was coming to an end and the crew was preparing to board the shuttle, Brynna graciously thanked the two for their hospitality and complimented them on their ability to entertain guests. She told them she would send word when they located the materials they needed to build their walls. Braxton and Lazaro gave the two men instructions on how to prepare the land for the stones when they did arrive.

Two days later the crew located a good place to establish a stone quarry and had taken a little time to relax. Jason, Laura, Thane, Aulani, Jake, Marissa, and Vesta were all very much in need of some downtime. They had spent most of their time routing the sick through the ship's infirmary or seeing to the needs of those waiting to be treated. Even Vesta seemed unusually tired and a bit cranky. Manton was used to her "temper," but this was different.

She had been quite active helping Thane and Jake with hunting food for their temporary refugees. He thought perhaps it was because she had been on her best behavior for the Sky People and it was starting to get old. Brynna was feeling better after her ordeal.

Brynna assigned Braxton, Lazaro, and Thane to start carving stones out of the side of a mountain with the lasers from the shuttle. Brynna took the Surf-Ve to Primus to let Cashel know they would begin bringing stones in the morning. It took about three days to get the large stones in place. The stones were cut large enough to be an impenetrable barrier against any of the native inhabitants. The only way to traverse the wall was to dig under it or build a ladder to go over it. The weakest points in the wall were the drainage ditches which were put into place to keep the area from turning into a lake, the gates, and the joints in between the huge rock slabs. It took about ten days using the shuttle, and the Surf-Ve and all the peasants and slaves the two cities could muster to get the wall built and secured. It took a few more days than the crew expected but was a surprisingly quick and smooth job.

The day they finished the job, Cashel and Medwin were standing in a tent outside the city overseeing the work. The two issued a command that the next day would be a day of feast and rest. They would rest for the day and celebrate, then start harvesting their crops the day after. The two again emphasized all available people would be needed for the harvest because the entire crop would be saved this year. The one thing he was not saying was there would be no slaves to harvest most of this year's crop. Jake overheard Cashel and Medwin talking about how hard it would be to plant and harvest without the slaves. He decided to plant some seeds for thought of his own. "Lord Masters, the data module our Commander is giving you will show you how to make tools to help you plant and harvest with less work. It should greatly improve your harvests, which will make you wealthier and more powerful than ever. If, however, you try to back out of the arrangement to release the slaves, well, it would be a shame if we had to take all these stones and put them back in the quarry." Cashel laughed and agreed with Jake. It would be a lot of wasted work for all of them.

Medwin felt a knot form in his stomach. He was genuinely trying to find out if his brother would consider going back on the agreement. It wasn't that he cared so much about the slaves. He was more concerned his brother would find out it was his fault Auryon was now a slave of the Sorley. If he could keep her hidden away because of her slave markings, he could control what she told Cashel.

As soon as Jake walked away, Medwin started in on his brother again. "Was that supposed to be some kind of threat? Who does he think he's talking to?"

Cashel had been leaning over a table, examining the plans for the wall, and surveying the progress, but he stopped and looked at Medwin. "I suppose it could have been a warning, but I don't have any intentions of reneging on our agreement, so I just took it as a joke. You do remember the firelight that comes from their flying machine is what cut those stones out of the mountain, right?" Medwin nodded, and Cashel continued. "Those same fire lights could cut down these walls or destroy our cities. I didn't agree to this alliance lightly. I understand what is at risk here. Do you?" Medwin continued to scowl. He didn't like feeling out of control. Cashel leaned back over the plans in front of him when Medwin didn't answer.

Medwin finally answered, but he moved very close to Cashel and spoke in hushed tones. "I do understand, and I don't like it. There are only twelve of them. We could capture them and force them to teach us how to use their machines. We could rule over the Sorley and the Akamu."

Cashel rolled himself back into a fully upright position. He looked around to see who was nearby. The only people close by were his own. "Clear the tent! Now!" He ordered. The others were high-ranking officials who weren't accustomed to being ordered around. From the sound of Cashel's voice, they knew now was not the time to argue. The men scattered quickly and kept their distance. Cashel kept his voice low. Medwin saw the blood begin to boil in his brother's veins, but this time he wasn't going to back down easily. "What is WRONG with you? They may be few in number, but their weapons are far greater than we can imagine. I have heard stories about them. Their weapons can strike a man from a great distance. The Sorley speak of the gods helping the captain of the Sky People. The gods saved him from certain death! Is this who you want to make our enemy? Is it?"

Medwin began to realize he didn't truly understand what they were up against, but it wasn't enough to deter him, yet. He also realized his brother's resolve wasn't going to be changed without a good reason. "I just thought there might be a chance."

"You thought WRONG! Let this go! I mean it, Medwin. Right now, they are asking nicely. They are powerful enough to simply tell us what to do. They didn't have to ask and give us choices. We need to stay on their good side."

"All right, Cashel, I get it!"

Medwin started to walk away, but before he did, Cashel caught his arm. "I hope you do 'get it' because if you don't, I'll stop you myself. Understood?"

Medwin jerked his arm away from his brother. "I said I got it!" Medwin took a couple steps away then said over his shoulder, "I think it best if we don't talk anymore today. I think we will get more work done separately."

Cashel watched him go. He wasn't convinced his brother would let this go. His brother was tenacious, but something was different about this. The men, including Jabre, who had been chased out of the tent, were hovering just out of earshot trying not to look conspicuous. Cashel waved at them to come back in and pulled Jabre aside to talk to him. In a few minutes, the man nodded and left abruptly.

Jabre took care of the first thing Cashel had given him to do then went to the stables to get a horse. Minutes later, he was riding toward the ship. David, Brynna, Manton, and Vesta were taking their turn staying with the *Evangeline* while the others got away for a while. Everyone else was helping with the construction of the wall. Auryon was also still with the ship. David was on the bridge monitoring communications and scanners. He saw Jabre coming in hard and fast. He gave Brynna and Manton a heads-up. The three met him as he reached the ship.

Brynna stepped forward as Jabre dismounted and led his horse toward her. "Jabre, what is it? Why have you come?" Her first thought was that he figured out who had harmed him and Auryon and had taken matters into his own hands.

Jabre quickly put those fears to rest. "The Lord Master Cashel is concerned his brother may act rashly and foolishly. He sent me to warn you. He is trying to keep Medwin under control, but Medwin is not acting normally. Cashel doesn't know what has gotten into his brother lately, but he wants me to warn you to take precautions."

David jumped in. "Precautions against what?"

"He is afraid Medwin may try to take your people as prisoners. Medwin wants your machines for himself. He thinks he can force your people to teach him how to use your machines. Once he has control of them, he wishes to destroy the Sorley and rule over the Akamu. The Lord Master Cashel is watching his brother closely, but he thought you should know. He also asks that if he does try something, you spare Medwin's life and let Cashel punish him."

David immediately got on his comm unit. "Attention all hands. Keep doing whatever you are doing but listen up. Stay alert to your situation. Don't wander away from each other. As soon as your duties permit, rendezvous with the shuttle casually, and get back here. Jake, report back to me when everyone is accounted for, and you're headed back."

After the captain's transmission, Brynna turned her attention back to Jabre. "Please thank the Lord Master Cashel for the warning. We will do our best to honor his requests. Thank you for your help as well, Jabre."

Jabre nodded and looked around with his attention landing on the ship's open doorway. "You're welcome. Thank you for helping Auryon and me. Is – Is Auryon still here? May I see her? Please?"

Brynna gave David a questioning glance who in turn nodded. Brynna looked back at Jabre and smiled. "Yes, Auryon is still here, and you may see her, but there is something you need to know first."

"What is it? Is something wrong?" The look on Brynna's face didn't indicate anything was wrong, but Jabre was concerned.

"No, she's doing beautifully. Our healer was able to repair all of the slave markings. She has been restored to her original beauty. You must NOT tell either of the Lord Masters about this though. It will help us determine who brought about these tragic events. If anyone were to know, it might put her in greater danger. Do you understand?"

Jabre indicated he did, but the dazed look on his face was not so convincing. Vesta had been standing just out of Jabre's sight with Auryon inside the ship. Brynna nodded to them. Auryon came slowly out of the ship and down the steps. She was clearly nervous. Jabre turned to greet her and gasped. Her face and skin were just as beautiful as the day he had lost her to the Sorley. "How is this possible? Wounds can heal, but there is always a scar."

"Our healer has tools to remove scars and heal skin within minutes," Brynna explained.

Auryon was so nervous and excited about her new appearance; she could no longer contain her excitement. She skipped the last few steps and jumped into Jabre's arms when she saw him smiling at her. A small piece of her was afraid he would reject her for using sorcery to change her appearance. She was greatly relieved when he accepted her. After spending a few minutes together, Jabre knew he needed to get back to Primus. He hugged her tightly and promised he would return as soon as he could. He had a great deal of difficulty letting her go. Finally, he pulled himself away. His strength came from the thought that he was leaving to keep her safe. Manton, who had been looking after Jabre's horse, now brought the horse forward. Jabre mounted quickly before he lost his resolve to leave. He looked at Brynna. "In case my master's brother finds out I was here, my job was to personally invite you, your crew, and the two Akamu warriors, to the celebration tomorrow when the slaves are released."

Brynna responded, "Tell the Lord Master Cashel, except for those who must stay with the ship, we will be there."

As Jabre rode off toward the city, David looked at Brynna. "So, who gets to miss the party?"

Brynna's face wrinkled in thought. "I'm thinking Thane is our best pilot, so he should fly us in and drop us off then come back to the ship. That keeps us from getting cut off from the shuttle and Thane can pick us up again from wherever we need it. It also prevents Medwin from knowing where we will be. I think Lazaro should man the weapons and either Aulani or Cheyenne man comms. What do you think?"

"Sounds like a good plan to me. Are you going to just pick one or take volunteers for comms?"

"I don't have a preference, so I will leave it up to them for now. If they can't decide, I will."

About sunset, Jake contacted the captain. "Security Chief to Captain Alexander."

"This is Captain Alexander, go ahead, Chief."

"All crew members are aboard the shuttle, and we are headed back to the ship. No incidents to report, sir."

"Understood, the shuttle bay is open and ready to receive you.

The Commander wants everyone in the dining hall for a briefing in thirty minutes."

"Yes, Captain. I'll pass the word."

Thirty minutes later, the crew was assembled as ordered. Brynna brought everyone up to speed on the warning sent by Cashel about Medwin. The cautious Commander ordered everyone to be fully armed at the celebration the next day and stay alert. It was decided Cheyenne would man the comms while Thane and Lazaro piloted the shuttle. Jake expressed concern that Cheyenne would be alone on the ship for a period of time. Lazaro was equally concerned. Vesta volunteered to stay with her, claiming she didn't feel up to an all-day celebration anyway. As soon as she spoke, Manton gave her a sideways glance of concern. In the last couple weeks, the entire crew, including Lexi and Braxton, had come to accept Manton and Vesta as trusted crew members despite their rocky beginnings. Brynna had no problem with leaving Vesta alone on the ship with Cheyenne. Jake was surprisingly comfortable with it.

As the briefing ended and the crew headed off in different directions, Manton pulled Jason aside. The two quietly talked and kept casting glances toward Vesta. As soon as they were done talking, Manton hurried out. Vesta and the rest of the crew had already cleared the room leaving only Jason, David, and Brynna. After Manton left, Jason approached the remaining couple. Brynna looked up at Jason, "What was that all about?"

Jason grinned. "Vesta is beginning to have the early symptoms of being pregnant, but they still don't know it yet."

David looked confused. "When are you planning on telling them? Why haven't you told them yet?"

"Captain, this is a technologically backward people. They basically believe if you can't see it, touch it, hear it, taste it, or smell it then it either isn't real, or the gods are responsible. If I tell them too soon, they will think I cast a spell on them, or I am a messenger of their gods. If we are trying to indoctrinate these people to the tenets of the Commonwealth, I don't think convincing them I am a messenger of the gods is a good way to start. Do you?"

David shook his head. "I suppose you're right. When will you tell them?"

"I told Manton to have Vesta to stop by the infirmary if she didn't feel better soon or if she felt worse and I would check her out. When this feeling gets worse, she'll come to see me, and I'll tell her then. Her baby already has a heartbeat; she can hear, so it will be easy enough to convince her this early. Don't worry Captain, I got this."

Brynna just listened to the two men and smiled knowingly to herself. Jason was used to dealing with both the physical and the emotional, but David was a problem solver. He felt like things should be handled directly and quickly. His battle strategies were more covert, but he didn't view this as a battle. Dealing with people wasn't his strongest skill. Brynna made a mental note to "advise" him on this aspect of "battle" later. Brynna's training in sociology gave her insight into the way Jason was handling this situation. It was also why she was such a good strategist.

The next morning, everyone had a chance to sleep in a little, as the celebration wasn't to start until the afternoon. The crew took the opportunity to get in some personal time for exercise, or pleasure reading or whatever they felt like doing. Thane and Aulani went for a run outside. A couple of the Akamu warriors came through headed to visit the Sorley to trade for some meat. They delivered the agreed upon tetrabradium ore for Lazaro to convert for use in the tachyon emitters. Manton discreetly asked the warriors to keep an eye on the ship while the crew was in the Kimbra cities.

As the afternoon approached, the crew loaded up into the shuttle and headed to the Kimbra cities. Thane made a pass overlooking the two cities and their new walls. Most of the crew was happy to see the fruits of their labor, but Brynna was strangely quiet. Thane put the shuttle down near an outside entrance and took off as soon as the crew had disembarked. Brynna took off at a fast-paced walk as soon as she was outside the shuttle. David and Lexi took off after her as quickly as they could. They caught up with her in one of the nearly empty passages. David wanted to grab her arm and stop her but decided to keep things professional and not personal. He called out to her, "Commander!"

Hearing his tone, Brynna stopped and turned to face him. David got closer and saw the anger and fire in her eyes. He took his tone and demeanor down one more notch before addressing her further. "Commander, I seem to have missed something. What's got you ticked off?" Lexi caught up to them in time to hear his question. She waited quietly to hear Brynna's answer.

Brynna was breathing fast, not from her fast pace, but from the anger she felt. She was trying hard to control her tone and attitude knowing she was addressing her captain again and not her husband. Finally, she spat her answer out. "Those greedy, selfish..." She was unable to finish the sentence respectfully, so she tried another train of thought. "Did you see their crop fields? They have harvested at least fifty percent of their crops since yesterday." The two continued to give Brynna blank stares. "They're freeing the slaves today. They had to have every slave in this city working all night to get that much of their crops harvested. They're trying to get as much out of them as possible before letting them go. Of all the greedy, selfish..." Her voice trailed off, and she blinked back tears.

"Commander, you don't know for sure that's what they did and if you go in 'guns blazing,' they will get defensive or lie to you," Lexi advised her to go in softly and ask questions. Brynna took a moment to steady herself. She knew Lexi was right, but she was just so angry.

"You can't expect to change their way of life overnight, Brynna." David gently reminded her. Brynna gave him a look somewhere between vexation and embarrassment. He apparently knew people better than she had given him credit for. Once she composed herself and the rest of the crew caught up, they started on through the passage. David gave her a quick smile and a wink before escorting her toward the celebration. He knew she could use the added encouragement from her husband instead of the sternness of a captain. They had talked about using battle strategies on people the night before. Brynna seemed to think he didn't know how to handle people very well. Maybe he didn't, but he did know how to handle Brynna.

Brynna and the others approached a series of pavilions set up around the fields. Jabre met them and escorted them to the Pavilions where the Lord Masters were. The two were lounging around a large table with several other high-ranking members of the Kimbra society. Brynna recognized this might not be the best time or place to challenge the two directly. Cashel stood up and greeted the crew. He introduced them to the other officials. It only took a moment for the Lord Master Cashel to pick up on Brynna's displeasure despite her courteous display.

While one of the Lord Master's officials conversed with Brynna, Cashel pulled David aside. "Is something wrong? Commander Brynna seems disturbed by something."

David weighed his answer carefully. "Yes, Lord Master, she is extremely upset, but I suggest you speak with her privately." David knew Brynna would not want to say much to Cashel in front of his subjects. He would not take kindly to being shamed or embarrassed in front of them.

Cashel glanced over at her then at Medwin who was staying close to Brynna. "Is this about the message I sent to her?"

David shook his head. "No, this is something she saw this morning that disturbed her."

The Lord Master had been relaxed, but now the look on his face was more sober. He was one who could read and manipulate people. Seconds later, the look on his face changed again, to one reflecting the merriment that had been there moments earlier. He picked up his cup from the table and a fresh one from a servant's tray. He walked over to Brynna. Handing her the fresh cup, he interrupted their discussion. "Forgive me, gentlemen, I hate to interrupt, but I need to speak to the Commander about the celebration and the upcoming peace negotiations with the Sorley. Commander, would you care to go for a walk with me?"

Brynna put on her best smile. "Of course, Lord Master. I would love to."

Jake grabbed Marissa's hand as casually as possible, and the two walked a parallel path as Brynna and the Lord Master. Jake intended to subtly surveil Brynna and the Lord Master, but they were acting more like young lovers. Marissa was getting used to being Jake's partner in these scenarios and enjoyed it.

As Brynna and Cashel walked out of earshot, one of the Lords known as Lord Ayele began to laugh. He leaned over to another Lord and said, "Lord Broona, I am sure the Lord Master will enjoy her company, whether she enjoys it or not."

Lord Broona joined Lord Ayele's laughter. "I am sure he will, as much as he enjoys every woman's company." The two men did not realize David was close enough to pick up their comments.

David moved directly in front of the two men who tried, unsuccessfully, to look innocent. "You should not disrespect your leader, my wife, or me in this manner." He leaned in closer to them. "My wife is a trained warrior. Despite her appearance, she can put a man down without breaking a sweat if she so desires."

Lord Broona didn't blink but laughed again. "Are you speaking from experience?"

David smiled. "Absolutely." He started to step away then leaned in close to the men again and whispered. "I trained her." The two men got quiet for a moment, and then awkwardly changed the subject. David hadn't trained Brynna in hand-to-hand combat. He did have a hand in training her for this mission, and they had sparred numerous times. She was a formidable opponent.

As soon as Brynna and Cashel were out of sight of the pavilion, Cashel got down to business. "I seem to have done something to upset you. What is it and what can I do to fix it?"

Brynna took a deep breath and chose her words carefully. "How is it you were able to harvest so much of your crops overnight?"

Cashel glanced at the field in front of him and the workers in it. "I see. You believe I am trying to get every last bit of work I can from the slaves before I free them. You are somewhat correct in your belief, but not totally. Maybe we should have delayed the celebration a couple of days so they would not have to work such long hours."

Brynna stood there stewing angrily. Cashel openly admitted the thing she wanted to accuse him of and seemed nonplussed by his own actions. Cashel continued his explanation. "We needed to harvest food for today's celebration, some to take to the negotiations, and the slaves will need food for their travels. The Sorley can't support so many slaves on their trip back to their homes. I had both, slaves and citizens, working through a good portion of the night. Is this what upset you? I do not intend to keep all we have harvested, and when I give the signal, ALL will stop working."

Brynna's anger relented. She still wasn't happy, but she did realize she had underestimated the man. She finally responded to him. "Forgive me, Lord Master, I assumed the worst about you. I made a mistake. You are a better man than I gave you credit for. If you needed more time, we could have put off the celebration another day or two."

Cashel shook his head. "Perhaps this is where you were right about me. I didn't think about any of this until late yesterday after your party had already left. I suppose I could have sent Jabre back to you a second time, but everyone was already preparing for the celebration. I decided to make the best of my own poor judgment."

Brynna looked at the tired workers. "Have they done enough to stop now?"

Cashel glanced at the wagons and piles of harvested food. A piece of him wanted to get as much of the harvest done as possible, but he didn't want Brynna to think any worse of him. "Yes, I believe they have. I will issue the order."

Jabre and two guards were also following Cashel from a discreet distance. Cashel waved him forward and instructed him to tell the workers to stop harvesting, get themselves cleaned up and to return for the celebration. Jabre left Cashel and the guards and did as he was instructed.

After Jabre had left, Cashel turned his attention back to Brynna. "Commander, how is Auryon? Is she well and safe? Are she and Jabre still in love?"

Brynna looked surprised. "Auryon is fine. You knew about their relationship?"

Cashel smiled. "I had not seen my baby sister happier than when she was with Jabre. I was prepared to send him with her as her guardian when she married the Sorley council member, so they would always be together. They could not be married, but they could still be in love."

"So, you didn't have a problem with their relationship being unequal?"

Cashel cocked his head, giving her a curious look. "I am the Lord Master. I make the laws and rules of this city. I can make it okay if I choose. Jabre is a good man despite his lower station, and he would have treated her well. I just enjoyed seeing her happy. If she had stayed here, I would have given Jabre property and title, whatever it takes to make her happy."

Brynna weighed her next words very carefully. "Do you trust me to do what is best for Auryon?"

Cashel thought this was a rather strange question, but he was certain the Commander had a reason for asking. "I believe so. Why do you ask such a question? Is there something I should know?"

Brynna glanced around to be sure that no one was within earshot. "I know who betrayed Auryon and Jabre, but I do not know if others were involved. I intend to find out for certain. I may be asking for quite a bit of trust from you at some point. I will not allow any harm to come to you or anyone else at the peace negotiations, but I have a plan to get to the truth. Can you trust me with your life as well?"

The Lord Master looked warily at her. Something told him she could be sly and sneaky, but she could still be trusted if she gave her word. "Give me your word that no harm will come to me, my sister, or my people, and you will have my trust."

Brynna nodded. "You have my word as an Officer and Representative of the Commonwealth. No harm will come to you or your people so long as they are innocent of this betrayal."

"I also want the lives of the traitor or traitors given to me."

Brynna shook her head. "I can give you the lives of those who are Kimbra citizens. I do not have the authority to give you Malek and any others among the Sorley. It is possible an agreement can be reached during the peace negotiations. You have a right to bargain for it."

"Fair enough. I want these traitors to pay, and pay dearly, for what they have done to my family."

Brynna gave him one word of caution. "Make sure the price isn't too high to pay to get that satisfaction. It could cost you more than you know."

Cashel eyed her cautiously. He knew there was a lot hidden in her words, but he also knew she had said all she was going to. He let the matter drop.

Brynna and Cashel talked about the arrangements for the peace negotiations and how to get the slaves out of the city without causing a riot. As much as Brynna didn't like it, Cashel insisted it would be best if the slaves were sent with the supplies for the peace negotiations and the end of slavery be announced at that time instead of tonight. Primus was providing tables, chairs, and some food for the negotiations. Kasen was bringing meat, wine, and cheese. The Akamu were bringing representatives as well. They were providing some of the security for the event as well as firewood. The Akamu's reputation for being fierce warriors made them ideal for the job. No one wanted to make enemies of them.

After finishing their discussion, the Lord Master made his way to a balcony where the Lord Master Medwin and the other Lords from both Primus and Corvan joined him. Cashel invited David and Brynna to join them. The bulk of the two populations gathered on the ground beneath them. Jabre announced his leader, and the crowd cheered and applauded mostly because it was expected of them. Cashel stepped forward and raised his hands to silence them.

"Citizens of the twin cities of Kimbra! This is a great day of celebration! We celebrate this day because we are now a protected people. The Sky People have helped us to build the walls we needed to protect our fields and our citizens."

Cashel's speech continued to drone on, thanking the Commonwealth for its help and giving the assembled crowd the expected pep talk. David listened, but he didn't pay as much attention to Cashel's words as he did to locating his own people. From the balcony, he could spot all of his people except one, Jake. He thought for a moment. The only reasons a security chief might disappear was he was either forced to disappear, or he was after something. Suddenly a voice in his ear said, "I'm above you and to the right, on the wall." It was Jake's voice. David slowly and casually looked the direction he was told and saw Jake perched like an eagle on the wall. From his vantage point, he could see the entire crew as well as the rest of the assembly. Jake had seen the captain eyeballing each of the crew. Since the two had not made eye contact, he deduced the captain was looking for him. David nodded thanks to his conscientious security chief. Sometimes he felt like a nervous dad with his crew.

David relaxed and tuned back into Cashel's speech. "Tomorrow we will work toward peace with our neighbors, but today, I decree from this moment on, no one will work for the rest of the day, not a Lord or Noble, not a tradesman, not a servant, nor even a slave. The food is prepared already, so no one else needs to work. Anyone caught giving orders to another today will face my wrath. If you wish for something to eat, you must show your own strength today and get it for yourselves. We will begin by allowing those who have worked the hardest to have the first chance to eat. The slaves will eat first, the servants second, the tradesman third, and the Lords and Nobles last. The guards will take turns because they must remain on duty, but it will be light duty. Let us feast!"

The crowd murmured in disbelief, and no one moved. The Nobles on the balcony were equally shocked. Cashel looked over at Jabre and asked him to see to the guard's rotation to eat and relax. Cashel looked at the stunned crowd and loudly proclaimed, "Slaves, please. Go eat. The servants, tradesman, and nobles cannot eat until you have, and we are hungry." The slaves moved slowly to the tables where they had laid out the food. They cautiously took plates, but still, put only meager portions on their plates. As the first ones sat down to eat and no one stopped them or chastised them, the slaves behind them were bolder in getting their food. The slaves still sat on the ground outside of the pavilions. As they finished, the servants moved in behind them. The groups each moved through without incident. The newness of the situation made everyone nervous and put most on his or her best behavior.

Some of the Nobles were less pleased by the day's events. They were not accustomed to waiting on themselves. Medwin warned Cashel he was stirring up a hornet's nest. The two of them happened upon a conversation precisely mirroring Medwin's warning. The same two nobles David encountered earlier were griping and complaining about the Lord Master's reversal of the societal roles. The two were sure the Sky People were a bad influence on their leader. Their words were coming dangerously close to treason. When Cashel approached them from their blind side, they were caught unawares. Cashel was undoubtedly angry, but he was trying hard to control himself. "Lord Broona, Lord Ayele, are you both blind to the opportunities that are upon us? The Sky People are bringing a great alliance to us, which will give us new machines, and in turn greater profits. They have asked for little in return. We will now be able to keep our crops for ourselves and sell them instead of having them stolen. We also will no longer risk our people's lives to protect our crops. My own sister was lost to us by one of those raids. Who has not been touched by such tragedy? Now it has been stopped. Do you not see why I am celebrating?"

Lord Broona and Lord Ayele looked at each other and were afraid to speak, but Lord Broona risked it. "My Lord Master, we understand why you celebrate, but why did you treat the slaves and servants better than you have treated us? We have worked hard as well, and we are more deserving to eat first. We feel you have dishonored us."

The Lord Master shook his head. He looked at the plump figures of the two men. "I doubt either of you have put in a hard day's work in your lives. I gave my servants a treat so they will remain loyal to me. They will think of me as a kind and benevolent Master who cares for them. Unlike you two, who are angry because you have to carry your own plates. You will be viewed as spoiled children. Threats, punishment, and fear only go so far in commanding obedience. Have I not always treated the two of you well? Perhaps I have been too benevolent toward you both. How would you feel if I withdrew my benevolence from you? Perhaps you would prefer to learn how to harvest the crops yourselves."

Lord Ayele tried to smooth things over. "Lord Master, please forgive us. We get a little cranky when we are hungry. Lord Broona was only concerned the Sky People were trying to take your power away from you. Our concern was for you."

"See that it is. It sounded like your concern was for yourselves. The Sky People will be gone in a short time. If I don't like the changes they introduce to us, I can change them to suit my own needs when they are gone. I have seen the power they possess. I would not want to make them our enemies. They are more powerful than the Akamu. Just remember, you rule at my sufferance. If I don't feel I have your complete loyalty and support, I will replace you with someone who can give me loyalty and support. Do you understand me?"

The two quickly replied individually, "Yes, Lord Master."

Medwin's ornery streak reared up as he and Cashel walked away. "Aren't the Sky People proposing we send an ambassador to live with the Akamu and another to live with the Sorley?"

Cashel put his arm across his brother's shoulders as the two walked away and answered. "Yes, I believe they are. Who do you think we should send?" As they got out of hearing range, Cashel laughed at his brother. "You do have a mean streak, don't you?"

The rest of the day went without incident. Everyone enjoyed a day of eating, fun, games, and drinking. The crew was careful to drink water instead of wine. The Captain, Commander, and Security Chief had all been adamant about staying sober. The crew made it back to the ship without incident. They even brought back some food for the crew members who stayed behind on the *Evangeline*.

PEACE AND TRUTH

The crew was up early the next morning getting ready for their guests, everyone except Vesta. Vesta was definitely sick this morning. She could deny it no longer. Manton asked Jason to come to her instead of going to the infirmary. Jason, knowing what was wrong, brought her something for nausea and a vitamin supplement. He told her to come to see him in the infirmary as soon as the nausea passed.

Soon after the sun was up, their guests began to arrive. The first to arrive were the Kimbra slaves bringing the food, tables, and seats as promised. The Sorley were only a few minutes behind bringing the additional tent and fresh game. Brynna and Lexi were busy directing the others where to put everything. Brynna wanted four tables arranged in a square under the *Evangeline* with the other tables placed under the tent from the Sorley. The food was placed on the tables under the Sorley tent.

The Kimbra slaves had not been informed of their impending freedom and did everything the crew asked of them. Brynna looked at their haggard, scarred faces. She wanted more than anything to have Jason start treating them and let them rest and relax, but there was so much work to be done. She felt guilty asking for their help, but she made sure she always asked and did not give orders. Brynna did give Jason permission to start treatments after the negotiations were underway. She cautioned him to keep those whose scars were healed out of sight until after Auryon's testimony.

The delegates from the Akamu and the Sorley arrived about an hour after the supplies. The Kimbra apparently partied too hard and were having trouble getting started this morning. The Akamu delegation included Tarin, his wife Gaia, Adan, and Caius. The other two members of the Akamu ruling council stayed behind to govern in Tarin's absence. They brought a couple young warriors to watch and learn, as well as the warriors providing security.

The Sorley delegation included Kasen, Tharen, and Gervas. Jager stayed behind in Kasen's absence. Kasen also brought Malek, Damar, and Tolem as witnesses along with a few warriors as guards.

Late into the morning, the Kimbra carriages were seen approaching slowly from the East. When they arrived and sullenly greeted Brynna with bloodshot eyes, she decided to introduce them to coffee. She also asked Jason to offer them something to ease their discomfort. The delegation was made up of Cashel, Medwin, Broona, and Ayele. They were also escorted by several guards.

Brynna had Thane and Lazaro manning the scanners and weapons from the shuttle, just in case. Jake, Marissa, and David were the designated guards for Brynna. Brynna's delegation included herself, Lexi, Braxton, and Cheyenne. Aulani, Laura, and Jason were dealing with people, food, and whatever else came up. Manton and Vesta did whatever was asked of them as well, but they wanted to spend time with their friends. They had not seen their friends since they left the caves nearly a month ago. As Brynna started the negotiations, Jason pulled Vesta inside to the infirmary.

Auryon had been sleeping in the infirmary since she had been with the crew. She was anxiously pacing because she knew Jabre and her brothers were outside. She wanted desperately to see them. She wanted to slug Medwin and hug Cashel. Having Jason and Vesta in the room provided a helpful distraction. Auryon watched curiously as Jason had Vesta lie down on one of the scanning beds.

As the image of her unborn child appeared on the screen, Auryon came closer. "What is that?"

Vesta looked up at the screen. Jason turned up the sound of the heartbeat. He turned the screen so Vesta could see it better. "Vesta, do you trust me and my machines?"

Vesta thought his question was strange. She gave him an honest, but hesitant, "Yes, Dr. Jason."

Jason smiled at her and patted her arm. "Good. My machines can see things while they are still forming inside the body. I know it must look strange, but it will look better later. You are carrying Manton's child."

Vesta promptly let out a blood-curdling scream. The scream resounded through the corridors and outside. Manton recognized his wife's voice and ran into the ship. David was closest to the doorway and quickly followed him. The negotiations came to an abrupt halt before really getting started. The two entered the infirmary together and saw all three occupants with pale faces. Jason was pale because he hadn't expected such a reaction from Vesta. Auryon was pale because she was unaccustomed to seeing inside a person's body. Neither was sure why Vesta had screamed or was pale.

As Manton reached Vesta's side, Jason managed to ask, "Vesta, what's wrong? I thought you wanted a baby. Why did you scream?"

Manton wanted to know the same things, so he didn't bother asking any questions. He simply held her shaking hand. Vesta began to cry. Manton looked at the doctor. "Vesta never cries. What is wrong with her?"

Jason, still looking rather shook up, answered. "I don't know, I just told her the reason she has been sick is because she is going to have a baby. I showed her an image of the baby as it is starting to form and let her listen to its heartbeat. She just screamed. I don't know why. Vesta, the baby is fine. You are fine."

Manton looked dazed for a moment then looked at Vesta and smiled. "We are going to have a child?" Vesta continued to cry. Manton's smile faded. "Why are you crying?"

Vesta managed to stop crying enough to speak. She looked up at Manton. Tears still streaming down her face, "We promised the gods a sacrifice if they gave us a child. We do not have a sacrifice to give them. What if they take away our child?"

For a moment, no one knew what to say. They understood her fear but didn't know quite how to address it. David touched his comm unit and gave Jake and Brynna a quick update. He specifically left out the details.

David stepped forward. Sitting on the edge of her bed, he picked up her free hand and asked her some very pointed questions. "How many years have you and Manton been together?"

"Seven."

"And in that time, you have never had a child. Right?"

"Yes, you know this is true."

"Who do you think gave you this child? Did your gods grant you a child?"

Vesta looked at Manton then back at David. "I do not know." David looked up at Jason, who now had color back in his face. He worded his explanation carefully. "Dr. Jason is the one who put Manton's child in your belly. Your gods did not help him, so you do not owe them a sacrifice. You simply owe Dr. Jason a thank you."

Vesta looked at Manton. "Do you think this is true?"

Manton was frightened as well, but he had grown to trust David and the rest of the crew. He had also seen David's miraculous recovery. Slowly, he nodded. "I believe the gods of the Sky People are the ones we need to thank not the gods in the mountain. They refused to help us. His god is more powerful than our gods."

David started to object and set the record straight, but Jason shook his head at him. "Just let it go, Captain. They aren't ready yet."

David rolled his eyes. He stood up and patted Vesta's hand. "By the way, congratulations to both of you." He laid her hand back on the bed and started to leave the room.

Vesta called out to him with fresh tears streaming down her face. "Captain! Thank you for helping us and for stopping us from making some terrible mistakes."

The captain was slightly embarrassed by the intensity of her gratitude but acknowledged her nevertheless. He continued toward the door and glanced at Auryon who was still somewhat pale. "Are you all right?" She gave him a weak nod. She sat down on her bed to stay out of the way for now. As he left, he heard the doctor giving the happy couple explanations about mood swings, morning sickness, and whatever else could go along with having a baby.

As David stepped outside the *Evangeline*, he had a strong desire to laugh, but this was not the right time or place. He took great care not to make eye contact with Brynna when he resumed his post. When their eyes did finally meet a few minutes later, a giant question mark was evident on her face. He covered his mouth quickly and looked away.

The beginning of the peace negotiations started rather well. The Sorley conceded quickly to their guilt in stealing from the Kimbra and agreed to stop all further attacks if peace were made today. It wasn't a difficult agreement, since the addition of the great wall around the Kimbra cities. All parties would trade for goods and supplies. If any two parties needed mediation, then all three parties would meet again in this very spot to come to an agreement. The spot where the ship sat would from this point on always be considered neutral ground. All parties were in agreement with the plan to stop slavery. Ayele and Broona were not happy with the arrangement, but they didn't dare challenge Cashel openly.

Brynna introduced a code of human rights. Everyone would be entitled to certain minimal rights. She wasn't expecting to rewrite their entire civilization, but she knew slavery would reemerge the second they left if certain rights were not laid down for all the subservient groups. The code of rights had to also be accompanied with a prescribed system of justice. Brynna allowed each group to work out the particulars themselves. Previously, if a slave were to commit a crime, their master could punish them however he saw fit. It was also possible for whoever caught the slave to punish the offender and then the master could punish the slave a second time. Servants weren't much different. If the master ordered the crime to be committed, he usually wasn't held accountable. Her goal was to establish a trial by a jury of peers prior to punishment.

At lunch, each delegation ate apart from the others. They were to each spend their time discussing how to establish a fair system of justice. The final say would rest with their leader. The Akamu and the Sorley were done quickly because their government was more tribal in nature. Heads of families were easily set up as judges between the Sorley and Akamu.

The Kimbra had no real hierarchy. There was a ruling class, and then there was everyone else. Cashel was careful to listen to his advisers, but little was achieved. The Lord Master finally requested Brynna join them and help them come to some sort of agreement. Brynna brought Lexi to their table and told the Lord Master she didn't think it would be appropriate for her to help them directly. She assured them Lexi was very wise and trustworthy and could help them. Broona and Ayele wanted to know why they and the Lord Masters could not just handle things themselves. Lexi tactfully explained they were "important and busy" men and it would be quite taxing for them to handle every minor squabble among the common people. The thing she didn't explain to them was, due to their positions of power, the chances for corruption and intimidation increased significantly. She didn't really need to explain it to them because Ayele and Broona had already been looking at it as a chance to accept bribes. The Lord Master Cashel, being an astute man, knew what Lexi was, and was not saying. He finally decided he would appoint judges. Difficult or appealed cases would come directly to him or Medwin, by-passing his greedy nobles. He also set up stiff penalties for judges who took bribes. He decided he would see to the comfort of the judges so there would be little reason for them to accept bribes. He wanted to make it clear the judges would work for him and no one else. Ayele and Broona were less than pleased.

Brynna didn't want to influence the Kimbra during lunch because she had a secondary agenda, to get at the truth of what happened to Auryon. She didn't want to accidentally put herself in the middle. The Kimbra took a while longer to come back to the table with their plan for justice.

Once all the delegates came back together, they each presented their plans for a balanced system of justice. Each delegation gave their approval over the other's plans. Then Brynna threw her wrench into the works. "It seems you have each come up with good plans to ensure the safety of your citizens from unlawful punishment but, what if, you who are rulers do not follow these plans? Who do you answer to? Whom do your citizens go to if you fail them?"

The Lord Master Cashel was the first on his feet. He was angry. "I am the ruler of my people! I answer to no one! I know what it means to be a leader! The people I rule over are like children. I am responsible for them. Do you think I would harm my own people? I will hold myself accountable!"

Brynna saw Tarin from the Akamu scowling. Kasen was holding his tongue, but he was also glaring at her. Brynna addressed the Lord Master directly. "Lord Master Cashel, I am not saying you would harm your people. I am not saying you would not hold yourself accountable. I am not suggesting anyone is guilty of anything. What if someone close to you did do something wrong? Could you judge them fairly? Could you judge your own sister or brother? Your own child? Your Nobles? Would your subjects view their punishment as just? I am merely seeking to remove the burden of bias."

The mention of sister or brother evoked two reactions. Cashel became calmer, but still wore a mask of suspicion on his face. Medwin was again suddenly afraid his secret was somehow out. He stood up and whispered into his brother's ear. Cashel shoved Medwin away from him. Looking back at Brynna, he responded. "I think I see your point. You want us to have a way of protecting ourselves from the appearance of being unfair and above the law, as well as the pain of judging one of our own."

Brynna smiled and nodded. "Exactly."

Kasen had held his tongue as long as he could. "What is it you propose?

Brynna proposed each ruler choose two fair and impartial leaders from their own ruling councils to be judges as situations needing them arose. No matter which society the accused was from, each would still provide two representatives. If the entire ruling body was under suspicion, then judges would be chosen by the other two societies. The judges would decide on guilt and punishment. The three delegations grudgingly agreed but did not see how it would be necessary.

The group took another more relaxed break. They mingled more with each other. The delegates were not anxious to mingle with people who weren't their own, but all three groups were comfortable enough visiting with the ship's crew. Brynna took this opportunity to talk to Kasen about getting the truth about Auryon out. The two came up with a plan. Kasen sent some of his men to construct a fire circle.

The council came back together. They saw Kasen's men working on the fire circle. They had heard about the Sorley's fire ring but had never seen one. The council now had questions, but Brynna didn't field them until she established one more thing. "I need your agreement on one more point. I want it agreed upon that everyone has a voice and speaks the truth unless it can be proven otherwise. I want a slave's word to be just as good as a nobleman's word."

Medwin knew where this was headed. He tried to circumspectly find a way to stop Brynna. "Servants and slaves generally cannot be trusted because they say what their masters tell them to say. It isn't that I doubt their honesty, but they are afraid of disappointing their masters."

Brynna turned the tables on him. "So how do you suggest we guarantee their safety and their honesty?"

Medwin stammered, "Uh, I would have to think about it for a time. I'm not sure this can be solved today."

Brynna smiled. "I'm sure we can come up with something easily enough. Does anyone have any suggestions?"

Kasen volunteered a helpful suggestion although it wasn't what Brynna was looking for. "If anything befalls the one who testifies or his family the same tragedy should be given to the one he testified against."

Brynna took a deep breath. "Although that would be sufficient motivation to leave the witness alone, it does lead to one problem, two problems actually. First, it doesn't prevent the witness from being bribed or threatened. Second, what if something bad happened to the witness by chance. Would you punish the one accused for an accident?"

Tarin offered a second solution. "The witness and his family can be moved to a safe location until the danger is past. We will offer to allow those of the Sorley or Kimbra sanctuary in our caves if they so desire. The Kimbra have the option of moving from one city to the other if the risks are small. Will they also offer refuge to our citizens if needed?"

Kasen jumped back into the discussion. "We are only present during the warm days, but we can offer refuge to the Kimbra or Akamu when we are here, and we can transport those who wish to move to another city in the far places. I still believe the accused should bear punishments given to any witness who is harmed. If it would make you happy, it can be decided by the judges whether the accused is responsible either directly or indirectly."

Tarin promptly responded. "I agree. Lord Master Cashel, what are your feelings?"

Cashel sat there thoughtfully. "I agree. So let it be done."

Brynna looked slightly vexed, but she let it go and again reminded herself they could not be civilized to the Commonwealth standards too quickly. They were making a lot of progress though. Her eyes landed on Medwin who looked like he had swallowed his own tongue.

Brynna did a recap of all they had agreed on. She included what the Commonwealth had brought to the table. With their data modules, each of them could improve themselves, or they could call on the Commonwealth if something was beyond them. The Commonwealth could bring in healers, medical supplies, food, or mediation if needed. Once everything was agreed on, Brynna asked if there was anything else needing to be dealt with.

Jabre stepped forward. "I have need of judges from the rulers of the Akamu and the Sorley to determine the guilt of the Kimbra Lords." Auryon stepped out from behind Jabre. She wore a tunic with long sleeves and covered her head and face with a cloth veil. Cashel and Medwin stood up suddenly. "Auryon!" The two were anxious to see her but were fearful. They did not wish for their sister to be disgraced by being seen as a slave.

Brynna had instructed Jabre to accuse the Kimbra at this specific time and place. His interjection was no surprise. "State your grievance Jabre."

Jabre was both afraid and angry. He spoke slowly and carefully. "I do not know who all the involved parties are, but the Lady Mistress Auryon, the sister to the Lord Masters, Cashel and Medwin, was betrayed. One or both of them are responsible for nearly getting me killed, for the Mistress being kidnapped, and held prisoner by the Sorley."

Cashel and Medwin were suddenly quite pale. Cashel thought back to the conversation he had with Brynna the previous day. Could he trust her? He was starting to have doubts, but he was sure they were brought on by fear.

Medwin balked quickly and loudly. "This was a trap! We will not stand for this! Cashel, let us leave here at once!"

Cashel carefully watched Brynna's eyes. "No. An accusation has been made, and we must give an answer. If we leave now, no one will trust us to keep our word about anything."

Medwin tugged on his brother's arm. "You're not serious!"

Cashel jerked his arm away from Medwin. "I gave my word, and I intend to keep it. I will not lose the respect of my peers, my rivals, or my subjects." He looked firmly at Brynna. "Choose your judges."

Brynna looked to Tarin. "Tarin, I need two from the Akamu."

Tarin didn't look any happier about the situation than Cashel or Medwin. Tarin nodded and turned to his delegation to discuss who should serve as judges.

Brynna looked at Kasen. "Kasen, I need two from the Sorley." Kasen nodded. He turned to Gervas and Tharen and spoke to them briefly.

Tarin chose himself and Adan to serve as judges. Kasen designated Tharen and Gervas for the Sorley.

Brynna pulled the four judges aside and instructed them to choose two from the Kimbra delegation. Since there were only four nobles present, the decision was relatively easy. Broona and Ayele were chosen.

Medwin was not happy with his fate resting in the hands of Broona and Ayele who were known to be power hungry. "Cashel, those two will find us guilty just to take our places ruling over the cities."

Cashel looked at his brother. He knew Medwin was right, but he was also afraid Medwin must be the one who was guilty. "If our innocence is obvious, they will have no choice, but to release us from guilt. We must find a way to prove our innocence and quickly. I believe the Sorley are preparing that fire circle for us."

Medwin had felt a lump growing in his stomach over the last few days. As he looked out at the fire circle, he felt the lump in his stomach getting bigger.

The group took a brief break and rearranged the tables to appear more like a courtroom. Two of the tables were placed together in a straight line for the judges to sit at. The other two tables were separated and angled toward the head table forming a triangle. She intended for Cashel and Medwin to sit at one of the tables and Jabre and Auryon to sit at the other.

Brynna took the time to tell Jason he could get started on taking care of the slaves. He and Laura had already done some triage work and decided who needed care the most. The two didn't waste any time getting started. Brynna did remind him to keep them clear of the proceedings. She didn't want it evident to Cashel and Medwin yet that Auryon no longer had slave markings.

The group came back together to start. Brynna specifically arranged the judges so they were not sitting by their own people. She wanted to encourage the different societies to work with each other. She directed the others where to sit. Once the group settled in, Brynna intervened in the proceedings one more time. "May I give you a little more guidance on your proceedings?"

Tarin looked back and forth at the other judges. No one seemed to mind, so Tarin nodded at Brynna to proceed. Brynna continued. "I propose you choose a lead judge to conduct the proceedings and keep order. In this case, since it is Cashel and Medwin are the ones being judged, I suggest it not be Ayele or Broona. The next thing I suggest is to have Jabre state his case exactly as he knows it. Do not allow him to speculate. Then let him and Auryon call whatever witnesses they have. After Jabre has presented his case, allow Cashel and Medwin to present their defense. Once both sides have presented their arguments allow the judges to ask any additional questions. Then withdraw to determine guilt or innocence and punishment. Does that seem fair?"

The judges looked back and forth at each other and nodded. Lord Broona suggested Tarin be the lead judge and the others quickly agreed. Lord Broona's only thoughts were that the Akamu believed in swift and harsh justice. He and Ayele had already seen their chance to move into complete power.

Tarin had one question. "Shouldn't the punishment be decided before we begin? They are accused of treason, and the punishment is death."

Brynna spoke slowly and deliberately so there would be no misunderstandings in translation. "I do not recommend you decide on punishment until you know all the facts. It is possible there has been a misunderstanding. I also suggest anyone who confesses their guilt voluntarily be granted leniency. This system is new, and it will serve to help all of us learn. Part of the reason a justice system works is because everyone knows it is there."

Tarin acknowledged her instructions and began. "Jabre, state your case, as you witnessed it."

Jabre told about the evening the Sorley raiding party attacked the Kimbra fields. He saw the party approaching and sounded the alarm sending the workers running for the city walls. The Kimbra warriors had headed into the fields to protect the crops and the workers. Jabre tried to get Auryon back to the city, but she was trying to help an elderly woman get back to safety. The three of them were cut off by the raiding party. Jabre reported one of the Sorley yelling to the others. "Malek! I have him! The woman is here too!" Jabre had thought at the time it was just because they had been spotted, not because he had significance. Jabre had drawn his sword and put himself in front of the two women. A man, he supposed was the warrior called Malek, rode toward them and shot an arrow into the arm Jabre was holding the sword with. Jabre pulled out a dagger with his left arm and tried to push the women toward the city. Malek had dismounted and used his spear to knock Jabre to the ground and unconscious. When Jabre regained consciousness days later, he had a stab wound in his abdomen, and Auryon was gone. The woman Auryon had tried to help was left alone. The woman was left behind because she was too old to be worth much as a slave.

Tarin asked Jabre, "What makes you think you were betrayed?"

Jabre looked at Auryon. "When Auryon was found and brought back, I learned the Sorley had been told when and where we would be."

Tarin thanked Jabre for his testimony then turned his attention to the veiled woman beside Jabre. "You are the woman known as Auryon?"

Auryon stood. "I am Mistress Auryon of the Kimbra, sister to the Lord Masters, Cashel and Medwin." Even though her clothing covered nearly every inch of her body, she was still clearly nervous. She fidgeted anxiously. Jabre reached up and squeezed her hand. She glanced down at him, and her eyes displayed the gratitude she felt. She cleared her throat and began her tale.

"Several years back, my brothers tried to arrange a marriage for me with a member of Kasen's ruling council. The man they wanted me to marry was a cousin of Kasen's known as Malek. The marriage was intended to bring peace between our two peoples. I refused to marry Malek because my heart belonged to another, and it would be an unhappy union for both of us. I could not love Malek as a wife should love a husband because of my love for Jabre."

As she spoke, Cashel sat there quietly listening, his visage displaying nothing of his thoughts. Medwin's demeanor was quite different. He acted like he was sitting on a cactus. He fidgeted incessantly. When Auryon spoke openly of her feelings for Jabre, Medwin looked like he was about to be sick to his stomach.

"Both of my brothers were angry with me for refusing to marry Malek. I told Cashel he should work out a peace treaty without relying on a marriage to seal the deal. Cashel was so angry he told me to stay out of his sight for a few days. I did as he asked. I went to the fields to help the workers. I had been going to the fields every day to help. Once we start the harvest, we must get it done quickly, or the Sorley send raiding parties to steal from us." Auryon looked directly at Kasen, "Forgive my bluntness, Lord Kasen." Kasen nodded in response.

He knew he was guilty, but it had been the way they had always done things. They allowed the Kimbra several days to gather food before they came to take a portion of the crop. The Sorley were not greedy, but they were routine opportunists. Auryon continued with her story. "Four days into the harvest, the Sorley came. Jabre saw them coming and blew his horn to call for the soldiers from the cities. He tried to grab me and take me back to the city, but there was an elderly woman who would never make it back to the city without help. I refused to leave her behind. Two of the warriors saw us and cut us off from the soldiers coming from the cities. The warriors called out to Malek. It struck me as odd, but I couldn't make sense of it then. They sounded like they had been looking specifically for us. I was too frightened to remember exactly what they said. Jabre tried to protect us, but he was shot with an arrow. I didn't see who shot him. Malek came."

Auryon took another slow deep breath as she relived the horror of that day.

Tarin, hearing her hesitation and seeing she was again shaking, intervened. "Do you need to take a break?"

Auryon wiped away a stray tear and shook her head. Lexi had stayed near the woman. She felt somehow responsible for her. Lexi poured a glass of water and handed it to her. Auryon gripped the glass tightly and took three hard swallows of the water. She quietly thanked Lexi, and then set the glass back down on the table. Taking another deep breath, she started again. Her words were broken up and slow.

"Malek came riding up. He hit Jabre in the head with the butt of his spear. Jabre was knocked unconscious, and then he turned his spear around to kill him. I – I tried to stop him. I pleaded with him not to hurt Jabre. He threw me aside and – and then stabbed him."

Her tears were flowing freely now. Jabre reached up and squeezed her hand again. This time he held her hand tightly and didn't release it. Auryon took another couple sips of her water and caught her breath.

"I thought Jabre was dead. I tried to get to him, but Malek pulled me away. He tied my hands together and threw me across his horse. One of the other warriors, Damar, asked what he should do with the old woman. Malek told them to leave her because she was too old. I had never met Malek before, but he knew who I was. When we reached the Sorley village, he told me I was supposed to be his wife. He gave me the option of marrying him or being his slave. I chose slavery. I could not marry the man who had killed my beloved Jabre. Malek was furious. He beat me and marked me. He nearly killed me."

Tarin saw Auryon was still shaking visibly. He decided to take some of the pressure off her. "How did you know you had been betrayed?"

The question forced Auryon to lay her emotions aside and refocus her thoughts. Auryon took a second to answer his question, but this time she was calmer. "A year after I was taken, the Sorley were back in this area. Malek got drunk. He would often get angry at the sight of me when he was drunk. I learned quickly to stay out of his sight if I could when he was drinking, but

I couldn't that night. He slapped me around, and then he told me my own family had betrayed me. They wanted rid of Jabre because he was a commoner. He told me my brothers tried to break us up by arranging our marriage and when that didn't work, they sold me out. They told him where we would be the day I was taken. Malek told me they paid him to kill Jabre. They paid him with me." Auryon began to cry again. This time Jabre grabbed her and held her tightly.

Tarin then had to ask the hard questions. "Is there anyone who can confirm what you have said? What about the old woman in the field with you?"

Jabre looked up at Tarin and shook his head. "The old woman passed away that next winter."

Tarin had one more question. "Auryon, who knew about your relationship with Jabre?"

Auryon lifted her head from Jabre's chest. Jabre loosened his grip on her so she could turn to face Tarin. "Both Cashel and Medwin knew."

Tarin nodded. "Do you know if anyone else knew?"

Auryon shook her head. "A relationship with someone of lower station is frowned upon. We had to be discreet. I am not aware of anyone else knowing about us. Some of the servants or slaves may have picked up on it, but we tried to be careful even around them."

Kasen stood up. "I have the three warriors here with me. Malek will tell you all he knows, and he will speak the truth to you. His life is forfeit if he lies and he knows this."

Medwin had reached his limit. He bolted out of his chair. "I told you this was a trap! Kasen just admitted he knew his warriors were needed here to testify today! And how can we be sure this really is our sister? It sounds like her, but I have not heard her voice in several years, and all I can see is her eyes. I'm tired of this charade. I am leaving!"

Tarin stood up and gave two of his own warriors a quick look that said plenty. The two warriors blocked Medwin's path. Medwin turned around and walked back toward the proceedings. He moved to the center of the floor area. He wasn't sure what to do next. He looked from Jabre and Auryon to Tarin, Kasen and his eyes finally came to rest on Brynna. He raised his arm and pointed at her. "You! You are the one who set us up!"

Tarin looked at Kasen then Brynna. "Commander, do you have an explanation?"

Brynna stepped forward. "I do. When the slaves were released, Auryon's story came to light. Jabre was here bringing us a message from the Kimbra when the two met again. Each thought the other was either dead or forever lost to them. When we found out about the betrayal, we knew Auryon could not return to the Kimbra without fear for her life or Jabre's. This issue had to be dealt with. I encouraged them to wait until a system of justice was set up. If it had come to light without this justice system, the ones responsible would simply have gotten away with it, and perhaps others would have died. So yes, I knew about it, and I persuaded them to bring it to this council after the negotiations were complete. It is completely up to you how to proceed. If you decide they are innocent of wrongdoing, then so be it. I suggest you hear all the evidence first though. I did tell Kasen about Auryon's situation. He has agreed to welcome her and Jabre as Sorley citizens if her safety cannot be guaranteed. He also guaranteed the cooperation of any of his people who were involved. Yes, we did plan for this, but it was not a trap. We are looking to right a wrong."

Tarin was clearly not happy. He felt like he was being used, but her reasoning was solid. Tarin looked at the other judges. "Is this arrangement still acceptable? We must all be in agreement on this issue."

Medwin looked at Ayele and Broona and ever so slightly shook his head at them. He wanted them to be dissenting votes, so this would finally be over. Ayele averted his eyes from Medwin and agreed to continue. Broona kept his eyes locked on Medwin as he expressed his agreement. Broona seemed rather pleased with himself. Cashel still sat quietly in his chair, but he was intently watching his two nobles. It was clear; the ride home wasn't going to be any fun for Broona or Ayele.

With the council in agreement to continue, Tarin moved forward. "Lady Auryon, I am sorry, but in order to confirm your identity, we must ask you to remove your veil. I know this will be difficult for you, but it must be done." Tarin strongly suspected she was covered to conceal slave markings.

Medwin tried to carefully conceal a smirk. He was sure when the council saw her scarred face, they would instinctively distrust her. He didn't really want to see his sisters scarred face, but he valued his own well-being more.

Auryon nodded. Jabre gently helped her remove the veil. As soon as everyone could see her face, there were gasps and startled exclamations all around. Cashel was the first to react. "What is the meaning of this?" Looking at Brynna, he demanded an explanation. "You told us she had been marked yet clearly she has not!"

Medwin, still in the middle of the area, had been standing there defiantly facing Tarin. When the startled look appeared on Tarin's face, and Cashel reacted, he had to turn and see Auryon's face for himself. Her face was as clear and beautiful as the day she had disappeared. Medwin gasped, "Auryon!"

Tarin shook off his own daze. "I will take that as confirmation this woman is your sister Auryon." Medwin was hoping to cast doubt on her identity because of the scars, but he messed that up himself.

Cashel was still looking at Brynna for answers. Brynna stepped forward again. "Our doctor is capable of healing old wounds as well as new ones. Auryon was scarred, but she has been healed of the physical scars. The emotional ones remain. Those don't heal as easily."

Tarin decided it was time for him to retake control. "Everyone go back to your places and sit down." Kasen and Cashel sat down, Brynna moved away from the triangle, Jabre and Auryon took their seats. Medwin remained defiantly in the center of the triangle. Tarin gave him a look suggesting he should comply, or else. Medwin wasn't ready to back down yet. Tarin gave him a reason to rethink his decision. "Lord Master Medwin, either take your seat willingly, or I will have my warriors take you forcibly back to your seat and tie you to it."

Tarin's warriors flanked the man and started reaching for his arms to drag him back to his seat. Medwin jerked away from their grasp. "All right! Fine! I'm going!" The two men followed him closely and remained standing behind his chair.

Tarin eyed Brynna closely. "Why did you have her conceal her face?"

Brynna stated calmly. "There were a couple reasons. Auryon has worn slave markings for several years now. She has only had them healed for a few days. She was nervous about having her brothers see her again. We also felt like we could learn the truth from the reactions of her brothers when they did see her face. I don't know if the judges have learned anything, but I have, and I believe Jabre and Auryon have."

Tarin looked very annoyed with her. "No more games."

Tarin looked to Kasen. "Bring your witnesses forward." Kasen waved the three men into the meeting. Tolem and Damar told the same stories roughly as Auryon and Jabre. Details varied a little, but nothing noteworthy changed. Malek had the entire story. He told the board of judges how Medwin had approached him with the peace agreement and the arranged marriage. Medwin had escorted him to the edge of the fields and pointed out his sister. Medwin had also pointed out Jabre who was with Auryon as one of her guards that day. Malek told the judges that Medwin had distastefully reported his sister's infatuation with her "guard" and he would do anything to end it. Malek's demeanor was extremely subdued compared to the rantings they had seen weeks prior. The man went on to explain the Lord Master Medwin returned to him a couple weeks later with a new arrangement. Auryon had refused to marry Malek because of Jabre. Medwin offered to give Jabre and Auryon to Malek.

Medwin jumped to his feet. "That is not true!" Tarin's men grabbed Medwin and put him back in his seat.

Tarin gave Medwin a stern look. "You will have your turn to speak. Allow Malek to finish."

Malek looked at Kasen warily then continued. "Medwin told me if I got rid of Jabre, I would be free to marry Auryon. He told me where Jabre would be and when. I did as Medwin asked, but Auryon still refused to be my wife. She's such a beautiful woman. I was drunk and angry at being rejected by her twice, and I punished her for it. I am sorry Auryon for everything I did to you. I hope someday you can forgive me. Jabre, I am sorry for the pain I caused you and for trying to kill you."

Tarin had a couple questions for Malek. "Did Kasen influence your testimony in any way?"

Malek glanced at Kasen then hung his head. Kasen folded his arms and threatened Malek. "Malek! Speak the truth no matter who is guilty or who it hurts!"

Tarin looked from Kasen back to Malek. "Answer my question! Did Kasen influence your testimony, either by threats or bribes?"

Malek raised his head and looked at Tarin. He couldn't help but see Kasen's son, Tharen who sat near Tarin. Tharen was a younger image of his father although his temperament was more like his mother's. He felt like he was betraying both father and son. "Yes, Kasen threatened me."

Tarin shook his head. "Your testimony is useless then."

Tharen, knowing his father, thought there must be more to it than this. "Tarin, may I ask him a couple questions?" Tarin eyed the young man. He wondered if Tharen was planted as a judge just to support his father. Tarin finally agreed just because he wondered how it could possibly help.

Tharen looked at Malek. "Malek, tell me exactly what my father said to you."

Malek looked around at the fire circle that had been prepared. He could tell there was rain coming in, but he knew even that wouldn't save him. The wood was already soaked with oil. He looked back at Tharen. "Kasen ordered me to speak the truth today and to hide nothing, no matter who it harms."

Tharen continued his questions. "What did he say would happen if you lied or hid a truth?"

"He told us, we would be stoned in the fire ring if we lied or hid the truth."

"Did he know what you were going to say when you testified today?"

Malek looked slightly confused. "Yes – No... I do not know. I assumed he knew the truth."

Tharen wanted to be sure everyone knew the situation. "Just to be clear, Kasen did not ask you what your side of the story was? He didn't tell you what to say?"

Malek shook his head. "No, he never asked me what the truth was, but he said he would know if I lied."

Tharen looked at Tolem and Damar. "Does he speak the truth?" The two men hastily agreed.

Tarin looked annoyed. He didn't know whom to trust at this point. He decided to see if anyone else had testimony against the two accused before allowing them to defend themselves. "Is there anyone else who has testimony against the accused?"

Cashel looked hard at Brynna. Brynna met his gaze but remained silent. Cashel couldn't get any kind of a read off her. She seemed truly neutral. What he didn't understand was, he had admitted knowing about the relationship to her. Why didn't she use that knowledge against him? It wasn't quite making sense. The other question was, "What did she learn from revealing Auryon's unscarred face?"

When Tarin saw no one else speak up, he turned to Cashel and Medwin. "You may now answer these charges made against you."

Cashel thought for a moment then stood up and asked. "May we have a break to prepare ourselves? I would also like to speak to the Commander for a moment."

Tarin nodded. "I think we could all use a break, but my men will remain at your sides."

Cashel looked pale. "As you wish."

Brynna approached the two men cautiously. Medwin was already spouting an angry litany of complaints. She didn't want to interrupt. Cashel waved at Brynna to come forward. He also promptly shut Medwin down with a disgusted look. "Medwin, you did this, didn't you? How could you do this?"

Medwin looked shocked his brother would suggest such a thing. "Cashel, I would never do anything to harm Auryon. I only want what is best for her."

Cashel grabbed his brother's arms and shook him. "Tell me the truth!" Medwin was suddenly dwarfed by his brothers posturing. He was now afraid to tell him the truth, so he flatly denied it. Cashel released his brother and made one last plea. "If they find us both guilty, then we will both pay the price for harming Auryon and Jabre. If you confess, I can help you. If you don't, who will look out for our family?"

Medwin gave him a blank stare. He didn't understand what he was up against. Cashel gave up and turned to Brynna. "You had evidence against me, yet you didn't use it. Why?"

Brynna softly explained. "It isn't evidence against you. Yes, you told me you knew about the relationship, but you also approved of it. That is evidence for you not against you."

Cashel looked back at Medwin with sadness in his eyes. Medwin became uncomfortable with Cashel's stares and walked away. Cashel looked back to Brynna and made one last request. He whispered quietly to her. Brynna backed away and shook her head. David looked up and saw Cashel grab Brynna's arm. As he moved closer to her, he heard Cashel say, "This is a private matter between my brother and me. Give me your word, you will say nothing!"

Brynna's eyes pleaded with him. When he wouldn't relent, Brynna finally answered him. "Fine! I won't volunteer the information to the tribunal, but if I am called on to testify, I will not lie."

David watched Cashel release her arm and walk away. David closed the gap between himself and Brynna. "What was that all about?"

Brynna sighed. "Cashel is going to throw himself on his sword."

David looked at Cashel who was pulling Tarin aside to talk to him. David looked back at Brynna. "Do you think Cashel is guilty?"

"No, I don't, but I think he's trying to protect his brother and his sister."

David looked confused. "How is that?"

"If Cashel claims responsibility, Medwin will remain in power and untouched, but he wouldn't dare touch Auryon and Jabre. If he did, his guilt and punishment would be assured."

"Is there anything you can do to stop him? Can you testify about the conversation you just had?"

Brynna scowled. "No, I gave Cashel my word I would not testify voluntarily. David, you can't interfere with the council either, none of us can."

David stood there a moment staring at Brynna. Brynna could see the wheels in his head turning. In a moment, he turned to walk away. He gave a less than reassuring, subdued parting response. "Understood, Commander."

David walked over to the crowded tent and grabbed a drink and a piece of meat from the table. He looked around and found Medwin standing by himself on the far side of the tent staring off into the distance. The two Akamu security guards were keeping a discreet distance, but an ever-watchful eye on the man. David went and stood beside Medwin. He just stood there a moment, waiting on Medwin to acknowledge his presence. Medwin finally gave David a sideways glance. "What do you want? Haven't your people done enough damage to us?"

David nibbled lightly on his food. "I just wanted to congratulate you on your accomplishments. You have gotten away with the near murder of Jabre, got us to build protective walls around your cities, your sister has been brought safely back to you, and before the day is out you will be the ruler over both Kimbra cities. You can even take credit among your people for the peace treaty. That's a pretty good list of achievements."

Medwin turned to face David. "What are you talking about? Are you trying to get me to confess to this horrible crime I am being accused of?"

David rocked back and forth on his heels. "Oh no, I'm not trying to get a confession from you. I was just inspired by your incredible ability to come out of this so cleanly." David sipped on his drink.

Medwin eyed him suspiciously. "What do you mean by ruler over both Kimbra cities?"

David wanted to appear to be at ease, so he took a large bite of his meat and chewed noisily. "Well, I really didn't realize how badly you wanted control of both cities." David continued to chew obnoxiously. As he started to take another bite of the meat, Medwin knocked the morsel from his hand. He grabbed David's clothes angrily and pulled him forward. The two Akamu were on Medwin in a split second with weapons drawn. Medwin, realizing his predicament, slowly released David. David waved the two men away. Jake had been drawn by the raucous as well and continued to get closer to the two men. David loudly proclaimed, "Just a minor misunderstanding, everything is fine here. Everyone go back to eating." Luckily, David had his back to Brynna. Even from across the grounds, which measured about one hundred yards, he could feel her angry glare on the back of his head. David subconsciously ran his hand over the back of his head and smoothed his hair back into place. His hair wasn't messed up, but Brynna's imagined stare made him feel like it was. Medwin still stood there glaring at David. David lowered his voice and smiled sarcastically at Medwin. "Look, I just didn't think you were power hungry enough to get rid of your own sister and brother. I'm impressed."

Medwin continued his angry glare. "I don't understand what you are talking about. Your machine must be broken."

David stepped closer to Medwin and lowered his voice even further. "I get it. You aren't guilty of anything. I just wanted to know how you got Cashel to voluntarily confess to everything. What kind of leverage are you using against him?"

Medwin swung his fist around and nailed David squarely in the jaw. David was expecting the punch and allowed his body to reel with the blow. He hit the ground. This time Jake was on Medwin faster than the Akamu, only his weapon was a Tri-EMP, rather than a sword. David got up and wiped a small spot of blood from his lip. "Jake, stand down. I've got this." Jake backed away and holstered his weapon. David stepped closer to Medwin again and put his message as plainly and bluntly as he could. "Cashel knows you are guilty of selling out Jabre and Auryon. He's going to confess to being solely responsible for it. You're going to get your brother killed. Can you live with that?" David let his words sink in for a moment then walked away.

By this time, Brynna had made her way to Jake's side. She wasn't nearly as angry as she had been moments earlier when the sounds of anger had reached her ears. It had been mere minutes after she ordered David to stay out of the situation and now he was in the thick of it. Once she reached Jake, she realized David was intervening in the only way possible yet still obeying her command. He was splitting hairs. Personally, she wanted a way to intervene. She wasn't sure she wanted it bad enough to take a punch to her jaw. She silently hoped David had gotten through to Medwin, but she also knew the captain deserved a severe tongue-lashing. This was her sphere of command, and he knew better than this. She debated about whether to say something to him now or wait until later. She decided not to air their dirty laundry here and now.

Moments before the council reconvened, Tarin walked up to Brynna. "Do you believe Cashel is guilty?"

Brynna was startled by his question. "You can't ask me that Tarin. I can't influence your ruling."

Tarin eyed her carefully. "You knew he was going to confess, didn't you?"

Brynna said nothing and looked away. Tarin continued to study her. "You know he's innocent, don't you?"

Brynna looked back at Tarin. "I can't answer that, Tarin."

Tarin folded his arms. "What would you do if I ordered you to testify?"

Brynna's eyes reflected a wide variety of emotions including alarm, worry and a plea for release. "Tarin, I would tell you what I know, and I would tell the truth, but I would like you to find another way. I gave my word I wouldn't intervene. Please find another way to get at the truth."

Tarin stroked his beard thoughtfully then gave Brynna her release. "Very well. I will find the truth another way."

Tarin called the judging council together and talked to them for a few minutes. Whatever he said to the men made them nervous. Each man looked around anxiously and avoided making eye contact.

To Lexi's trained eye, the council appeared to be harboring some dark secret. Lexi approached Brynna and inquired about it. Brynna saw the same things. She knew Tarin was up to something. She gave Lexi a brief update and suggested she prepare Auryon for it. "Auryon knows it was Medwin, not Cashel. Warn her not to fight this, just let it play out. I won't let anyone hurt Cashel." Lexi returned to Auryon's side and warned her as best she could.

Tarin called the meeting to order. "May I have everyone's attention? I wish to announce; no further testimony is necessary. Cashel has confessed to being solely responsible for the betrayal of Jabre and Auryon. This council has agreed to accept his confession and will now render judgment."

Despite the warning Lexi had given Auryon, the woman could not help herself. She began to weep then cry out. "Cashel, how could you? I thought you loved me. How could you do this to me?"

Tarin didn't want the meeting to get out of control, so he took over quickly. "Mistress Auryon, I know you are distressed, but please allow me to finish this. I will allow you time to demand the answers you seek."

Auryon continued to cry, but she allowed Lexi and Jabre to help her sit back down. Medwin sat there in shock. Captain Alexander had just told him this was about to happen, but he was still unprepared. Tarin looked at Cashel. "Give your confession Lord Master Cashel." Somehow, this time, when he said, "Lord Master," it didn't have the same ring of importance.

Cashel stood slowly. He took one last sip of his drink to wet his lips. His mouth was uncomfortably dry despite the drink. "Tarin has spoken the truth. I claim all responsibility for what happened to Auryon and Jabre. I forced Medwin to take the message to Malek. Medwin tried to protect Auryon, but I told him I would slaughter his children starting with his firstborn if he didn't do as I ordered."

The longer Cashel spoke, the sicker and more stunned Medwin became. Cashel kept his eyes on Tarin alone. A look of sorrow engulfed his face, and he finally looked down at the ground. Knowing Auryon needed a reason, he gave her one. "Auryon, you are of the ruling class, an heiress, yet you ignored the boundaries which are there for our protection. You flagrantly fraternized with Jabre. Medwin and I tried to arrange a marriage for you to help protect our people and remove you from temptation. You rejected our attempts to provide a better life for you and for your people. You put your own desires ahead of your people. You are the one guilty of betrayal, not me."

Cashel took another drink of his water and steadied himself again. "I did not intend for you to live as Malek's slave. That was not the agreement. He was to take you as his wife and provide a good life to you by Sorley standards at least. He is also guilty of betrayal. That is why I did it, but I have had years to think about my choices, and I was wrong. If I could undo this, I would. I would not have betrayed you or Jabre. Once I saw Jabre's injuries and heard how he tried to protect you, I knew I was wrong to keep you apart. I kept him alive, for your sake. I hope someday, you will forgive me."

Cashel looked back up at Tarin. "I have one last request before you pass judgment." Tarin nodded, and Cashel spoke again.

"Auryon, Jabre, as some small recompense for what I have done, I turn all my property, holdings, and authority over to the two of you. Jabre, you are now ruler over the Kimbra under one condition. You are to love and care for my sister to the end of her days. It cannot make up for all the pain I have caused, but perhaps it's a start."

Jabre was caught between shock and anger. He was ready to run the guilty party through with his sword, but his own Lord Master? Medwin was still in shock over Cashel's confession. When Cashel turned everything over to Jabre, Medwin snapped out of his stupor. "Cashel, what are you doing? You can't do this. This is wrong!" The group of onlookers was all in shock at the events playing out in front of them. Murmurs and whispers began spreading throughout the crowd.

Tarin struggled to stay in control of the situation. "Quiet! Silence! Silence!" The crowd got quiet again. "Cashel and Medwin, please stand for your judgments." Cashel and Medwin stood. Cashel looked resolute, and Medwin looked like a lost little boy, despite being a grown man. Tarin stood as well. "Medwin, this council has determined the testimonies today do not bear sufficient evidence to your guilt. You are free to return to your home. Cashel, your final request is granted. Jabre and Auryon will now speak for Primus, and all you own is now theirs. Cashel, by your own admission, you are guilty, and this council accepts your plea of guilt. As this council is new to our peoples, it must be taken seriously and seen as a firm establishment. No one should view this council as powerless or a puppet of our new Commonwealth allies. As an unfortunate consequence of this situation, punishment will be severe. Betrayal of one's own kin by one who is meant to lead by example is the most heinous of crimes, and you are hereby sentenced to death. Because you confessed willingly, this court will offer the following leniency. You may choose your method of execution, but the sentence will be carried out by sunset. Do you wish any of your family still within the city to be brought out before your sentence is carried out?"

Cashel looked up and quietly answered. "No, Medwin can explain it to them after it is over. I don't want my wife or children to see my shame." Cashel hoped by making Medwin explain to his family, perhaps he would feel some sense of remorse.

"Do you have a preferred method of execution?"

Cashel shook his head. "It does not matter. Dead is still dead, just make it a fast death."

Tarin took a deep breath and considered his words carefully. "Very well then. Although your crime deserves a slow, painful death, the judgment of this tribunal is you will be executed by a warrior's death. You will face a joint firing squad of our best archers at sunset."

Cashel gave Tarin and the council a simple, "Thank you."

Tarin ordered his men to take Cashel into custody and release Medwin. Cashel looked up at Brynna and gave her a nod of thanks for not saying anything. Brynna still wearing a look of consternation, acknowledged his thanks. This is not how the system was supposed to work. The guilty were not supposed to get away with their crimes. Auryon continued to cry softly. A strange hush fell over the crowd. Medwin looked pale as a ghost.

Tarin wanted to close the meeting out by making sure everyone understood the council's purpose. "This council will exist for the sole purpose of keeping the peace between our three nations. The crimes committed by the Kimbra have kept the conflict alive between the Kimbra and the Sorley. This council will only deal justice out to crimes of such a high nature they affect more than a single nation. All other crimes will be handled internally. Any leader may call a meeting of the council at any time, but any leader who does not abide by the council's agreements will suffer dire consequences. Does everyone understand this and are all in agreement?"

Kasen nodded his agreement. Tarin looked to Jabre and Auryon.

Jabre was not accustomed to power, and it took him a minute to give his consent, but he had no questions or objections. Medwin was still reeling from the current events. He pulled himself together enough to offer a last objection to try and save his brother's life. "I don't agree. I object to your judgment against my brother. You are punishing him for a crime committed six years ago. This council did not have an agreement or jurisdiction six years ago."

Tarin was prepared for this argument. "You are correct. The crime precedes the council's jurisdiction, but the results have lasted until today, and the crime was just discovered today, so our decision is just. Unless he is not actually the one who is guilty. Your objection is noted, but you are outvoted. Kasen, will you deal with the guilt of your men or do you wish to bring them before this council for punishment?"

Kasen stood to address Tarin. "I believe the crimes my men have perpetrated are equal to that of Cashel's guilt. I give them to you for equal punishment. Give them the same warriors death."

Malek jumped up. "Kasen! No! You promised us leniency if we spoke the truth!" Damar and Tolem were on their feet in panic.

Kasen whirled around to face his three men. "Be Silent! This is leniency! My choice would be to have you stoned in the fire ring! You were supposed to be my trusted advisers! You kept a truth from me that kept us at war with the Kimbra for six years. How many of our warriors died at the hands of the Kimbra because of you three? I could think of a thousand slow, painful deaths far more deserving!"

Malek and his cohorts felt a sick feeling develop in the pit of their stomachs. They did as they were told and sat down and kept their mouths closed. They knew Kasen could and would kill them slowly and painfully if he so desired.

Tarin spoke again. "So be it. Let today be the end of the death and destruction. Let us begin anew tomorrow with leaders who respect the lives of others. Unless there is a reason to reconvene sooner, we will come together again at sunset."

Tarin moved to make arrangements for his and Kasen's best archers to be brought in for the execution. His face didn't show it, but he knew this was a mistake and it bothered him a great deal. He wasn't sure how to get at the truth though.

Medwin was starting to come to terms with his own guilt. He stood there by Cashel. "Cashel, why did you confess to this? You're not guilty." He paused and looked around to be sure the guards weren't close enough to hear what he said and spoke softly. "You know I did this."

Cashel looked relieved to at least hear the words come out of his mouth. He didn't know if he could convince Medwin to formally confess, but it was a start. "I know you're guilty, but the chances of me being proven innocent and you being found guilty were pretty slim. If we were both found guilty, our families would suffer, and Auryon would be left at the mercy of those two vultures." Cashel nodded in the general direction of Ayele and Broona. "You seem to be pretty good at protecting yourself, so you should be able to protect yourself and Auryon from them. One of us has to survive."

Medwin still looked confused. "So why didn't you tell them I'm the guilty one?"

Cashel angrily looked at his brother. "Because I had no way to prove it and I shouldn't have to do that. You should have been man enough to take responsibility for your actions. I really hope you're man enough to live with my death. I'm counting on you to take care of my family. Don't disappoint me – again."

Medwin was too choked up to speak. He simply nodded and walked off by himself.

David and Brynna were standing together watching the exchange. Brynna shook her head. "I may have to shoot that man myself if he doesn't come clean."

David folded his arms across his chest and turned to wander off himself. "There may be a line of people ready to do that."

Brynna suddenly gasped and called out, "David!" David whirled around in time to see Medwin grab a Sorley horse and ride off toward Corvan. It happened so quickly no one had time to react. Tharen and Gervas grabbed two of the remaining horses and took off after him, but his head start was too great. They quickly realized they would never catch him.

Tarin walked up to Brynna and made one simple statement. "If he does not return and confess, I will call on you to testify to what you know."

Tarin moved away from her, but not before she could ask one question. "Tarin, what will you do to him if he confesses?"

Tarin shrugged. "I do not know. At this point, he deserves a coward's death, but I will have to consult the other judges. We have no intention of executing anyone today. I chose the death penalty to put more pressure on Medwin. Perhaps I chose wrongly. I will not allow an innocent man to die."

David took precautions in case Medwin was attempting to bring back a rescue party. He changed things up a bit this time though. He put Marissa and Jake in the shuttle and Lazaro on the bridge manning the scanners. This particular trip, Thane, Aulani, and Cheyenne had spent a lot of time inside the ship. Their time here on Medoris was getting close to being done, and he didn't want them to get space sick or claustrophobic once they were back in space.

Clouds began to move in and get heavier. It was still at least an hour until sunset, but Tarin knew everyone needed to get to shelter. The area under the *Evangeline* and inside the Sorley tent wasn't going to be enough to protect everyone from the elements. Tarin knew he needed to finish the matter even if it wasn't sunset. He had Cashel and Kasen's three men placed inside the fire circle and lit the fire. He did so more to get everyone's attention focused on the seriousness of the situation. The archers stood armed and ready outside the circle. Tarin commanded the attention of everyone present.

"As a condition of our alliance with the Commonwealth and our alliance with each other, all slaves of the Sorley, Akamu, and Kimbra are free. For those of you who were taken from distant cities, the Sorley will help you return if you wish. If you wish to remain here, the Kimbra and the Akamu will make places for you to live. The choice is yours. You are free.

"Another condition of our alliance is there will be a system of justice holding every man and woman under accountability. No matter what his or her rank or station is, everyone will receive justice. That is why we are here now. A grave crime was committed against Auryon and Jabre, and a price must be paid."

As Tarin continued to address the crowd, David got a message from Lazaro. Three riders were coming in fast from the direction of the hive cities. David advised Lazaro to keep scanning all directions. He wanted to make sure this wasn't a diversion. He seriously hoped it was Medwin returning to face the music. David passed the information on to Brynna discreetly then went back to listening to Tarin.

"This punishment was agreed upon by the council, but it is NOT JUST. There is doubt to the actual guilt of Cashel. Can anyone here add to what has already been spoken?"

Brynna shifted nervously. She knew her hand was about to be forced. David sensed her tension and whispered, "Try to stall until those riders get here. Maybe whoever is coming can end this without you testifying."

No one stepped forward to give any further information. The men in the fire ring, except Cashel looked nervously at each other. They were silently hoping somebody would say something. Tarin's eyes searched the crowd. He was looking for any sign that someone wanted to speak or was hiding something. His eyes finally landed on Brynna. Just as he was about to call out her name, Auryon spoke up "Wait, please. I know Medwin was the one who made the deal with Malek, but I cannot believe Cashel forced him to do so. Are there not any who witnessed this? Were any of his servants present? Can Medwin confirm this? Cashel never seemed to mind my relationship with Jabre."

Cashel raised his head when he heard Auryon speak. Hearing her questions, he shouted to Tarin. "There were no witnesses. No one was with us. My confession should be enough for you. Get this over with."

Jabre looked at Auryon. "I was so angry when I found out we had been betrayed I was ready to kill whoever did this with my bare hands, but I agree. This is not right. I have served Cashel nearly all my life. I do not think he is capable of this." Jabre turned to Tarin and called out to him. "Tarin, may I withdraw my charges?"

Tarin shook his head. "It is too late for that."

Jabre glanced down at Auryon. "Then may we, who were the injured parties, ask for leniency? We are concerned justice will not be served with Cashel's death."

Tarin glanced up to where he had seen Brynna standing. She was no longer standing there. He searched the crowd for her again. Brynna slipped up behind Kasen and told him about the approaching riders. She asked him to try and stall until the riders arrived.

Kasen stepped forward. "Tarin, do what you want with Cashel. He no longer concerns me, but those three deserve punishment now if they can be of no further use. Archers! Ready your bows and take aim at Malek, Tolem, and Damar!"

Tarin was caught off guard by Kasen's apparent impatience. He wasn't sure if he should intervene or not. The three men weren't under his jurisdiction, but he might need them.

Malek, obviously troubled, fidgeted nervously and begged Kasen for mercy. "Kasen, please don't do this. I am your kinsman. I am loyal to you. We are all loyal to you. Have we not proven it many times over? We sought to end the fights between our people and the Kimbra. That's why we made the deal with Medwin for Auryon."

Kasen moved to the edge of the fire circle. Tarin tried to discourage him, but he lacked the motivating force because of the questionable nature of the situation. Kasen continued his verbal assault on the men. "You broke your deal with Cashel and Medwin! Archers! Take aim!"

Malek stood there a moment and replayed Kasen's last sentence in his mind again. The Sorley archers had done as Kasen ordered and were standing with bows drawn and aimed at the three men. They were waiting and listening very carefully for the command to fire. Malek looked up at Kasen and finally responded. "Kasen! Our original deal was made with Cashel and Medwin both, but Medwin came to us with just two guards when he offered us Jabre. He said she would agree to marry me if we got rid of Jabre. It was only Medwin, not Cashel! He said Cashel didn't know about this, and we shouldn't mention it to him. When we found Auryon with Jabre we thought Medwin was giving her to us. We didn't know she wasn't supposed to be there. Kasen! Please!"

Tolem and Damar jumped in. "Kasen, he speaks the truth!" Kasen raised his arm to order the archers to fire their arrows. He looked at each man's face carefully. He was looking for any signs they were holding anything back from him. Each man now had a look of resignation on his faces.

Cashel was now worried again about his brother. He called out again. "I already told you. I ordered Medwin to keep my name out of it. I knew about it. Medwin was following my orders!" The crowd around stood there silently waiting for Kasen's decision.

Malek and his two companions steeled themselves for the inevitable. They were not tied to anything and could have moved around the ring, but they knew it only meant a slower more painful death. They remained as still as possible despite their fight or flight instincts. Time seemed to be suspended as everyone held their breath, waiting for the arrows to be released from their suspension.

A voice rang out from the edge of the grounds, "Stop! Archers! Stand down!"

Tarin looked to see Medwin and two riders approaching. He turned to the archers. "Archers! Stand down!" The archers glanced nervously at Kasen who nodded at them to lower their weapons.

Cashel, upon seeing Medwin, called out again. "Medwin! Don't do this! Tarin, you have my confession. Nothing else is needed! Get on with this! Please, Tarin!"

Tarin glanced at Cashel then looked at Medwin and his two companions. Medwin had gotten close enough now to get off his stolen horse and walk up to Tarin. "I thought I had until sunset, Tarin."

Tarin looked up at the sky. "There's a storm coming in. It looks to be a bad one. We need to seek shelter. If you have something that will change this outcome, say it quickly."

Before Medwin could speak, Cashel jumped in again. "Medwin, this matter is settled! Say nothing else!" Medwin glanced at his brother. For the first time, Cashel had a look of fear on his face. Tarin took Medwin and the other council members away from the fire ring. The group reassembled under the ship.

The four men were stuck in the fire ring until the fire burned down. Kasen had the archers begin digging up dirt to throw on the fire later. He knew this was about to be over. The archers also stood guard over the four men to make sure they didn't do anything foolish. Kasen then moved over to the edge of the ship to hear what was about to transpire.

Once everyone was in place, Tarin moved quickly to get things moving. "Start talking, Lord Master Medwin. What do you have to add?"

Medwin had resolved himself to Cashel's fate and taking responsibility for what he had done. "Cashel lied to you. He knew nothing of my plan to have Jabre killed. These two men can testify they accompanied me when I met with Malek, Tolem, and Damar.

They can also tell you I ordered them not to speak of this to anyone."

Tarin looked at the two men. "Why should I trust that these two men have not been bribed or forced by you just to save your brother?"

Medwin hadn't really thought that far and was not sure how to answer. After a moment of thought, he continued. "And how do you know Cashel speaks the truth? His punishment is mine and mine alone. You have the testimony of Malek and the others that I alone spoke to him. Now you have my confession. I alone am responsible and these two witnesses who will agree with me. I ask you to release Cashel and punish me instead."

Tarin wasn't going to be persuaded easily. "Why would you do such a thing to your own sister?"

"Auryon was young and foolish. She allowed herself to fall for a man whose station was below her own. She could never marry him. She would not even consider a noble marriage. It was a disgrace to her station, her family, and to herself. Jabre should have known better and discouraged her, but he was no better. It turned my stomach. I didn't know Auryon would be with Jabre that day. My intention was to get Jabre away from her. I didn't care whether they took him as a slave or killed him. I just wanted him out of her life. I never meant for this to happen to Auryon." Medwin looked over at Auryon. "Auryon, I am so sorry. I know there is nothing I can do to make up for all of this. I hope someday you can forgive me, even if I am not here to know it."

Tarin had determined early on Medwin was guilty, but he wanted to be sure all deceit was now gone. "Why have you waited until now to tell us this?"

Medwin hung his head in shame. "I didn't think we would be found guilty. I thought I could escape from being found out. I also didn't know Cashel would take the blame for me. I guess I didn't realize what was at stake until it was too late. I'm sorry I didn't say anything sooner and take responsibility for what I had done. I am ready to face my punishment."

Tarin motioned to two of his warriors to step forward. "Take him to the far side of the grounds and hold him there. I want to talk to these two witnesses without him."

As soon as Medwin was out of earshot, Tarin started to question the two men. "Before I ask you two anything about Medwin, answer this question for me. Do you two have families? Wives, children, parents, brothers, or sisters?"

The two men looked confused, but each man nodded. "Yes, Lord Tarin."

Tarin was just as hard of a leader as Kasen only more straightforward. "Then let me be perfectly clear. If you lie to me, if I even think you have lied to me, I will have your families dragged out of the Kimbra cities and thrown into that fire ring. I will throw everyone from the oldest, sickest grandparent to the youngest child in there where they will be stoned to death if you lie to me even once. If you think I can't get to them because of your new walls, you are mistaken. I will send Jabre to retrieve them for me. He will tell them a lie they will believe and gladly follow him willingly out of the city where my men will take them captive. Do you understand?"

The two men looked shocked, but each agreed to speak only the truth. Tarin questioned them rapidly. He accepted each of their testimonies, then threw a barrage of rapid-fire questions at them, and even repeated some of his questions. He wanted to be sure they had not been coached by Medwin. The two men passed Tarin's test confirming Medwin's story. They included testimony of Medwin's angry rants about his sister's indiscretions and Cashel's weaknesses in dealing with them. The two men were escorted out to the fire ring where Malek, Tolem, and Damar also confirmed the two men had been with Medwin the day he had told Malek where Jabre would be.

Once Tarin was satisfied the two men were telling the truth, he asked Brynna for someplace private the council could go to deliberate. Brynna escorted them to the dining hall and shut the door so they could have privacy. It took about thirty minutes for them to reach a consensus. It took them another few minutes to figure out how to get the door open again so they could get out. Fortunately, Brynna had posted Manton outside the entrance, and when he heard them start pounding on the door, he opened it for them.

Before the group retired to the dining hall, Tarin asked Kasen to get the four men out of the fire ring. Jake and Marissa were relieved of their duty on the shuttle and returned to guard duty on the grounds. Once David saw that Medwin was only bringing two men with him, he had them stand down. Lazaro was still on the bridge watching the scanners to be sure that a late war party didn't show up. Jake and the other crewmen helped put out a section of the already dying fire and threw dirt over it to create a walking path. Kasen's men were happy to be able to walk out of the circle under their own power. Cashel was less than happy. He didn't want to die, but he didn't want his brother to die either.

The group reassembled under the *Evangeline*. The storm was nearly on them at this point. David sent Jake to pull the shuttle out of the shuttle bay so both the shuttle and the bay could be used to house people when the storm hit. The other crewmen started rolling the sides of the tent down and anchoring them into place. David had the crew move people into shelter in the gym, cargo bay, and shuttle bay. The shuttle itself could be used as a last resort. The Surf-Ve was pulled out to make room for more people. Anything that couldn't be fastened down was stowed away aboard the ship.

Tarin called the meeting to order. He had Cashel and Medwin stand before the judges' council. He didn't take the harsh tone he had used earlier and spoke to Cashel. "Lord Master Cashel, we have testimonies that now tell us it was your brother Medwin, and him alone, who is responsible for this crime against Auryon and Jabre. The testimonies include Medwin's own confession. Medwin has also shown remorse for his actions. Did you claim responsibility for this just to spare your brother's life?"

Cashel stood there silently, refusing to answer. He was at a loss for what the best course of action now was, so he chose to say and do nothing.

Tarin tried one more time. He didn't want to be aggressive with his tactics, but he would if that was what it took. "Cashel, nothing can be gained from your silence or from you taking blame that is not yours. You are the Lord Master of Primus, speak the truth."

Cashel raised his head to meet Tarin's gaze. He wet his dry lips and slowly admitted his lie. "I did not want both of us to die, so I admitted guilt. I knew nothing of Medwin's plan to get rid of

Jabre. I did know he didn't approve, but I didn't know he was capable of such treachery."

Tarin quickly located Brynna and called her forward. "Commander Alexander, I believe you have testimony regarding this case."

Brynna was caught off-guard. Testimonies were supposed to be held before deliberations not after. She stepped forward and tried to find a way out of it but was not successful. "Tarin, I was not here to see any of these events years ago."

Tarin knew why she was being evasive. He gave her a certain amount of leniency, so her word would still be honored. "How many people have confided in you about these events?"

Brynna was grateful for his straightforward approach. She wanted very much to say what she knew, but she couldn't in good conscience volunteer it. "Three."

"And were those three Jabre, Auryon and Cashel?" Tarin wasn't about to beat around the bush anymore. The wind had picked up and the air smelled of rain. Thunder and lightning were rolling closer with each passing moment.

"Yes, Tarin. Those are the three who spoke to me about the events of six years ago. Before you ask, the conversation you want to know about is a private conversation I had with Cashel yesterday. He was glad to know his sister was returning, and he told me he knew about and approved of the relationship between Jabre and Auryon. He said, as Lord Master he could make it right, even though it wasn't."

Tarin asked just one more question. "Did you believe him?"

Brynna looked over at Cashel. "I have not known him for very long, but yes, I believe he spoke the truth."

Lord Broona interrupted. "How do you know when Cashel heard of his sister's return, he didn't have that conversation with you to hide his guilt over ordering Medwin to betray Jabre six years ago?"

Lord Ayele seconded Broona. "He makes a good point. How do you know Cashel didn't orchestrate all of this including Medwin's witnesses?"

The looks on Cashel and Medwin's faces were a mixture of shock and anger. They now knew for a fact that Broona and Ayele were not trustworthy.

Brynna also picked up on the fact the men were not to be trusted and since they had posed the questions, albeit rhetorically, she answered. "Cashel had no way of knowing Auryon's scars would be healed so she could appear publicly. We kept that information from him and Medwin. They also did not know we would call him into account for something occurring six years ago. Also, if he disapproved, why save Jabre's life? His innocence is plain to see."

Tarin turned to the judges' council, and they whispered quietly for a moment. Lord Broona and Lord Ayele didn't seem happy, but they appeared to acquiesce. Tarin stood and faced the two men. Brynna retreated from the circle and went to stand near David who was carefully watching the weather yet listening to the proceedings. Tarin gave the judge's decision. "Lord Master Cashel, this council believes you to be innocent of the crimes brought out today. We no longer hold you accountable. You are a free man. Lord Master Medwin, this council finds you are guilty of these crimes and no longer fit to rule over the Kimbra. Cashel, you are to find another who is fit to lead and put him in the place of Medwin to rule over Corvan. Lord Master Cashel, can you do this?"

Cashel nodded sadly. "I will turn his holdings over to Jabre and Auryon. It is the least I can do for them after the treachery he committed against them."

The rain was starting to fall, so Tarin cut it even shorter. "Good, then justice has been served. Let us get to shelter."

Medwin and Cashel both looked confused. "Tarin, wait. We don't understand. What about Medwin's execution?"

Tarin dismissed everyone to get out of the weather and walked over to the two confused men. "The council never agreed to execute you, Cashel. We knew early on you were confessing just to protect Medwin. We only gave you a death sentence to put pressure on Medwin to confess. No one died as a direct result of Medwin's actions, so death is too strong of a punishment. You may do what you want with Medwin, but he is not to rule over others. He must be placed in a position of servitude. He cost Auryon six years of her life. No one knows what she suffered at the hands of Malek, but her. He needs to understand some of her pain. After six years, he can be returned to a leader's role, but not over the people of Corvan. Do you understand now?" The two men still seemed to be in shock. Tarin went on to explain a little further. "Cashel, we decided on Medwin's punishment based on your order to turn all you owned over to Jabre and Auryon. That seemed appropriate for Medwin. You saw your own execution as your punishment, but you tried to make restitution by giving your property and position to Jabre and Auryon. Medwin confessed also believing execution was his punishment, so we gave him the same punishment you gave yourself."

Cashel seemed to understand, but Medwin still looked stunned. When the realization began to hit him, he looked at Cashel. "Cashel, what will I tell my family?" Cashel hesitated before answering. "I don't know yet, but we will figure it out."

Tarin stepped closer to Cashel and Medwin so as not to be overheard. "By the way, you need to do something about Broona and Ayele. Those two are dangerous men."

Cashel nodded. "I agree. I think Medwin had an idea I might use."

"What idea?" Tarin queried.

"We need ambassadors from the Kimbra to go live among your people and the Sorley. I can split them up and send one to you and one to Kasen."

"You want to give us your problems?"

Cashel's smooth politician's tongue began to put a polished spin on his idea. "If I split them up and send them away, they lose their allies. I also think perhaps you and Kasen are leaders who are better equipped to keep them under control than I am. After all, I have allowed a travesty of justice to occur within my own household."

Tarin grinned and walked away. He didn't like being out in the open during a storm. Kasen and his people were more comfortable in the tent. Cashel and Medwin followed Tarin aboard the ship. The crew secured the extra tables and chairs in the cargo bay, and the horses were tethered to the landing struts, which gave them a small amount of shelter. David kept Lazaro on the bridge monitoring the storm. He had Jake keep a close eye on the tent. He tried to convince Kasen and the others to come aboard the ship, but they insisted they would be fine.

DISASTER

The storm continued to worsen. As the sun's light faded from the sky, bright lightning kept the sky lit up. Lazaro suddenly made a blanket call to all ship's personnel although he addressed the Captain. "Captain! We've got a funnel cloud forming directly four miles southwest of here. It's headed this way."

In turn, the captain started issuing orders. "Thane, get aboard the shuttle and get it out of the storm. Keep whatever passengers you have on board. Aulani, go with him to help secure the passengers. Jake, get the Surf-Ve under the belly of the ship. Braxton, get ready to activate the ship's shields. Doc, you and Laura prepare for patients with fresh injuries. Brynna, you have the bridge. Manton, get those horses under the ship or turn them loose. Vesta, direct Kasen's people where to go when they reach the ship, Marissa, Lexi, and Cheyenne, you help me get those people out of the tent and into the ship." The crew had no time to don rain gear. The funnel cloud could be on them in less than four minutes, or it could dissipate and never get there. Tarin and some of the Akamu warriors picked up that something was wrong and quickly asked Vesta what she knew. As soon as they heard what was happening, they followed the crew out to the tent to help get people inside the ship.

David led the charge into the tent. He burst through two of the flaps. "Kasen, we have to get these people into the ship! There's a tornado coming!" Kasen had to wait for, what seemed to David, to be an interminably long time for the translation to go through and Kasen to understand him. As soon as it came through, Kasen drew his dagger and took several long fast steps to the side of the tent facing the ship. In two quick moves, he sliced a large "X" into the wall. He ordered everyone to the ship. Tharen grabbed the closest people to him, pulled them abruptly to their feet, and pushed them toward the new opening. David and the crew followed suit. Cheyenne helped a young mother with her two small children. Most were able-bodied adults, but some in the crowd were elderly, some were very young, and some were injured who were here to see if Jason could help them. Lexi grabbed another two children by their hands and pulled them hastily toward the ship. David grabbed the arm of an elderly man with a cane and helped him. The other strong, able-bodied men followed the crew's example. Marissa picked up a little girl whose big brown eyes reminded her of the little girl she held on her lap on the shuttle ride on Galat. The girl was a little older. When Marissa started to whisk her away, she started to scream and cry. She was reaching for something over Marissa's shoulder. The child suddenly twisted out of her grasp and hit the ground running away from the ship. Marissa turned to run after the child. She found the child now clutching a hand-sewn doll. Marissa grabbed the child again and ran for the tent opening. The wind speeds picked up so much Marissa was now having trouble navigating her way to the ship. David was standing at the bottom of the steps helping people climb up into the ship. Jake had secured the Surf-Ve and helped Manton with the horses. As soon as the horses were secure, he headed to move the last remaining people into the ship. He saw Marissa struggling against the wind and rain and ran to help her. Hail began to form and started pelting the ground. The hail started about the size of a pea but quickly grew much larger. Jake grabbed his portable shield from his belt and held the shield over the three of them. Marissa was struggling so badly to walk and hold the child; she placed the child in Jake's free arm. Jake yelled over the howling winds. "Stay right on my six. Don't fall behind!" Marissa gave a quick "Got it!" She grabbed the back of his shirt and hung on tightly.

Brynna was anticipating needing the shields to surround the ship quickly. She ordered Braxton to configure the shield to cover the top and as much of the sides of the *Evangeline* as possible. She waited for David to give the signal to close the shield completely.

Jake and Marissa were the last ones to reach the ship. David ducked under the steps for protection while he waited for Jake and Marissa to reach him. Jake kept his eyes glued to his destination.

It was taking all his strength to hold onto his portable shield, the child and walk toward the ship. If the wind caught his shield the wrong way, it could easily break Jake's arm. Marissa looked up and saw the tornado was nearly on them. She slipped in the mud and lost her grip on Jake's shirt. Jake was just two steps away from the stairs. He turned to go back for her. David jumped from behind the steps to the protection of Jake's shield and hollered. "Get the child inside, I'll get Marissa."

Marissa was hit by a fist-sized ball of hail and was now fighting her own pain as well as the slick mud and harsh wind. She managed to get to her feet and staggered back toward the ship when swirling debris struck her again and knocked her to the ground. David dove for her hand. He managed to grasp her forearm and pulled her toward the ship. He grabbed the stair handrail and wrapped his arm around it for security. In his ear, he could hear Brynna calling out. "Captain, I need to close the shield! Are you and Marissa clear? Captain, please respond!"

David managed to give her a quick, "Stand by!" He and Marissa were struggling right in line with where the shield would form. David continued to pull Marissa toward him, but the funnel was so close, he was having trouble pulling against it. The two of them were now soaking wet and covered in mud. David felt Marissa losing her grip on his arm. "Marissa! Hold onto me! DO NOT LET GO!" Another fist-sized chunk of hail hit Marissa in the head. David felt her hand and arm go limp as she lost consciousness. The wind was now lifting the lightweight lieutenant off the ground. David felt the urge to panic, but quickly recognized it for what it was and squelched it. He tried calling out to her to rouse her. "Lieutenant! Marissa! Wake up! I can't hold you like this!"

Jake dropped the child inside the door and raced back down the steps to help his wife and the captain. Just as he neared the bottom of the steps, another chunk of ice hit David's arm. A groan of pain forced its way out of his mouth, and David lost what little grip he had left. The funnel grabbed Marissa and whisked her quickly away. David called out, "No! Marissa!"

The captain let go of his grip on the rail and started to launch himself in the general direction he had seen Marissa disappear. Jake jumped faster. He grabbed onto the captain and rolled the two of them under the ship. Jake tapped his comm unit and yelled. "Close the shield! We're clear!"

A second later the shield came down to the ground blocking the wind, rain, and hail. Jake released his grip on the captain and pulled himself into a sitting position. He sat there staring at the ground. David didn't like losing. He jumped to his feet. He paced back and forth along the edge of the shield like a caged lion. He watched the swirling wind and debris looking for some indication of where Marissa was. As the storm roared around them, it caused the ship to rock and groan, despite its size and the protection of the shield. Seeing a small chunk of hail lying on the ground, he angrily kicked it. He looked down at Jake. The captain touched his comm unit. "Commander, I need you to track Lt. Holden's comm unit. Keep track of its every move."

Brynna started to question the order but thought better of it. She quickly acknowledged him and did as she was ordered. She watched the signal from the comm unit spin, spiral and twist, and then it went dead. Brynna marked the exact track and continued to mark the tornado's track after the comm unit went dead.

When Jake heard David's order, he looked up at David appreciatively. "Captain, thanks for trying to save her." It didn't make David feel any better to know Jake wasn't blaming him.

David was busy enough blaming himself. "Jake, why did you stop me from going after her?"

Jake rolled his eyes. He was hurting thinking about his wife, but the captain's question was so ridiculous, it bordered on being laughable. "Captain, I have a lot of confidence in you, but I seriously doubt you can hold your own against a tornado. Marissa was already gone. There was nothing more you could do."

David paced back and forth still mentally kicking himself. "Jake, I'm so sorry. I failed you, and I failed her."

Jake finally stood up. He walked up to the captain. He was afraid to make eye contact with David. As a crew member, they were taught there was a time and place to give in to their emotions and how to compartmentalize just long enough to get their jobs done. Jake was afraid if he looked David in the eye, he might lose what little control he had. His eyes finally made contact. "Captain, it wasn't your fault. It was just circumstances."

David put his hand on Jake's shoulder. "Jake, I really am sorry. Please let me know if you need anything. I need to get inside and start tracking her signal. Take whatever time you need."

David went up the stairs into the ship. He headed to his quarters for a quick shower and change of uniform. He touched his comm unit to let Brynna know where he was headed. Fifteen minutes later, David stepped onto the bridge. The look on Brynna's face when she saw him said more than he wanted to hear. Brynna stood up to give him a full report, but just she was about to speak, Jake stepped onto the bridge. David glanced up at him. "Are you ready for this?"

Jake appeared calm but preoccupied. He nodded at David and Brynna, "I'm fine."

Brynna had the forethought to have Lexi on the bridge. Lexi kept her distance from Jake for the moment but carefully watched him. David turned back to Brynna. "Commander, report."

Brynna nodded and updated him as ordered. "Captain, we kept track of the Lieutenant's comm unit until the unit stopped functioning. The computer has continued to analyze the storms course speed and pattern. We can track her comm unit well beyond its functionality. The one problem is, we don't know if she's still wearing it or not. Weather forecasts indicate the funnel cloud will dissipate in the next few minutes and the rest of the storm will be out of the area within the hour."

David looked at the storm path on Brynna's computer screen. "As soon as the shuttle returns, we can start sending out search parties. Put me on shipwide comms and tie in the translator."

Brynna pressed the appropriate buttons on her console then looked back at David. "You're on."

"Attention all crew and guests! This is Captain David Alexander. The ship has one crew member lost in the storm. We will start a search and rescue mission within one hour. Any help would be greatly appreciated."

The captain turned around to face Jake. "Chief, are you fit for duty?" Jake was sitting down in one of the seats on the bridge and leaned over with his face buried in his hands. When the captain interrupted his thoughts, it took a second to process what he was being asked. Jake did a mental assessment of his own well-being before answering.

In a second, he looked up at the captain and gave a firm, "Yes sir!"

Lexi had been standing next to Jake with her hand gently on his shoulder. As soon as she heard the question, alarm bells began to go off in her head. "Captain, may I speak to you for a moment? It's important."

David looked at her and knew exactly what she was going to say. He also already knew how he was going to answer her, but decided it was best to at least go through the motions. He stood up quickly and said, "My office."

As David disappeared through the doorway, Brynna hastily grabbed Lexi's arm. "Don't push him. He knows what he's doing and now isn't the time to push."

Lexi glanced back at Jake who still sat slumped over in his chair. "That's what I'm afraid of. He's pushing Jake too much."

Brynna gave Lexi a wry smile. "I was talking about David, not Jake." Lexi walked on into the captain's office feeling slightly confused and trying to put Brynna's comment into the correct context.

David was in a hurry to get organized for the search and rescue mission, so his patience was limited. "State your case Lt. Flint." The captain had reverted back to rank and names to set the appropriate tone for this part of the mission and for their impending conversation.

Lexi hesitated for a split second as Brynna's comments fell into perspective. "Captain, I feel like you already have your mind made up about this, but I'm not sure Jake is fit for duty right now. He needs to be a grieving husband, not a security chief."

David tried not to respond too quickly, but he felt like this conversation was a colossal waste of time since he had indeed already made up his mind, as Lexi suggested. "Lieutenant, I appreciate your concerns, really I do, but you're right. My mind is already made up. This job is as much a part of Jake's life as his wife is. If I take both away from him, he has nothing left. When we find her, he can be her husband, but right now, he and I both need him to be the security chief. Do you even think for a second, he's going to sit still in this ship and not go out there and look for her? I would, however, appreciate it if you could stay close and let me know if this becomes too much for him. I don't expect him to be a hundred percent, but if he goes too far down, I'll ground him."

Lexi stood there, dumbfounded. "Captain, why did we even have this conversation? I'm not sure if you can call it a conversation."

David felt his impatience nearing its limits. "First, you asked for it. Second, I need you to know I value your input. Third, I also need you to know I am fully aware of the situation. I know Jake's state of mind is questionable. I plan on giving him things that don't require more than the most simplistic levels of thought, nothing complex. It will be enough to keep him active. For now, I'm the security chief, not Jake. Is there anything else?"

Lexi shook her head. "No, sir, that covers it." She was also grateful he hadn't bitten her head off. She sensed if she had said anything more, that it was a definite risk.

David stood up from his desk and headed toward the bridge. "Good, we've got work to do."

David stepped onto the bridge and Brynna called out. "Captain on the bridge!" Jake and Lazaro snapped to attention.

David glanced appreciatively at Brynna, "As you were. Chief, I need you to find Kasen, Tarin, and Cashel. Ask them who, among their people who are present, might be able to help us search. Jake, we're just looking for volunteers, so don't pressure them, just ask them how much help they can offer. Also, tell them we will meet in the dining hall in a few minutes to discuss search patterns. I just need search leaders, not everyone, because the dining hall can't hold that many. If we have people in there, we will need to relocate them elsewhere. Questions?"

Jake shook his head. "No, sir." He headed off to do as he was told. Lexi followed after him. Jake knew why and even though they didn't speak, her presence was appreciated.

David looked back to Brynna and Lazaro. He started to point at the map with his right arm, but where the hail had hit it was still hurting, so he switched arms. He pulled his right arm in close to his body as a reminder to himself not to use it. With his left arm, he indicated where he wanted to start searching. He also wanted one crew member with a comm unit with every group. The search would start about a hundred yards before her comm unit went dead and spread out a hundred yards on either side of the tornado's path. He told Brynna to forward the map and data to the dining hall. He gave Lazaro the responsibilities of coordinating the search teams from the ship and seeing to the needs of the refugees who would be staying on board the ship. He left Cheyenne and Vesta to assist him. Once the shuttle returned, they would need to get the passengers off and load it with equipment for doing search and rescue. David, Lazaro, and Brynna discussed the best way to deploy their assets for the most widespread coverage of comm units, scanners, lanterns, medical equipment, and other necessary items. David assigned Thane to pilot the shuttle and Jason to accompany him. He put Jake, Laura, and Lexi in the Surf-Ve to follow the path of the tornado. He split the rest of the crew up to travel down the right and left sides of the tornado's path. David and Brynna planned to lead the ground teams on one side of the path, and Braxton and Aulani would take the other side.

David and Brynna left the bridge and headed to the dining hall. Lazaro contacted the shuttle to update Thane and Aulani on what was happening and gave them their orders once they returned to the ship. The two were clearly rattled when Lazaro gave them the news Marissa had gone missing and had quite probably not survived the storm.

Just before David and Brynna entered the dining hall, Brynna reached out and stopped him. "David, what happened out there?"

"We can talk about it later. We've got to get this search and rescue organized."

Brynna wasn't going to be put off that easily. "Captain, we can't get started until the shuttle returns, and I need to know how this is affecting you."

David was expecting this, but he was hoping to avoid it until later. He started pacing again, which gave Brynna her first clue to his state of mind. "I know I need to talk about this, and I will, but I'd rather stay busy for now and not think about it. The short version is I sent one of my crew members on a mission, and it has probably gotten her killed. I was trying to pull her to safety. We got hit with some hail, and I couldn't hang onto her. Yes, it was my fault."

Brynna's eyes narrowed. "How many lives were saved?"

David looked annoyed again. "What?"

"You heard me. You went out there to save lives. How many lives would have been lost if you hadn't sent her out there?"

"I don't know. I didn't count. If we hadn't gone out there, all of Kasen's people might have been killed. Marissa was carrying a small child when she reached the ship."

"David, you know as well as I do you can't win them all. Yes, you are the captain. Your decision and its consequences rest on you, but this is not an issue of fault. Kasen's people have you to thank for not losing their leaders. You made the right call. I know it hurts to lose someone, but you have to move forward. This crew doesn't need you to put up walls and keep them out. We're not just co-workers. We're family. Don't be afraid to show both pain and strength."

Instinctively, David raised his right hand to reach for Brynna's and when he felt another twinge of pain. He turned away slightly so hopefully she wouldn't see him wince, or if she did maybe she would think it was mental, not physical. In a moment, he turned back to her and reached up with his left instead and gave her hand a quick squeeze. He hoped she hadn't noticed he had switched hands. He really didn't want to take the time to have Jason look at it right now. He would gladly let him look at it after they found Marissa. "Brynna, I will take the appropriate time to grieve. I promise. I also promise not to take anyone's head off in the meantime. Fair enough?" Brynna was just about to respond to him when David's comm unit sounded and interrupted her.

Lazaro hailed the captain to let him know the storm had finally settled down, and the final coordinates would be on the map when they displayed it. David acknowledged the message as Thane and Aulani walked up. David moved on into the dining hall before he had to answer any more unpleasant questions. He motioned for Brynna to take over the computer station. In the room waiting for them were Tarin, Manton, Kasen, Tharen, Cashel, Medwin, and Jabre along with the rest of the crew. David showed the group Marissa's picture and briefly told them what had happened to her. He showed them the map and described their intended search patterns. Jake reported that despite the large number of people on board, only twenty to thirty were able-bodied men or women capable of helping with the search. The search team would have crew members with a comm unit evenly interspersed between them, so help would never be more than a few yards away. The crew would also have the benefit of scanners, which could help with the search. The captain had Kasen, Tarin, and Cashel organize their people to put together what horses and torches they could come up with, while his people loaded the shuttle and Surf-Ve with medical and debris removal equipment. David gave one last warning about the dangers of the storm damage. He didn't want anyone else getting hurt.

Twenty minutes later, everyone was ready to move out. David and Brynna went through the airlock and stopped at the top of the steps. The place where the tent and tables had been, was totally empty except for splinters of wood and tree branches. There was no sign of the tent, only empty postholes where the tent poles had been. Kasen emerged behind them and looked at the area. He gave David a look, showing just how thankful he was to be alive. "Captain Alexander, you saved my life and the lives of several of my people. We owe you a great debt."

David would like to have offered Kasen a smile, but he couldn't muster one right now. "Kasen, we are allies and friends now. I couldn't let anything happen to you or your people. I am glad we were able to save your people."

A look of sorrow crossed Kasen's face. "I am sorry it has cost you one of your own to save my people." David thanked him for his sentiment and got busy again.

The shuttle and Surf-Ve were loaded up with those going on the search and rescue mission. David reserved the shuttle for those who were accustomed to the sensation of flight, namely the crew, including Manton, Kasen, Tharen, and a few others Kasen vouched for. The others were on horseback or in the Surf-Ve.

The three groups departed for the rendezvous point. The shuttle made the first pass to look out for obstacles and to identify a landing site. The area was still rather wide open, but the further northeast the more trees there were. The ground also became steeper as you moved into the hills and mountains.

The shuttle found a good place to land. While the passengers were unloading, Thane linked to the Surf-Ve and let the others know what sort of terrain and obstacles they were dealing with. David attempted to help with the unloading, but his arm, wrist, and hand were beginning to swell, and he was having more trouble dealing with it. Jason caught sight of David cradling his arm as he walked away. The Doc grabbed a scanner and med kit and chased after David.

When Jason caught up to him, David was noticeably pale, even in such poor light. "Captain? Want to tell me what's going on?"

David turned toward the Doc's voice. He immediately saw the med kit in his hand, and he knew his secret was out. "Sorry Doc, I thought it wasn't that bad. I thought I could keep going for a little longer. I just wanted to find Marissa first."

Jason pulled a scanner from his kit. "Let me see what I can do for you to keep you in the game for now. How did this happen?"

"I got hit with a large chunk of hail. It's why I lost my grip on Marissa."

Jason looked at the diagnosis on his display. "My word, Captain, it's a wonder you're still functioning at all. You've got numerous fractures in your hand and wrist, not to mention the soft tissue damage. I can give you something for the pain and swelling, but I need to immobilize it until I can treat it completely. It's no wonder you lost your grip on Marissa. That chunk of ice nearly crushed your hand." David pulled his jacket off to give Jason more room to work. Jason quickly put a splint on David's hand and wrist, and then secured it by placing it across his chest and wrapping a bandage around it and his torso. Jason dosed him with the medication he promised, then helped David put his jacket back on over his left arm and hung the right sleeve over his right shoulder.

By the time they were done, the Surf-Ve had arrived and unloaded the passengers. David gave one last set of instructions and divided the ground team members out and started them on their way. Jason got back aboard the shuttle. The shuttle crew made passes to warn the Surf-Ve of upcoming debris, which might need to be circumvented. They also used the spotlights and lasers on dense debris. The group searched through the night covering nearly a twenty-mile stretch. They took two brief breaks to get something to eat and rest a few minutes.

Laura had joined the ground crew during the night. As the sun started to rise in the early morning, she picked up something on her scanner. The scanner was programmed to scan for the refined metals found in Marissa's uniform in addition to scanning for human life signs. The thing that was disturbing her most was that nothing showed up on the human life signs. She already knew the chances of finding Marissa alive were small, but she was still holding onto some small amount of hope. She didn't want to get Jake's attention until she had something definite to report. Kasen and Tharen were closest to her, so she enlisted their help to search the pile of debris.

David saw the three converge on the pile. He didn't move any closer but kept his eyes on them. Since they were nearing the end of their search grid and the point where the funnel cloud dissipated, their chances of finding her were going up. Their chances of finding her alive were going down in an inversely proportional manner. The further the funnel had carried her, the greater her chances were for life-threatening injuries. It also meant it would take longer for the crew to find her and treat her injuries.

When Laura and the others reached the debris pile. Laura could see a body underneath the pile of trees, and her heart sank, as she couldn't confirm any life signs. She also couldn't confirm it was Marissa. Laura discreetly called for the shuttle to cut away some of the debris. Groups had done the same thing throughout the night, so she hoped it wouldn't get Jake's attention just yet. Laura got on a private line with Jason and asked him to have Thane bring the shuttle low enough for him to jump off. She told him what she knew so far. Laura repeated the message via a private comm link with the captain. David told her to call him as soon as she could confirm they had found Marissa. David sent a couple more men to help with the debris removal. Jake had already passed the debris field Laura was working on, so his attention was focused in front of him.

Minutes later Laura sent a message to the captain. The body was Marissa's. They were still trying to reach her to confirm there were no life signs. Laura was still holding out hope that Marissa was too far from their scanners, although she knew deep down the scanners were better than that. David sent a private message to Jake. "Chief, I think Laura may have found her. Bring the Surf-Ve back around to Laura's location." Jake didn't bother to acknowledge the order or ask any questions. He knew the chances of her being alive were slim to none, and the flat tone of David's message didn't offer any hope either. David watched the Surf-Ve come to an abrupt stop. Jake quickly turned the vehicle around and headed toward Laura. While Jake headed for Laura's location, David passed the information on to Brynna and headed to Laura's location himself. Brynna ordered the search to come to a halt and moved everyone back toward the Surf-Ve. In the distance, she saw the shuttle land. She saw Jason slowly walking away from a pile of debris. She hadn't seen him leave the shuttle, so it took her a moment to realize they had already been working for a few minutes. Jason reached Jake and David at the same time. Jason put his hand on Jake's shoulder. Presently Jake spoke to the two men then walked by himself over to the pile of debris.

David struggled to program his comm unit one-handed. Brynna was now at his side. She looked at his immobile arm and scowled at him. This wasn't the time for a discussion about his arm or lack of communication skills, so she silently helped him program his comm unit. He sent out a message to all ship's personnel except for Jake and Marissa. "Attention all hands, the body of Lt. Marissa Holden has been found. Our thoughts are with her husband, Security Chief Jake Holden. More information will be provided as it becomes available."

The crew gathered around David and Brynna. They watched as Jake knelt down beside Marissa. Jake spent a few private moments with her. His voice could be heard as he softly talked to her lifeless body. He gently brushed her hair out of her face. Jake went from kneeling to sitting on the ground beside her. From a distance, they began to watch as he leaned over and pulled her into his arms. When the crew began to hear gentle sobs coming from Jake, they turned away to give him a little more privacy. Brynna, Aulani, and Laura were in tears. No one spoke for a long time.

Kasen approached the crew. "Captain Alexander, we are very sorry for the loss of your warrior. We would be glad to give her a warrior's funeral if you wish."

David thanked Kasen quietly. "I'll tell Jake about your offer. Our people come from different worlds, and each one has different plans for their funerals. I'll have to find out how Marissa's people want it handled. I will let her family know you would honor her this way."

Kasen nodded his understanding. The three societies all had different ways of dealing with the dead, so he had no trouble with the concept. "May we be permitted to carry her back as we would one of our own fallen warriors?" Kasen went on to explain they would place her body on a stretcher and raise it up on their shoulders and carry her all the way to the ship. David asked if he was sure he wanted to do that. It was going to be a long walk back to the ship. The two of them finally agreed on a compromise. The men would carry her onto the Surf-Ve, sit beside her for the ride back, and then carry her onto the ship. Kasen took six volunteers, and they quickly constructed a stretcher for her. Jason had a medical stretcher, but the men were adamant about doing it their own way. David took the top of the Surf-Ve down.

In a few minutes, they saw Jake emerge carrying the woman who had been his bride for only a few short months. He was no longer crying. Seeing the stretcher Kasen had prepared for her, he gently placed her body on it. No one had to explain their intentions to Jake. Thane took over driving the Surf-Ve and Jason moved to fly the shuttle back. As they loaded the two vehicles back up, Malek was over-heard asking a rather strange question. "Why does Captain Alexander not ask his gods for help? His gods restored him, why won't they heal the woman?" Jake heard the question but was in no condition to respond.

David looked at Malek. "We have no gods. The one who healed me is not my god. He is my enemy, and I never asked him to heal me."

Malek was undoubtedly not a wise man, as his actions had shown over the years. His sense of timing was quite poor. He scoffed. "An enemy who heals you against your will is not much of an enemy. If he had healed me, I would serve him as my god. If this doesn't earn your trust, what does?" After a stern look from Kasen, Malek stopped talking. Despite his lack of social graces, Malek did have a valid point.

David was sitting across from Jake during their conversation. He glanced at Jake and saw conflict displayed on his face. David leaned forward. "Jake? What about it? He said all I had to do was call his name."

Jake had been holding his head in his hands. He looked up at the captain. "Captain, as much as I want my wife back, we can't go down that road. It would be too high a price. At the very least, it's high treason."

David leaned back again. "I know. I just don't like failing, especially when this is the price of my failure." David let his mind wander. He considered the price of failure versus the cost of treason. He winced at the thought. It was his life or hers.

David sent the shuttle on ahead to the ship. The solemn procession arrived forty minutes later. The men who carried the young lieutenant were Kasen, Cashel, Tarin, Tharen, Gervas, and Jabre. They quietly carried her up the stairs into the ship. Jason directed them to the infirmary. Jake and the crew followed them in. As soon as the lieutenant's body was placed in the infirmary, her escorts moved back into the corridor. David stepped inside to talk to Jake and the Doc. He wanted to know what sort of arrangements to make for Marissa. Jake wasn't sure what Marissa would have wanted. Each of the crew had their preferences on file before they started this journey, so the information was in the computer. Jake moved over to the computer terminal and called up Marissa's file while David and Jason talked.

"Captain, no matter what her wishes are, I need to do a scan to determine the cause of death. Afterward, I can put her body in the stasis chamber until we are done here."

"That's fine. I'll ask Jake to get a clean uniform for her. I want her cleaned up. I know she wouldn't want to be seen like this. I want to have a memorial service this evening just before sunset."

"Why so quickly?" Jason was concerned David was moving too fast.

David flatly asked. "Will waiting improve the grieving process?" Jason was taken aback by the question. "I suppose not, but Jake and the rest of the crew will need more time than one day to grieve."

Jake walked back over to the two men. "Her records indicate she had no particular preference. She was very pragmatic about death. She said whatever I want is fine, but if she has to pick, she prefers to be committed into space. I can show you the video if someone needs to witness it."

David shook his head. "That won't be necessary. We trust you. Listen, Jake, can you get her a clean uniform? The doc needs to determine cause of death, and he can get her cleaned up. He's going to put her into a stasis chamber until we get back into space. Is that acceptable?"

Jake nodded. "How soon can we have her memorial service?"

Jason did a double take. "Jake, you can't rush through your grief."

Jake looked both perplexed and annoyed. "Doc, I'm not trying to rush through this. We have a job to do, and we all need to grieve, but I need to... I'm not sure how to explain it. A memorial service isn't going to put an end to my grief. I'm still going back to an empty cabin every night. I need to say my good-byes to her, but we still have a job to do. Once we leave Medoris, I will need to decide where to go from here. I'm probably not making a lot of sense, but I need to get this done."

David understood. He told Jake he would be on reserve status until further notice. David wanted to make sure Jake had as much time as he needed. He was only going to give him assignments if it was absolutely necessary. Jake went to get the clean uniform for Marissa as requested. Laura went into the infirmary to help Jason.

David stepped into the corridor to talk to the group waiting for him. He told them they would have a memorial service for their fallen comrade that evening. He asked the others to go home and check on their people and their cities. He invited them to come back for the service later that evening. Kasen volunteered to take the newly released Kimbra slaves with him and get them settled into tents of their own. There were many who still needed medical treatment. The Kimbra were not as apt to mark their slaves, so only a few needed the slave markings removed. Kasen said he would send them back for treatment in another day or two. Soon the ship was empty of everyone but the crew and the two Akamu.

David sent the crew to get some rest since they had all been up all night. The captain wasn't quick to take his own advice. He volunteered to take first watch then tied in the ship's scanners and comms to his datapad. He then went for a walk down to the creek. He sat down on the same tree trunk Brynna sat on the day they talked to Jabre about Auryon. He sat there quietly for a long time contemplating his own shortcomings and the "what ifs" of the situation. Suddenly he felt the presence of someone behind him. He had not heard a single twig snap, no rustling, and no sound of footsteps. He expected Brynna, Lexi, or perhaps Jason to chase him down to "talk." He knew however the person behind him was none of the ones he expected.

"You told me to call your name. I didn't call out for you."

"I know. I know you wanted to, and I know why you didn't."

"Did you come to taunt me or tempt me to commit treason?"

"Neither."

David still had not turned around to see his visitor. For a trained soldier, this required serious trust or a serious lack of care. "So why are you here, Arni?"

"Because I knew if you called me, it would be considered treason. This way I kept you from committing treason. I am here by my own choice."

Arni stepped into David's peripheral vision to take in the same view David had. He waited quietly for David to continue. "You're right. I wanted to call you very badly. I screwed up, and one of my crewmen paid the price. If I called you, you might save her, but it would cost me my life. Granted, I don't value my life over hers, but I can't commit treason just to get my crewman back. If I could trade places with her, I would in a second."

"You would leave your wife a widow in order to have your crewman back?"

"No, I don't want to do that, but if I thought it would save Marissa's life then yes, I would."

"But you couldn't call my name to save her?"

David was annoyed. He felt like the conversation was going nowhere. "It would cost me more than my life to call you."

Arni smiled and nodded. "Indeed, it would, but I'm not the one who attached a price tag. Your Commonwealth did that."

David sat there quietly for another minute thinking about what Arni said. He finally looked at Arni. "It's my fault she's dead. I would give you my life if it meant saving hers."

Arni laughed. His laughter only served to make David angry. "You think this is funny?"

Arni shook his head. "No, I think it's ironic. She has been kicking herself for getting herself killed. She feels like she's upset you terribly."

David stood bolt upright. "What? You know what she thought when she died?"

"She's with my Father right now. I know her thoughts and feelings right now. She has seen all you've done since you lost her to the storm. She's seen the tears being shed for her already. She is saddened by the grief she has caused all of you. She wants -"

"Marissa is dead! She no longer hears, sees, feels, or thinks. When people die, they're just gone! Having a spirit or soul has been proven by scientists to be false. It's an ancient superstition just to make people feel better."

"I see. Let me ask you this. How many of your scientists have experienced death? Can they really prove or disprove something they have no real experience with? I'm not going to say something untrue just to make you feel better."

David had no answer for Arni. It rattled every fiber of his being to have his entire belief system challenged.

"Marissa wants me to bring her back here, but she's afraid to ask. She knows it would be treason. She believes she is a prisoner of war. Your lieutenant doesn't fully grasp the complexity of her situation."

David finally had enough. "What do you want from us? Are you dangling your power in front of us hoping we'll take the bait?" David was now in Arni's face.

Arni's face was deadly serious. "I want to give you sufficient cause to trust me. I'm going to bring Marissa back to you. I would love it if you trusted me enough to ask for my help, or if she did, but you don't. Since you don't, I'm going to help you anyway and maybe when the right time comes you will trust me enough to call on me. If you had just called on me, none of this would have happened. I could have prevented all of this."

"You could have kept her from being snatched away by the tornado?"

Arni's face was still markedly serious. "I could have stopped the tornado."

With his one free arm, David shoved Arni up against the tree. "So why didn't you stop it? Why did you let her die? What did she ever do to you?"

Arni spoke softly and kindly. "I wanted to stop it, but I wanted you to ask for my help even more. Marissa is fine. I will restore her completely even though you still haven't asked."

David released his hold on Arni and backed away from him. He was torn between being grateful and angry.

Arni continued softly. "David, this is a gift. It isn't going to cost you anything. No treason involved. When Jake tests you, you didn't ask for my help. Get some rest now. This is over."

David blinked, and Arni was no longer in front of him. David was still angry. He wanted to punch something very badly. It didn't help that his dominant hand was still splinted and bound to his chest. He had gotten tense while talking to Arni and his arm started to throb, but now it suddenly felt warm, and the pain was gone. He looked up and saw Jason and Brynna walking toward him. David sat back down on the tree trunk. He didn't quite know what to do. He was exhausted. He felt frustrated and manipulated. When Jason and Brynna reached him, David grabbed onto Brynna with his one good arm and hugged her tightly. He suddenly realized it could have been Brynna instead of Marissa. He wondered if he would have hesitated to betray the Commonwealth if it had been her. Brynna was ready to wring David's neck when she walked out to meet him. Being a discerning individual, she felt the anguish in his grasp and held her tongue, again. He wasn't crying, but she could tell he was extremely tense.

After a few minutes, Brynna felt David relax. He turned to Jason and sighed. "Arni was just here. I don't think I'll be needing your services again."

Jason looked fretful. "Is he trying to put me out of a job?" Jason was making a subtle attempt at humor because it was clear David needed some relief from whatever was going through his head.

David looked down at his feet. "I'm not sure what he's trying to do."

"If he were trying to put you out of a job, Jason, he would have saved Marissa," Brynna responded bitterly.

David looked at her sharply. "He says, he can, and he will."

Jason shook his head. "She's dead all the way down to the cellular level. No amount of science can bring her back after this long. I suppose he could clone her and perhaps there is a way to replicate some of the chemical signatures in her brain responsible for her memories, but she would not be the same person."

Brynna looked at David suspiciously. "David, why does he want to restore her life?"

David looked down at his feet again. "He wants me to trust him. He told me he could have saved her from the tornado, but he didn't because I didn't ask him for help."

Now it was Brynna's turn to be angry. "He just wants you to feel guilty. He's trying to imply this is all your fault. It's not your fault, David! If I ever get my hands on that, Ar-"

"STOP!" David abruptly interrupted her. "He told me all I had to do is speak his name, and he would hear it. Don't say it, just in case."

Brynna was now more concerned about how much Arni had rattled David than about Arni himself.

The three headed back to the ship. Jason unwrapped the captain's hand and checked it out. It was indeed healed perfectly. There were no signs of fractures at all. Jason did double-check the stasis chamber after he had made sure the captain's hand was fine. Marissa's body was just as he had left it.

Before the captain went back to his cabin to get some rest, he did have one final question. "Doc, what did you determine was the cause of death?"

Jason's mood had lightened while attempting to treat David, but he became somber again. "She had several life-threatening injuries. Any one injury could have ultimately killed her, but her final injury was what took her life. Her neck was broken probably when she hit the ground the last time as the storm was dissipating."

"So she was alive through the entire storm?" Brynna marveled. "She felt every bit of the beating it gave her?"

"I suppose it would depend on if she were conscious or not. She did have a rather nasty concussion."

David shook his head and hoped he was right about this. "She was knocked unconscious by a large chunk of hail before the storm took her. It's part of the reason I couldn't hold onto her."

Brynna and Jason both knew David needed to vent. "What's the other reason?" Brynna asked.

David looked down at his hand. Opening and closing his now healed hand. "Another chunk hit my wrist."

Brynna glanced at the doctor. "Captain, I believe I am more fit for duty than you are at the moment. Dr. Adams, I trust you will concur with me. I recommend thirty minutes in the gym with a punching bag, then sleep. You need at least six hours of off duty time, starting now. You can do it voluntarily, or we can put it in the record and make it an order, your choice."

David was too drained to argue, he simply nodded and headed to the gym. With his arm working again, he was more than ready to punch something. He smiled briefly. Brynna was a wise woman. He had chosen well when he married her and made her his co-commander.

Later that evening, after some much-needed rest and a good hot meal, everyone seemed better. The captain knew he needed to write up a report about Arni's visit, but he wanted to get Marissa's memorial service ready first.

As the day came to an end, everyone gathered outside for the memorial service. The leaders and several warriors came from the Kimbra, Akamu, and Sorley populations. Since a large portion of the tables and chairs provided by the Kimbra were blown away by the storm, David decided an informal service might be in order. Cheyenne programmed one of the data modules with holographic images of Marissa. There were images of Marissa from the ship's logs working, playing, laughing, and smiling.

David began by inviting everyone to make himself or herself comfortable. They were free to stand or sit on one of the ship's chairs, the ground, or random logs dropped by the storm. David had the crew come together and stand in formation as he read a copy of Lt. Holden's service record. The lieutenant had been an exemplary soldier, and her service record clearly reflected that. She received numerous awards and commendations for her service. When the captain finished reading her record, he added that he would be recommending her for the Medal of Honor. He read the recommendation for everyone to hear.

"Lt. Marissa Holden risked her life to save the life of another. She did not shirk her duty and gave no thought of her own safety. She thought only of the life of the child in her arms, a child she had no physical or emotional ties to. She followed the orders of her commanding officers without question. In so doing, paid the ultimate price. Even though her career was cut short, she served as an exemplary officer during the time she served aboard the *Evangeline*. She was loved, respected, and admired by all her shipmates. I can think of no one more deserving of the Medal of Honor than Lt. Marissa Holden. Respectfully submitted, Captain David Alexander."

David dismissed the crew from formation then continued. "Lt. Holden leaves behind an emptiness no other individual can fill. Another officer can do her job, but no one can take her place in the life of her husband Security Chief Jacob Holden, or in the lives of we who considered her both friend and family."

Jake sat down in a chair placed nearest the data module. He sat there as if frozen in time. There was no hint of emotion on his face. Lexi sat down on one side of him and despite their early rivalry. Thane sat on the other side of Jake. David's voice droned on in Jake's ears. Jake was also blaming himself for Marissa's death. For a split second, he wondered if he should have asked the captain to get Arni's help. He shifted suddenly in his seat as he tried to shake off the thought. He was not about to fall into that trap.

As the sun set over the horizon, the traditional funeral dirge of the Commonwealth Interstellar Force emanated from the data module. It was the type of melody conveying a different sentiment depending on how it was played. It could be majestic, victorious, or deeply sad. As the music played, several of the crew were moved to tears. Jake stood at attention and never flinched. David also stood at attention. He had not given an order to bring the crew to attention. He left it up to the individual to do as he or she needed. As the music came to an end, David's eyes focused on the landing at the top of the stairs. He had caught movement out of the corner of his eye. When he looked in the direction of the movement, he saw two figures emerge from the ship. One was Arni, and the other was Marissa. The captain failed to realize the music had stopped, and everyone was standing there looking at him.

Captain Alexander was torn about how to react. Arni was his sworn enemy, but he had done nothing harmful to the crew. He had been nothing but helpful to them. The crew and visitors grew concerned over the captain's awkward silence. Brynna and Jake were the first to turn to see what the captain was staring at. Gasps could be heard escaping from several of the crew members. The captain never said a word, but he set his datapad down and walked to the bottom of the stairs. He reached his hand up to Marissa. Jake was a mere two steps behind him. Marissa came down the steps looking slightly dazed. David met her part way up the stairs and took her hand. He backed down the stairs and handed her off to Jake. He looked back up at Arni. Arni had a look on his face that David had trouble interpreting. He expected to see smug self-satisfaction. It looked more like care and concern.

The Sorley, Akamu, and Kimbra looked at each other in confusion. This was the dead woman warrior they were here to mourn?

David kept one eye on Arni. As soon as Marissa was safely in Jake's arms, David addressed Arni directly. "Arni, I appreciate what you have done for Marissa and Jake, and for me, but you know this doesn't change things. I won't betray the Commonwealth. You're still my sworn enemy."

Arni came slowly down the steps. The look on his face never changed. Arni stopped at the bottom of the stairs and said two simple words. "I know." He then walked through the gathering and into the darkness. He never looked back.

Kasen and the other leaders approached David. "This is your enemy?" David nodded. Kasen looked to where he had seen Arni disappear in the darkness. He then looked back at Marissa. "Malek was right. If he is not a god to be worshiped, then he is at least a powerful man to be feared, and one you would do well to not have as an enemy."

David looked at Marissa then back at Kasen and said the only thing he could. "I know."

The captain walked back over to the data module and shut it off. He picked up his datapad and asked for everyone's attention. He thanked all three societies again for their help in locating Marissa the previous night and for attending her funeral. The next part was the hardest part for him to say to the group around him. "We are grateful our fallen comrade has been brought back to us. The man you saw return her to us is the same man we warned you about. He is very powerful. He healed Marissa to buy our loyalty. We believe his goal is to corrupt the crew of the *Evangeline*, and once we leave here, he will not concern himself with you. If he does come here again, use your data modules to contact us. We will be leaving in a few days. If you need our help in the next few days, let us know. Send those who need slave markings removed to see Jason. We will arrange for someone from the Commonwealth to come and travel with Kasen's people to continue removing slave markings among the other populations on your world. It will take some time to get a team out here, but we will get someone here as soon as possible. It has been a difficult day for all of us so everyone, please head back to your homes. This crew needs a time of rest and relaxation. We will be glad to spend more time with you over the next few days."

David walked over to Brynna and asked her to organize a quick cleanup of the grounds while he took Jake, Jason, and Lexi inside to meet with Marissa. Commander Alexander didn't want to miss any more than she had to of that meeting, so she organized it quickly and got the crew moving. As soon as the guests were gone, the fires put out, the data module and chairs put away, the crew all hurried back into the ship. They all had questions for Marissa as well as a desire to simply hug her and welcome her back.

Brynna found the group in the infirmary. Marissa was sitting on the edge of the scanning bed. Jake was hovering around her nervously. He was glad to see her alive, but he was paranoid about it at the same time. Brynna looked at David. "What did I miss?"

Jason looked up from his datapad. "It is one hundred percent Marissa. She's not a clone, and she's one hundred percent alive and well. Her memories appear to be intact. Lexi wants to spend some time with her tomorrow doing a full psych evaluation.

It's too late in the evening to get started, and everyone is exhausted. I suggest we all take the night off and work on this in the morning."

The captain nodded. "Lieutenant Holden, I need to ask a favor of you."

"Yes, Captain?" Marissa had no idea what he could possibly want at this late hour.

"The information we have on the Liontari conscripts is that they are able to get out of locked doors. I am going to ask you to voluntarily confine yourself to the infirmary tonight. Can you do that for me?"

Marissa looked nervous. She knew she needed to answer his question first and defend herself second. "Yes, Captain. I promise I'll stay here." She hesitated for a moment then added. "Captain, I didn't betray the Commonwealth. I swear I didn't."

David gave her a reassuring smile. "I just need to be sure. Jake, I think you need to spend a few minutes with your wife. I would prefer you return to your own quarters for the night though. I don't really think we have anything to worry about, but I need to talk to you before you retire for the evening."

Jake's paranoid nature had him conflicted. He wanted his wife back, but he was concerned if she was now under the influence of the Liontaris, then she wasn't really back. He was also concerned about whatever the captain wanted to talk to him about.

Jason set the infirmary up to monitor Marissa through-out the night including video monitors. He thought maybe he was being too cautious, but it wasn't going to hurt anything. It would certainly make Jake feel better.

Jake spent a few reassuring minutes with Marissa who was genuinely afraid of being labeled a traitor. Marissa wasn't the type to cry easily, but one small tear managed to slide silently down her cheek. Jake's paranoia finally gave way to the kind, caring husband Marissa knew and loved. After comforting her, Jake told her he would send the other crewmen in to visit with her for a few minutes.

Most of the crew was hanging out in the dining hall. Jake stopped in and told them they could visit briefly, but to use caution because she had been under the influence of their enemy. Most hadn't really thought about it. They were just excited to know she was alive and well. The crew didn't want to overwhelm their comrade, so they went in to see her two at a time and welcome her back. They exchanged numerous hugs. Marissa didn't consider herself to be the hugging type, but she had to admit the hugs felt good.

Jake went to the captain's office. Brynna was there with him. The captain filled Jake in on his encounter with Arni down by the creek. David explained his doubts that Marissa committed treason just to get her life back. He also told Jake this was probably Arni's way of trying to buy the crew's loyalty.

Jake sat in his chair with a distinct look of consternation. Finally, he addressed the captain's arguments. "Captain, how do I know neither one of you have turned? Maybe you both have turned, and you are protecting each other."

The captain nodded thoughtfully. "I suppose that is a possibility, but until you can prove our disloyalty, you can't take action. I can still swear loyalty to the Commonwealth, but feel free to watch both of us for any actions contrary to our mission. Lexi can interview both of us tomorrow if it will make you feel more at ease, Chief. In the meantime, I am preparing a report to send to CIF HQ. As soon as we are back out in space, we can get these reports on their way and get updated orders on whether we can question Arni or not. It's possible we could even get the chance to capture him."

"Yes, Captain." There really wasn't much for Jake to object to. He had no proof anything was wrong with the captain or Marissa, other than being alive and in perfect health.

"I'll make sure, whatever our orders are, both of you get a copy. Jake, do me one favor though."

"What is it, sir?"

"If you decide we are compromised, just maroon us on a planet. I really don't like the idea of being spaced."

Jake gave the captain a strange look. The look on David's face was deadly serious. When Jake realized he was serious, he offered David a compromise. "If we are in space, I'll put you down first."

David agreed. "Fair enough. Let's make sure we offer the same to anyone else if the matter comes up."

Brynna shook her head. "You two are terribly morbid."

David and Jake both looked at her. "Have you thought about it? Spacing would not be a good way to die." Jake nodded his agreement.

The next morning, Lexi interviewed the captain and Marissa and determined they were not compromised. Jake was glad to hear it and glad to have his wife back. He hadn't allowed himself to accept her until she was appropriately cleared. The captain arranged for everyone to take short duty shifts which basically gave everyone the day off. Lexi and Brynna agreed this was a good call on his part. The crew's tension levels were extremely high right now.

As the crew sat around eating dinner in the dining hall, everyone wanted to know what happened to Marissa. They tried to be polite and wait for her to volunteer the information. She and Lexi discussed it in Marissa's evaluation, but Lexi wasn't about to share.

Cheyenne finally said what everyone was thinking. "Marissa, so tell us what happened to you. What's it like being dead?"

Marissa was taken aback by the abruptness of the question. She wasn't quite sure how to answer. She glanced nervously at Jake and Lexi. Lexi came to the rescue. "Listen, everybody. This has been a traumatic thing for Marissa. You shouldn't pressure her. She can talk about it when she's ready."

Marissa felt relieved. Cheyenne looked both disappointed and slightly embarrassed. Marissa knew they were all wondering the same thing. She decided to give her and the rest of the crew some semblance of an answer. "I don't know where I was. It was very bright, brighter than anything I've ever seen. I felt warm and safe. Arni came and talked to me. I was afraid when I saw him. I thought he had taken control of me. He told me..." As Marissa relived the memory, fear began to show on her face.

Jake jumped in. "Marissa, you don't have to do this."

David echoed his security chief with greater voracity. "Lt. Holden, you are under no obligation to satisfy the crew's curiosity." David gave a warning look to the rest of the crew who prudently decided to go on about their business.

Cheyenne gave an apologetic look to Marissa. Her child-like enthusiasm and curiosity were now gone from her face. "I'm sorry Marissa. I didn't mean to upset you. You're back as good as new, so I guess I didn't think about it being scary."

Marissa gave Cheyenne a weak smile. "It's okay. I'm not sure I understand exactly what happened to me. I didn't feel dead. I suppose I would be just as curious if I were you. Let me sort it out in my head first, then maybe I can talk about it."

Cheyenne's youthful smile came back. She gave Marissa a quick hug then gathered her dishes and went on her way.

The next morning Brynna sent Thane out with the shuttle to bring back the former slaves waiting for healing at the Sorley encampment. It took a couple more days to get everyone taken care of. Jason spent several days working with the local healers on using the data module and some basic ways to improve general health. Sometimes he grew tired of teaching people about hand washing. Sometimes he just wanted to teach surgical procedures.

The rest of the crew spent more time working with the leaders to continue cementing their new governmental changes, as well as get some new projects started for various improvements. The crew was able to relax and enjoy the rest of their time on Medoris IV. The highlight of their last week on Medoris was to attend the wedding of Jabre and Auryon. It was a fitting end for a stressful mission.

The day before their departure, Jason gave Vesta another thorough exam to be sure her pregnancy was progressing, as it should. David sat down and talked to Manton and Vesta to see what they learned from their experience. He was not disappointed. They learned the value of negotiating, how to treat people fairly and equally and they lost confidence in the gods of the mountain. David had no doubt these two would impart what they learned to their people and would spread it even further.

As he was preparing to take Manton and Vesta back to the Akamu, surprisingly Lexi asked David if she and Braxton could go. David agreed, but he wanted to know her reasons. The thing David was concerned with was who could monitor the mental health of his only clinical psychologist when she was recovering from a trauma. Lexi confessed her desire to find the man Gabe, who helped her when Manton and Vesta took her captive.

David asked what seemed to be an obvious question. "Did you ask Manton and Vesta about him?"

"I've been afraid to ask because I didn't want him to get into trouble for helping me."

David frowned. "From all Manton and Vesta have learned from us, I no longer believe that to be an issue."

Lexi thought about it for a moment. "I suppose you're right. I'll ask them about him."

Lexi got up to leave, but David motioned for her to stay seated. He hit the comm button and called them to come to his office. David didn't want to leave this to chance. It felt like Lexi needed some closure on the issue. Perhaps by finding this man and thanking him, she could get what she needed. A minute later the couple entered David's office. David invited them to take a seat. Glancing at Lexi, he asked, "Would you mind if I...?"

Lexi shifted nervously in her seat but nodded. She had gotten comfortable enough with the couple to handle business and even relax, talk, and joke with them, but rehashing their earliest encounters still made her uncomfortable.

At David and Lexi's combined presence and exchange, Manton and Vesta started to get nervous. "Is something wrong?" Manton ventured.

David smiled to put the two at ease. He leaned back in his chair. "No, not at all. This may not be the easiest of conversations for any of us, but there's no problem." David watched the couple relax before continuing. "When Lexi was being held in the caves, she was helped by someone, and she wanted to convey her thanks. No one knew she was helped and she didn't want there to be any repercussions against the one who helped her. Can you help us with this?"

Manton and Vesta seemed genuinely puzzled by the captain's request. Vesta had been fairly subdued throughout their stay with the crew, but the longer she was with them, the more she seemed to get her nerve back. She jumped in before Manton had a chance. "Captain David, Lt. Lexi, we did a great wrong when we hurt you and your husband. We will do whatever you ask of us to make this right again. I do not know who else had access to our area in the caves, but we will be glad to help you find the one you seek. We will not harm the one who helped you in any way. I think perhaps we owe them a debt of gratitude. Who is it you seek?"

439

Lexi felt her own confidence returning as David paused and glanced at her. He wanted to see if she was strong enough to take up her own story. She was. "A man came into the cave, and he brought some water to me. He took the gag out of my mouth and gave me a drink. He, well, he said some things to reassure me I was going to be okay. He was an old man. I really don't know how he moved those stones. He seemed so small and frail. His hair was white and thin, and it barely reached his shoulders." She went on to describe the man down to a scar on his right cheek. Lexi was surprised at how well she remembered someone she had only met for a few brief minutes.

Manton and Vesta still had a blank look on their faces. "Did he tell you his name?" Vesta asked.

Lexi was still hesitant about telling them. Her concern was for the old man's safety. She finally gave in and told them. "He said his name was Gabe."

As soon as she told them the man's name, Manton and Vesta gave each other terrified looks. David expected either recognition or another blank stare. "What is it?"

Vesta lost her courage once again. Manton picked up for her. "Please, tell us exactly what he said to you."

Lexi wasn't sure why it mattered, but she answered their question. "He told me he wasn't going to hurt me, and he was sent there to protect me. He said your people didn't know he was there. He told me not to mention him to you. He instructed me, not to try and escape." Lexi's face displayed a rather quizzical look.

Manton and Vesta's faces were now pale. Manton pushed Lexi to go on. "What else did he say?"

"He said you wouldn't hurt me no matter what you said, and he said a couple of strange things. I just thought it was because he didn't know Intergalactic Standard very well, but it didn't make sense."

Now David was curious. "What was it?"

"He said Braxton was fine, you were coming for me and I still had a job to do."

Manton and Vesta grabbed each other's hands and talked in hushed whispers to each other. They spoke so fast and so softly the translators weren't picking them up.

David looked at the couple for a moment and waited for what appeared to be a consensus between the two. "What is it?"

Manton sat up on the edge of his chair. "The man you described was Vesta's grandfather. He was the spiritual leader of the Akamu. He died many seasons ago. I knew him before Vesta and I were joined. Our people believe messengers of the gods may appear as those who have gone to the land of the dead. These messengers come to protect or to bring messages to those who still live. We would have done a horrible wrong if we had harmed you, Lt. Lexi. May the gods forgive us? It was a far greater harm than we could have imagined. The gods sent their messenger to protect her from us. The gods were against our plans to use her to have children from the very beginning. If we had tried, even if you had not found her, the gods would have punished us for taking her." The couple quickly got on their knees and began to pray to their gods for forgiveness.

David and Lexi were left looking shocked at each other and at the couple kneeling on the floor. David finally gathered his wits and attempted to interrupt their prayers. "Manton, Vesta, you didn't harm Lexi. She's safe, so you're safe. Manton, Vesta, listen to me."

The couple stopped their chant and looked up at David. "If the gods were trying to protect Lexi, she is fine, so you haven't offended them. Vesta, they've even allowed you to carry a child. There is also something that makes me think this was not the work of your gods, but the work of our enemy. Our enemy told us he has a job he wants us to do for him. Our enemy has great power. He can see inside our minds. He may have taken the image of your grandfather and used it to keep you from harming us. You have no reason to be afraid. Our enemy is using this to try and turn our loyalty away from the Commonwealth."

Vesta glanced up at the captain and Lexi. "You are certain?" David got up and went around the table and helped Vesta to her feet. "I'm certain. Our enemy is seeking to destroy us, not you." David wasn't sure what to really make of it. He offered the only explanation he could think of to reassure them. David was doing his best to discourage their trust in the Mountain gods. The thing he didn't realize was, he was planting seeds for Pateras Liontari.

After David and Lexi were sure the couple was satisfied, they escorted them back to the Akamu caves. David, Brynna, Lexi, and Braxton spent some time with Tarin and his council. David and Brynna praised Manton and Vesta openly in front of Tarin and his people for their service to the crew and to the Commonwealth. Most of the crew said their farewells to Manton and Vesta on the ship. The rest of the crew said their goodbyes now. The two had fit in with the crew well. Although they had primitive beliefs, they were highly intelligent and learned to use and accept the ship's technology quickly and easily. The crew was sorry to see them go. Manton and Vesta were also sorry to leave the crew, but they were glad to get back to their friends and family. The crew bid the Akamu farewell and headed back to the ship.

The crew spent the rest of the day finishing their departure preparations. Manton and Vesta's quarters were cleaned. Lazaro calibrated the converted tetrabradium ore for use in the tachyon engines. Marissa plotted her navigation for their next destination, Drea. The shuttle and Surf-Ve were cleaned and secured on board the ship. The ship's water reserves were refilled. The crew got a good night's sleep then took off for space the next morning.

Once in space, Captain Alexander sent off their official reports. He also sent a request for additional instructions. To find evidence of the Liontari presence and walk away from it was one thing. To have Arni Liontari pursuing him was another issue entirely. He still filed for Marissa's award, despite the fact she was now alive again. Her accomplishment and bravery still deserved to be awarded. He was glad she would be alive to receive the award this time. With all that completed, David set up the duty roster for the next few days. The stress of the recent weeks would certainly take its toll on the crew. David made the schedule as light as possible. He eliminated all training shifts and limited duty shifts to six hours at a time.

David sat back in his chair and reflected on the last few weeks. The Commonwealth had declared war on the forces of Pateras El Liontari. Something just wasn't sitting right about this. Your enemy isn't supposed to follow you around and save your life. David had been involved in a war shortly after he graduated from the CIF academy. It was one of the ugliest times in his life. The time on Medoris was not the most pleasant, but it would have been worse if Arni hadn't intervened on their behalf. David wondered if this was a political war instead of a physical one. As much as he hated war, he hated political wars more. Political war or not, David intended to defend the Commonwealth, unreservedly.

David got with Lexi and encouraged her to schedule heavy recreational activities. He also encouraged her to keep a watchful eye on the crew. This mission was bound to have a lasting impact on them. Hopefully, the next mission would be less dramatic. Drea was a more technologically advanced society. Surely, they were advanced sociologically.

DISASTER

EPILOGUE

"Come in Gentlemen. Please have a seat." Executor Hale waved the three men to seats across from his desk. "What brings my Defense Minister and two of my Admirals to my office this fine day?"

Being the superior, the Defense Minister began the explanation. "Admiral Garcia and Admiral Deacons have brought a problem to my attention. Your orders were quite clear, sir, but they seem to believe this problem is an opportunity."

"By all means Gentlemen, please explain."

"Admiral Deacons received a request for additional orders and a clarification to standing orders from one of the twelve search teams. It seems the Liontari may be targeting our search teams. A majority of the teams have already encountered his influence. The team requesting additional orders has just left their second planet. It seems the Liontari influence was not found on the second planet but has initiated contact with the team itself. He's healed two of their crew members from rather extensive injuries and one from death."

Executor Hale leaned forward in his seat. "Have these two crew members been compromised?"

Admiral Deacons had been silent up until now. "From the reports I received, the two at risk have been carefully evaluated by the ship's psychologist. The security chief expressed concerns, although his report supports the others."

Admiral Garcia scowled at his companion. "You've left out some vital details, Robert."

Executor Hale scowled. "What details?"

EPILOGUE

"The ship in question is the *Evangeline*, my nephew is the captain. Arni Liontari healed him, twice. The crew member who was healed from death was the security chief's wife."

"Could the reports be inaccurate?"

The Defense Minister jumped in, "This is what I was talking about. They seem to think this isn't a problem, but the entire crew could be infiltrated."

Executor Hale leaned back in his seat for a moment. He finally asked, "What are the clarifications and additional orders they are seeking?"

Admiral Deacons didn't want to appear to be hiding anything or protecting his nephew. "They've noticed the interest Arni Liontari has in them. They stated he seemed willing to discuss his needs and plans with them openly. They asked about pursuing such discussions to determine enemy plans and movements, or if they should still follow their previous orders to avoid contact at all costs. Captain Alexander stated in his report, he believed the enemy is trying to 'buy' their loyalty through acts of benevolence."

Executor Hale thought for another moment then leaned forward again. "Admiral Deacons, since you are personally involved with Captain Alexander, do you believe you could make an honest and impartial assessment of his state of mind?"

Admiral Deacons hesitated. "I believe so, Sir."

"Fine, investigate the captain and crew as you feel necessary. Report your findings to the Defense Minister. After I have the final reports, I will issue any changes in the orders. Does that cover everything?"

Sensing the meeting was done the two Admirals stood up. They acknowledged their assignment and thanked the Supreme Executor for taking the time to see them. The Defense Minister remained a moment longer at the Supreme Executor's request.

"Minister Payne, I asked you to stay behind because you are clearly not biased in this situation. Once you have Admiral Deacon's report, look into it yourself. Forward your report to me, directly. I want to handle this personally."

"Of course, Supreme Executor, is there anything else?"

"Not right now, but if things don't go the way I hope, I may have more for you to do."

"Yes sir." Defense Minister Hamilton Payne was loyal and paranoid. He was a good man to have in this office. He and the Supreme Executor got along well. Minister Payne left the office and caught up with the Admirals as they were stepping onto the elevator. The three chatted a bit as they went back to their respective offices.

Now alone in his office, Executor Hale spoke aloud in an unknown language. Two large figures appeared in his office. "It seems we have a problem."

"The prophecy?" The first figure inquired.

Luciano nodded. "He's trying to entice my scouts to join him."

"You knew this would happen," The figure said bluntly.

The second figure spoke, "Perhaps if you took some of the pressure off. They aren't going to understand the threat. If they find out what Pateras is capable of on their own perhaps he will no longer fascinate them. He's going to appear benevolent to them, for now. Once they learn the truth, he'll no longer appeal to them. His ways are beyond the understanding of men. Let them learn. They will only confuse themselves."

Luciano scowled. "The prophecy can't be thwarted. They are the words of Pateras. They are however vague, and they can be influenced. It says some will remain faithful to me. I must keep as many as I can. I'm going to keep them moving as fast as I can. I don't want them to have time to think and consider what's happening."

"What do you want us to do?"

"Just keep watch for now. Focus on my twelve teams. If anything significant happens, I want to know about it right away. I know it's early, but I'll destroy this entire galaxy if I have to."

The figures grew immensely larger, and their visage changed to something clearly not human. In a second, the two figures faded from sight.

Luciano glared out the expansive window in his office. "I know I can't defeat you, but I'll destroy your precious human race inside and out."

CONTINUED IN:

DEFENDED
THE DEFENDER SERIES

Thank you for reading this story, we hope you enjoyed it. We invite you to explore the rest of the books in The Defender series. Reggi's other books are available through your favorite book retailer! If you don't see it on the shelf, ask them to order it for you.

Tell us what you think!

Leave a comment online with your favorite book store!

Visit us at ReggiBroach.com for the latest information!

Search for "Reggi Broach Defender" in your favorite search engine.

PRONUNCIATION GUIDE

Adan	AY - duhn
Akish	A - kish
Alexia	uh - LEX - ee - uh
Arni Sotaeras	AHR- nee - SOH- teh - rahs
Aulani	AW - law - nee
Auryon	AR - ee - on
Ayele	EYE - el
Broona	BROO - nuh
Brynna	BRIN - nuh
Caius	KAY - us
Cashel	CASH - ill
Damar	DAY - mahr
Donnel	DON - nel
Duard	DOO - ard
El Liontari	EL lee - on - TAHR- ee
Eston	ES - tuhn
Gaia	GAY - yuh
Galat III	GAL - at - 3
Gervas	GIR - vos
Iresh	ear - ESH
Jabre	JAH - bruh
Jager	JAY - gir
Joren	JOHR - en
Kainda	KAYN - da
Kasen	KAY - sin
Lazaro	LAZ - ah - roh
Luciano	LOO - shee - ah - noh
Malek	MAL - ik
Manton	MAN - tin
Medoris IV	meh - DOR - is - 4
Medwin	MED - win
Nasha	NAH - shuh
Pateras	PAH - te - ross
Slaina	SLAY - nuh
Tarin	TAIR - in
Tharen	THAIR - in
Tolem	TOH - lem
Vesta	VES - tuh
Winda	WIN - da

REGGI'S WRITINGS

THE DEFENDER SERIES

BIRTH OF THE DEFENDER
PREQUEL

How did it all start? How could anyone put something like this together? Did anyone design this or did it just "happen"? What brought David's parents together? How many lives did the birth of Arni touch? These seemingly unconnected events on opposite sides of the galaxy set Pateras' plan in motion.

THE MISSION
BOOK 1

Captain David Alexander commands an Explorer Class Starship known as the SS Evangeline. Their Commonwealth assigned mission is to locate and identify a new enemy encroaching on Commonwealth territory before it's too late. Their new enemy has unidentifiable technology that turns people against their own government. No methods of persuasion have proven effective in restoring the enemy conscripts. The Supreme Executor of the Commonwealth, Luciano Hale, has authorized extreme sanctions. He wants the Liontari forces stopped, at all costs.

THE DEFENDED
BOOK 2

The Crew of the Evangeline continue their Commonwealth mission to make allies of the non-space-faring planets in the galaxy. Drea III is a technologically advanced world shrouded by a dark history with the Commonwealth. Drean officials agree to hear the crew's proposal of an alliance with the Commonwealth. A series of startling discoveries land the crew in jail, charged with several capital crimes. Captain Alexander finds himself caught between his Commonwealth mandates and protecting an entire planet from disaster. David does the only thing he can. He throws himself on the mercy of the courts, defending his crew to his last breath. The secrets keep growing older and deeper. What else can be learned? Who is responsible for so many secrets? Who is Captain Alexander – really?

TREASONOUS ACTS
BOOK 3

Who enjoys the story of a good boy gone bad?

Captain David Alexander is just such a man. He followed the rules, dotted every "i" and crossed every "t." Service to the Commonwealth Interstellar Force was his life… until now.

Treason; the only crime punishable by death. The entire crew wavers in their loyalty. Only one man remains true, Security Chief Jake Holden. Can he save them from themselves? Can he stop Captain Alexander from taking the entire crew down? Can he protect the primitive world of Tudoren? If he can't, Admiral Robert Deacons, David's uncle will have to. Can he arrest or execute his own nephew?

IN EVIL'S GRASP
BOOK 4

Betrayed… Imprisoned unjustly… His body racked with pain… Evil voices whispering… Taunting him…

Pateras gave him a mission. Can Captain Alexander go on? Can he survive this darkest night of the soul? The desire to die grows stronger with each passing moment. His crew now believes he is either dead or their own betrayer.

Pateras prevents the Captain's captor from executing him outright. The one who betrayed him returned as an angel of light offering him a way out… a way to die.

MISSION ABANDONED
BOOK 5

The crew of the Evangeline is now united in following Pateras. The entire Galaxy is out for blood – theirs. The military base on Romajin was destroyed as the Evangeline escaped the solar system. Ten thousand men and women are dead, and Chief Security Officer Jake Holden stands accused of the crime. Supreme Executor Hale tries to coerce Jake into returning to his service by any means necessary.

A new army of super soldiers is dispatched to destroy the Evangeline and other potentially wayward crews. Captain Alexander seeks out the other eleven ships to warn them. Will his best friend from the Academy believe him? Can he convince them of the danger before the Nefil arrive? What about the local population? Will they become casualties of war?

BIRTH OF A REVOLUTION
BOOK 6

Captain Alexander finishes searching for the other eleven Explorer Class Ships. Their Drean allies set up a secret meeting for all the ships willing to come. Captain Alexander proposes an alliance of the renegade ships to confront the Commonwealth. The odds of success are phenomenally against them. Will they agree to his proposal or will someone report them to the Commonwealth?

The fear that someone will discover them keeps everyone looking over their shoulders. Captain Alexander has more than the Commonwealth looking for him. An ugly secret is revealed as enemies from his past get lucky. Trapped in a maintenance duct under a mine shaft with Lt. Marissa Holden in labor, David's life is in the hands of men bent on settling an old score. The crew searches frantically for their missing people, but the only one who can save him is another figure from his past. Can this man be trusted?

QUESTIONS OF TRUST
BOOK 7

The newly formed Pateran Resurrection Movement is severely outnumbered and outclassed. The potential for traitors in their ranks remains. Captain Alexander is immediately plagued with a manpower shortage aboard ship, along with a confessed Commonwealth spy. Arni, not one prone to violence, has asked one thing of the newly formed alliance; destroy the Nefil base on Ahnak III.

What else could possibly go wrong? Captain Alexander is elected to be the lead Admiral in the new alliance. Being nearly the youngest of the Explorer Fleet captains, David feels inferior to his peers. Personal tragedy strikes the new young Admiral adding to his load. Executor Hale allows a secret out designed to hurt one person, the new Admiral. How much more can Admiral Alexander take before he crumbles under the pressure?

CPSIA information can be obtained
at www.ICGtesting.com
Printed in the USA
LVHW111448230120
644585LV00001B/32